GONE
TO HER
GRAVE

BOOKS BY WENDY DRANFIELD

GONE
TO HER
GRAVE

WENDY DRANFIELD

bookouture

Published by Bookouture in 2022

An imprint of Storyfire Ltd.
Carmelite House
50 Victoria Embankment
London EC4Y oDZ

www.bookouture.com

ISBN: 978-1-80314-233-3
eBook ISBN: 978-1-80314-232-6

For Joseph

PROLOGUE
SIX YEARS AGO

Mrs. Rosemary Hendricks is the last person still at the church on this cold November evening. She assured Pastor Graham she was happy to lock up. There's no sense in them both hitting the rush-hour traffic and he knows he can trust her, unlike some of the other people who help out around here. It's dark outside now and the wind is howling through the single-pane windows, but at least it's not raining. Mrs. Hendricks is trying to tidy away the toys from this afternoon's play group in preparation for tomorrow's Sunday service, but it's difficult for her to scoop things off the ground since she has bad arthritis in her hands, hips *and* knees now. She's told the children more than once that they should tidy after themselves instead of leaving their playthings scattered around the church as if it's their own bedrooms, but they just ignore an old woman like her.

Her knees creak as she bends forward. Her back barely gives an inch as she tries to reach the soft toy at her feet. She could give up, leave everything a mess and let someone else clear away, but she'd hate to be thought of as lazy. Her fingers find the teddy bear's ear and she manages to grab it. Now begins the job of straightening up, something she used to be able to do without a second thought, but these days takes considerably more effort. Her spare hand clutches a wooden pew as she uses that to unbend her resistant spine. A few vertebrae crack back into place along the way. Eventually, she gets there. Throwing the toy into the box, she chuckles. "There's life in the old dog yet."

Behind her, the large oak door at the front of the church bangs closed, shattering the silence. The noise echoes through the building. Turning, she tries to see into the shadows where the light doesn't quite reach, but her eyesight fails her. She calls out, "Who's there?"

She's met with silence. Mrs. Hendricks doesn't scare easy— eighty-nine years on God's earth has taught her that when it's your time, it's your time, and no amount of fear will halt it—but something about the silence fills her with dread. She stands still, listening. There are no footsteps. So why did the door bang? Maybe Pastor Graham didn't close it properly on his way out.

"Looks like my hearing's the next thing to go," she mutters before pulling on her woolen hat, followed by her old winter coat, which she ties closed with a belt. She can't manage buttons or zippers anymore, and she's only going as far as her car. Picking up her purse, she walks toward the door, turning off the lights as she goes. Once outside, she stands at the top of the concrete steps that lead down to the parking lot. They look like a mountain to her these days, and they're covered with slippery wet leaves. Like her, the handrail is decrepit, and its strength can't be trusted. She looks out over the parking lot, her back to the church's door, as she fishes for the keys in her purse.

A shiver suddenly runs down her spine when she feels warm breath on her neck. Before she can turn around, she feels a hand push her hard from behind, right between the shoulder blades. The wind is knocked out of her in an instant and she just has time to register the fact that she's falling forward. Her purse is dropped, forgotten. Her left hand grasps for the rail but misses. Her head makes contact with one of the concrete steps, sending blood rushing to her ears and a searing pain through her skull and down her neck. She can tell from the impact that she can't survive this. Not at her age. Yet, somehow, she remains conscious.

Once she's landed in her final resting place, she manages to open her eyes. Confusion sweeps over her because of the angle she finds herself in. She's upside down, her head on the ground, the night sky at her feet. She can do nothing but watch as leather shoes descend the steps toward her. "Please," she groans. "Help me."

Her attacker looms over her in the dark and it quickly becomes obvious that this person has no intention of helping her up or summoning an ambulance. It's then that Mrs. Hendricks knows for sure this was no accident. This person meant to hurt her.

Her body starts to violently tremble as the shock that protected her from the worst pain wears off and fear sets in. Her eyes move up the attacker's body before settling on their face. She just has time to gasp before everything turns black.

CHAPTER ONE

PRESENT DAY

Troy Randle had a rough night, that much he remembers. As he slowly wakes up in his customary place after a liquor-fueled night out—the couch—he has a hazy recollection of what went down in the bar. Flashbacks of downing vodka shots, brawling with a motorcycle gang and then... firing his weapon? He desperately tries to remember whether that actually happened or not, but his memory is unreliable at this point.

Groaning as he turns onto his back, he tries to figure out how he made it home. He drove himself to the bar, that much he remembers clearly, but if he drove himself home after getting wasted, he could have hit an animal or a person and he wouldn't remember it. Not with the amount of liquor he put away. His left hand moves to rub his eyes but he winces at the pain in his fist, which barely opens. So the fight was real. He'd been hoping it was a dream. Being on parole, a bar fight would be enough to put him back inside, never mind a hit and run. Or firing his illegal firearm. Still, if he's waking up at home instead of in a police cell, he figures he can't have caused too much damage.

Slowly dropping his feet to the floor, he carefully sits up and blinks at the weak morning light streaming through the open drapes. Terri must have left them open all night. Through squinted eyes he glances at the clock over the TV. It's almost 10 a.m. already. "Shit."

He hadn't meant to sleep in that late. He was supposed to start work at the gas station at eight and being this late will get him fired, which means his parole officer will hassle him. She's a real hard-ass who barely lets him take a crap without permission. He sighs before yelling, "Terri? Why didn't you wake me? I probably just lost my job because of you."

There's no answer. In a house this small he'd hear her even if she was cursing him under her breath, something she likes to do. He stands as anger builds in his chest. Terri won't have left for work yet, it's too early for her afternoon shift at the care home, so she should be in the house. He shakes his head. She can be so goddam infuriating. And now she's going to *ignore* him? The room starts spinning from the alcohol still in his veins.

Taking a second to ride out the dizzy spell, he notices a faint smell. It's just strong enough to override the scent of the pumpkin spice candles Terri has dotted around the house. They started appearing before Halloween and she's adamant they won't be put away until after tonight: Thanksgiving. The sweet aroma aggravated him at first but he only notices it now when he's been outside the house for a period of time. The other scent he can smell has him sniffing his pits in case it's emanating from him. It's hot in here as Terri likes to have the heat on all night. He sure doesn't smell fresh but that's not what's bothering his nose. He wonders if the garbage needs taking out. Then he remembers the gunshot.

His mouth, already dry from a night spent wide open and drooling, suddenly feels like sandpaper. He looks around for a glass of water. Hell, he'd take a shot of whiskey if it'd stimulate some saliva. There's nothing to hand so he goes to the sink to drink from the faucet. After wiping his mouth dry, a feeling of dread washes over him because of the silence in the house.

Slowly, he moves past the small kitchen to the dark hallway beyond. "Terri? You home?"

No answer.

He desperately tries to remember whether the guys took him hunting while he was wasted. That would account for the gunshot. A glance into the bathroom on his left tells him it's empty. When he reaches the only bedroom in the house, he finds the door ajar. The coppery smell is slightly stronger here, mainly because there are no candles to mask it. He hesitates to push the door open so he uses his foot instead, and then braces himself as he peers inside.

Terri is lying diagonally across the bed, on her back and fully clothed. But she's not asleep. The blankets beneath her are saturated with blood. His girlfriend stares through the ceiling and the bullet hole between her eyes is black.

Troy's first thought isn't to try to revive her—she's too far gone—and it isn't to call the cops. It's to get the hell out of there.

CHAPTER TWO

Detective Madison Harper stands outside Detective Don Douglas's detached home as she sips hot coffee from her stainless-steel thermos travel mug. She has to use this instead of takeout cups to be eco-friendly because Owen, her seventeen-year-old son, believes that her generation is destroying the planet at a faster rate than any other. It's easier to reuse this than to listen to the lecture again. Secretly though, she's glad her son cares about things like that. He's thinking of specializing in environmental law when he goes off to college next year.

She knocks on Douglas's door and waits. This will be his first day back on the force after being suspended for drinking while on duty a month ago, and Madison couldn't be more relieved to have a partner again. The pressure to solve cases has been solely on her while he's been gone, but it's more than that. She had been worried for Douglas. He spiraled so quickly and secretly into alcoholism that she thought Chief Mendes would fire him. But, to her credit, Mendes stuck by him and gave him time to pull his life back together.

That time runs out today.

Madison shudders in the cold November wind and glances

at her watch. It's lunchtime. She's been at work since seven this morning, but Douglas prefers to work the later shift, when things are relatively settled like they are at the moment. Since last month's shocking murders—of a visiting crime writer and a convicted sex offender—things have been quiet in Lost Creek, southern Colorado. It's like the town has had its fill of drama and just wants to enjoy the holiday season in peace. Which is fine by her.

She sighs. Douglas should be awake by now. She knocks again. "Come on, Douglas," she shouts through the door. "If you leave me waiting any longer, I'll disinvite you to dinner later."

Although Douglas was the detective who wrongly arrested her for murder some years back, Madison's got to know him since her return home to Lost Creek earlier this year. More so since his recent suspension. She's been checking in on him regularly and even joined him at an AA meeting to try to understand what he's going through. Tonight, he's invited to Thanksgiving dinner at her house because he doesn't have family in Colorado and she didn't want him to be alone. But leaving her standing outside in the crisp autumnal weather is testing her patience.

She cups a hand over her eyes as she peers in through his front window. Blinds obscure her view, so she steps back and sighs. He could have already left for work without her. His garage is closed so she can't tell if his car's gone but assumes it is. He probably forgot she even offered him a ride to work. She would rather that was the reason he's not here than the alternative: that he's wasted somewhere or nursing the hangover from hell upstairs.

The second heavy downpour of the day begins, so she runs to her car and gets in. Switching the wiper blades on, she feels her cell phone buzzing in her pocket. It's Stella from dispatch. "Hey, Stella."

"Hi, Detective. If you're on your way back to the station, don't bother. I've had a call about a suspected homicide."

Madison's stomach flutters. She should have known the peace and quiet wouldn't last long. "Give me the details."

"Terri Summers. Thirty-four years old. Her mom found her with one gunshot wound to the head. She lives at 1321 Trent Road. I've already dispatched Officers Goodwin and Vickers."

Madison knows where Trent Road is. She starts her car and pulls out of Douglas's drive. "Could it be a suicide?" It's a myth that suicides increase during the holidays but that doesn't mean Terri Summers didn't take her own life.

"Her mom said there was no gun at the scene, although she was pretty cut up, so she could've missed it."

Madison doesn't know what's worse to attend, a murder or a suicide. Both have devasting consequences for the victim's families. "Does anyone else live at the property?"

"Troy Randle. He's the victim's boyfriend and a convicted felon," says Stella. "Aggravated battery."

She sighs at the predictability of it. "Do we know his current whereabouts?"

"Officer Goodwin was first on the scene and he says the only other person there is the victim's mother. She doesn't know where Troy is."

The poor woman. Being the one to find her own daughter murdered must have been horrific. "Understood. Ask Sergeant Tanner to get patrol looking for Troy. I'm on my way to the address now and I don't want him surprising me."

"Sure thing."

Before she ends the call, Madison asks, "Has Douglas arrived at the station yet?"

"Not that I've seen," says Stella. "The *Welcome Back* banner you bought is up and ready for him though."

Madison smiles. He's going to hate that. He hates all forms of affection—showing and receiving. She knows it's just a front to deal with past trauma, so she's doing her best to break down his wall one brick at a time with small gestures. It's better than giving up on him. She slips her cell phone back into her pocket and speeds over to Trent Road. It's not far from where she lives but more rural, deep into the woods. If she remembers correctly, it's a private road with no through traffic. A perfect spot to get away with murder.

As the rain pelts hard against the car's windshield, she struggles to see out. Lost Creek may be Madison's home town but it's not the only place she's lived. She spent six years incarcerated at La Vista Correctional Facility in Colorado before moving to California to seek help with overturning her wrongful manslaughter conviction. Like prison, that was a temporary address too, until she could eventually come home to clear her name. Now she's able to put that whole sorry affair behind her she's starting to settle back into life here, but it hasn't been an easy adjustment. The locals have short memories when it comes to their own crimes but when it comes to Madison's history, they remember everything. She's still trying to convince them her conviction was overturned not because she knows someone high up who pulled a favor, but because she wasn't the person who killed her fellow officer seven years ago.

Now she's hit the ground running back at Lost Creek PD, she's starting to care less about people's opinion of her. She's back in the stride of a regular routine: a half-assed run in the early morning followed by a sneaky cigarette—her only cigarette of the day, unless it's a bad day—breakfast with her son, and then a ten-to-thirteen-hour workday as one of only two detectives at LCPD. The town is pretty small, with a population figure that tends to go down quicker than it goes up. The town is nestled among impressive mountains and beautiful vast woods, off the beaten track, so they don't get many strangers passing through. If you come to Lost Creek, it's because you once escaped as a young person and are now reluctantly returning to visit the family members who chose to stay behind. Either that or you're fleeing something, and hoping never to be found by the outside world.

The only neighboring town, Gold Rock, is about a half hour's drive away, but that's just a small ghost town consisting of old mining families. They're slowly dying off, so the town is crumbling around them. Madison had a hand in killing off one particular resident and seeing another locked up, but she doesn't want to think about them. The day Angie McCoy's murder trial is finally scheduled will be the day Madison faces that whole mess. As one of the main witnesses for the prosecution, she'll have no choice. The McCoys' ranch is abandoned now, the scrapyard empty and quiet. Just like the rest of that town.

You can drive through Gold Rock in the blink of an eye and not even know you've been there. The nearest large town to Lost Creek is Prospect Springs, almost a two-hour drive away, depending on traffic. That has the bustle of a city but on a smaller scale. It's where you'd go if you ever found yourself needing some fancy—non-flannel—clothes, or a special anniversary gift for someone.

Madison pulls off the road at a long dirt track that's home to just one row of houses spaced well apart. The majority of people who live out here rarely venture into town, preferring their peace and quiet. Or their privacy, for a variety of reasons. LCPD doesn't generally get many call-outs to this location. The residents get on with their neighbors because they know they're likely stuck with them for good, so it's easier to just be cordial and keep the peace. When she sees a mailbox with 1321 on it, Madison pulls off the dirt road, which is basically a swamp of mud now thanks to the downpours, and into the victim's front yard.

Beyond the huge pine trees that surround the property she sees two police cruisers parked alongside a black Ford and a brown Honda. Officer Shelley Vickers is crouched next to the open door of the Honda, talking to an older woman who's sitting in the driver's seat. As Madison approaches them the rain tails off.

Shelley stands when she sees her approach. "Hey, Madison." The other officers refer to her as "Detective" but Madison mentored Shelley as a young rookie and they've become friends. "This is our victim's mother, Mrs. Sylvia Summers."

Madison looks at the woman and her heart goes out to her. She appears to have collapsed into the seat. With her pale, dazed expression and shaking hands, it's clear she's in shock. She looks to be in her seventies. Madison leans in. "I'm sorry for your loss, Mrs. Summers, and I hate to do this to you at such a terrible time, but I need you to stick around a little longer so I can ask you a few questions. Is that okay with you?"

Sylvia stares up at her with watery eyes and launches straight into what happened before Madison can venture inside and see for herself. "She's dead! I knocked on the door and there was no answer and the door was unlocked, so I went inside and she wasn't in the living room." She finally pauses for breath before continuing. "So I kept hollering her name but she didn't answer and I smelled something bad, so I walked up to her bedroom and I saw her there! Dead! On the bed." She starts sobbing and hyperventilating at the same time.

Madison crouches next to the car and places a hand on Sylvia's. It's cold and it feels like she's too fragile to cope with finding her daughter that way. "I'm so sorry. That must've been terrible."

Sylvia nods through her tears. "She was my only child and I wasn't there to protect her. Why would someone hurt my Terri? I just don't get it."

Madison feels bad for keeping her here because she doesn't seem in the right frame of mind to answer any questions, but right now is the best time to hear her account of what happened, while it's fresh in her memory. She turns when she hears a vehicle pulling onto the property and is relieved to see an ambulance and not a reporter.

An EMT, Jake Rubio, gets out. He pulls a bag out of the vehicle and strides over to her and Shelley. He nods at them both before asking, "What have we got?"

Shelley says, "Just one person inside the house, but they're already deceased."

Madison leads Jake away from the car. "That's our victim's mother, Sylvia. She's not taking it well and I need to question her. Would you check her over first? She's understandably upset but she's also struggling for breath."

"Sure."

"Thanks." Madison turns to Shelley. "Is Goodwin inside?"

"Yeah." With a roll of her eyes, Shelley says, "He's acting like he's a detective or something."

Madison understands her annoyance. Since Detective Douglas was suspended, Officer Dan Goodwin has been acting like he's in the running for promotion to Douglas's role. That will never happen unless Douglas gets fired and Goodwin beats more experienced applicants to it, but it's still irritating.

"Stay with Mrs. Summers," says Madison. "I need to take a look around."

"Will do." Shelley hovers behind Jake, who gets busy checking Sylvia's heart rate.

Madison turns to the victim's home. It's a modest-sized, white, single-story building, just one step up from a trailer. The front yard isn't well maintained; the lawn is patchy and overgrown in places, and the house needs a lick of paint and some repairs. Walking up the porch steps, she can see no obvious signs of forced entry. The front door doesn't look especially secure, with just one flimsy lock, but it's intact with nothing other than some shallow scratches around it. The kind of scratches made by someone too inebriated to get their key in the first time, if she had to guess. The lightbulb above the door looks like it's permanently on, which is wise as there are no street lights out here. The fact the bulb hasn't been smashed suggests the killer wasn't worried about anyone seeing them here.

After slipping some protective covers over her ankle boots and snapping on a pair of latex gloves, Madison takes a step inside. It's stuffy and could do with a window being opened. A sweet, sickly odor hits her and she instantly thinks of rotting pumpkins. That's when she notices the fall decorations everywhere. They make the living room look warm and inviting.

The living room and kitchen share a space, with just a narrow breakfast bar separating them, and the house is tidy. There are no dirty dishes in the sink, the counter is wiped clean and there's almost no clutter apart from framed photographs and candles on a sideboard, along with the fall decorations. She leans in toward the photographs. Various women and children grin at the camera but Madison doesn't yet know which one is Terri Summers. A look at the carpet tells her it's been vacuumed recently. Madison wonders if Terri always keeps a tidy house or whether her killer has been covering their tracks.

The only thing that looks out of place is a sweat-stained pillow and a crumpled blanket on the couch. They suggest someone slept there last night, maybe after a heated argument. Moving past the kitchen and on to the narrow hallway, she peers in at the bathroom on the left. It's small and dark, containing just a toilet, sink and a shower, with no room for storage cabinets. She switches the overhead light on and can see no obvious bloodstains anywhere. It's as clean as the other room. She'll still ask her forensic technician to do a full sweep of the place, even though there are no signs of a struggle anywhere.

A cough behind her makes her turn.

"Afternoon." Officer Goodwin points to the bedroom. "Our victim's in here." She follows him. He's in his late twenties, tall, with short black hair. He has an arrogance about him that's unappealing and since she got her job back at LCPD she hasn't had too much to do with him. She's heard from the others that he thinks he's some kind of hotshot. She doesn't mind that in a young officer, as long as they have something about them to back it up.

She enters the bedroom and sees the victim lying awkwardly face-up on the bed. Madison's hand instinctively goes to her nose as she approaches, although the body isn't smelling too bad yet, signaling she hasn't been dead long. But the sweet, somewhat coppery smell of blood, mixed with urine from the body and the heat from the house, makes Madison crave fresh air. She looks at Goodwin. "Open that window behind you, would you?"

He does, and the burst of cold air is a relief. It doesn't make this small room feel any less claustrophobic though. Aside from the queen-size bed in the middle of the room, one nightstand on the left and a large closet on the right, there's no room for anything else. The bedroom's door opens onto the end of the bed and you'd need to close it to get around to the closet.

Madison focuses on the bed. The victim's pink comforter is soaked in blood, but it's already drying in places, suggesting this murder didn't happen within the last couple of hours, maybe not even today. The victim has fallen diagonally, with her head pointing to the far corner of the room, which means both walls behind her are sprayed with a mist of blood, tissue and brain matter from the bullet's exit wound. She must've stood facing the doorway when she was shot. The fluid on the walls looks dry and Madison can see a bullet hole. It appears that the bullet went through the victim's head *and* the drywall beyond, before exiting the house. She crouches to look under the bed. Nothing but a couple of shoeboxes stored away. A quick rummage through them shows nothing of concern. She stands, satisfied there's no gun in here, so they can definitely rule out suicide. "What time exactly did her mom say she found her?"

Officer Goodwin shrugs. "No idea. I couldn't get anything out of her, so I let her wait outside."

She looks back at Terri Summers and it's hard not to feel for her. To be attacked in her own home—somewhere she should have been safe—is horrifying. She's dressed in what was a white T-shirt and a short black denim skirt, with black ankle boots on her feet and bare legs. She's wearing makeup and jewelry and looks like she could have been on her way out somewhere, or maybe on her way home, depending on when she was shot. Half of her blonde hair has been stained red by the blood from the exit wound to the back of her head. There's only one trail of blood to the front of her face, from the bullet wound in her fore-head. It snakes down to her right eye where it's pooled, obscuring the pupil. Her left eye is glazed over.

"Looks like a home invasion gone wrong to me," says Good-win. "I'm willing to bet that when the perp discovered he had an attractive woman alone in the house he tried to get her in the bedroom to sexually assault her, but she resisted."

Madison frowns. "That's the least likely scenario I could think of. I mean, look around, Officer. Nothing's been disturbed, there are no signs of forced entry, she's fully clothed and, to rule out robbery as well, she's still wearing a diamond ring on her hand."

Goodwin crosses his arms defensively. "Okay, so it was her boyfriend. I hear he's a loser who has a rap sheet for beating women."

Madison looks back at the victim. "She took a bullet to the face. Not to the back of her head, or a random shot to her body. To her *face*. This was definitely done by someone who knew her. Someone who looked her in the eye as they fired the weapon." She turns to Goodwin. "And I can guarantee you it wasn't a stranger."

CHAPTER THREE

Madison watches as Alex Parker—LCPD's only forensic technician—walks through the hallway just as Officer Goodwin exits the house to search for the bullet outside.

Alex is British, in his early thirties and always dresses the same: a T-shirt with a vintage band motif, black skinny jeans and sneakers. But now, his clothes are covered in a blue protective suit and he's holding a face mask. As he enters the bedroom he smiles widely. "Good afternoon, Detective. How are you today?"

She likes how he always asks that before anything else, no matter how bad the crime scene is that they're standing in. It's almost like a dead body is just part of the furniture for him. "Good. And you?"

"I'm very well, thank you. It's hard not to be on a stormy autumnal day like today. We won't have many more like this before winter sets in." Finally, he looks at the victim. "Oh dear. The poor woman. The only consolation is that her death would've been instant." He looks at Madison. "I assume you've already ruled out suicide?"

She nods. "There's no gun present in the room. And no

shell casing." The bedroom is as tidy as the rest of the house, so she would have found the shell casing easily in a room of this size.

"Hmm. So our assailant either took both with him when he left or he used a revolver." Alex goes silent as he leans in to look, not at the victim, but at the surrounding area. He scans the bed, then the wall and the objects around it. There's a book on the nightstand; it looks like a crime novel as it has a noose on the cover.

"We opened the window," says Madison. "Needed some fresh air."

He nods. "I'd say she was shot at close range for this kind of blood spatter pattern behind her and because of how small this room is. The killer probably stood exactly where you are now, in the doorway. She'll have a large exit wound to the back of her head no doubt." He stands up straight. "Have we found the bullet yet?"

"I just asked Officer Goodwin to find where it settled outside so that you can work your magic."

He smiles. "Excellent. Apart from photographing and processing the scene, is there anything specific you'd like me to do?"

She thinks and runs through the list out loud. "Fingerprints, blood swabs, fibers, fingernail scrapings, in case she had a chance to grab her attacker. I'd like to know what type of gun was used. And the rest of the house is pretty clean but look for evidence of a struggle elsewhere." She sighs. "Find me some foreign DNA."

"Ah, DNA." He winks. "My favorite three letters of the alphabet."

Madison smiles faintly. To call him a geek would be a simplified cliché but he certainly acts like one sometimes. It makes her wonder what he's like outside of work.

"I'll get straight on it."

"Thanks," she says. "Dr. Scott's on her way. Hopefully she can estimate how long ago this happened." Lena Scott is the town's medical examiner.

"I'm sure she will. Let me fetch my kit from the car." Alex squeezes by her to exit the small room.

She looks back at the bed. Something about the awkward way Terri's body has landed has her intrigued. Her left arm is behind her lower back, taking the weight of her body, as if she's trying to hide something. Madison carefully rolls Terri's body onto her right shoulder, just enough to see her other hand, which is closed around an object. A single red bead pokes out. It must be some kind of jewelry.

She frowns, trying to figure out why Terri was clutching it. Maybe it was just something she wore out last night and was in the process of taking off when she was attacked. Madison uses her free hand to try to pull the item from Terri's grasp but her grip is too tight. Her body is clearly in full rigor mortis. Madison will need to ask Lena to extract it once the rigor passes.

While she's level with the victim, she has a closer inspection of her face. The lips are blue with what Madison first thought was a fading layer of red lipstick on top, but on closer inspection she can see it's actually red wine stains. "Huh." A quick look around the room shows there are no wineglasses in here.

She gets up and walks to the kitchen. No wineglasses, or any dirty dishes, here either. Rifling through the trash, she can't find an empty wine bottle. Terri must have gone out to a bar or restaurant last night. If Madison can find out where she went, she can pull surveillance footage to see who she was with at the end of the night. Maybe Troy Randle caught her on a date with another guy and waited for her to get home before confronting her. In which case, who was the other man? And could Troy have killed him too? She sighs at the thought she could get called out to the mystery man's house soon, once he's discovered dead.

Then it occurs to her that she hasn't seen Terri's purse or cell phone anywhere. Another look around confirms it, which means whoever killed her took them. But why? It can't be robbery or they would have taken the diamond ring from her finger and searched for other items they could sell, including the car outside. Nothing else looks like it's been touched and Terri's car keys are on the coffee table. Perhaps there is something incriminating on Terri's phone. Messages. Her call history. The service provider should be able to help with her call history.

Alex heads past her to the bedroom as Madison steps out of the house. The air is notably cooler and fresher outside and she takes a deep breath to clear her lungs. They need to find Troy Randle immediately. He's their best suspect at this point. She walks over to the victim's mom. She's still in the passenger seat of her car and it looks like Jake has given her something to calm her nerves as she's less agitated. "She's ready to talk now," he says, as he packs his things together.

"Thanks." As Jake heads back to the ambulance, Madison crouches down next to Sylvia. "Mrs. Summers? Do you mind if I get in and ask you some questions?"

"No, but I only know what I saw in there." Sylvia wipes her eyes with a tissue.

Madison goes around and slips into the driver's side, leaving the door open. She pulls out her notebook and pen. "Does Terri have any children we should be looking for?"

"No. She hadn't had children yet. One miscarriage, but no babies." Sylvia tears up as she realizes the consequences. "Which means I'll never be a grandma."

The sadness in this woman's eyes makes Madison blink hard. Her own mom died when Madison was in her twenties. The only family she has around, other than her son, Owen, is a sister in prison and a father who moved away when she was a teenager. He had split with her mom and started a new life up in Alaska without them. She often wonders why he didn't get in touch when she was imprisoned. Shame, probably. "Could you give me Terri's cell number? Her phone's missing and I need to contact her service provider, see if they can locate it."

Sylvia closes her eyes before reeling off the number from memory.

Madison writes it down along with Sylvia's number and home address. "Thanks. Do you know what Terri was doing yesterday? Did she have a job or was she home all day?"

"She worked as a care assistant for the elderly, but it was her day off. She usually works five or six days a week and varying hours, depending on her schedule. I didn't speak to her at all yesterday but the night before she told me she was planning on staying home. Her boyfriend was down to work all day, so I think she was looking forward to having the house to herself."

"Her boyfriend is Troy Randle?"

Sylvia nods. "This is his home, but you wouldn't know it since Terri moved in. She cleaned it up good and proper. She keeps it nice and he doesn't even appreciate it. *He* must've done this to her. I told her so many times to get out while she still could because I was sure he'd started hurting her."

It's an age-old story that Madison's seen play out many times, but she can't jump to conclusions because if Troy turns out *not* to be responsible for this, she'll have wasted valuable time that could have been spent tracking down the real killer. "You've seen him hurt her?"

"Never with my own eyes." Sylvia pushes the tissue to her wet nose. "But I've seen the bruises. I was mortified that she'd let him treat her that way. She was an intelligent woman, Detective. I assumed she'd never put up with that kind of thing from a man."

Madison has heard this before too, from the friends and family of other domestic violence victims. But leaving an abuser isn't as easy as everyone wants to believe. "This is really important; do you know where Troy might be now?"

Sylvia shakes her head. "Either on the run or in some bar somewhere. He's a drunk. I can't understand what she saw in him. He works at the Fill-up gas station." Sylvia's cell phone rings and she leans behind Madison to retrieve it from the purse on the back seat. To Madison, she says, "It's my sister, Maggie. Oh God, I've got to tell her what's happened."

Madison squeezes Sylvia's spare hand. "I'll give you some privacy." She gets out of the car and overhears Sylvia trying to explain while sobbing. It's gut-wrenching to listen to. Madison approaches Shelley. "If Troy Randle turns up, don't let him in the house. Cuff him and take him down to the station for questioning. Meanwhile, ask dispatch to issue a BOLO. I want him brought in immediately."

"Roger that."

A car pulls in and Madison watches as Dr. Lena Scott gets out. A coroner's van pulls up right behind her.

"Afternoon, Detective," she says. Even on a blustery cold day like today Lena manages to look gorgeous in her skinny jeans, ivory silk blouse under a warm winter coat, and knee-high leather boots that look newly polished. All the guys at the station like Lena and not just because of her good looks and long brown hair. She's still new to town, so she's considered somewhat of an anomaly *and* a challenge. Not many new people move to this town and Madison's yet to find out what attracted her to it. Or what she's running from.

She gives Lena a rundown of what she knows so far and tells her where the body is. "Alex is processing the scene. There's not much to go on, so he shouldn't be long."

"Sounds like I won't find anything on our victim other than the gunshot wound then?" says Lena.

"Right. Unless she's got any drugs in her system. It looks

like she's clutching something in her left hand, but I couldn't retrieve it. Could you bag it up for me when you get a chance?"

"Of course."

An awkward silence falls over them and Madison wonders why Lena appears nervous. "You okay?" she asks.

Lena smiles, embarrassed. "Sure. I just... I wanted to ask you a question about your friend Nate."

Madison finds herself unexpectedly tensing. Nate Monroe is a PI she met earlier this year when she was at her lowest point, after her release from prison. As a result of what they've been through together since then, he's now her closest friend and she's fiercely protective of him. But she can't understand why she would bristle at the thought of Lena asking about him. "Go ahead."

Blushing, Lena asks, "Are you two an item?"

Madison laughs. That's not what she was expecting. She knows there's a lot of speculation about her and Nate's relationship because he was staying with her and Owen until he got his own place recently, but they've never dated or slept together. Madison's been single since she split up with her ex—Stephanie Garcia—ten years ago. She hasn't been in a relationship with anyone—male or female—since before she was imprisoned. It's a little hard to trust people once those closest to you have let you down so badly. "No, nothing like that. Why?"

Lena takes a deep breath. "I just wanted to check as I don't want to step on your toes. I keep bumping into him around town and he seems like a good guy. I mean, I know he has that whole death row history going on and all, but... I like him."

Death row history. Madison smiles. That's one way to describe Nate spending seventeen years on death row in Texas for a murder he didn't commit.

Lena averts her eyes to the ground. "I just wanted to check if he was single. Just in case I ever want to ask him for coffee or something. I mean, I probably won't because who has time to date these days, right?"

Madison thinks Lena would be great for Nate. She's warm and intelligent and he deserves someone in his life, especially now he's moving on from his past. But she doesn't want anyone wasting his time. "I'm pretty sure he's a free agent. Just..." She chews her lip as she tries to think how to word it delicately so as not to offend. "Just make sure you're ready for a relationship before you ask him out. He's been through a lot, you know?"

Slowly nodding, Lena says, "I read all about him online. Do you think someone can ever get over spending that long waiting for an execution date without serious psychological damage?"

Madison crosses her arms. She thinks of the nightmares Nate has. How he dreams he's in the death chamber, strapped down for his lethal injection. And of his past depressive episodes. One time he was so bad he wanted to step in front of a truck. Suddenly she wishes Lena would leave him alone, let Nate make the first move if he's interested. But it's not her place to say. So instead, she smiles. "He's about as screwed up as any other resident of this town."

Lena laughs. "I'll bear that in mind. Thanks. I better get inside."

Madison watches her walk into the house and wonders if she just ruined things for Nate. The roar of a car's engine distracts her. She spins around. A gray pickup truck skids through the mud to an abrupt stop beside the coroner's van and a stocky, aggravated guy gets out.

Madison watches as Shelley pulls her weapon and says, "Hands where I can see them, Mr. Randle."

Troy Randle glances at Shelley, but he's still advancing. "I need to talk to you." He's pointing at Madison now. Her hand hovers over her own weapon. "You better not try to pin this on me!" he yells.

With force, Madison says, "Mr. Randle, I need you to stop

where you are and put your hands over your head where I can see them."

He doesn't slow down but Madison can't see a weapon. She gestures to Shelley to lower her gun so as not to aggravate him further. "I'm happy to talk to you about this but I need you to stop where you are."

"But you're not listening to me!" he shouts. "I didn't kill her. It could easily be me dead in there instead!"

Madison wonders how he knows his girlfriend is dead if he hasn't been inside the house yet today. And if he *was* in the house earlier, why didn't he call the police when he discovered his girlfriend's body?

Before she can ask him anything he reaches into his coat pocket and suddenly a gunshot rings out and echoes through the trees, sending birds flying.

Madison gasps.

Mrs. Summers screams behind them and Troy Randle drops to the ground.

With her gun now outstretched, Madison swings around to see who fired a shot.

Officer Goodwin is standing next to the house, lowering his weapon. "He was reaching for a gun."

Madison doesn't have time to chastise him right now. She runs toward Troy and shouts to Shelley, "Get the ambulance back here right now!"

CHAPTER FOUR

Nate Monroe switches the car's engine off after finding a parking space outside Ruby's Diner. Turning to his passenger he says, "You want to stay in the car or do you want to stretch your legs?"

He gets the silent treatment.

"Look, I know you don't like waiting outside but I'm here on business. I need to focus."

His passenger looks away, unimpressed.

"I'll order something for you, if you like?"

Nothing.

"You don't want a sausage?"

The dog's head whips around so fast his tongue sticks out the side of his mouth. Nate smiles. "Oh, so *now* you're talking to me?"

Brody—a German shepherd, Siberian husky mix—barks excitedly. His tail loudly whips the seat.

"Sausage it is, buddy. Stay in the car." Nate opens the back windows for air, knowing full well the back seat could get drenched in a downpour, but it's for Brody. "Remember what to do if anyone tries to steal my car?"

Brody sits up straight and barks menacingly.

Nate laughs. "Oh my God, you're killing me." Brody is a stray he picked up from a previous investigation. Nate might be a private investigator, but Brody's the real deal—a trained police dog who lost his handler in the line of duty. After that he was left to his own devices as a guard dog for a summer camp in Shadow Falls, California. That's where Nate met him. They've been inseparable ever since and Brody has played a big part in helping him overcome his tumultuous past. He rubs the dog's neck before getting out of the car and entering the diner.

It's loud inside, with the bustle of chatty customers, the scraping of knives and forks, and the noise coming from the TV above the counter. The smell of fried food hits him immediately. To some, that would be comforting, but to Nate, it smells like prison food. There were never any healthy options inside. Everything was swimming in grease or dry as a bone. There was no in-between.

At the counter Vince Rader—owner of Ruby's Diner—notices him. He nods over to a spare booth. "Take a seat, I'll be right over."

Nate slips into the booth and checks on Brody through the large glass window. Brody's staring back at him and Nate can't tell if he's just imagining the drool coming from the dog's mouth.

"Hey, sweetie."

He looks up and sees Carla, one of the full-time waitresses. "Afternoon, Carla. How are you?"

"Good." She fills his coffee cup then looks over her shoulder. "Vince is acting all gruff as usual but you better believe he's excited about today. He's been waiting for your car to pull in for the last hour. Don't tell him I told you that." She winks before walking away.

Nate feels the heavy burden of having a new case to solve.

His clients always get their hopes up, no matter how much he tells them he might not find the answers they're looking for. And, many times, if he does find answers, they're not the ones his clients were hoping for.

Vince slides into the booth opposite him. He's tall and slim, sporting a buzzcut that he's probably favored ever since his days in the U.S. Navy. He's in his late fifties now but he bought this diner with his wife, Ruby, eight years ago. His legs don't fit under the table so he leaves them poking out, crossed. "Where's Brody? I've got some breakfast scraps ready for him."

"I left him in the car so we wouldn't get you in trouble with the health inspector. He'll be okay out there."

Vince nods. "You finished sorting your friend's estate yet?"

Nate's thoughts turn to Rex Hartley, his only friend in the world upon his release from death row two years ago. Last month Rex was murdered in his home and it fell to Nate to settle his affairs. He's missed him every day since and still picks up his phone with the intention of calling him. "Yeah. The rescue shelter he worked with now owns his ranch in San Diego, along with all the animals he cared for. Although I was under strict instructions to bring back an animal for Owen. I think he was expecting a dog but Madison said it had to be a cat so it could look after itself once Owen gets bored of it. So he now has an energetic kitten."

Vince laughs. "I bet the journey home from San Diego was interesting with Brody *and* a kitten in the car."

Nate smiles. "The cat was in a carry case but he kept reaching out to grab Brody's tail. Poor dog couldn't wait to get home."

"Won't Owen be off to college next year?"

"Yeah, then Madison will have a cat to keep her company." Nate thinks Vince is stalling by asking about anything other than what he came here for, and he can understand that. After all, he's here to investigate what happened to the guy's wife and grandson.

Six years ago, Ruby Rader and four-year-old Oliver Rader vanished after a day spent together. Neither of them has ever been seen or heard from since. There are no leads and LCPD is no longer investigating the case. The grief Vince carries weighs on him and shows in his face, which is heavily lined. "Can I get you anything to eat?" Vince asks.

"No, I'm fine." Nate pulls out a legal pad and pen, ready to take notes. "I'm not going to lie, Vince. This isn't going to be easy for you, going over old ground and digging up the past, but I wouldn't do it if I didn't think you could handle it."

Vince's hands tremble slightly as he sips his steaming coffee. According to Detective Douglas, who, along with Madison's predecessor Mike Bowers, investigated this case back in the day, Vince was the primary suspect when Ruby and Oliver disappeared. Lost Creek PD did a thorough investigation at the time and although they've never found the bodies, Douglas has previously given the impression that he still believes Vince had something to do with it. But to Nate that doesn't ring true. Vince asked him to investigate the cold case. He wants to find his loved ones so that he can bury them and try to move on. If he was their killer, he'd be reluctant to pursue any of this.

There's always the chance—no matter how slim—that Vince is playing Nate, and by asking him to investigate their disappearance he wants it to appear as if he wasn't involved. If so, it's a risky strategy.

"I'm ready," says Vince. "I need answers. It's time."

A middle-aged woman walks up to them. "Sorry to interrupt you and your friend, Vince, but what case are you covering on your podcast this week?"

Vince smiles broadly. He's proud of his *Crime and Dine* podcast, broadcast from his apartment above the diner. It's something he started after his wife's disappearance. He focuses on true crime cases and sometimes has interesting guests such as Shane Kennedy, the crime writer who went missing last month. Unfortunately for Shane, appearing on the podcast proved deadly. "I'm focusing on Beth Smith this time, Hattie."

Hattie frowns. "Which one is she again?"

"She was the British female serial killer who wreaked havoc in New Hampshire. She terrorized that poor detective guy." When Hattie still doesn't show any recognition, Vince waves a hand. "Just tune in tomorrow and you'll hear all about it. It's a good one, I can guarantee you that. The woman was batshit crazy."

Hattie turns to Nate and smiles. "I like those ones."

Nate laughs.

As she walks away, Vince says, "It's always the ones you'd least expect who love hearing all the gory details."

Nate gets down to business before they're interrupted again. "So, to get my investigation started I intend to question everyone Ruby had contact with on the day she vanished. It'll help me piece together a timeline of events. Are you comfortable with that?"

"Of course," says Vince. "I've got nothing to hide. But what if no one remembers that far back?"

Nate sips his coffee and glances out the window. The rain is holding off for now and he can see that Brody's jumped out of the car's back window and is watching people come and go from the diner. He won't stray too far. Not when he's owed a sausage. "In my experience, witnesses usually remember the events of a significant day. I'm sure Ruby and Oliver's disappearance was all over the news that night and for the weeks after. It would've triggered people to talk about where they were when they last saw them. That should stick in their memories. Besides, thanks to Kate Flynn's report a couple of days ago, everyone knows I'm investigating it for you. That's sure to have got people talking about it again." Kate is one of the local TV reporters.

Vince nods. "I hope so. I always got the feeling that some people didn't want to speak to the cops at the time, but maybe now that enough time has passed, they'll be more helpful."

"Do you know why they weren't forthcoming?"

Vince looks him in the eye. "Detective Douglas. He hadn't been in town long and he was an asshole. You've met the guy, so you know what he's like. He's not exactly approachable."

Nate hasn't had any good experiences with Detective Douglas either, but Madison's managed to forgive and forget, so he must have some redeeming qualities.

"Besides," continues Vince. "Living somewhere like this you soon realize the locals are happy to keep the town's festering secrets away from outsiders. Douglas was an outsider. He hadn't been here long when this happened. They're all scared of outsiders upsetting the status quo."

"I'm an outsider," says Nate.

"True. So it could go one of two ways; they'll either talk to you, or they'll see you off for daring to speak their secrets aloud."

Nate sighs. "Great."

Vince laughs. "I don't think a handsome young guy like you will have anything to worry about if you target the women. They'll be flattered you want to talk to them."

Nate's recently turned forty so he's not young anymore, but people do open up to him. Unless they're hiding something that is. "Tell me about the last time you saw Ruby. What was she doing?"

Vince's attention turns to the entrance of the diner and his face goes deathly pale. His mouth drops open as he slowly stands up. "Well, I'll be damned."

Nate follows his gaze. A guy not much younger than him is standing in the doorway. He's not all the way inside and appears reluctant to let go of the door behind him, almost like he's just realized coming here was a bad idea.

"Matty?" says Vince.

Nate stares at the stranger. This must be Matt Rader; Vince and Ruby's estranged son.

CHAPTER FIVE

Facebook Messenger

Hey.

Have you thought any more about what we discussed?

It's all I think about.

I'm sorry.

Maybe I should come visit.

I would appreciate that.

I feel like I'm going crazy.

Besides, we haven't seen each other in forever.

I heard some PI is looking into the cold case now.

Is that right?

Right.

People are starting to talk about it again.

It won't ever go away.

I agree.

I'll message you when I'm in town.

Look forward to it.

CHAPTER SIX

Madison heads into the police station through a side door. She has a mixed history with this place but she still gets a thrill every time she walks in. Policing is all she's good at, which she found out after being released from prison. She was forced to waitress at a nasty burger joint to make ends meet. She could never memorize people's orders, so everything would get delivered with an item missing, and the tiny pencils she was supposed to use were no good to her, she snapped every single one of them. Her boss said she was so highly strung that she was taking her rage out on the pencils, and he was probably right. She was relieved to ditch that job and knows that if she ever gets fired from LCPD, she should avoid anything in customer service. Fixing a fake smile on her face for the more obnoxious customers isn't something that comes naturally.

The station's small kitchen is her first stop. She needs a refill. The kitchen always smells strongly of stale coffee and it's messy as usual, so she wipes away the coffee stains and rinses some cups before pouring a drink. After her first gulp, Sergeant Steve Tanner approaches her.

"Hey, Madison." He sighs like he's delivering bad news.

"Chief Mendes is pissed. She told me she wants to see you as soon as you step foot in the building."

"Lucky me. Did you hear what went down?"

He nods. "Shelley called it in to Stella, so everyone knows." Stella's job in dispatch means she needs to disseminate information quickly and to the relevant people, but she also spreads it to anyone else—internally—who will listen. Madison can't hold that against her, after all she's gone to her for the inside scoop on more than one occasion herself. Stella has worked the graveyard shift since forever but is transitioning to days now she's nearing retirement. She used to foster kids when she was younger, while working here part-time. Never had any kids of her own though. Occasionally those she fostered come back to visit her but most have moved away and moved on with their lives, something Madison knows Stella struggles with as she loved them all as if they were her own children.

"I can't believe Goodwin shot someone," says Steve. "As well as a pain in the ass, he's a liability."

"You can say that again. I just hope Mendes doesn't blame me for what he did."

Steve looks sympathetic as she leaves the kitchen and heads to the chief's office. Madison glances through the glass panel before knocking. Chief Mendes is staring at her computer screen. Being a neat freak, she keeps her desk almost empty, with just a computer, a keyboard and a coaster with no coffee-stained mug sitting on top. Her looks are just as pristine; long black hair swept back into her signature ponytail, not a strand out of place. There are no signs of gray hairs, despite Mendes being in her mid-forties. The same gold necklace she always wears hangs from her neck and she's wearing a dark pantsuit, probably designer. A stranger would be forgiven for thinking this woman has never done a hard day's work in her life, especially not in law enforcement, but Madison knows she started her career as a police officer before working as a special agent in the Colorado Bureau of Investigation. She came to Lost Creek just months ago, after her predecessor's retirement. She's still new enough to the PD for everyone to be wary around her. Potty mouths are kept to a minimum for now too.

"You wanted to see me?" says Madison, tentatively stepping a foot inside the office but remaining close enough to the door to give the impression she's too busy to stand around talking.

Chief Mendes looks up over her glasses. "What the hell went down out there, Detective?"

Madison takes a deep breath. "Apparently, Officer Goodwin thought our murder suspect was about to draw a weapon and harm one of us."

"And *was* he about to draw a weapon?"

Madison didn't think he was at the time and her instinct had proven right. "No. Troy Randle was unarmed. But he didn't stop advancing when asked and he was obviously aggravated as he reached into his coat pocket. Anyway, he's on his way to the hospital."

"How serious is his injury?"

"Lucky for him and us, Officer Goodwin is a bad shot. The bullet hit Randle's shoulder. A couple of inches over and it could've proven fatal. He was making a lot of noise, so the EMT thinks he'll be fine after treatment. I've sent Officer Williams to the hospital; she'll keep me updated. I plan to go and question Randle as soon as he's well enough."

Chief Mendes stands up. "There's going to have to be an investigation into Officer Goodwin's actions. You shouldn't have let this happen."

Madison tenses. "He didn't exactly consult me first. And with all due respect, Chief, I was at the crime scene with just two uniforms for support while trying to brief both Alex and Dr. Scott, and keep the crime scene secure in case the killer returned. I really could've done with more backup. Detective Douglas for example."

Mendes frowns. "I assumed he was there with you." She leaves her desk and walks toward Madison, who steps aside. Poking her head around the door, Mendes scans the cubicles in the open-plan office. "Sergeant Tanner. Where's Douglas?" she asks.

Steve stands up. "He's not in yet, Chief. I've tried calling him but he's not picking up." Then, out of some kind of loyalty he adds, "I'm sure he's on his way."

Mendes checks her watch before returning her attention to Madison. "Swing by his place, would you? It's almost two o'clock. He should've been in by now. You can tell him from me that if he's not at work by the end of the day, there's no point him coming back at all. I've already been more than generous with my patience when it comes to Douglas."

Madison nods. She doesn't bother explaining she was at his place earlier and got no answer, because she doesn't want Mendes to know he might be drinking again. "I'll go there now. Dr. Scott's prioritizing the autopsy on Terri Summers but I'm not expecting any surprises. I can't say for sure yet whether her boyfriend killed her but he has a history of domestic violence."

"I don't want you to say that to the press," says Mendes. "You need to know for sure before you go slandering the guy our department just shot. The press will be all over us for this mistake." She sighs. "I just hope he *is* our victim's killer, for Officer Goodwin's sake."

Madison suddenly feels sorry for Goodwin. She's experienced what it's like to be the focus of negative press attention and she wouldn't wish it on anyone—but part of her wonders whether anyone will care that he shot someone like Troy Randle.

As she leaves the station her phone buzzes and she sighs when she sees who it is: Kate Flynn, Madison's friend from high school, who now hounds her for the inside scoop on the latest crimes so she can be the first reporter to break the story. She must have found out about Terri and Troy, but Madison can't talk to her now, so she declines the call and shoots her a message saying she'll call back when she gets a minute. It's more important that she finds Detective Douglas.

Once in her car she gets a text from her son.

The turkey's been delivered. It's huge. Can I eat a leg for lunch?

In preparation for Thanksgiving, she'd ordered a precooked turkey, knowing she wouldn't have time to cook a full roast for four people on a worknight. She was intending to cook the potatoes and vegetables herself, but with how today's panning out she's probably going to have to get them from Ruby's Diner on her way home. She had warned Vince that might happen, so he's prepared. She replies to Owen.

Don't you dare touch it! And if Nate and Brody turn up before I get home from work, keep it out of the dog's reach.

Then, as an afterthought, she adds:

Keep Bandit away too.

Bandit is Owen's new kitten. He's completely white all over except for a thick black line of fur across his eyes, making him look like a bank robber.

Owen instantly replies with a facepalm emoji. It makes her smile. Sometimes it's easier to communicate with him through messaging than it is face to face. Owen may act hard done by but he's looking forward to dinner tonight. He's close with Nate and couldn't understand why he wanted to move out of their place and into his own. Madison worries that Owen's in desperate need of a father figure since his own dad died. She also worries he's relying too much on Nate to fill that role.

Detective Douglas is good with Owen too, which surprised her since he isn't a people person. Owen manages to bring out the light-hearted side of him and Douglas has given him advice on which colleges to apply to. In a show of support for Douglas's fragile sobriety, Owen has hidden Madison's wine from view and they'll all be drinking nonalcoholic options with dinner later. Nate's promised to bring a couple of apple pies for dessert. Her mouth starts watering at the thought of all the food laid out on the dinner table. This will be her first Thanksgiving in eight years, because of her time in prison.

The closer it's got the more she's been thinking about her father. She's never really allowed her thoughts to go there since he moved away when she was a teenager, but Owen has been asking about him and it made her realize there's no reason not to reconnect with him one day. He's really her only other remaining family member. She doesn't count her sister for reasons she'd rather not think about right now. Of course, it's possible it's just the holiday season that's making her sentimental, but maybe when she gets a chance she'll try to track her father down. After all, it can't be that difficult to locate an FBI agent in Alaska. Unless he's retired by now. Or dead. That's always a possibility.

Before Madison can start the car, Shelley pulls up alongside her and gets out. She shivers in the cold as she's not wearing a jacket over her black uniform. Leaning down to Madison's open window, she says, "Goodwin and I have been called in to speak with the chief. Have you just come from there?"

"Yeah. She's mad. Just stay quiet and let Goodwin explain himself. There's nothing you or I could have done to stop him shooting Troy Randle."

Shelley nods, but she looks uncertain as she watches two other officers heading out of the parking lot. "When I first started here I used to have nightmares about pulling my weapon on innocent bystanders by mistake. You know, actually shooting them dead." Her hands shake as she pushes her windswept hair out of her eyes.

Madison can't tell if she's shaking because she's rattled by what's happened or she's just cold. "Well, we don't know whether Troy's innocent yet. He's the most likely suspect for our homicide. But, yeah, Goodwin shouldn't have reacted that way." She sighs. "So who's at the crime scene now?"

"Aside from Kate Flynn and a couple of other reporters, Alex is still processing the scene and Officer Sanchez is stationed outside, securing the property. Terri Summers has been taken to the morgue."

She should've known Kate would be there already. "Has anyone questioned the neighbors yet, to see if they saw or heard anything?"

"Yeah, I spoke to a couple of them and Goodwin spoke to the rest. As far as I know, no one heard anything out of the ordinary except for the next-door neighbor, George Ryan. He thought he heard a gunshot last night but he didn't check the time. Apparently, he and his daughter have heard a lot of gunshots this week, on account of people illegally hunting turkeys for Thanksgiving."

Madison rolls her eyes. "Why pay for one when you can get one for free, right?"

"Right. He was genuinely upset to hear Terri Summers had died. Said she sometimes babysat for him, and his daughter will be devastated by the news."

"That's sad." It sounds to Madison as if Terri was someone people liked. Which makes it harder to understand why anyone would want to kill her. "Terri's cell phone and purse were missing from the house. Keep an eye out for them, would you?"

"Sure. I'll tell the others."

"Thanks. Did Douglas turn up after I left?"

Shelley shakes her head. "No. Sorry. Do you think he's back on the booze?"

Madison's stomach flips with dread. "I hope not. Because Mendes isn't in the mood to give him one final chance." To change the subject she asks, "What are you doing tonight? You're not working, are you?"

"No." Shelley sighs. "I'm that sad, pathetic thirty-one-year-old single woman who has to spend Thanksgiving getting quizzed by my aunts and uncles as to why I haven't met a nice man and settled down yet."

Madison shoots her an amused but sympathetic smile.

"Every time I see my Aunt Gina she asks me how come I haven't met someone through work. I have to remind her that everyone I meet is either dead, drunk or handcuffed." Shelley rolls her eyes.

"No luck with Jake Rubio yet then?" Madison knows Shelley has had the hots for Jake—the EMT—since forever. But he's a notorious womanizer and Shelley's back and forth as to whether she wants to go there or not.

Shelley stands up straight. "No, I've decided I don't need the hassle, no matter how hot he is. I don't want to be just another notch on his bedpost."

Heavy drops of rain start hitting the windshield, so Madison starts the engine. "If I were you, I'd hide in the kitchen until Goodwin gets here. You need to face Mendes together or you'll be the one who gets it in the neck. I'm heading to Douglas's place. Good luck."

Shelley grimaces as Madison pulls away.

CHAPTER SEVEN

On the way to Douglas's house Madison gets a call from dispatch telling her one of Troy Randle's friends has heard what's happened to him and is demanding to speak to her.

"He wants the lead detective," says Stella. "Wouldn't tell me anything else."

Madison sighs. "Fine. Where does he live?"

"He owns the bar over on Deacon Street: Joe's Saloon. Says he'll be there all day. His name's Joseph Manvers."

Madison has been in the bar a couple of times but she couldn't say which bartender was Joe. She swings her car around in an empty parking lot. "I'm on my way."

The windshield wipers click back and forth, as she drives the short distance to the bar. Through the rain she can see a guy waiting in the open doorway with the bar lit up behind him. It's only mid afternoon but she'd bet the place is busy already.

As she parks out front, she wonders why one of Troy's friends would want to speak to her. If he's as aggressive as Troy is and he's mad at his buddy getting hurt by a police officer, he might want to take it out on her. She instinctively touches the gun at her hip before getting out of the car and decides it's better for him to come to her in case he has buddies inside waiting to ambush her. She motions him over to the car. At first, he raises his hands as if to say "You want me to get wet?" but she's insistent, so he runs on over. "Get in," she orders.

He does. Rubbing the rain out of his hair and onto the car's interior he glances at her. "You know it's warmer in the bar, right?"

She can't see a weapon on him. "It's quicker this way and I'm busy. I'm Detective Harper. So, what did you want to see me about?" She assesses him as he dries his hands on his shirt. He has Mediterranean features, with jet-black hair and olive skin. His eyes are the greenest she's ever seen. He looks about the same age as her; thirty-seven.

"Is it true Troy's dead?" he asks. "It was on the news that someone died up at Trent Road and I recognized Troy's house, but they didn't name the victim."

She has to be careful not to reveal too much, but he might know something that could help the case. "No, he's not dead. He's wounded, but he'll be fine." Relief washes over his face and she can't help feeling annoyed that this guy cares about someone like Troy Randle. "It's Terri who's dead."

He looks at her properly. "Shit. Not Terri." He shakes his head. "She was a great girl. I thought she'd change Troy. Make him less..." He doesn't finish his thought.

"Angry? Volatile? Less *abusive?*"

He slowly nods. "Troy used to be a good friend of mine but after he did time for assaulting a previous girlfriend, I distanced myself from him. Once he got out he started drinking heavily, always spending time at the bar. The liquor just got a hold of him, you know?"

She knows. She thinks of Detective Douglas and his fast downward spiral.

"I had to throw him out a couple of times. That was awkward."

"Was he here last night?" she asks.

"Yeah. He arrived early evening and got progressively drunk before getting into a stupid fist fight with some bikers. It sprawled out into the parking lot and next thing I know I heard a gunshot over the music. I was about to call the cops but thought I'd better check if anyone was dead first. If *Troy* was dead." His eyes well up. He's clearly upset by how much his friend's life has changed, which means Troy can't be all bad. "One of the bikers fired a warning shot into the sky. No one was hurt, and Troy's so-called friends dragged him into a pickup truck and drove away."

"What time was that?" she asks. She can check with Lena whether the time he was dropped off was before or after Terri's approximate time of death. "Before midnight?"

Shaking his head, he says, "No. The fight was just before closing, around one-thirty."

"And who was in the pickup with him?"

"The only guy I recognized was Mark Wheeler. He lives out near Fantasy World but I don't know where exactly." Fantasy World is the town's run-down amusement park. It attracts nothing but trouble, always has. Madison's son can attest to that.

She looks him in the eye. "Do you think Troy is capable of killing Terri?"

Joe looks away, slowly shaking his head. "I don't think he has the smarts to *plan* a murder. But even if it was a spur-of-the-moment thing caused by a drunken rage, I doubt he was capable of standing up for longer than a few seconds judging by the state he was in when he left here." He pauses. "How was she killed?"

Madison hesitates to tell him but figures she'll be telling the press later anyway. "Bullet to the face."

Raising his eyebrows, Joe says, "There's no way Troy was capable of shooting in a straight line by the time he got home."

He gets an idea. "What if he shot her by accident? Maybe he was aiming at something else."

Madison gives him a stern look. "What, at the wall? Come on, Joe. Why would he shoot anything in his own home if not to cause injury?"

He lowers his eyes. "Right. I guess I just don't want it to be true."

It's clear that whoever shot Terri did it with precision. Judging by the description Joe's given of Troy's state when he left here in the early hours of this morning, it's unlikely it was him. But Joe's his friend, he could be covering for him. For all she knows Troy left the bar sober. She points to the security cameras. "I'll need a copy of your footage from the last twenty-four hours."

He looks surprised that she wouldn't just take his word for it. "Sure."

Madison would prefer that Joe is lying, because if Troy isn't the murderer, it means Terri's killer is still free, and she has no idea what their motive was and whether they'll strike again.

Madison finally makes it to Douglas's house just after three-thirty. It's the time of year where daylight is already fading fast and the heavy black clouds that continue to build overhead make it darken even earlier. Walking up Douglas's front steps, she realizes his porch light isn't on, unlike that of his neighbors. There doesn't appear to be any light coming from inside, either. She bangs his door loudly and steps back. A curtain twitches next door but the neighbor doesn't wave.

"Come on, Douglas," she mutters. When it's clear he's not answering, she tries phoning him. His blinds are still closed, so a look through the window doesn't help, but she does hear his cell phone ringing. It's only faint, suggesting it's either somewhere near the back of the house or upstairs. Presumably that means he's hiding inside, ashamed. She sighs. She thought they had a good enough rapport by now for him to know he can greet her in any state.

The backyard is easily accessible so she wanders around the house, giving him time to get up. At the back door she knocks and waits. No answer.

"Come on, Don," she says to the door, trying to keep her voice down so the neighbors don't hear. She's assuming Douglas doesn't share details of his private life with them. "Just open up and show me you're still alive. You don't have to invite me in."

Silence.

She's starting to worry now. He could have choked on his own vomit for all she knows. "If you don't say something, I'm going to force the door open."

She tries the handle. It's locked. There's no sound at all from inside and her mind is convincing her that he's hurt in there. But if she forces her way in and it turns out he's just out buying groceries, he won't thank her for it. In fact, he'll probably never speak to her again.

She hesitates, and decides to call Chief Mendes. Maybe Douglas has turned up at work since she left. Mendes answers immediately.

"Hey, Chief. I'm outside Douglas's house for the second time today and there's no answer. I've tried his cell and can hear it ringing inside, but he's not picking up."

"He's not answering my calls either."

Madison has a sudden sinking feeling. He'll know they will be wondering where he is, so why isn't he getting in touch to reassure them he's okay? "I think he's inside his house. Maybe he's—"

"Drunk himself into a stupor?" suggests Mendes.

She hates to admit it, but she can't think of any other explanation. "Right. His doors are locked but I could probably get in easily enough. What do you think? Shall I break in?"

"I think that's a bit dramatic," says Mendes. "Let's give him until tomorrow to turn up."

"You sure? What if he's done something stupid and needs medical assistance?"

Mendes hesitates. "And no one has a spare key to his place?"

"No. You know how private he is."

Silence... until: "I'm not paying for a new door. Try not to cause too much damage and call me immediately once you've checked inside."

Madison nods. "Understood."

She slides her phone into her pocket and ignores the heavy rain drops that soak her hair. "Douglas?" she yells loudly. "You better have some pants on 'cause I'm coming in."

CHAPTER EIGHT

As Nate is still new to Lost Creek, he never met Ruby Rader, but her son, Matt, looks just like his dad: tall and slim with short brown hair, although Vince's hair is turning gray now. Vince steps forward as Matt sheepishly approaches him. Everyone in the diner appears to stop their chatter in order to watch the overdue reunion. The locals will be well aware of the history between this pair.

"It's been too long," says Vince before embracing his son.

Carla and a couple of the other waitresses are staring with genuine smiles on their faces. They probably know better than anyone how much Vince has missed him. But Nate gets a feeling Matt doesn't want to be here. There's no smile and he doesn't hug his father back. Vince had previously disclosed that Matt and his wife, Jo, seem to hold some resentment toward him for what happened but he doesn't know why. Ruby and Oliver disappeared while Ruby was babysitting their four-year-old for the day. That's not Vince's fault.

Matt pulls away first. "How have you been, Dad?"

Vince wipes his eyes. "Surviving, son. Just surviving. Not a day goes by that I don't think about your mother and son."

Matt looks away, like he doesn't want to talk about that right now. "Can we go upstairs?"

Someone walks into the diner and Nate recognizes Kate Flynn. She's without her cameraman and is checking her purse for cash, so it looks like she's come for coffee, not a story. But it's not long before she picks up on the mood in the room. She stops dead when she recognizes Matt Rader. The urge to throw questions at him must be overwhelming for an ambitious news reporter like her.

Vince spots her. "You go on upstairs, son. It's unlocked. I'll be up in a second with coffee and something to eat. You must be hungry after your journey." Vince turns to Carla, who nods before preparing some food.

Matt forces a grateful smile at his dad, which falters the minute he spots Kate. Without a word he heads behind the counter and out of view, where the stairs to Vince's apartment are. The diner chatter resumes as everyone talks among themselves about what just happened.

Vince turns to Nate with excitement in his eyes. "I never expected to see him again. It's been five years since he and Jo moved away." He sits back in the booth as if he's just had a shock.

"You okay?" asks Nate, concerned.

Rubbing the back of his neck, Vince says, "I think so. I'm starting to wonder why he's come home now."

Nate tries to reassure him. "After you gave me his number a few days ago I tried calling him. He didn't answer, so I left a voice message."

With raised eyebrows Vince says, "You work fast."

"I told him I was looking into the case at your request and that I wanted to get his perspective. I didn't expect him to show up though. Maybe Thanksgiving and the anniversary of their disappearance persuaded him to come see you. Lots of people feel the pull of family at this time of year even without that kind of anniversary looming over them."

Nate doesn't have any family to speak of. His parents are long gone and his brother and sister are presumably still back home in Kansas. He wouldn't know, they broke off all contact when he was arrested for murder almost twenty years ago. They didn't contact him once during his time on death row and he tries not to think about them, or about whether he's an uncle, and how much family life he's missed out on. When he was first exonerated and released, and trying to return to some kind of normality outside, he thought they might try to find him, to apologize for their lack of support. But they never did.

"That must be it." A huge smile breaks out on Vince's face. "I guess I better go and find out." He stands. "Sorry to mess you around. We'll have to do this another time."

"Not a problem," says Nate, standing. "Maybe Matt would be open to meeting with me once he's settled in."

Vince nods, then collects the food and drinks Carla has put together for him. Kate steps forward as if she's about to ask him a question, but she must think better of it, which is unlike her. At the counter Nate pays for his coffee and collects a sausage for Brody.

"That was Vince's son," says Kate alongside him.

"So I gather."

"Is he back to help you with the cold case?" she asks.

Nate hesitates. The minute Kate found out Vince had asked him to find Ruby and Oliver, she announced it on the news. That not only put everyone on edge and potentially gave a head start to their killer—*if* they were killed—but it means all eyes are going to be on him now. He understands the whole town wanting to know what happened to Vince's wife and grandson, but Nate doesn't want Kate reporting every step he takes during his investigation, like she does with Madison's cases. He's not law enforcement so he doesn't have to tell her anything he doesn't want to. But he also doesn't want to be rude. She's Madison's friend and actually pretty likable. "I had no idea he was coming back, neither did Vince. Sorry, but I have to get this"— he gestures to the sausage—"to Brody. Have a good day, Kate."

As he goes to pass her, she rolls her eyes. "You could be about to unearth a dangerous killer who's been living in this town in plain sight since he abducted Ruby and Oliver Rader six years ago, and you don't expect me to want to report on it?"

He turns back to her. "Listen, if I find out anyone else is at immediate danger of this person, I'll be telling LCPD. That's when you'll find out. Until then, it's best to assume I've got no leads."

He leaves the diner. Brody's clearly been watching him this whole time because he's standing right outside the diner's door, tail beating hard against the glass in excitement. His nose nuzzles the greasy takeout bag and he almost rips it from Nate's hand. "Whoa! Hold on a second."

Walking to his car, he pulls the sausage from the bag. Brody instinctively sits his ass down and stares intently, like it's a perp about to make a run for it. Nate holds it out. "Here you go." Brody takes it gently but he barely chews it. It's gone in seconds. "Did you even taste that?"

He opens the passenger door and Brody jumps straight in. Once Nate's in the driver's side he watches the rain lash against the windshield and considers where to start with the cold case now he has to wait longer to speak to Vince. He doesn't have all the facts yet, so he googles Ruby Rader's name. Several articles jump out at him. The first is from the week after her disappearance six years ago.

LOCAL WOMAN AND GRANDSON STILL MISSING

Ruby Rader, 53, and her grandson Oliver Rader, 4, have now been missing for eight days. They were last captured on

CCTV at 4.25 p.m. on the Saturday before Thanksgiving in the Fresh Is Best grocery store, where they purchased a selection of food items.

Nate watches blurry surveillance footage of them walking around the store. Oliver looks tiny on screen and he has his hand in Ruby's. Her other hand is carrying a shopping basket. Ruby appears to have shoulder-length dyed red hair and is wearing jeans and a pale blue T-shirt. The footage cuts to them leaving the store, with Oliver running ahead to the car. He appears to be smiling, enjoying spending time with his grandma, no doubt. Nate has a sudden sinking feeling. Oliver looks so small and fragile and like any other four-year-old: a happy, playful boy who's full of life. He'd be ten now, if he's still alive. Nate can't imagine how he would be. His heart goes out to Matt and his wife. To have lost their son *and* Matt's mother at the same time must have been devastating. That must be why they cut all contact with Vince when they moved away. Vince and this town are too much of a reminder of what happened and what they were missing.

He continues reading.

Mrs. Rader was due to drop Oliver at his home by six that evening. Unfortunately, they never made it to the property and they haven't been seen by anyone since leaving the store. Lost Creek's investigating detective, Don Douglas, confirmed there have been no tip-offs or potential sightings. "We firmly believe Ruby and Oliver Rader are in danger, but I cannot confirm what leads we are working on." When asked whether Mrs. Rader's husband was a suspect, he replied, "We have spoken to Vince Rader extensively and while he remains a person of interest, he has not been arrested at this time."

Nate shakes his head. Just seeing how happy Vince was

when Matt walked back into his life is enough to convince him that Vince was purely a victim in all this.

He clicks on the next article in the list, which was written a year after their disappearance.

Local couple leave town without their missing son

Matt and Joanne Rader have decided to leave Lost Creek for good after the disappearance of their four-year-old son, Oliver. Oliver went missing with his grandmother a little over twelve months ago and the pair were never heard from again. When asked why they were moving away Joanne Rader commented, "Every room I'm in at home reminds me he's missing. Every store I go to has his missing person poster up, reminding me someone did something awful to him. I can't drive past his kindergarten without crying. The police tell me they're no closer to finding him and I can't cope with living among people who know who did this. Someone is covering for Oliver's abductor. How am I supposed to work and shop in this community knowing that?"

Matt Rader added, "We haven't given up hope that Oliver could be found alive, but by the time he comes back to us, we might not be, because the weight of his disappearance is killing us. I just hope he's with my mom somewhere and they're happy, because if I consider the alternatives, I don't want to get up in the morning."

We contacted Lost Creek PD for an update on the case and were told by Detective Don Douglas that he is still considering this a missing persons case as there is no evidence to suggest they were killed. "We won't rest until both Ruby and Oliver are found, but it's true that we have currently exhausted all leads." He repeated his pleas for the public to get in touch with any information they might have and stated, "We remain committed to bringing Ruby and Oliver home to their family."

Once the talk of the town, this case appears to be a dark shadow hovering over the community, and one they would rather forget. The majority of locals believe both victims to be dead, with some even pointing the finger of blame at Vince Rader. "After Ruby went missing he started that stupid Crime and Dine *podcast," said one resident who wishes to remain anonymous. "At first, I thought it was to appeal for information about his wife's case, but now he interviews all kinds of people on there: suspects, victims, crime writers, and one time he even interviewed a woman who's on death row!"*

Detective Douglas insists Vince Rader has never been arrested in connection with his wife and grandson's disappearance and asks that people keep an open mind.

Nate lowers his phone and sighs. With no potential suspects then or now, it's clear he's got his work cut out for him.

CHAPTER NINE

SIX YEARS AGO

Ruby Rader is restocking the clean white cups on the tray behind the counter when she feels arms close around her and a kiss on her cheek. She smiles before glancing around the diner to see if anyone caught that. Carla's busy clearing tables and the breakfast waitresses are taking orders. The customers are either staring at their phones or watching the news on the small TV above the counter.

She glances up at the TV. As usual the media is covering the story about the town's first female detective who, last Christmas, was convicted of the murder of a fellow cop. Although she's been in prison for almost a year already, every time Madison Harper loses an appeal or releases a statement about her innocence, the local TV stations understandably give it a lot of airtime. She was all the town talked about when she was arrested and most people still follow her progress with interest.

Ruby's seen this footage already as it's repeated from last night's late bulletin. Madison Harper is once again insisting she was framed for Officer Levy's murder and that someone in Lost Creek was responsible. She's scaring people by saying they shouldn't trust anyone. Ruby doesn't know what's worse—that a detective could murder someone or that a local from their town could frame her for it. It's left a feeling of unease among the community.

She's only ever talked to Madison on a casual basis, when she would come in for coffee in the months before her arrest, usually with her adorable little boy, Owen. Madison always seemed pleasant enough, and totally incapable of what she was convicted of. Her sister, on the other hand, is devious and Ruby would be happy never to see Angie McCoy or her husband, Wyatt, in here ever again. There's something menacing about that couple. Luckily, they don't come to Lost Creek much, even though they live in nearby Gold Rock.

Ruby turns around to look at her husband, who hasn't yet let go of her. "Vince! Not in front of the customers."

"Oh, shush, woman. If I can't steal a kiss from my own wife, what can I steal?"

She laughs. "You're just a randy old man who can't keep his hands to himself."

"Isn't that why you married me?" He winks at her before going to have a word with the cook.

The bell above the door—which she knows Vince hates with a passion and swears he'll destroy it if she ever leaves him—rings, making her look up. Matt and Oliver walk in and she feels her whole face light up. Her son and his wife, Jo, have to work all day today, even though it's a Saturday, so she gets the pleasure of spending a day with her precious grandson.

"Hey, Mom," says Matt, pulling off his gloves. He's frowning as usual.

"Grandma!" says Oliver. Matt lifts him onto one of the stools at the counter, giving Ruby a chance to lean in for a kiss on his cute little cheek. He's swaddled in a hat, scarf and gloves on account of the cold spell they're having. It feels more like winter than fall out there.

"Here they are," she says. "My favorite boys."

"What about Grandpa?" asks Oliver.

"I'm too old to be a boy," says Vince, returning to the counter and leaning in. "I'm a wise old man now."

"Like a wizard?"

"That's right. Just call me Gandalf."

Oliver laughs and it makes Ruby smile. She can see his wobbly front tooth just itching to fall out. It's the first one he'll lose, so she's been explaining the concept of the tooth fairy to him. Jo told her that ever since he learned he'll get money for his teeth he cleans them better, in a bid for a higher payday.

Vince pours coffee into a takeout cup as Matt asks, "Can you have him home for six? Jo should be back by then, and I won't be far behind."

Jo works as a bookkeeper for various employers and Matt is a home security installer. They're at the stage of their lives where they're trying to work as much as possible in order to earn enough for a mortgage and a brother or sister for Oliver. "Sure. We have a fun day planned, don't we, sweetie?"

Oliver nods emphatically. "Dinosaurs."

Matt frowns harder. "There are dinosaurs in Colorado? Why didn't anyone tell me?"

"Don't be afraid, they're contained in the new museum," Ruby says with a smile. "That's where we'll head first."

Matt takes a slug of his coffee before leaning in to kiss his son's forehead. "I better go. Have a good day, okay?"

"We will," Oliver replies.

Matt says goodbye to her and Vince before heading out to his car. Ruby watches him through the diner's front window. Her heart swells with pride at having such a hardworking son. She has everything crossed that he and Jo will get pregnant soon so they can give her more grandchildren. Matt's her only child but she and Vince did try for more. It just wasn't to be. Which is what makes Oliver so special.

"You okay, honey?" asks Vince.

She turns to him and smiles. "I honestly couldn't be much happier right now."

He squeezes her hand before turning to prepare Oliver's breakfast.

CHAPTER TEN

Madison tried the shoulder-against-the-door trick, but the door didn't budge, so she went to speak to Douglas's immediate neighbor. As suspected, they didn't have keys for his place and they knew very little about his comings and goings. So as her final option she phoned Nate and asked him to help her break into the house. She could hear the smile in his voice as he agreed.

She listens as footsteps approach the rear of the house. Nate appears and her shoulders relax. It's like having a partner in crime. He's always there to help in difficult situations.

He smiles broadly and gives her a quick hug before saying, "Two questions: Why are we breaking into Douglas's place, and won't he shoot us if he's in there?"

She takes a deep breath. "He didn't show up for his first day back at work and he's not answering the door." Nate looks alarmed, which makes her feel justified in wanting to break in. "I can hear his cell phone ringing inside too, which means he could be in need of assistance."

He picks up a discarded piece of wood from the backyard.

"Wait!" she says. "Mendes says I've got to limit the damage. He could just be sleeping off a hangover for all we know."

He raises his eyebrows. "What does your gut tell you?"

She swallows. "That he's in trouble."

Nate nods. "Turn away." He hits the door's glass panel with the wood and the impact shatters the silence.

"I thought you had some clever technique for opening locks that you learned in prison." Madison looks at him. "I could've done *that!*"

He smiles. "But I won't get into trouble with Chief Mendes. You would have."

She rolls her eyes as Nate feels around inside for the key. After a couple of seconds, he stops.

"What?" She takes a step forward, and that's when she smells it.

Death.

Her chest fills with dread and she gets goosebumps through her entire body, making her shudder. "No."

Nate reaches out and touches her arm. "It might not be him. Stay here."

Nate means well but he sometimes forgets *she's* the police officer here, not him. She goes right ahead and turns the key from the inside, almost catching her wrist on a shard of glass. The door swings open and she pulls out her weapon. "You probably shouldn't come in."

Nate's not a cop; he's a private investigator. She shouldn't even have asked him to come, but none of that matters right now.

He scoffs. "Madison, I'm coming with you."

She's glad. Because if this smell is Douglas, she doesn't know what she'll do. Slowly edging forward, she hears faint voices. Cocking her head to listen, she can't tell what she's hearing.

Behind her Nate says, "Sounds like the TV."

Madison takes another step forward before shouting, "This is Lost Creek PD. If anyone is here, make yourself known." She doesn't wait for a response and there is none. Moving through the kitchen is like forcing herself through a fog of putrid stench.

When they step into the living room, she involuntarily gags more than once. She needs to keep her hands on her gun and her eyes on the room, but it's hard. She's only been in here twice before, and briefly. The place looks neat and tidy, but it's difficult to see much with the blinds closed. The TV is switched to infomercials. Her eyes move to the couch, which is empty. The only other seat in here, a leather recliner, is facing away from her. A wooden side table sits next to it and she can see an arm outstretched, the hand resting on the table as if the occupier is asleep.

"There," says Nate, clocking it at the same time as her.

She stays where she is, frozen to the spot, as Nate goes around her. He switches a lamp on and steps in front of the recliner. When he sees who's in it, he closes his eyes for a second. "Don't come any closer, Madison. You don't want to remember him like this."

Tears spring to her eyes and she hesitates, but she needs to know what happened. She steps in front of the recliner and sees Douglas's head leaning back against the leather. "Oh, God." His cloudy eyes are lifeless. She trembles as she sees a bullet wound to his right temple. The wall next to him is sprayed with blood spatter. His right hand rests in his lap, the rigor mortis gripping his gun tight.

Douglas shot himself with his own service weapon.

She leans forward, overtaken with dizziness. "I can't believe he would do this. I... I don't understand." She breaks down in tears and feels Nate pull her to him. Thoughts of the guys at the station and how they'll react spring to mind. Madison's witnessed three suicides in her life: two of her cellmates in prison, plus her predecessor, Detective Mike Bowers. They all left her feeling angry, useless and hopeless. And finding Douglas is no different.

A tight knot grips her chest and she can feel it growing with each breath she tries to take. She has to pull away from Nate, she needs room. And air. She attempts to inhale deeply, but the feeling of panic grows and her lungs constrict. The smell of Douglas doesn't help. It feels like she's swallowing the putrefying gasses from his body. She looks at Nate, trying to convey her panic.

Nate leads her to the couch and sits her down. Crouching in front of her, he talks her through it with the calm, reassuring voice of a doctor. "You've got this, Madison. It's the shock and anxiety trying to fool you into feeling unsafe. It'll pass shortly, it always does. You *are* safe. We just have to ride it out. I'm here for you."

She can't even nod. She knows it's a panic attack but she hasn't had one for a while and she'd forgotten how overwhelming and scary they are. How out of her control they are. She's at the mercy of her anxiety right now and it feels unbearable because she can't predict how her body will react.

She can't control her racing heart rate. Her chest is constricted. She wants to sit and stand at the same time. She leans forward to put her head between her legs to stop the dizziness. Tears stream down her face.

Nate's rubbing her back and purposefully blocking her view of Douglas. "You've got this, Madison. It's starting to let up. You're going to be okay."

She sits up and pushes his hand away. She's glad he's here with her but being touched is irritating. He doesn't appear offended. He probably has more experience of panic attacks than anyone she's ever met.

After a few awful moments that feel never-ending, her breathing finally returns to normal. Pulling a tissue from her coat pocket with trembling hands, she wipes her face and composes herself. She can't help feeling a little embarrassed at causing a scene.

"You okay?" asks Nate.

She swallows before nodding. "I need to distract myself because I really don't want another one of those." She takes a slow deep breath and looks around the room, anywhere but at Douglas. The furniture is mis-matched, with a mixture of old solid oak tables, a cheap white entertainment unit and a large flat-screen TV. It's tidy, as usual, with nothing out of place. She doesn't for one second think he tidied before killing himself, this is just how he was; meticulous.

"Let's get out of here," says Nate. "We need to call this in."

With a feeling of dread, she stands up on shaky legs and approaches her detective partner. Crouching in front of him she slowly reaches out to touch his empty hand. It's cold and clenched, and the lifelessness brings home how final this is. "You were an amazing detective, Don. Your daughter would have been so proud of you." Hot tears escape her eyes as she gets up and strides out of the house, craving a cigarette like never before.

She may have only recently started working with Don Douglas again, but she had got to know him better while she tried to bring him back from the depression that took him down-hill so quickly. She had tried to be there for him when he started turning up at work with alcohol on his breath. She had been naïve. Because she hadn't realized that, by then, it was already too late.

Don wasn't from Lost Creek. He had moved here after the loss of his six-year-old daughter and his detective partner, both killed by an ex-con with a grudge. He and his wife divorced shortly after, as so many couples who lose a child do, which was when he'd moved down here to start afresh. To forget. But he was never able to forgive himself for being unable to protect his daughter. It's clear to Madison now that his PTSD had taken hold of him and he felt the only way out from the guilt and grief he carried with him was to end his life.

In the backyard she feels Nate close his arms around her again and she gives in to the embrace. "It shouldn't have ended this way, Nate. We were supposed to be partners. I had so much to learn from him."

"I know," he says into her hair. "I'm sorry."

He holds her there in the rain as she releases all her frustration at Douglas. Suicide is so final. There's no opportunity to help the person back from the brink. If she had thought for one second he might do this she wouldn't have let him out of her sight. But why didn't she see it coming? What did she miss? Guilt threatens to overwhelm her.

Her cell phone rings. They both ignore it when it rings twice in a row, but she can't ignore it a third time. She pulls away from Nate and wipes her eyes with her hands before retrieving it from her pocket. "It's the station."

"Let them wait," he says, pushing a strand of her wet blonde hair back behind her ear. "Take the time you need."

"I can't. It might be urgent." He doesn't try to argue because he knows what she's like. "Hello?" she says.

"Hey, Madison. It's Steve. Chief Mendes wants to know if you've located Douglas."

Madison looks at Nate. He rubs her arm. "He's dead, Steve."

"What? Say that again. I can't hear you over the rain."

Madison takes a deep breath. "Don's body is here at his house. He shot himself in the head. There's nothing we can do for him." Her voice falters at the end and she puts a hand over her mouth.

Steve is silent for a long time before he lets out a long sigh. "Holy crap."

"Would you tell Mendes for me?"

"Sure." He sounds shaken. "I'll be there right away. Leave everything to me."

"Thanks," she whispers, before ending the call. To Nate she says, "Sergeant Tanner is on his way. He'll take over."

Nate nods. "You're soaking wet. Let's go wait in my car."

She lets him lead her around to the front of the house. When she slips into his car, Brody leans in from the back seat and starts licking her ear. She can hear his tail banging the interior with an excitement she can't match. She musters up the energy to stroke his gorgeous face. "Hey, boy."

Nate tells him to lie down and he does what he's told. Then Nate takes her frozen hands and rubs them in his. The rain beats against the windshield as they sit in silence.

CHAPTER ELEVEN

Everyone who's currently free has been called back to the station. Chief Mendes is standing front and center of the large briefing room. Madison is off to the left, leaning against a table and staring at her feet. The room is cold as someone's left a window open. Madison shudders and crosses her arms to warm herself. With Nate not being part of the team, he's gone to her house to break the news about Douglas to Owen.

When it's clear there will be no more arrivals, Chief Mendes asks Officer Goodwin to close the door. News hasn't spread yet so only Madison, Steve and Chief Mendes know Douglas is dead. Everyone else—officers, admin staff, dispatch—are quietly talking among themselves, wondering what's so bad that they've all been called in.

"Okay," says Mendes. Normally unshakeable, she looks pale and dazed. Like she can't quite believe what she's about to say. "I have horrible news and it's for our ears only. Nothing that we discuss in this room should find its way into the press. Everyone understand?"

A silence falls across the room and everyone stands a little straighter.

When she's satisfied they're all listening, she continues. "I'm sorry to report that Detective Douglas has recently passed away. It appears he's taken his own life."

Gasps. Followed by disbelief. All anyone can do is look around at the person next to them to see if this is a sick joke.

Stella speaks first. "You've got to be kidding? Please tell me that's not true."

Madison can't look at her because she can hear the emotion in her voice.

"I'm afraid it's true. Madison found him at his home not long ago." Mendes takes a deep breath. "Some of you may know that Don had been suspended for battling an alcohol problem, but no one in this department had any idea he was considering taking his own life."

Stella walks over to Madison and puts an arm around her shoulders. Madison has to close her eyes. She can't look at any of them and she's determined not to cause a scene, but she's barely holding back the tears that threaten to fall.

"Sergeant Tanner is at the scene with one of the medical examiner's assistants. He'll oversee arrangements until I manage to speak to Douglas's family. I'll be doing that next." Mendes pauses and softens her tone. "If any of you need to take a minute, please do. My door is always open for any of you. If I can stop this happening to anyone else—" She doesn't finish her sentence and Madison can't resist a glance at her. Chief Mendes turns away slightly.

Madison's never seen her upset. In order to give Mendes a minute to compose herself, she clears her throat and says, "Let's go for a drink tonight. Joe's Saloon at eight. We'll raise a glass to Detective Douglas."

Everyone nods in agreement, even though it's Thanksgiving. It would be difficult to find the appetite for turkey and all the trimmings after this. The only person who's shaking his head is Officer Goodwin. "Sorry, I can't." He turns to the officer next to him and mutters, "I promised my girlfriend I'd meet her parents."

Shelley looks at him, incredulous. "You can't do that another time?"

"No. I've put it off so long that she's threatened to dump me if I don't turn up."

Chief Mendes throws him a look of contempt as she walks to the door. "I'll be in my office if anyone wants to talk."

"Will you be coming tonight, Chief?" asks Officer Sanchez. Madison hasn't worked with him yet. He looks too young to be a cop.

Mendes pauses at the door. "I have my parents coming in from out of town, but I'll try to stop by."

Madison's relieved she's willing to come. The previous chief wouldn't have spent time with any of them outside of work. She feels her phone buzz in her pocket. It's the ME's office. Madison stays behind as the room empties. "Hello?"

"Hi, Madison. It's Lena. Do you have a minute?"

"Sure."

"First of all, I just want to say I'm devastated about Detective Douglas, so I'm sure you and your department must be too."

Madison nods, even though Lena can't see her. "Chief Mendes has just told the team. It's going to be a difficult few days."

"Of course. My assistant is with him now and she can't see anything untoward. It's highly likely I'll be ruling his death a suicide once he's been brought in and I've confirmed everything."

Madison closes her eyes. She can't believe they're talking about Douglas. "Chief Mendes will be calling his family shortly. Expect them to be in touch about arrangements for his body."

"Of course." Lena takes a deep breath. "I hate to change the subject but I'm starting the toxicology tests for Terri Summers and I have to ask; did you know she was pregnant?"

"What?" She had no idea. Terri's mom can't have known either or she would have told her. Her heart sinks. "I didn't."

"It's likely she was at the start of her second trimester; approximately thirteen weeks into pregnancy. It's possible she didn't know yet."

Madison thinks of the red wine stains on Terri's lips. She considers it unlikely that Terri knew. "I'll have to tell her mom."

"I'm sorry. These are the worst kind of cases."

A thought comes to her. "Can you do a DNA test on the fetus? Because if it's not Troy's that could be a possible motive for Terri's murder."

"Of course."

"Thanks. What was Terri holding when she died?"

"Oh yes, that was a beaded bracelet, possibly a child's as it looks cheap. I've bagged it up. Maybe Alex can pull something from it."

Madison frowns, then wonders if it could belong to the neighbor's daughter who Terri used to babysit. "I'll be interested to know if she was drinking alcohol when she died, as I saw the red wine stains on her lips."

"That will show on the toxicology results, which take a couple of days."

"Okay. Let me know if you find anything else."

"Will do. And Madison? Take care of yourself today."

Taking a deep breath, Madison says, "Thanks."

She walks past Chief Mendes's office, planning on going to see Terri's mom with the awful news that she was close to becoming a grandmother. Chief Mendes calls her inside. "Close the door."

She worries she's in trouble.

"How are you doing?" asks Mendes.

Madison swallows, unsure how to answer that. "I'm angry

about Douglas. I just wish he'd said something, you know?" She looks down. "He didn't even give us a chance to help him."

Mendes nods. "I know, but there's no telling if we could have prevented it, even if he'd told us how he was feeling." She checks her watch. "It's past five already. You should go home. Go and spend some time with your son and have a break before you go to the bar later."

Madison raises her eyebrows. She's never been told to leave work early before. Maybe Mendes thinks she's at risk of hurting herself.

"Not only did you attend this morning's crime scene but you found your partner's dead body this afternoon. That's too much for anyone to cope with in one day."

When she puts it like that, Madison suddenly feels drained. She's been worrying how Owen reacted to the news about Douglas, so it would be good to get home and discuss it with him. "What about Terri's killer? Because I don't think it was Troy. He was too inebriated to shoot straight, according to a witness. What if the killer strikes again tonight?" She starts panicking. "With Douglas gone and me at home, who would stop it from happening?"

Mendes steps forward. "You need to learn to rely on the team around you, Madison. All our officers are aware of the homicide and are out in force across town. I'll hold a press conference once I've spoken to Douglas's family. I'll make the media aware of his passing and update them on the homicide. Plus, Sergeant Tanner will coordinate anything that comes in overnight. You know what he's like; he practically lives here by choice. He'll contact you if you're needed urgently."

It's true that Steve hardly ever goes home. He's in his early forties and single with no kids. He lives for his job and seems content for it to be that way. "And what about you?" Madison asks. "When are you going to give yourself time to process what's happened?" She doesn't know much about Mendes's personal life. She's never heard her mention a partner or children, but it's not unusual for a police chief to keep their personal life private.

Mendes turns away and walks behind her desk. "You don't need to worry about me." She smiles sadly. "Now, get out of here. That's an order."

As Madison leaves her office she can't help glancing at Douglas's desk. The *Welcome Back* banner is still there. Never to be seen by the intended recipient.

CHAPTER TWELVE

Nate's unsuccessfully trying to keep Brody and Bandit away from the turkey. He always thought cats and dogs didn't get along but this pair actually team up to steal food. "Help me out, would you, Owen? Get your cat away and put Brody outside."

"I'm trying!" says Owen. He lifts the white kitten but Bandit is clinging onto Nate's sweater, so he removes each claw one at a time. The cat makes high-pitched protest noises, making Owen laugh. "He makes it sound like he's never fed!"

Nate turns to Brody, who's sitting at his feet, alert for any dropped meat. "You know better than this. Stop encouraging the cat."

"Come on, boy. You'll get the leftovers." Owen leads Brody out the door to the large backyard beyond. Before Madison and Owen moved in, this house used to be a small farmhouse, and still has a large barn out back and, beyond that, cornfields that are surrounded by expansive views of the mountains. Madison inherited it after her ex-girlfriend was murdered. Until then, she didn't own anything and had nothing but the money Nate paid her for working their first case together in Shadow Falls, California. The house is a three-bedroom two-story, just the right size for her and Owen. It was a little snug while Nate was sleeping in the spare room.

He hears the front door slam shut and after a few seconds Madison walks into the kitchen. She'd called in advance to say Mendes had sent her home, which was when he and Owen started preparing dinner.

She gives him a weary smile. It's clear she's exhausted by everything that's happened today. Her hair is tied back in a messy ponytail and her eye makeup is badly smudged from all the tears. Looking at the food, she says, "This smells amazing. I thought I wasn't hungry but now I'm starving."

"Wash up and take a seat. Owen fetched the side dishes from the diner, I'm just reheating them."

"Hey, Mom." Owen hugs her. "Sorry about Detective Douglas. I can't believe you had to find him like that."

When Nate told him what had happened, Owen was genuinely upset. The first thing he asked was how his mom was. Owen and Madison spent seven years apart while she was in prison and it hasn't been smooth sailing getting to know each other again. But things are slowly improving.

"Thanks," she says. "Are you okay?"

"I guess. Suicide sucks. I had a friend at school who took his own life, back when you were in prison."

Madison looks shocked. "I'm so sorry. I had no idea."

He shrugs, clearly not wanting to talk about it.

Madison turns away, blinking back tears. She takes her time washing her hands at the sink, probably wishing she had been around to comfort him.

With Owen's help Nate plates up the food in silence and takes it to the dining table. They chose not to set the table with the special Thanksgiving plates Madison had put out in preparation this morning. It didn't seem appropriate. However, Nate does light a candle in the center and says a silent prayer for those they've lost this year, who should be joining them tonight.

When Madison sits opposite him, she forces a smile. "Thanks for doing all this, you two. I know it's not exactly what we had planned, but I guess we're getting good at improvising. What's that saying? God laughs at our best-laid plans?"

"Something like that." Nate squeezes her hand across the table before they all tuck in. He can't think of anything to talk about that isn't work related or depressing, so they listen to Owen as he distracts them with talk of school and video games until Bandit suddenly leaps onto the table from the nearby breakfast bar and sticks his head in the turkey's carcass.

"That damn cat!" says Madison.

Owen picks the tiny kitten up and keeps him on his lap while he eats with one hand. Occasionally he feeds Bandit small pieces of white meat to keep him happy. Brody must see the cat's getting preferential treatment as he starts barking at the back door. Nate rolls his eyes and gets up to let him in. Brody heads straight to the dining table and sits patiently, watching them and the floor for any drops or spills.

After a few minutes Madison says, "Nate? Your dog's staring at me."

Nate tears off a large chunk of turkey breast and drops it into Brody's food bowl. It keeps him occupied for now.

They eat in silence for a while, and there's no hiding the fact this isn't the joyful meal they had hoped for. The fourth seat at the table is conspicuously empty and Madison's not eating much. Eventually she says, "Do you find yourself wondering what your family are doing tonight?"

He leans back as he considers the question. "Sure. But I doubt they're sparing a thought for me."

She nods before looking at Owen. "What about you? Do you wish we had a bigger family?"

He shrugs as if he isn't bothered but Nate thinks he's holding back. "I guess. Why? Do you?"

Madison thinks about it. "I've been thinking about my dad a lot lately."

"Really?" says Owen. "So you'd consider a reunion with him?"

"It's not that simple." She sips water before returning to her food.

Once they've had their fill, Nate, with Owen's help, takes the dirty dishes and loads the dishwasher. Madison clears the table before saying, "The guys and I are getting together shortly to remember Douglas."

Owen says, "Does that mean I can go to Jason's house tonight? His mom has baked all these pies for dessert and they've got the whole family round. He said that once everyone starts getting drunk, all the great-aunts and -uncles start handing out random cash to the kids. Jason got *two hundred bucks* last year!"

Nate tries not to laugh, especially when he sees the disappointment on Madison's face. It's clear she wishes she could provide that kind of family environment for him.

"Sure. You can stay over if you want," she says. "Once I get home from the bar I'll be hitting the sack so I can get up early for work tomorrow. I attended a homicide today and the killer is still at large. So that case will keep me busy over the coming days."

Nate heard about the murder of Terri Summers on the news earlier but he hasn't had an opportunity to ask her about it yet.

"Will you feed Bandit for me in the morning?" asks Owen.

They all look at Bandit, whose smooth pink belly is rounded with Thanksgiving dinner.

Madison rolls her eyes good-naturedly. "I knew I'd be the one left caring for the cat."

"But he loves you, look!" He holds Bandit out to her but the cat isn't happy at being taken away from Brody's food bowl, so he hisses. He's only tiny but he's vicious. "Sorry," says Owen. "I'll take him upstairs while I get my stuff together."

When they're alone Madison turns to Nate. "I'd invite you to come along but it's cops only, sorry."

"That's okay. I've got the cold case to work on anyway." He slips his coat on. "Vince's son turned up at the diner today."

She looks surprised. "Really? That's interesting. Why now?"

"He knows I want to talk to him about the case, so I'm hoping it's because he wants to help. Vince was over the moon to see him, but Matt didn't look as happy to be here."

"I'm not surprised. Douglas told me that Matt's convinced his mom and son are buried somewhere. I can't imagine what he and his wife went through back then." She sighs. "I'd love to investigate that case for myself one day."

"Did Douglas ever tell you what he thought had happened to them?"

She pushes her hair behind her ears as she thinks. "Yeah, he said he expected their remains to be found by joggers one day. He was convinced they were killed here in Lost Creek and not abducted."

He nods thoughtfully. "I guess I need to start from scratch and give it a whole new perspective. I love cold cases."

She smiles at him. "I know you do. I still remember the terrible analogy you gave me when I first met you."

He playfully frowns. "Me? Give a bad analogy?"

She crosses her arms. "Now let me see if I can remember this right. You said something about cold cases being the same as other investigations except they've been frozen in time and all they need is fresh pair of eyes on them to"—she gestures air quotes—"*defrost* the evidence. Or something as lame."

He laughs sheepishly. "Yeah, that sounds like me." Zipping his jacket up, he asks, "Need a ride to the bar so you can have a couple of drinks?"

Shaking her head, she says, "No. I'll only have one. I need to be clear-headed for tomorrow." She steps forward and hugs him. "Goodnight."

He opens the front door. "Come on, Brody. Time to go home." The dog runs ahead of him to the car and Nate looks back at Madison before leaving. Worried about how she'll cope with Douglas's suicide, he offers what he hopes is a reassuring smile before stepping out into the dark.

CHAPTER THIRTEEN

Madison's nerves are affecting her stomach as she approaches the entrance of the bar. A feeling of dread is building in her chest again. Her phone buzzes with a welcome distraction.

I'm so sorry to hear about Don Douglas. Are you okay? We need to catch up.

It's from Kate, which means Chief Mendes has held her press conference and the media now know what happened today. Madison's touched that she'd reach out.

Thanks. I'll call you sometime tomorrow. Busy now.

She gets a thumbs-up and a heart emoji in response, then pockets her phone. As she pushes open the door to Joe's Saloon, she takes a deep breath. Somehow, even though smoking is banned indoors, it's still dark and smoky in here. Her craving for a cigarette, which hasn't really left since she found Douglas, gets stronger.

She spots Shelley and Alex over in a dark corner, and something about the way they're leaning in as they talk to each other makes her wonder if they're getting close. It makes her smile. The rest of the department is over by the pool table. Not everyone is here yet, including Chief Mendes, but it's a good turnout considering what night it is. There's no sign of Officer Goodwin and she's surprised he didn't bring his girlfriend's parents here to kill two birds with one stone. He seems the type to be disrespectful.

Madison approaches the bar and nods at Joe, the owner, who stops drying glasses. He pulls out a flash drive from the cash register and slides it along the bar to her. "Security footage from last night."

She pockets it. "Thanks." Normally people take forever to provide their footage and sometimes they refuse without a warrant. She's glad it was easy this time. "I'm supposed to give you a receipt for this, so you can reclaim it when I'm done."

He dismisses it with a wave of his hand. "Keep it. It's just a copy." He leans forward. "Are you here for more information about Troy?"

"No. I'm here because I need a drink."

He smiles. "In that case what'll it be? Actually, let me guess. You look like you enjoy bourbon, neat, on the rocks. No nonsense."

She cocks her head with a faint smile. "Why do bartenders always think they've got everyone figured out? I'll have a bottle of Bud." She does like bourbon but he doesn't need to know that. And she wants a long drink she can nurse for a while, so she doesn't get tempted to have more than one. Right now, it would be really easy to get drunk.

"I heard those guys"—Joe nods to the officers around the pool table—"talking about your partner's demise. Is that why I'm surrounded by cops tonight?"

She nods but can't find the words to explain further.

He turns to the refrigerator behind him and that's when

Madison notices Chief Mendes on the TV above the bar. It's a rerun of her press conference. "Would you turn that up for a few minutes?"

Joe finds the TV remote and then passes her a Bud. Madison takes a seat on a barstool and listens in as Mendes talks. She senses a crowd building around her and turns to see Shelley, Alex and some of the uniforms. All eyes are on the TV.

"Detective Harper will be leading the investigation into the death of Ms. Summers," says Mendes, coming to the end of her briefing about this morning's murder. "And I can confirm it *is* being treated as a homicide. If anyone saw or knows anything, you're advised to contact the station as a matter of urgency. We don't want to give her killer a chance to harm anyone else. We would advise the community to remain extra vigilant until we have a suspect in custody."

A journalist asks, "Will the officer who shot Troy Randle be suspended from duty? And would you confirm which officer it was?"

Madison raises her eyebrow, interested to hear the answer.

"I won't be releasing any information about that until an internal investigation is finished, and I won't be releasing the officer's name at this time. Troy Randle is recuperating in hospital. His injuries are not life threatening." Chief Mendes pauses to clear her throat and change pace. "I now need to share some upsetting news about one of my detectives. Most of you will know Detective Don Douglas through his hard work and dedication to this police department and the local community." She pauses and Madison can imagine all the reporters sitting a little straighter in their chairs. "It saddens me to have to tell you that today he was found dead at his home from a self-inflicted gunshot wound."

There appears to be a whole minute of silence as not one journalist asks anything. They're obviously stunned by the news. Eventually, Madison hears Kate's voice. "Do you know why he took his own life?"

Mendes is unable to hide her contempt. "It's not for me, or anyone else for that matter, to speculate on Detective Douglas's state of mind. I've notified his family and they wish for their privacy to be respected at this difficult time. Thank you." Mendes gathers her things and leaves the room as fast as possible. The footage cuts away to a news anchor in a studio, who goes on to speculate what caused Douglas to do it.

"Good riddance to bad rubbish."

Madison gasps. She looks around to see who said that out loud but the uniforms have already rounded on the guy. Officer Sanchez has him out of the bar in seconds and all Madison can hear is, "He's an asshole who tried to pin a robbery on me!"

Shelley slides onto the stool next to her. "How you holding up?"

Madison sighs. "I could do without idiots like that tonight." She checks where Alex went and sees he's sitting alone in the corner. "Anything going on between you two that I should know about?"

Shelley immediately blushes. "I don't know. He's not really my type but he's interesting to talk to. He doesn't do Thanksgiving because he's British and has no family over here, and I couldn't handle another second with my family, so I think we're both in the same boat tonight. I've left my aunts discussing why I can't get a man. I'm tempted to take Alex back there later, just to shut them up."

Madison laughs. Then, gently elbowing Shelley, she says, "Alex is cute. And he'll probably treat you better than Jake Rubio ever would. Get back over there and see what happens. You don't need to babysit me."

Shelley looks reluctant to leave her alone. "I assumed you'd bring Nate."

"He already had to sit through dinner with me and Owen. I

didn't want to force him to come here too." She watches as the uniforms pile back into the bar. She doesn't know what they did to the heckler but Steve has turned up and is barking orders for them all to get their asses inside.

He approaches her and Shelley. "Mendes and I have spoken to Douglas's dad. He's in Seattle and he's going to arrange for a cremation and then for the ashes to be sent to him so that he can scatter them near the resting place of Douglas's mom.

"So his family aren't coming here at all?" asks Shelley.

"Nope," says Steve. "They're not inviting anyone to the cremation either."

Madison can't believe they won't get to give Douglas a proper send-off. "Was his dad even upset?"

"Yeah, he was. I get the sense he's not the kind of guy who shows his emotions, which must be where Douglas got it from, but he choked up when Mendes gave him the news. Once he found out how Douglas died, he didn't appear to want any more details, and who can blame him, right? He phoned back later to talk about the cremation. I've let Lena know she can release the body once she's done her thing."

Madison feels herself tearing up at the thought that Douglas will soon leave Lost Creek without any of them saying their goodbyes. But it's up to his family what happens to him now. "I wish I'd got to know him better."

Steve rests a hand on her back. "Madison? You knew him better than any of us and you worked with him for the shortest amount of time, so you have nothing to feel guilty about, trust me."

She looks him in the eye and can tell he has his own regrets. Douglas was a hard man to get to know, but some people prefer to keep others at arm's length and you have to respect that.

Officer Sanchez approaches them. "Stella's about to do Douglas's end-of-watch call. You coming?"

Madison's chest fills with dread. The end-of-watch call is a final call to the deceased cop over the radio. It's something she knows she'll break down at hearing, but it's the least she can do for her partner.

The bar empties of law enforcement and Shelley squeezes Madison's hand as they go out to a cruiser in the parking lot. Officer Goodwin has made an appearance, alone, but there's no sign of Chief Mendes.

They silently gather around the open door of the cruiser, drinks in hand, waiting for Stella's voice to come through on the radio. Some onlookers from the bar stand in the doorway watching. Not one person films them on a cell phone. Even the kind of people who frequent Joe's bar know about honor. Except for them it's honor among thieves.

Finally, the radio crackles to life and Madison turns her face up to the stars.

"Attention all units. Clear the air for priority traffic."

Silence.

"Dispatch calling Detective Douglas, do you copy?"

Madison squeezes her eyes shut.

"This is a final call for Detective Douglas," says Stella, as professional as ever.

The silence stretches out, long and bleak. Even Joe has switched off the music in the bar. Madison holds her breath, wishing that radio would crackle into life with Douglas's surly reply.

Eventually, Stella continues, "No response... Detective Donald Douglas, we thank you for your professionalism in your work life, your integrity being beyond reproach, and your commitment to law and order. You can rest in peace. Your watch has ended and we have it from here. Dispatch out."

Madison breaks down and walks away from the crowd, toward the aspen trees. When she woke up this morning, she was excited for Douglas to return to work. She was excited for it to be Thanksgiving. She thought it might be a quiet day on the job while the community comes together with their families. She thought no blood would be shed today. She never expected to end the day feeling more upset and alone than ever before. She considers calling Nate and telling him to come back to her house with a bottle of something strong. She even pulls her phone out. But then she's reminded of what Lena asked her today, about whether he's a free man. It makes her slip her phone back into her pocket.

She can't keep relying on Nate to help her out every time she's having a bad day. He needs to get on with his own life, without her weighing him down. So instead, she gets in her car and drives back to her empty house alone.

CHAPTER FOURTEEN

Facebook Messenger

Hey.

Still want to meet?

Of course.

What time and where?

How about evening at your place?

I want to avoid crowds.

I can let you know an exact time in the afternoon.

Sounds good.

It's my day off so I'll be home all day.

Just do me a favor and don't tell anyone I'm coming.

I don't feel like talking to anyone I don't have to.

We need privacy for what we're discussing.

Sure. I get that.

Thanks.

See you tomorrow.

CHAPTER FIFTEEN

In the early morning frost, Madison checks if anyone's watching her from the road in front of the building behind her. She takes a long drag of her cigarette as she stands outside the medical examiner's office, about to see Lena for an update. Her nicotine craving finally got the better of her. This is the last cigarette from the pack she's had hidden at home for the last two months, so it's not like she's addicted again or anything. Sometimes you just need that one thing that relaxes you the most.

She sighs as she exhales the smoke. The weak morning sunshine feels warm on her face, but it's not strong enough to warm the rest of her body. Cars speed by, all in a hurry to get to work and not considering the black ice they were warned about on the morning's weather report. She thinks of Douglas, about how he should also be on his way to work. That reminds her of the last conversation they had. She had asked for his advice about a sexual assault that she was investigating, committed by an unknown assailant. He'd told her that her theory was completely wrong and that she was thinking like a rookie. She was pissed with him at the time but the memory brings a smile to her lips now because it was just so typically Douglas.

Her smile falters when she remembers the disturbing nightmare she had last night, when she finally managed to drop off. In it, she'd found Douglas still alive, just before he pulled the trigger. She pulled his hand away and grabbed the gun from him, relief swamping her body. But when she looked at his face she realized he'd already shot himself, yet somehow he was still alive. He said something she couldn't make out at first. When he repeated it, with blood running down the side of his face, she heard, "Help."

But of course, it was too late to help him in her dream, just like in real life.

She shakes the thought away before taking one final drag. After stubbing the cigarette out on the wall of the building, she places it back in the empty packet and takes a deep breath. Time to see Lena. Inside, she announces herself to the receptionist and Lena appears shortly after.

"Morning, Detective. How are you?" Lena has her hair tied back in a French braid and a white coat covers her clothes. Her wide smile reminds Madison of the actress Julia Roberts, and it's easy to see why she's popular with men.

She's not Madison's type though. Chief Mendes is her type. Not that she'd ever go *there*. "I'm good."

She follows Lena into the morgue. The room is cool, with a vague chemical smell, stronger than you'd get in a hospital. Lena's assistants, Skylar and Jeff, say hi before carrying on with their work.

Madison is afraid to look too closely at any of the covered cadavers they've pulled from the refrigerator in case one of them is Douglas. He must still be here.

"Before we begin," says Lena, her voice lowered. "Don't take offense at this but I can smell cigarette smoke on you."

Madison raises an eyebrow.

"I know it's not my place to say this, or maybe it is given my job, but if you were ever considering giving up cigarettes, now's the time to do it. I mean, if you saw inside the lungs of smokers compared to those of nonsmokers, you wouldn't even hesitate. I can show you some day, if you need further persuasion." She steps back, hands up. "Okay, lecture over."

Madison's face reddens. She already feels guilty for smoking and it's not like Lena's telling her anything she doesn't know, but somehow, it's different when it comes from a medical examiner. "That was the last in the pack, so I'll try not to buy another one."

Lena turns and changes the subject. "Okay, this is Terri Summers." She doesn't pull the sheet back. "I don't need to do an autopsy unless you insist, because in my opinion the damage from the gunshot wound she sustained was enough to kill her instantly. I don't believe a defense attorney could argue anything else. Apart from the bullet hole between her eyes there were no other injuries to her body except one large fading bruise on her shin. I can find no evidence of sexual assault. Tox results are due back in a day or two. I can do a paternity test on the fetus if you can provide Troy's DNA for comparison."

Madison nods. "I'll get it for you today. Do you know the sex of the fetus? I have a feeling Terri's mom might ask."

"Not without performing certain tests, no. From the scans I've done I believe the fetus was around thirteen or fourteen weeks. It obviously died with mom. Even if there had been a coffin birth—"

"I'm sorry, a what?"

"A coffin birth. I know, it sounds horrible, right?" says Lena with a sigh. "It's when the decomposition of the mother forces the fetus out through the vaginal opening. It's to do with the buildup of gasses in mom's body. It's extremely rare, but it can happen. I'm glad for you and whoever originally found her that this wasn't the case here. I mention it only to say that even if we could see the fetus, it's likely they won't have formed genitalia yet, so we'd have to perform other tests in order to establish sex.

I would assume Terri's mom won't want the fetus to be put through any invasive tests, but it is an option."

This whole conversation is depressing and Madison wishes she hadn't asked. "Were you able to determine a time of death for Terri?"

"I think so. She was in full rigor when we got to her, and the warm temperature in the house probably hastened her decomposition a little, so I'd say she was killed the evening before she was found."

That's what Madison assumed, based on the red wine stains. After all, it's unlikely, although not impossible, that Terri would have opened a bottle for breakfast that morning. Her mom found her at lunchtime. "Are we talking around midnight?"

"I'd give a window of between 8 p.m. and midnight."

Madison shudders. Joe told her that Troy didn't leave the bar until around 1.30 a.m. and she had watched the security footage when she got home last night. Troy arrived at the bar just after six and he was there the whole time. He disappeared from view of the internal cameras a couple of times but was picked up on the exterior camera that overlooks the parking lot. He'd gone out to smoke a cigarette and check his cell phone.

With Terri's approximate time of death being *before* Troy left Joe's Saloon, he can't be her killer. Whoever shot Terri is still free and could strike again. Thinking out loud, Madison says, "That suggests whoever she spent the evening with was our killer. It wasn't her boyfriend because Troy was at a bar, drinking himself into a stupor."

"It's not my place to speculate," says Lena, "But perhaps she was seeing someone else without her boyfriend's knowledge, and it was them who killed her?"

Madison nods. "I guess the baby's paternity results will help with that. If the baby isn't Troy's, we could have our killer's DNA."

"Oh, before I forget," Lena fetches something from a drawer. "Here. This is what Terri was holding at the time of her death."

Madison takes the clear evidence bag from her and looks at the item inside. It's a multi-colored beaded bracelet: red, white and blue. It doesn't look expensive, so she doesn't think Terri was hiding it from her killer. She must've been in the process of taking it off or putting in on when she was ambushed. It's scuffed in places and the elastic holding it together looks like it's snapped several times over the years and has been tied back together. "Thanks. I'll see if Terri's mom recognizes it before giving it to Alex."

Lena chews the inside of her lip nervously before asking, "Want to discuss Detective Douglas next?"

Madison takes a deep breath, knowing she can't put it off any longer. "Sure." Lena walks over to the refrigerator and opens a door. Madison tenses. "That won't be necessary."

After a second's hesitation Lena closes it again. "Of course, sorry. I've ruled his death a suicide and his father has already been in touch. He wants his son released for cremation. It's booked for three o'clock tomorrow afternoon."

She swallows. That soon. Madison wants to think of some reason to delay the inevitable. It doesn't feel right to have him cremated so soon. But of course there's nothing she can do. She saw with her own eyes that it was his choice to die. But there's something about it that feels wrong. Probably only because she knew him. An image of his living room springs to mind. It was so sparse. She shakes the thought away.

Lena walks over and places a gentle hand on her shoulder. "I know how difficult this must be for you. Maybe it's worth speaking to the police department's therapist to help you get through the next couple of weeks?"

Madison scoffs. "What therapist?"

"Oh, sorry. I just assumed there would be one on call for all officers. Especially at a time like this."

Madison's never heard anyone mention a therapist, but it wouldn't be a bad idea. Maybe if the department had one, Douglas would still be alive. She realizes that's something positive she could do as a result of his death. If she could talk Chief Mendes into hiring a therapist, she has no doubt the team would keep them busy, what with all the horrors they witness on a day-to-day basis. "I better go. I've got to pay Terri's mom a visit. She'll want to know when she can bury her daughter. Thanks for your help."

"No problem. I'll call you with the results we're waiting on."

Madison turns to leave, her heart heavy with the knowledge that this is the last time she'll ever be in the same room as Don Douglas.

CHAPTER SIXTEEN

Seated on the top step of his porch, Nate's waiting for Vince to arrive. The morning sunshine makes a nice change, and everything is blanketed with a glimmering white frost. Brody bounds up the porch steps to sit next to him, his thick husky coat—a mixture of creams and browns—keeping him warmer than Nate in his sweater.

Nate offered to meet at the diner but Vince wants to check out his new place and make sure he hasn't been conned into leasing a rundown shack. According to him, realtors in Lost Creek have a bad reputation. Using just a fraction of the compensation payout from his exoneration, Nate is leasing this detached family home on a quiet rural street. He could have bought a place easily enough but he doesn't know yet if this is where he'll settle. He still has a lot to figure out.

This house in particular appealed to him because his neighbors are spaced far apart, giving him privacy, and the magnificent evergreen trees that surround his home aren't tall enough to hide the mountain peaks in the distance. Having grown up in flat, vast Kansas, Nate can spend hours staring at the mountains. Knowing they've been here longer than any person really has a way of putting all your problems into perspective. They signify freedom to him. He's never been as free as he is now. And truth be told it can get a little lonely, which is something he never anticipated.

Brody barks once but there's no car approaching yet. Nate strokes the dog's neck. Having some land with the house was important to him for Brody's sake. Brody loves the backyard because it's filled with trees and therefore squirrels. There's nothing the dog likes chasing more than squirrels—except maybe perps.

Having only moved out of Madison's place a few weeks ago, Nate feels comfortable here already. It's not like he was meant to be living with Madison anyway, it was temporary while they got their lives back on track, but he'd registered the disappointment in both her and Owen's eyes as he'd left for the final time. He put it down to them being afraid of being alone, in case all the pain of their enforced separation rears its ugly head.

He finally hears it—the distant rumble of an engine. Vince is here. Brody must have heard it before he did. Nate stands up and blows warm air into his cupped hands. It feels like winter is starting to bite already. Brody thuds his tail in excitement. He loves Vince because he smells of all of Brody's favorite foods.

"Morning!" says Nate as Vince exits his car. He's carrying a six-pack of beer.

Brody runs down the steps and up to Vince, almost pushing him over with the weight of his paws against his chest. "Hey, boy! Are you behaving?" Vince rubs the dog all over, before heading for the porch. He hands over the beer. "Housewarming gift."

"Appreciate it."

"It's a cold morning."

"It is," says Nate. He leads him into the house and Brody follows, just a step behind Vince, his nose sniffing the air around him. "Coffee?"

"That'd be great but do you have decaf?" Vince raises his hands defensively. "Now don't laugh at me. My doctor says I need to reduce my caffeine consumption. So I'm in the process of looking for a new doctor."

Nate laughs. "Sure, I've got decaf." Nate developed a sensitivity to caffeine once he left prison. The coffee they had to drink inside was so weak it barely had any taste, never mind any kick, so once he got out and tasted a chain-store variety, he almost passed out. The caffeine surged through his veins making him hyper and nauseous all at once. It was like the worst kind of high, and nothing like when he first tried cocaine. He gradually built up his tolerance to stronger caffeine, but there are still some chains he can never drink from unless it's decaf.

Vince spots a problem with one of the kitchen cabinets and starts messing around with it while Nate makes the drinks. "I can fix this for you if you like? The hinges need readjusting."

Nate smiles. "It's fine, I'll get around to it at some point. I don't expect my guests to do odd jobs while they're here."

"It's no problem." Vince pulls out a Swiss army pocketknife which comes with a variety of other functions, one of which is a screwdriver. He has the door hanging right in a matter of minutes. The satisfied look on his face tells Nate he likes to feel useful. "Have you checked the place for mold? You don't want to develop allergies."

"I'm pretty sure the house is fine, Vince. You don't need to worry about me." With their drinks, Nate leads him to the dining table where he has a notebook ready. He needs to get from Vince what he can't get from the internet: the inside facts about what happened the day Ruby and Oliver disappeared.

Taking his seat, Nate asks, "How's your son doing?"

Vince groans. "Good question."

"Why? What's wrong?"

Taking a deep breath, he says, "Matt's angry with me for

asking you to look into the case. He wants me to ask you to drop it. Thinks it's a waste of time to have you dig up the past and get the media all excited about it again."

"Is he worried they'll come after him?"

"I think so. He doesn't want him or Jo to be hounded again. It was pretty bad last time. I should know. Business tailed off at the diner and I had *child killer* sprayed on my windows more than once. I was Douglas's main suspect but he didn't disguise the fact that Matty was his second. Maybe he thought we were in on it together, who knows?" Vince pauses. "I can't believe Douglas killed himself. I may not be his number one fan but I can still appreciate how horrible it is that he went out that way. I bet your friend is upset."

Nate nods. "Madison's blindsided. Thinks she could've talked him out of it if she'd known."

"That's not how suicide works. She might have talked him out of it once but those feelings would soon come back without proper help in the meantime." He looks Nate in the eye. "I lost a navy buddy way back. I managed to stop his first attempt but turns out all I did was delay the inevitable."

Nate doesn't agree that it's inevitable. He's been suicidal more than once but lately he hasn't even considered the idea. Things can get better. He wouldn't have believed it when he was at his lowest, but his life has changed a lot since then.

"And she has that homicide to deal with too," says Vince. "Terri was a wonderful young lady. It doesn't make any sense that someone would want to hurt her."

Nate knows violence is rarely logical. Wanting to focus on his investigation, he asks, "Does Matt have an alibi for the day his mom went missing?"

Vince shoots him a look, probably trying to figure out if Nate's going down the same path as Douglas just because it's the most obvious. "He used to install home security systems and was in between appointments during the so-called window of opportunity—the time between when Ruby and Oliver left the grocery store and before they were due home. The only thing that stopped him being pulled in as a suspect was the fact his cell phone placed him where he said he was."

"Which was?"

"Pulled over near Fantasy World. He was having a bite to eat between jobs, a takeout sandwich."

"Any footage of him there, or witnesses?"

Vince visibly tenses. "Didn't you hear me? His cell phone confirmed he was at that location at the time."

His cell phone could have purposefully been left there. These days people are savvy to how incriminating their devices can be. Nate's always amazed when someone gets caught because they were dumb enough to take their cell phone *to* the scene of the crime. But he changes the direction of his questions. "Is there anything about that day that I need to know?"

Vince sips his coffee as he thinks. "Everything was perfect. Ruby and I had a happy marriage. Matty and Jo were all good. Oliver was like all kids that age, funny and energetic." He looks down at Brody who's staring at him intently. "I can't understand what happened. But even worse, I can't understand why they haven't been found."

Nate's sympathetic. Six years is a long time to go without answers. "Were her bank cards used after that day?"

"Nope. Never again."

"What about the groceries she bought that evening. Were they ever found?"

Vince shakes his head. "It's like a spaceship beamed them up to another planet. Car, groceries and all. It was bizarre then and it's bizarre now."

He's not wrong. "What about plans for the rest of the week; had she made arrangements to be anywhere or to meet up with friends?"

"It was Thanksgiving the Thursday after they vanished. We

had plenty of plans to celebrate that with Matt and Jo." He fixes his eyes on Nate. "I know what you're thinking, but she wasn't canceling plans or giving away her possessions as if she was planning on splitting town or harming herself. She wouldn't leave me and Matt behind, not willingly."

Nate nods before sitting up straight. He's not looking forward to asking the next question but it's important. "Don't take this personally but I've got to ask. What were you doing on the day they vanished? What's your alibi?"

Vince doesn't react. He must have known it was coming. "I was working at the diner all day and run off my feet because Ruby wasn't around to help out. At the time they went missing that evening, I was up in my apartment doing some paperwork: preparing a food order, paying invoices, that kind of thing."

"Was anyone able to verify that?"

"Plenty of people saw me working at the diner. But I was alone in my apartment. Some think I could've slipped out the side entrance and gone to kill my wife and grandson." He looks away. "They'd be wrong."

Nate can tell it's like it happened yesterday for Vince. The emotions are contained, but barely. They sip their coffees in silence for a while until Vince speaks. "You know, I keep the diner open in case they ever come back. God knows Ruby would kill me if she turns up one day and finds I've sold it to some godawful coffee chain. I felt bad enough just removing the irritating bell over the doorway, but I had to. It was so distracting and my heart would jump into my mouth every time it rang." He wipes his eyes. "The more time that passes, the more I feel like I'm losing my grasp on them, Nate. I feel like they're slipping away."

Quietly Nate asks, "What does your gut tell you happened? Where do you think they are? Is there anyone in town you suspect had anything to do with it?"

Vince sighs. "I don't feel like they're dead, but I can't tell if it's wishful thinking. And would I really know if they were? Some of my podcast guests—a couple of local mediums—believe we have psychic links with our loved ones, that we feel an internal emptiness when they're no longer alive."

Nate remains quiet. Unlike Madison he's open-minded about mediums and psychics, but he doesn't condone those who charge grieving families for their services.

"And while I feel empty because I don't see them every day, to me it just feels like they're still on their day out. I feel like they might walk into the diner any minute. You know?"

He nods. That sounds like unresolved grief to him. "I think you told me Matt and Jo split up after the disappearance, is that right?"

"Right. Not straight away. They left town around the one-year anniversary, wanting a fresh start. They moved to Nebraska, but they didn't stay together much longer. They went their separate ways sometime after that. Matt didn't tell me at first, so I don't know exactly when it happened. All he said is that Jo had moved to California to be with her mom, who she was already visiting a lot. Probably seeking comfort. I never heard from Jo at all once they left town. I got the impression she believed some of the news reports that speculated I was the killer." He shakes his head and Nate thinks he's close to tears. "She *knew* me. How could she believe I'd hurt my grandchild?"

"She was suffering and looking for someone to blame," says Nate. "I bet she doesn't believe that now."

"I guess I'll never know. I asked Matt yesterday if he ever hears from her and he said he saw on Facebook that she's remarried, but she didn't get in touch to tell him. It's crazy how you can share a missing child with someone and drift apart."

"You'd be surprised how common that is. I guess being together is a constant reminder of their loss." He pauses. "What are my chances of having a one-on-one with Matt?"

"Actually, he said he wouldn't mind putting you right on some things."

Nate's surprised. "Tell him I'm free whenever he's ready."

Vince nods before sipping his coffee.

Looking at his notes, Nate asks, "What was Ruby's state of mind that day? Did she ever suffer with mental health problems?"

Considering the question, Vince says, "I've thought long and hard about that over the years and she definitely appeared a little out of sorts in the days leading up to her disappearance."

"How do you mean?"

"It's hard to explain. She was preoccupied by something. I felt like she was trying to come to some kind of decision."

Nate hates to ask but it's an obvious question. "I know there were rumors she might have been seeing someone else and possibly moved away to be with them. Maybe she didn't have the guts to tell you she was leaving?"

Vince shakes his head wearily. "There's no way. We had a rock-solid marriage, of that I'm certain. Besides, she didn't have time to cheat. That diner was important to her and, like me, she worked long hours, alongside looking after Oliver when needed. She helped Jo a lot with babysitting because Jo was working hard."

"What did Jo do for work?"

"She was a bookkeeper who worked freelance for various local businesses, as well as doing some volunteer work, if I remember right."

Nate notes everything down. "And Ruby didn't ever suffer with poor mental health? Depression, anxiety?"

"She suffered with postpartum depression after Matt was born but she never had any other issues, nothing that needed medication anyway." He gives Nate a stern look. "I hope you're not looking to go down the murder-suicide route."

"If you tell me she's not capable of that then, no, I won't." Not unless he finds evidence that would support it.

"I'm telling you you're way off if you're considering that as an option. Ruby doted on her grandson, and besides, wouldn't their bodies have been found if that were the case? And what's her motive? It doesn't make any sense."

"I agree, but I have to remind you of what I told you when I agreed to take this case on; sometimes the answers I find aren't the answers my clients want. You need to be prepared for any outcome. Because I simply follow where the evidence leads."

Vince stands, as if it's too painful to even consider Ruby was involved in this. He looks around the kitchen diner. "This is a nice place you've landed. It has good energy, lots of light."

"Thanks."

"Big for a single guy though. You could fit a partner and a couple of kids in here if you get busy."

Nate smiles good-naturedly. "I think it's a little late for that."

"It's never too late. Don't be blind to what's right in front of you, Nate. Don't hold back. Life's too short. You of all people should know that."

He isn't sure what Vince is implying but suspects it has something to do with Madison.

"If you ever want company on the long winter nights, I'm partial to a beer or two. We could sit out on the porch and put the world to rights. Or I could help you decorate. It seems fun at first but it doesn't take long to realize an extra pair of hands makes light work."

"Thanks, I appreciate it." Nate thinks Vince is lonely. His son probably won't stick around for long and he'll be right back to where he started: sitting in that apartment over the diner trying not to see Ruby everywhere.

Brody barks.

"I thought you'd never ask. Here." Vince pulls a grease-stained paper bag from his coat pocket. Brody licks his lips and keeps his eyes on the prize as Vince unravels some roast chicken. With a soft mouth Brody takes it from him and it's gone with one chew. The dog looks around to see if he misplaced it, unwilling to accept that's all there is.

Nate leads Vince to the front door, sensing he's done with rehashing the past for today. "Tell Matt to give me a call. Like I said, I can meet him whenever he's ready."

"Will do. Maybe he'll open up to you. He's never wanted to talk about it with me."

"Why's that?"

Vince shrugs. "You'd have to ask him."

Nate waves him off. It's strange that Matt wants him to stop investigating his mother and son's disappearance. Shouldn't he be relieved someone's looking for them again? Nate considers whether he's underestimating the lasting effects of losing a child in those circumstances. But as he watches Vince drive away, he's unable to shake off the thought that Matt could know more than he's letting on.

CHAPTER SEVENTEEN

SIX YEARS AGO

Ruby has had her fill of dinosaurs. Three hours walking around a museum dedicated solely to them will do that to someone. She'd bought Oliver almost everything he wanted from the gift-shop and now he's hungry for lunch. They both are.

"Are we going to see Grandpa?"

"No, he'll be busy with the lunch rush. Let's leave him to it so I don't get roped in to helping." She grins at him.

Oliver's hand is tiny in hers as they exit the museum, and she knows she has to cherish these days while he's still happy to hold hands. If he's going to be anything like his dad, once he turns eight or nine, he won't want to show her any affection in public for fear of his school friends seeing them.

She secures him into the car seat while he plays with his plastic T-Rex. Once strapped into the driver's seat she pushes her wet and windswept hair out of her eyes and carefully pulls out of the parking lot. Downtown is pretty quiet today, maybe because of the rain. It's relentless and, even though it's only lunchtime, the swollen dark clouds are blocking most of the daylight. Everyone has their headlights on as car tires swoosh through the standing water.

The sound of the windshield wipers creaking back and forth is almost hypnotic. Her mind wanders and she feels her stomach knotting as she thinks of what's been bothering her lately. She recently discovered something so awful that she hasn't even told Vince about it. She plans to double check whether it's true before speaking to her husband or confronting the person involved. A false accusation could have terrible consequences, but if she's right, confronting the person could cause even more problems. She feels sick with worry. If only she could forget she was ever told. But that's not possible.

She turns to look at Oliver on the back seat. "You okay, sweetie?"

He nods. "Can I have a chocolate milkshake?"

Smiling, she says, "Sure. If you eat all your lunch."

The car stops with a shuddering jolt, sending pain down Ruby's neck. Wincing, she carefully turns to check on Oliver. "Are you hurt?"

His eyes widen as his bottom lip trembles with the shock of the collision. "What happened, Grandma?"

She's hit the car in front. Luckily, she wasn't going fast because of the poor visibility, but she knows instantly it was her fault. She wasn't paying attention and didn't see the other car brake. Rubbing her neck, she leans back against the headrest. "It's okay, we're okay. Don't be scared."

Ruby watches as someone gets out of the black SUV in front. She panics at the thought they might attack her for colliding with them. After all, how many times has she seen reports of road rage on the news? People are highly strung these days, ready to snap at a second's notice. About to lock the doors just in case, she breathes a sigh of relief when she sees Detective Douglas approaching. It's not ideal to hit a cop's car but at least she won't be shot by a vengeful stranger. She lowers her window, feeling rain catch her arm and thigh. "I'm so sorry, Detective. That was all my fault."

When he recognizes her, his expression softens slightly. He looks past her into the back, his face full of concern. "You okay, son?"

Oliver nods, trying to hold back tears.

"That a T-Rex you got there?"

"Uh-huh."

"He's not going to eat me, is he?" He winks.

A giggle. Ruby closes her eyes with relief.

Detective Douglas looks at her. "I'm sorry, Mrs. Rader, but I've got to ask; have you consumed any alcohol today?"

A car honks their horn behind them. "Get out of the road!"

Douglas ignores it.

"Of course not, it's only lunchtime," she says.

"So you just weren't paying attention?"

She bristles at his statement, but he's right, she wasn't. She was thinking about the discovery that's got her all churned up inside. "I glanced back to check on Oliver. It was just a second."

"That's all it takes to kill someone." He moves to the front of her car and checks her fender and then his car. When he returns, his jacket is soaking wet. "Your car took the brunt of it. We should exchange insurance details."

She raises her eyebrows. "You're not going to arrest me?"

"Not this time. But if you're involved in another collision in the future you'll go straight to the station. That's if you're not injured. Understand?"

She nods. "Sure." She scrambles around in her purse for her cell phone so she can send him her details. Smiling up at him, she says, "Your next dinner is on the house, Detective. My way of apologizing for the trouble."

He doesn't smile. "I'd rather you take care of your grandson properly. He can't be brought back to life with a free meal."

Detective Douglas isn't from Lost Creek and Ruby knows he has a reputation for being a little serious, but his statement makes her feel even worse than she already does, even if he is right.

"Forgive me," he says, softening again. "You have to understand I've attended a lot of RTC's in my time where the outcome was more serious. I wouldn't ever want to deliver bad news to your family."

She has to blink back tears. If she hadn't been worrying so much about what she'd recently been told, she wouldn't be in this situation. That decides it for her. She's going to deal with the issue head on, because until she does, she won't be able to relax.

CHAPTER EIGHTEEN

Madison is wandering around the hospital searching for Troy Randle's room. He's being released later today and she wants to question him before he has an opportunity to skip town. She's heard rumors he's worried she's going to frame him for his girlfriend's murder. Sounds like a guilty conscience to her. As she works her way through the maze of corridors Madison tries not to notice the unpleasant sterile aroma that always makes her feel like she won't get out of here without receiving a worrying diagnosis first, even though she's only here to visit someone.

She finally locates the correct room. Officer Shelley Vickers is sitting opposite the bed, reading a newspaper. Troy's in the bed, his leftovers from breakfast are discarded on the table next to him. He's wearing a blue hospital gown and his right shoulder has a large bandage over it. As far as she can tell he's not hooked up to any machines but he looks like death warmed up, as her mom used to say.

Shelley looks up first. "Hey."

Troy sits up when he sees her. His hospital gown drops from his neck, exposing his chest which is covered in thick black hair. He looks older than forty, with a weathered face and a heavily lined brow. Madison wonders what Terri saw in him.

"You here to arrest me?" he asks.

"That depends. Have you done anything wrong?" He may not have been around to shoot Terri himself but she's considering the possibility he hired someone to do it for him. Maybe he wanted out of the relationship for some reason. Or maybe he discovered something that pissed him off, such as that Terri was having an affair.

Shelley takes the opportunity to use the restroom, so Madison takes her seat. "Your friend Joe Manvers showed me security footage from his bar. I know you were there when Terri was murdered."

He sinks back into the bed, clearly relieved. "Thank God."

"I'm sorry for your loss." She means it, despite what she thinks of him. "Everyone I've spoken to says wonderful things about Terri."

He looks down at his hands. "She was a good girl. Difficult to fight with, you know? Too damn patient with me."

Madison doesn't smile because she knows what he's been convicted of in the past. "What was she doing that evening while you were at the bar?"

"No idea. As far as I knew she was staying home all day. It was her day off work and she said she just wanted to watch TV and chill."

"I assume you found her after you woke up the next morning?"

He looks at her properly, and she can tell he's weighing up whether he'll get in trouble for not calling the cops. "I was so drunk that night I could barely stand when I woke up the next day. I wasn't thinking straight. All I could think about was how it looked like I'd done it."

"So you saved yourself by fleeing the scene." It's not a question.

"You'd do the same thing in my position."

"Actually, no, I wouldn't." She pauses and fixes her eyes on his. "Did you pay someone to kill her, Troy?"

He shakes his head in surprise. "What? You've gotta be kidding me."

"I don't hear a denial."

He takes a deep breath and she sees a flash of anger cross his face. "Listen, if I paid someone to kill her, there's no way I would've slept in that house knowing her body was rotting in the bedroom. What kind of psycho do you think I am?"

She resists the urge to reply to that. He could be telling the truth, but she'll keep an open mind at this stage. "So tell me what you think happened. Was she seeing someone else? Did she invite someone over that evening? Had she—or you—upset anybody?" Madison's also not ruling out the possibility that whoever killed Terri actually came to kill Troy.

He slowly shakes his head again as he thinks. "She wasn't the type to cheat. But I don't know if she invited anyone over. Normally she'd go to her friends' houses if she wanted a girls night." He snorts. "I think she was ashamed of being with me or something. As for having a beef with anyone, I haven't upset anyone lately but I can't speak for her. Who knows what she gets up to when I'm not there? You'd have to ask her friends from the care home."

She's surprised there are no signs of the grief he should be feeling after the loss of his girlfriend. Still, it doesn't give her any pleasure to have to tell him about the baby. "Did you know she was pregnant?"

His mouth drops open and he doesn't speak for a full minute. "No, she wasn't."

For the first time Madison feels bad for him. "I'm sorry, she was. It was still early days, and I'll need to take a swab from you to test whether you were the father. I'm not saying Terri was cheating on you, but if the baby isn't yours, that might be a motive for the father to have killed her."

He looks away. "She always wanted kids."

"Were you trying?"

He hesitates. "She talked about it all the time, but I guess I didn't commit either way. I already feel like an old man. Who knows if I'd have the energy to take care of kids at my age?" He takes a deep breath. "But I wasn't against the idea. I guess I was just weighing it up. Terri would've been a great mom. She had the neighbor's kid over all the time, showing her how to bake or make craft shit."

"Do you think she knew she was pregnant?"

Troy considers it for a long time. "If she did, there was a reason she didn't tell me. Maybe she *was* screwing someone else and thought he was the baby's father." He pauses. "Or maybe she was ashamed that I was."

Madison thinks he might be right. She pulls out the evidence bag containing the bracelet Terri was holding. "Does this look familiar to you?"

He takes the bag from her and stares hard. "It probably belongs to the neighbor's kid. Maybe they made it together."

Madison nods. That's what she was thinking too. She takes it back from him and asks, "How's your shoulder doing? I hear you'll be released soon."

He looks at it. "Hurts like a bitch. I hope you know I intend to make a formal complaint against the asshole who shot me. You make sure your chief knows about it."

She wouldn't expect anything less. "I'm sorry that happened, and I know Chief Mendes will be in touch with you. But next time a police officer tells you to stop advancing, I'd recommend you listen." Standing, she says, "I need to take a swab from inside your mouth now. For the baby's paternity test."

He lets her do it, and she seals the tube before writing his details on it.

"So, what, am I supposed to go clean up the bedroom when I get out of here or do you guys do that?" he asks. "Because I have no stomach for blood."

"Your home is a crime scene, Mr. Randle. You'll need to find somewhere else to stay for the foreseeable future."

"I haven't got money for motels!" He shakes his head. "I knew the minute I met that girl that she would cause me problems. All women do. If you ask me, I'm better off single. Less drama that way."

Madison glares at him. Again, he's showing animosity toward his dead girlfriend. Shouldn't he be upset that someone entered their home and killed her? He hasn't asked what happens next in the investigation, or if they have any suspects in mind. Maybe he's in shock, or maybe it's the pain meds dulling his senses, but his reaction has her wondering again whether he could be involved somehow. He'll remain a person of interest for the time being. "If you think of anything that might help us find Terri's killer, get in touch with me immediately. You never know, the killer may come back for you, so it's in your interest that I find them as fast as possible."

His eyes widen. She leaves her card on his nightstand before departing.

Madison drops the DNA sample in at the medical examiner's office on the way to visit Terri's mom with an update. The sunshine is quickly thawing the frost as she waits outside the home of Sylvia Summers. There was no answer to her first knock so she tries again. Sylvia hadn't answered her home phone either. Madison's about to give up when a car pulls into the driveway. An older woman gets out. She looks tired and upset, and when she spots Madison she says, "Can I help you?"

Madison steps forward. "I'm Detective Harper from LCPD. I'm here to speak to Sylvia."

The woman walks past her and opens the front door. "Come in out of the cold."

Once inside, the woman removes her jacket and looks at Madison. "Sylvia had a stroke last night. She's in the hospital."

Madison's mouth drops open. "I'm sorry to hear that."

"I'm her sister, Maggie. I take it you're here about what happened to Terri?"

Madison nods and follows her into the living room. "Is Sylvia going to pull through?"

"The doctor thinks so, but she can't speak at the moment. They're making her rest, so I've been sent to collect some clothes and toiletries for her." Maggie's face suddenly crumples. "First my niece, now my sister. I'm having the worst week." She removes her glasses to rub away tears.

Madison places a hand on her shoulder. "I'm sorry. I can come back another time?"

"No. Take a seat. I want to know about Terri. Sylvia was convinced her boyfriend killed her and I saw on the news that he got shot too. Did he try to get away or something?"

Moving a *TV Guide* magazine out of the way, Madison perches on an armchair. She's not surprised Sylvia fell ill. It was clear yesterday that she was suffering after the news of her daughter's death. Maybe Jake Rubio should have taken her to the hospital then. She takes a deep breath. "Right now, it doesn't look like Troy killed Terri. I'm going to have to look elsewhere for answers."

Incredulous, Maggie says, "But how can that be? No one else would want her dead. She was just living her life without bothering anybody. It doesn't make any sense!"

Nodding, Madison says, "I know, but I have no leads yet. I want to assure you and Sylvia that I'm considering all possibilities. Do you know of anyone besides Troy who might have a grudge against Terri? Even if it was a stupid argument over social media, or a co-worker who was harassing her."

Replacing her glasses, Maggie gives it some serious consideration. "She always attracted male attention because of how pretty she was, but I can't think of anyone in particular. You'd have to ask her friend Antony. He works at the care home too. He's a care assistant but he also offers beauty treatments to the residents. According to Terri, they all love him."

"What's the care home called?"

"Mountain View Senior Care. You asked about grudges. Terri wasn't the kind of person who got into stupid fights, Detective. She never talked politics or argued for the sake of it. She was more of a peacemaker." Her eyes well up again. "There are so many bad people in this world and someone chose to take *her*. I just don't get it."

Madison feels horrible for her and doesn't want to upset her even more, but she has no choice. "I have something to tell you. I don't know if you'll want to tell your sister this right away, although she may eventually hear it on the news if you don't tell her; the ME found that Terri was pregnant at the time of her murder."

Maggie gasps before covering her mouth with her hands. "Please say that's not true."

"I'm sorry. It was still very early days for the fetus, so we don't know the sex, but I know that won't make it any easier for you."

Collapsing back into the couch, Maggie's overwhelmed by the news.

"I'm waiting on DNA testing to see if Troy was the father."

"Well, who else would it be?" she snaps. "Terri didn't sleep around, Detective."

"That's not what I'm insinuating, at all, but we have to know for sure. After all, it wouldn't be that surprising if she'd started seeing someone else in order to get away from Troy, would it?"

Maggie slowly shakes her head before dabbing her eyes with a tissue. "Is there any chance her killer wants to come for the rest of her family? Are we in danger?"

Madison has to be honest. "There's no way of knowing that until I find a motive, but I can't rule it out. Be extra vigilant; lock your doors and windows, don't let anyone into your home unless you know them well and don't announce your whereabouts on social media."

Maggie scoffs. "My granddaughter's terrible for that. She posts her life story on Facebook. I keep telling her she needs to make her account private just for family and friends to see but she laughs at me. She's at the age where she thinks she's invincible."

Madison considers explaining that, while it's a good idea to keep her account private, her daughter is more likely to be hurt by someone *inside* her family and friend bubble. She would recommend closing her account altogether. "Was Terri on social media much, do you know?"

"We're all on Facebook. We use the messenger thing for group chats. It's easier than calling everyone individually."

She makes a note to look at Terri's account. It could yield a lot of information about the days leading up to her murder. Pulling the bracelet Terri was clutching out of her pocket, she holds it up for Maggie to see. "Do you recognize this?"

Maggie leans in. "Not really."

"You don't know whether it was Terri's or not?"

"No, sorry. It doesn't look familiar."

Madison pockets it again. "Sylvia wouldn't have taken Terri's purse or cell phone from the house, would she? We haven't been able to locate them."

They both glance around the living room and then Maggie

checks the kitchen, returning empty-handed. "I can't see why she would. Surely your officers wouldn't have let her?"

"They shouldn't have but I just wanted to check. When Sylvia's up to speaking, would you ask her for me? I won't get in touch with her myself while she's in the hospital, not unless it's urgent. I don't want to make her any worse."

Maggie nods.

"When was the last time you saw or spoke to your niece?"

"Last weekend."

"Did she tell you what she had planned for yesterday or, more specifically, last night?"

"No. We were making arrangements for Thanksgiving, deciding who was going to bring what. It was going to be here at Sylvia's house, but obviously that never happened. I had to throw the uneaten turkey out this morning." She lowers her eyes.

This will be a Thanksgiving that both she and Madison will never forget. "Was Troy planning on joining you all? Or does he have family in town?"

"He was invited, but not his family. We've never met any of them, they're up north somewhere." Maggie licks her lips as if she's thirsty. She looks pale and drained.

Madison thinks it's a good time to leave. Standing, she says, "I'll keep my fingers crossed that your sister recovers quickly. If either of you has any questions, don't hesitate to call me. She has my number, but I want you to have it too." She hands her a card.

"When can we bury my niece, Detective?"

Madison hesitates. "We're still waiting on some results, but I'll let you know as soon as we can release her to you."

Maggie nods. She's being strong, but Madison can tell the full weight of her grief will hit her the minute she's alone again.

CHAPTER NINETEEN

Madison's desperate for coffee but before she allows herself a break, she wants to visit the Mountain View care home. It sounds like that's where Terri spent most of her time, so perhaps one of her co-workers knows something that her boyfriend and aunt don't.

GPS has Madison there in five minutes and as she gets out, she looks around. The home's name makes sense as soon as she sees Grave Mountain looming over it, casting a huge shadow and blocking the morning sunshine. It's not the best mountain to have a view of when you're frail and elderly, not with that name. The building looks a little like a motel from the outside, because of the way it sits back from the road with a large parking lot out front and no attempt at making it homey. There are rows of windows for the residential rooms inside, but no doors apart from the main entrance.

She walks up the wheelchair ramp and enters the building, relieved to find that the inside couldn't be more different to the bleakness of the outside. The lobby is well lit, with flowers arranged in large vases on the reception desk and a fresh perfumed scent hits her nose. There are residents shuffling around, some clothed, some in pajamas and robes, but almost all with a walking aid of some kind. To her right she can see a large day room with a huge TV on the wall. To her left is a long corridor that must lead to the residents' rooms. She spots a black cat emerging from one of them but a uniformed member of staff guides it back inside. Madison hopes they have a litter box in there.

A young woman behind the counter looks up from her seated position and offers a bright smile. "Good morning. How can I help you?"

"Morning," says Madison. "I'm Detective Harper from LCPD."

The woman's smile falters before she can say anything else. "Are you here about Terri? We're all devastated by what's happened. I still can't actually believe it." Her eyes well up.

"I am," says Madison. "I wanted to speak to her manager."

The receptionist nods. "Mr. Kane's with a family at the moment—their mom passed last night—but I'll get him as soon as he's free. Why don't you wait in the day room? I'm sure some of our guests would love to chat about Terri. She was a real favorite here."

"Thanks." Madison heads to the room with the TV. There must be about ten residents inside, all sitting in mis-matched armchairs. They look uninterested in the TV, probably because it's switched to a soap opera.

Two men are playing a slow game of chess. One of them reminds Madison of her dad, which is strange as he doesn't look anything like him—although it's been so long she doesn't really know what he looks like these days. She feels a pang of regret at going so long without getting in touch. There's so much he's missed out on: seeing her join the force and get a job at the same police department he used to work at, as well as meeting his only grandchild. But equally, there's a lot she's glad he wasn't around to see.

A tall, elderly man enters the room behind her and says, "Watch out, guys, we've got a cop in our midst." He holds his hands up with a grin on his face. "It wasn't me!"

She smiles. "Hi. I'm Detective Madison Harper from LCPD."

"We know," he says. "We watch the news."

She wonders if he's referring to her history or the press coverage of Terri's murder. "Mind if I take a seat?"

"Sure, go right ahead. I assume you're here about Terri?"

She sits next to three older ladies who have brightly colored, manicured nails. "Right. I wanted to speak to her boss."

The guy rolls his eyes, "Kane's useless. He probably doesn't even know which employee she was."

The woman closest to her says, "Charles is right about that. He's never here. You ask us anything you need to know, Detective."

Madison's grateful they're willing to talk to her. "I guess the most important question is whether any of you have any idea who might have killed her. Did she have any fallings out with other staff or any of the residents' family members?"

The woman laughs. "Lord, no. You couldn't argue with Terri. She wasn't interested in drama. She was one of the kinder staff, who just got on with her job and treated us like human beings, not senile old fools." Her eyes turn watery. "She'd even come in on her days off if we needed anything fetched from the store."

"Really? Did she visit on the day she died?"

They all look at each other and shake their heads. That's when a young male staff member joins them.

"This is Antony," says Charles. "Detective Harper is here to discuss Terri."

"He's been ever so upset because they were close," says one of the other women. "Are you feeling any better today, sweetie?"

Madison looks up at Antony. He's probably five-six, with a slim build and brown hair. His eyes are red-rimmed and he looks like he'd rather be anywhere other than at work today. "I'm okay," he says with no enthusiasm.

Madison stands. "I'm sorry for your loss. It's clear that Terri was well liked by everyone who knew her. I'm in charge of investigating her death and I don't want to upset you further, but do you mind if I ask you some questions?"

He shakes his head.

"Do you have any suspicions about who might have wanted to hurt her?"

"No, that's just it; it doesn't make any sense."

She leads him away from the others. "Do you know if she was seeing anyone besides Troy?"

"No way. She wouldn't cheat. But I guess…" He hesitates.

"What is it? It could help me find her killer sooner if you're completely honest with me."

He looks torn, like he's about to betray his dead friend by giving away a secret. "She was planning on leaving Troy eventually. She told me he hit her."

"Did you ever see it for yourself?"

"No, but she wouldn't lie. She broke down one day and it all came out. I think she was planning on moving back home with her mom, but she hadn't asked her mom yet. She was nervous about it and didn't want a lecture about choosing the wrong guys. I think she felt like she let her mom down by getting mixed up with someone like Troy."

"That's understandable," says Madison. "I'm struggling to see why Terri would be attracted to him in the first place."

Antony smiles. "She had a thing for the underdog. Troy isn't all bad, or at least he wasn't. I think she felt sorry for him and then got in too deep. I don't think she really wanted to move in with him, but she was ready to start a family with someone and we're not exactly spoiled for choice in a town this small."

Madison smiles. He's right about that. "Did Troy know she was planning on leaving him?"

"I doubt it, but I don't know for sure."

"Was she fearful for her life?"

Antony shakes his head. "No, it wasn't that bad yet. They did love each other at one point, but Troy hid his aggravated battery conviction from her and started drinking heavily. Every once in a while, he'd lash out and slap her across the face for no reason and with no warning. She wasn't cowering in corners or anything like that. She would've left before it got that bad."

Madison thinks that's probably where it was headed if Terri stayed with him much longer. "And there's no one else you can think of who might have wanted to hurt her?"

"No. If it wasn't Troy who killed her, it must've been a random attack, because there was no reason to hurt her. She was—" His voice hitches and he covers his mouth with his hand.

She rests a hand on his shoulder. "I'm sorry to upset you. I'm working as hard as I can to find her killer, okay?"

He nods.

"If you hear any rumors or remember anything that might be significant, give me a call." She hands him her card. "Any time of day."

"I will." He walks away from the day room.

Madison sighs as she watches him. It's becoming clear with each hour that passes that this case isn't going to be easy to crack.

CHAPTER TWENTY

Terri's boss had no useful information, so on her way to the station Madison takes the opportunity to drop by Ruby's Diner for coffee. It's almost lunchtime and she needs an energy boost. Once inside she places her order at the counter with a waitress who was hired just recently, to replace Kacie Larson.

"Have you seen Kacie lately, Detective?" the waitress asks.

Kacie worked here until last month when she went missing. She was eventually found by Madison and Nate, but now she's in jail awaiting trial on some serious charges. Not the outcome they had anticipated.

Madison smiles sadly. "Afraid not. Her trial date's not been set yet, but I did bump into her daughter just last week."

The waitress's eyes light up. "How's little Ellie doing?"

"She's being spoiled rotten by the foster carers, and I understand she gets weekly visits with her mom." Thanks to her young age the baby hasn't yet been negatively affected by everything that happened. She was happily laughing away at Madison's attempts to entertain her. That could change depending on the outcome of her mother's trial and as the years advance, but Madison knows Ellie will be well cared for regardless of what happens.

"That's great news. I'll let the others know," says the young woman, after filling Madison's travel mug and passing her the club sandwich she ordered to go. "Enjoy your lunch."

An old guy sitting at the counter says over his shoulder. "You found the killer yet?"

Madison raises her eyebrows. "I'm working on it."

He won't look at her. "Yeah, well don't wait too long. Maybe you ought to be out there doing your job and not in here yapping with the waitresses."

She rolls her eyes. She's dealt with his type before and refuses to feel guilty for taking a minute to grab lunch. "Good advice. Thanks." She looks around the diner on her way out and spots a guy she vaguely recognizes in the far corner booth. It's Matt Rader. He's staring at a laptop on the table in front of him. She hesitates to go over there but he's someone Nate wants to speak with. If she were investigating Ruby and Oliver's disappearance, she'd want to question him as a matter of urgency too.

Curiosity gets the better of her. She approaches his booth. "Sorry to bother you," she says.

He looks up, initially annoyed at the distraction, but when he recognizes her, he leans back and crosses his arms. "I saw on the news that you were out of prison and back in town. How can I help you, Detective?"

His hostility is evident, despite them never sharing more than a casual greeting before. This is the first time she's seen him in seven years. "I just want to say I'm sorry about Ruby and Oliver. I was in prison when they disappeared, but I'm sure Detectives Bowers and Douglas did everything they could to find them."

Matt scoffs. "You've gotta be kidding me!"

She senses she's about to get an earful.

"They did jack shit, actually. And now *they're* both dead. Some might call that karma."

She shakes her head at his attitude. "There's no need to—"

"You know what?" He's getting louder and Madison can sense other customers listening in. "There's every need to. Detective Douglas never took it seriously. He slandered my mom's name by suggesting she could've run off with another man. I think that turned the community against her, making them less interested in helping the investigation because they thought she invited trouble by cheating on her husband. And for that reason, I can't say I'm sorry he shot himself."

Madison tenses. She sympathizes for what he's gone through and all but she's disgusted by his comment. "No police officer is perfect, Mr. Rader, because no human is perfect. Douglas would've considered every possible motive for your mother and son's disappearance, because that's how investigations work. The fact he couldn't find them would've kept him up at night, so don't assume he didn't give that case one hundred percent of his time and energy."

Matt looks away, somewhat subdued.

She takes a seat across from him, trying to keep their conversation private. "He took his job extremely seriously. I mean, I should know; he didn't cut me any slack when he thought I was guilty of murder, even though I was a cop and he knew me." She holds his gaze.

He looks surprised. "So why don't you feel the same way I do about the guy?"

She shrugs. "Because I'm in the same position he was—looking for missing people, solving homicides. If you think that we don't absorb every single emotion that comes from the victims' families, you'd be wrong. We work the case as if it's *our* family members missing." She leans back. "Besides, cops have big egos. We don't like to be wrong ever, and we don't like killers, rapists and child abusers getting away with their crimes.

Why else would we be in this job? How else could we deal with the horrors we attend if we didn't believe we could catch the perpetrators and get justice for the victims?"

He takes a deep breath and rubs the back of his neck. "I hear what you're saying. I'm just frustrated."

"You're allowed to be," she says. "And you're right to hold law enforcement to account. But Douglas didn't deserve to die. He'd suffered plenty too. He lost his young daughter to a targeted drive-by shooting and was never the same because of it. He had a soft spot for kids. That's how I know he would've done everything in his power to find Oliver."

He looks her in the eye. "I didn't know any of that."

"Not many people do. He didn't let anyone in." She sips her coffee, relieved she's been able to make him see the reality of Douglas's job at that time.

"Do you know anything about the guy my dad's paying to investigate the case?"

She smiles. "Nate Monroe is my closest friend. I'd trust him with my life."

Matt raises his eyebrows. "Wow. You two dating or something?"

"No." She sips her coffee before standing up. "Speak to Nate, and soon. He's trying to help you and your dad." She walks away.

Madison arrives at the station just after midday. The morning sun has all but disappeared behind clouds. On the way to her desk she looks in at Chief Mendes, wanting to catch up, but Mendes is speaking on the phone so she heads straight to her desk and hangs her jacket on the back of the chair. The desk opposite hers was Douglas's. Someone's taken his *Welcome Back* banner down and cleared the few personal effects he had. She's glad she didn't have to do it.

The dispatch operators share the cubicle behind her desk, with Stella positioned directly behind Madison. Stella turns to her now, removing her headset. "How are you holding up?"

"I'm okay." She doesn't mention the sleepless night, the nightmare about Douglas, and the awful conversation she had to have with their victim's aunt about her murdered niece's dead baby. It's all part of the job and something she's expected to deal with, but it reminds her to talk to Mendes about getting a department therapist. "Has anyone called in with any tips about Terri Summers?"

Stella turns to her desk, which is covered with plants, romance novels and hundreds of sticky notes, something they're not meant to use anymore because of the environment. Owen told Madison about them but she can't remember why they're so bad, something to do with not being recyclable maybe. Stella picks up a sheet of paper before facing Madison again. "Nothing other than a few sightings of her coming and going from the care home where she worked on the day before she died. Sergeant Tanner's been trying to narrow down who her cell provider is so he can request a call history."

It's a relief to know Steve is filling the gap left by Douglas until a replacement is recruited. It makes her think of Officer Dan Goodwin. She shudders at the thought he'll apply for it because he's nowhere near ready. Shelley would be Madison's first choice, but she probably doesn't have the confidence to go for the job when the time comes. "Where's Goodwin? Do you know if he got suspended for shooting Troy?"

"No idea. He's not on duty today."

Madison wouldn't be surprised if that's who Mendes is talking to on the phone. "Is Steve around?"

"He's on his way back to the station now."

"Good, I want a briefing so we can all catch up. It's odd that there are no tips coming in about Terri's murder. Someone should know something."

"I'll let him know to hurry." Stella pulls her headset back on and turns to her computer.

Madison walks to Chief Mendes's office and knocks. Mendes is just finishing her phone call and she waves for her to enter. "Thank you for your understanding. I'll be in touch." Mendes hangs up and sighs heavily. She looks like she needs a strong coffee. "How are you doing today, Detective?"

Forcing a smile, Madison says, "I'm okay. Eager to find our killer. There's not much information coming in from the public, so I'll be holding a briefing as soon as Steve arrives."

"Good. I should tell you that Officer Goodwin won't be suspended."

She raises an eyebrow. "How come?"

"I believe he was justified in firing his weapon, as it looked like Mr. Randle was pulling out his own gun. Goodwin believed he was stopping you from being shot, and I accept that explanation. Case closed."

Madison isn't surprised. Perhaps if the department wasn't short-staffed the outcome would be different.

"I'll let Mr. Randle know," continues Mendes. "And in the meantime, we keep our fingers crossed that he doesn't acquire a lawyer."

"I've just come from visiting him at the hospital and I have no doubt he'll milk this situation for all it's worth. He's that kind of person."

Mendes leans back in her seat. "Great. That's all I need."

Madison hesitates. "About Douglas. I think it's time we hired a department shrink." She crosses her arms. "Even if it's on a casual basis, we need someone we can call on when things like this happen."

Mendes stares at her. "Is this your way of telling me you want to talk to someone about his death?"

She swallows. "Maybe." Then she attempts a laugh, "But I'd probably consume all their time, what with my history. We might start out talking about Douglas's suicide but what if the dam breaks and all my unresolved issues over my time in prison come up? I mean, the therapist would need a therapist by the time I'm done with them."

Mendes offers a faint smile. "You didn't seek counselling once you were released?"

As if it's that easy. "No. I was broke and homeless. I had no friends or family to take me in. I was eventually offered a halfway house and found work in a shitty burger joint with other ex-cons. I had nothing." She swallows the lump in her throat, surprised at how raw her emotions from that time still are. Perhaps Douglas's death has something to do with it.

"I'm sorry, I didn't know what it was like for you after your release," says Mendes with genuine concern. "I realize now that I actually know very little about what you went through. You seem to come in and get the job done with no unresolved anger about your wrongful arrest."

"That's what you do when you need money to live. This job is my lifeline back to normality. I have a son to support." She laughs. "And now a damn cat too."

"You don't give yourself enough credit." Chief Mendes looks at her for a long minute without speaking. "Let me check the budget, see where I can free up some cash for a therapist. If we get one, just make sure you make use of them. Got it?"

Madison nods, surprised that she was so easy to convince.

CHAPTER TWENTY-ONE

Sitting at his dining table, with Brody asleep at his feet, Nate tries calling Matt Rader. It goes straight to voicemail just as he suspected it would. For some reason Matt's still playing games. Nate looks at the list of other people he wants to speak to about Ruby's disappearance. The next name on the list is Joanne Rader—Matt's ex-wife and mother of Oliver.

All he knows is that she moved to California to live with her mom after splitting from Matt. Nate has a landline number and a cell number for her that Vince gave him. Although Vince wasn't sure they're still correct after all these years. Matt gave them to him after the divorce, in case Vince ever needed to speak to Jo, but he's never called her. Nate tries the landline number first in the hope she's at home and can talk in private. He doesn't want to upset her while she's possibly at work or with friends. It rings four times before a woman answers.

"Hello?"

"Hi. My name's Nate Monroe and I'd like to speak to Joanne Rader if she's home."

There's a slight hesitation from the end of the line. Before, "Are you a journalist? You sound like one."

It's good that she's wary of talking to strangers. "No, nothing like that."

"Jo's at work. I'm Patricia, her mother. You want to leave a message?"

"No, that's okay. I guess I can try her cell number."

"She doesn't answer that if she doesn't recognize who's calling."

That's understandable. "Fine. If you could pass her my cell number, I'd love a call back."

"What's this about?"

He can tell her suspicion is borne out of all the media coverage that surrounded the disappearance of Jo's son at the time. Nate decides it's best to be honest from the outset. "I'm a friend of Jo's father-in-law, Vince Rader. And I'm a private investigator."

Silence.

"Vince has asked me to look into Ruby and Oliver's disappearance. I understand that's going to be difficult for you and your daughter, but I'm hoping she'll speak to me. Maybe there's something she remembers that can help give me a lead."

Patricia appears to thaw. "I'm sure you can appreciate it's a difficult subject, Mr. Monroe. She doesn't talk about it to just anyone."

"I can understand that. I've helped find missing people before, so I'm hoping I can bring fresh eyes to the case. I'm also not a local of Lost Creek, so I have no allegiances to anyone."

"Except Vince. You said you were friends."

She's sharp. "New friends, but if the evidence leads me to him, then we won't be for much longer."

There's silence while she considers what he's said. Eventually she says, "Give me your number." When she's taken it, she adds, "Have you spoken to Matt yet?"

"Not yet. He's back in town, so I'm hoping—"

"What? He's gone home?" She's clearly shocked.

"Right. But I've yet to speak to him."

"Well, *he'd* know more than my daughter." There's hostility in her tone.

"Are you saying you think Matt could've been involved somehow?"

"Are you recording this call?"

"No, of course not."

"The journalists do. They record everything and then use it against us." She inhales deeply. "My daughter has been through hell and back, Mr. Monroe, and we just want to be left in peace. But I'll tell her you called. I guess it's up to her whether she wants to reopen old wounds and get her hopes up again. Goodbye."

Nate looks at his phone. The call has ended. He sighs. Patricia's anxiety about the case being reopened is understandable. Jo tried to start afresh with her move to California, and to speak to him would take her right back to the worst time in her life. But he also knows that parents of missing children rarely give up hope, so he suspects she'll call him back before the day is through.

Next on his list is Barbara Evans, Ruby's closest friend.

Thirty minutes later, Nate pulls up outside Barbara's home. She'd agreed on the phone to speak to him if he visited her. She's in a wheelchair and struggles to get around since her husband died.

Nate walks up the ramp that leads to her front door and knocks. He left Brody at home this time. He looks around while he waits for an answer. The neighborhood is middle class and the front yard is a proper garden with an herb patch, home-grown pumpkins that are on the turn and a lot of evergreen shrubs. When the door behind him opens he turns around.

"Admiring my squashes, were you?" asks the woman who

greets him. She's in her late sixties and her hair is dyed a strange orange color, with gray showing at her hairline. She's wearing about six bracelets, four necklaces and has chosen some bright eyeshadow and lipstick. She's dressed entirely in bright pink, including her slippers. There's a small white dog on her lap but Nate is unfamiliar with the breed.

He can't help but smile. "I sure was. You care for them yourself?"

"Of course. Just because I'm in a wheelchair doesn't mean I can't garden. I have a friend who gardens with her feet because she lost the use of her hands a decade ago. Don't write us off, Mr. Monroe. We're still capable of a lot of things, including murder if the mood takes us." She turns her electric wheelchair around. "Come on in."

He smiles. This is going to be interesting.

The inside of the house is less bold, but it's filled with ceramic dogs. They're on every hard surface and they all look like Barbara's dog. There are paintings covering the walls and the couch and armchairs are flowery. Nate never knew his grandmother—she died when he was still young enough to forget her—but this place makes him wish he did.

"Can I get you a drink? Please say yes, because I have a new tea set I've been dying to use with a guest. You'll have to have tea though, so I can make full use of it. My daughter brought home some proper English tea bags from her last trip abroad. Unfortunately, I can't get any of my friends to try them."

"Tea would be great, thanks." He takes a seat on the couch and instantly melts into it. His whole body relaxes and it makes him wonder where he can buy one of these. Brody might sleep on this at night instead of on the bed.

When Barbara has finished preparing their tea, he takes a sip. It tastes like dishwater, but he smiles. "Nice."

She looks delighted. "So what do you want to know, Mr. Monroe?"

"Please, call me Nate. As I said on the phone, Vince has asked me to find out what happened to his wife, and I understand you and Ruby were good friends. I thought you might have some information or thoughts on what happened to her."

"Oh, I have thoughts alright. I never spoke to Vince Rader again once the police named him a person of interest."

He raises his eyebrows. "Why's that?"

"I just can't. I don't want to believe he was involved, but the police must've had their suspicions. My friend Annette says they just don't have enough evidence to charge him with it."

He's disappointed that she'd listen to rumors. "I happen to know for a fact that there was no evidence at all to suggest Vince was involved. And he's paying me to look into the case. Would he do that if he were guilty?"

She considers it. "Maybe he's playing mind games with you."

He smiles politely. "You said yourself you didn't want to believe it, presumably that's because you knew him well?"

She nods. "He and Ruby had a great relationship from the outside. My husband liked Vince too. He was nice to me and Missy once Bob passed away. He'd come and fix things around the house, do you remember, Missy?" She looks down at the dog in her lap. "I guess I allowed myself to get swept up in the rumors from the women at my bridge club. It's hard not to when you watch those crime shows on TV. But I should've known better. Maybe I'll give him a call and apologize."

"I'm sure he'd appreciate that." He pauses. "Tell me, when did you last see Ruby?"

"The day before she went missing. She called me and was clearly upset. I couldn't get much out of her, but she left me with the impression she'd learned something disturbing."

Putting his cup on the coffee table, he asks, "What exactly did she say, can you remember?"

"Mr. Monroe, I'll never forget that conversation as long as I live." She pauses. "She said if I knew what she'd learned, I'd be horrified. She didn't want to believe it, and said she was going to need to do some more digging, just to make sure."

"Did she tell you what she'd learned?"

Shaking her head, Barbara says, "No. She wasn't ready to tell me until she was one hundred percent certain of it. It was personal for her, I know that."

He assumes Ruby didn't tell Vince or he'd already know what it was by now. Vince did mention Ruby seemed out of sorts in the days leading up to her disappearance. Nate suddenly wonders what happened to Ruby's cell phone and whether it went missing with her. The call logs and messages might reveal what she'd discovered. Presumably if the police had her cell phone at the time, they would've already checked all that out. He doesn't have access to the police files and if Madison shared them with him, she could get into trouble for it, but that doesn't mean she can't check it out for herself. "Is there anyone you think she might have confided in?"

Barbara seems offended. "I was her best friend. The fact she didn't tell me can reassure you that she didn't tell anybody." Her dog yaps in her lap, so Barbara leans forward to get a cookie. She breaks it into pieces and feeds it to the furball.

"How was Ruby's relationship with her son?"

"Oh, she doted on Matt of course, and that grandson of hers. She just loved it when she got to babysit. Her opinion of Jo went up the minute she got pregnant."

"She wasn't keen on her before then?"

Barbara waves a hand. "Oh, nothing like that. It's a mom thing. No woman is good enough for your son, and no man for your daughter. Not until they give you grandchildren, at which point the sun shines out of their ass. You don't have children, I take it?"

He shakes his head.

"Jo used to work for someone Ruby wasn't keen on, so that

would start arguments sometimes, but nothing serious. I know Jo was grateful for all the support Ruby gave them with Oliver. And both Ruby and Vince loved looking after their sweet little grandchild."

Nate leans in. "I heard Jo worked as a freelance bookkeeper and volunteered at various places. Which employer was Ruby not keen on?"

Barbara hesitates for the first time in the conversation. "You're not from around these parts, so I take it you've probably never heard of the McCoys from Gold Rock?"

Nate's stomach flips with dread. Not only has he heard of them, he played a part in their demise this summer. Angie McCoy is Madison's older sister and she's probably the meanest woman Nate's ever met. She and Madison couldn't be more different. "I know them."

She doesn't seem surprised that their reputation is well known, even to outsiders. "Wyatt's dead now of course, and Angie's locked up." She shakes her head. "That ranch of theirs, along with the attached scrapyard, must be going to ruin without them. It's a shame; an old property in a historic town like that should be sold off and cared for by a new family, or it won't be long before there's no one left and the town becomes a distant memory to old-timers like me. Anyway, Jo did some bookkeeping for Angie. I don't think they liked each other much from the sounds of it, so it didn't last very long, thankfully."

Nate considers whether Jo working for Angie could have a bearing on what happened, because if there was enough animosity between them, it could be a motive. His gut tells him Angie wouldn't hurt a child. She took Madison's son in while Madison was locked up, and treated him as if he were her own. A little too much like he was her own, but that's not the point. It shows she has a soft spot for children. Still, he writes it all down, knowing he has to follow where the leads take him. Madison won't be happy though. She wants to forget Angie even exists.

"Did they fight about something and that's what ended their working relationship?"

Barbara shakes her head. "No, I don't think so. I think Jo just decided they weren't a good fit. She worked there for less than a year, and that ended before anyone went missing."

He nods before asking his final questions. "I'm assuming you've lived here your whole life?"

She nods.

"So what does your gut tell you about what happened to Ruby and Oliver?"

She sips her tea before answering. "I think it's inevitable they're dead, otherwise they would've been spotted somewhere. I think if it wasn't Vince who killed them then a serial killer must've swept through our town on his way elsewhere. Because I can think of no one around here who would hurt that little boy."

Nate isn't so sure about a serial killer as they're responsible for less than two percent of homicides in the U.S. And it's not like Lost Creek is a through road to anywhere else. It ends at the mountains. There's only one way in and one way out. Why would a town like that attract a serial killer?

"I just hope they didn't suffer," she adds.

He nods, but he suspects that however Ruby and Oliver were killed, they would have suffered plenty.

CHAPTER TWENTY-TWO

Madison waits until the last person enters the briefing room and then closes the door. The mood is still somber at the station, following Douglas's death. Steve, Shelley, Officers Sanchez, Goodwin and Williams, as well as Chief Mendes and Alex, all stand looking at her expectedly.

"Okay, I won't keep you long. I just want to make sure we're all fully briefed about where we're at with the Terri Summers homicide." She looks at Officer Williams. "Gloria? Would you lead some officers in a search of the immediate area around the victim's home? I know there was a preliminary search but I want to be sure we didn't miss anything. Check the whole road, the neighbors' yards, Terri's vehicle, and so on. Maybe we'll get lucky."

Gloria nods. "Happy to."

"I especially want to find a wine bottle and possibly two glasses, because the victim had been drinking red wine just before her murder. I'm working on the assumption she was at home and invited someone to share a bottle, because her boyfriend said she was planning on staying in all day. I also need the murder weapon." She looks at Alex. "Do you know what kind of gun we're looking for?"

He smiles. "Actually, Detective, I've found what I believe to be the murder weapon."

Madison's shoulders relax for the first time since this happened. Finally, a breakthrough. "Where was it?"

"Hidden under the victim's couch. There was a trail of blood spots on the floor that had been wiped clean but not clean enough. They must've fallen from the barrel of the gun as they led all the way from the bedroom where she was killed to the living room. The gun is registered to Troy Randle."

"Damn." She sighs. "Troy has a cast-iron alibi, so he didn't shoot Terri." Registering the disappointment on Alex's face she quickly adds, "But good work finding it. Does it have any prints on it?"

He nods. "Only Mr. Randle's. If you're saying he's not our killer, then the killer obviously wore gloves and was trying to frame him."

Madison agrees. "It suggests the killer knew Troy would be a good suspect for this." She takes a deep breath and focuses on everything else they still need to do. "We're also looking for Terri's cell phone and purse, so it's safe to assume the killer took them with him."

Steve speaks up. "I'm trying to narrow down which cell provider she was with so I can request her records and try to get the current location of her phone."

"Would Troy know who she was signed up with?"

He shakes his head. "I called the hospital and spoke to him. He said he had no idea about stuff like that and he doesn't have access to her emails or bank account to check who she makes her payments to. She didn't own a computer or laptop and she used her phone for everything online."

"It's important we find her phone as soon as possible then," says Madison. "Because her aunt told me Terri favored Facebook Messenger as a means to chat with family, so I want to be able to access her account through her phone, but I suspect the killer took it with him for that exact reason. Without it I'd need to ask Facebook for access to her account but they're notorious for denying information requests."

"You appear certain this murder wasn't committed by Troy or a random stranger," says Chief Mendes.

Madison nods. "There's nothing to suggest this was a random home invasion. And I've ruled Troy out as a suspect because he was so inebriated he could barely stand that night. Besides, Lena told me earlier that she thinks Terri was killed during the four hours before midnight. Troy didn't leave the bar he was drinking at until 1.30 a.m. I've seen the CCTV footage. With that being said though, let's not rule out the possibility that Troy could have hired someone to kill her. But it would be pretty sick to knowingly sleep in the same house as your dead girlfriend all night."

"Killers are capable of all kinds of depravity," says Steve. "Maybe Troy is banking on us believing he's not capable of doing that."

Madison nods. "True. My gut tells me we're looking for someone else though. Someone who thinks they've got away with it."

"If that's the case," says Mendes, "the public is still at risk, because if he thinks he can get away with it again, he may attack someone else, and soon. I'll step up patrols in the area and I want all officers on high alert for any suspicious behavior."

Madison feels unnerved. The killer is one step ahead of them. She's inclined to believe Joe Manvers when he said Troy doesn't have the smarts to plan a murder. They're dealing with someone who planned Terri's death and the cover-up meticulously, and with no credible motive for wanting her dead, it's going to be a difficult case to solve.

Alex says, "Regarding her online presence, I'm sure it'll be easy for me to find her Facebook account and view the basics. I could see if her Facebook friends are accessible and check what she posted in the run up to her death, unless she had all her privacy settings on, in which case we're reliant on Facebook handing over the information."

"Do it. Thanks." She turns around to the table she's perched on and picks up an evidence bag containing the bracelet. "See if you can pull anything off of this. No one knows whether it was Terri's or not and she was clutching it when she died."

He steps forward and takes it from her. "Will do."

A knock at the door interrupts them. Stella steps in and hands a note to Madison. "Donna Jones from the Fill-up gas station wants you to know that Terri stopped by there around six on the evening she was murdered."

Finally, they have something concrete in the timeline of Terri's day.

"Her number's on there," Stella nods to the note, "but she says she's working until four this afternoon if you want to stop by and watch the security footage."

"Thanks." Once Stella leaves, Madison turns back to Alex. "Did you find anything of interest at the crime scene other than the gun?"

"Surprisingly little. Which leads me to believe the house was cleaned by the killer, because even the vacuum was empty. I would've expected that to have something in it considering the floors were immaculate. There certainly wasn't any debris in the bins inside or outside the house. Which begs the question; where was it emptied?" He pauses for effect. "Our killer obviously didn't want to leave any hairs or fibers behind. I've dusted everything he would've had to touch, to see if he left any fingerprints behind. I just need time to process them all."

Something about the fact the killer vacuumed the place bothers Madison. "Terri's murder was clearly premeditated, so we need to figure out the motive." Pausing, she adds, "Any questions, thoughts or theories?"

No one has anything.

"Then I need to go and pay Donna Jones a visit."

The Fill-up gas station is about two miles north of Terri's address. Madison knows that Troy Randle was working there the day she was killed, but he didn't turn up for work the morning she was found. She pulls into a parking space and gets out. As she approaches the entrance, she sees Matt Rader leaving.

He holds the door open for her and smiles. "Detective."

She nods. There's something about him that she finds unsettling. He doesn't stop to talk and she watches as he slips into his Toyota and drives away. She'd bet he won't be in town much longer. Not unless Nate gets a breakthrough in the cold case. She'd love to help him with that but she's too busy right now.

Inside the gas station it's warm and it smells strongly of coffee thanks to the coffee machine that sits next to a microwave on the counter. There are two customers in line so Madison waits her turn. The woman at the cash register is Donna, according to her name tag, and she's multitasking, serving customers while talking to a friend on her cell phone. When it's Madison's turn, Donna tells her friend she'll call them back. Then she yells at the top of her voice. "Darryl! You need to cover the counter. The cop's here."

Madison watches with amusement as a tall teenager with long hair appears from behind her. He works his way around the counter while Donna motions Madison to the back room. Inside there are four surveillance monitors all with different shots of the gas station, two out front and two inside. Without a word, Donna lines up the footage of Terri's visit and hits play.

Madison watches as headlights emerge from the dark,

approaching the forecourt. The timestamp says it's 6.01 p.m. A woman Madison recognizes as Terri gets out of the vehicle and starts pumping gas. She isn't dressed how she was found the next morning. She's in sweatpants and a sweater. This is only two hours before Lena thinks Terri could have been shot.

Eventually Terri enters the store and browses the aisles as Madison watches. It's always a strange sensation to watch a dead person walking around in the hours before their murder. Terri's completely oblivious that this is the last time she'll ever buy something. That once she changes out of those sweats, she'll be wearing the outfit she'll die in. Madison wishes she could reach into the security footage and warn her.

"She bought a pack of M&M's," says Donna, over her shoulder. "Said they were to go with some red wine she had at home."

So it seems Terri did drink the wine at home, not at a restaurant or a bar. They need to find the empty bottle and glasses. Madison watches Terri shoot the shit with Donna for a few minutes and then leave. "What did you talk about?"

"I asked if she'd had a good day and she said she'd spent it lazing around the house alone. It was her day off work and she said she caught up on her sleep."

"Did she have any makeup on?"

"Not a scrap. Not that she needed it."

The fact that Terri was dressed differently when she was killed suggests she invited someone over to share a glass of wine. That could be a friend, or a lover. If it wasn't the killer, it's likely they would have come forward by now to get themselves ruled out as a suspect. It also explains why the bottle was missing from the house, along with the used wineglasses; they're evidence. "Her boyfriend works here, right?"

"Who, Troy?" Donna rolls her eyes. "If you can call it that. My boss has a thing for recruiting ex-cons. He's one of those bleeding-heart liberals. Doesn't care that he's putting the rest of us in danger by helping out the criminals."

Madison raises an eyebrow. "The world needs people like your boss. Otherwise, these ex-cons would find themselves without work and even more desperate. What do you think they'll do then? I mean, doesn't everyone deserve a second chance?"

"Troy was living his second chance and he used it to kill his girlfriend."

"No. He didn't kill Terri."

"Well, I heard he used to beat her," Donna says defiantly.

Madison takes a deep breath, trying not to show her irritation. "When was the last time he was here?"

"The day before her body was found. He arrived ten minutes late, just after eight in the morning. He left at five. Said he was getting food from the taco place before going to Joe's Saloon."

Madison writes it all down. Troy went from work, to a fast-food joint, to the bar. It's likely he didn't see Terri at all after leaving home that morning. "Ever see Terri in here or around town with a guy other than Troy?"

Donna smiles. "Are you saying she was cheating on his sorry ass? I sure hope she was. The guy's a pig."

"Is that a no?"

Donna nods.

"Do you know who Terri's friends are?"

"I've seen her in here with a couple of women from the care home where she works. I can't say if they hang out together all the time."

Madison doesn't think Terri was drinking with a friend as they would have come forward by now. It must've been a guy she was into, otherwise Troy would have known about it. She turns back to the screen. "I'll need a copy of that footage."

CHAPTER TWENTY-THREE

On her way back to the car, Madison gets a phone call. It's Owen. "Hey," she says. "Everything alright?"

"Okay, don't be mad at me," he says, "but I did something you might not be happy about."

She stops walking and tries not to panic. "Have you been arrested?"

"What? No, of course not." He says it as if that would never happen to him, even though it did and not too long ago.

She leans against the car. "What have you done?"

"Just hear me out. Remember, don't be mad."

"As long as you didn't kill someone, I think we're good."

"Maybe I should just tell you later."

Madison stands straight. "Owen? Don't leave me hanging. What is it?"

She hears him swallow. "You said at dinner last night that you're missing your dad, right?"

She frowns. "Right. So what?"

"Well, I tracked him down on Facebook a week ago and sent him a message telling him I'm his long-lost grandson and that we'd love to have him visit sometime." He says it all in one breath.

"You did *what*?"

"I already knew you were missing him and he was really easy to find, so I thought what the hell. Anyway, we've exchanged a few messages and he seems cool, but I wasn't sure how you'd react, which is why I've held off telling you. Then I figured he might get in touch with you directly and you should probably be prepared for that just in case. Okay, gotta go! I've got homework to do."

She looks at her phone but he's disconnected before she can give him an earful. Her mouth is open in disbelief. She hasn't discussed her father much with Owen. All he knows is that Bill Harper lives in Alaska. That's pretty much all she knows about him now too, together with the fact he works for the FBI. He was a detective at LCPD when she was a kid and she's always wondered how he would react to knowing she followed in his footsteps. She wishes she was the one to make contact, but has to admit she might not have been brave enough. After all, her dad never got in touch after her arrest. He never visited nor wrote to her in prison. And he didn't offer her sanctuary upon her release. He must be ashamed of having a daughter who went to prison. That would have been professionally embarrassing for him—if he ever heard about it all the way up in Alaska.

She sighs and pulls the car door open. Before driving away, she checks the time. It's almost two o'clock. Douglas is due to be cremated in twenty-five hours. She leans her head back against the rest, struggling not to think about it. That's when she realizes what's been bugging her about his death. Douglas didn't leave a suicide note. Not that she saw anyway. Maybe Steve found one while he was arranging for the body to be moved. For some reason it bothers her. Wouldn't Douglas have left a note for his dad? Sure, he was a man of few words, but don't most people who take their own life leave some kind of message? She investigated one suicide where the guy left all his financial documents and passwords next to his farewell note, making sure his family could access everything in the aftermath.

She pulls out her phone and calls Steve, watching cars come and go through the gas station's parking lot as she waits for him to answer.

"Sergeant Tanner."

"Hey, Steve. It's me. Quick question: did you find a suicide note at Douglas's place?"

He doesn't hesitate. "No. But I can't say I was looking for one, probably because I was in shock. I'd have thought it would have been on or near his body if he left one."

"That's what I'd assume." She pauses as she thinks. "Would it be okay if I take a look around his house?"

"For a note?"

"Yeah. I don't know, something's bugging me about the way he died and I just want to satisfy my own curiosity. He's being cremated tomorrow afternoon and this is my only chance to make sure I was thorough, you know?"

Steve sighs down the line. "Sure, I guess it can't hurt. I'll drop his keys at the front desk for you."

"Has his back door been fixed then?"

"Yeah. The glass has been replaced and Mendes is paying for it."

"From the budget?"

"No, from her own money."

Madison raises her eyebrows. She's heard the team complaining among themselves that Mendes didn't make it to Joe's Saloon to honor Douglas. Maybe they should shut up and consider what she *is* doing for him. "I'll swing by in five minutes for the keys."

The only problem is, she doesn't want to go back to Douglas's house. Not on her own. Douglas's blood will still be on the chair and wall. His belongings will still be around the house, where he left them. Everything will be there but him. She decides to shoot Nate a text.

Do you have an hour to come back to Douglas's house with me?

Even though she doesn't offer any explanation she gets an immediate response.

On my way.

She smiles, and part of her wishes he was her detective partner, but she knows there's no way he'd ever consider joining the force. It was a crooked cop who secured Nate's wrongful conviction and it's taken a long time to convince him all cops aren't like that one.

She drives to the station and collects the keys before continuing on to Douglas's house. Preferring not to go inside alone, she waits in her car. Nate pulls up behind her just minutes later and they approach the front door together.

"What are we looking for?" asks Nate, pulling his jacket collar up for warmth.

"He didn't leave a note," she says. "Don't you think that's weird?"

"Not really. I read an article once about how fewer than fifty percent of suicides leave a note. I'd be willing to guess that's even less for men."

She nods. "Maybe that's it. But I don't know... It's bothering me."

"Then let's check it out."

She loves how he's willing to listen to her. Most guys would blame her suspicions on her grief or stress. Some assholes would even assume it's her time of the month, but Nate's always championing her. He trusts her instinct. It gives her the confidence to follow her gut.

Putting the key into the lock, she turns it and the door opens. They cautiously step inside.

CHAPTER TWENTY-FOUR

Nate enters the house behind Madison. The smell of decay has mostly abated, but as they enter the living room he can see a swarm of flies hovering over Douglas's bloody recliner. He opens a window and swats them away with a newspaper.

Madison's quiet as she assesses the room, so he says, "If he left a note, it has to be in here. I can't imagine he'd leave it upstairs."

She nods. "That's what I'd assume, but there's nothing here." She even looks under the recliner, using her phone's flashlight.

"Does that really surprise you though? You know what Douglas was like."

She looks up at him with a pained expression. "I know. But I feel cheated, somehow. I guess I'm looking for confirmation that he did this to himself. And answers as to why." She shakes her head. "It's selfish, I know." Then, looking at the floor, she says, "Do you remember whether the carpet looked recently vacuumed when we came in yesterday?"

He frowns and looks straight at the floor. The rest of the

downstairs has hardwood floors but in here a gray carpet is covered in dirty footprints from everyone who attended the scene yesterday during the middle of a heavy downpour. A few decaying leaves have found their way in on the bottom of boots. "I can't say I noticed."

"It's tidy in here though, right?"

He looks around. "It's minimalist. Exactly how I would expect Douglas to live."

She sighs, clearly frustrated. "Let's check upstairs."

He follows her up. The hallway is narrow, showing two doors that lead to bedrooms and one that leads to a bathroom. He checks out the bathroom. It's small and square. The bathroom cabinet has a mirrored door which he opens. Band-Aids, Q-tips, floss, toothpaste and aftershave sit on the shelves. An electric razor is plugged in on the shelf next to the cabinet, flashing to show a full charge. Nate instinctively pulls the plug out. There are no pill bottles anywhere, not even painkillers.

Madison enters and looks over his shoulder. "The master bedroom is sparse. Nothing in his drawers except clothes, books and these." She opens her hand. "His AA sobriety coins." There are four coins: one given for twenty-four hours' sobriety, and then one for every week he's managed to stay sober since. She shakes her head and from her reflection in the mirror he can tell she's struggling to hold back her emotions.

He turns to face her. "You sure you want to be here?"

She nods. He follows her into the spare room, which is small and rectangular, with a single bed and closet and a few storage containers stacked neatly in the corner. Madison gasps as she notices the four large framed photo collages of what must be Douglas's wife and child. He's in a lot of the photographs too and they were clearly taken in happier times.

After a minute, Madison becomes upset and leaves the room, but Nate can't tear his eyes away. Douglas looks like a different person in these photographs. He's positively beaming from ear to ear. Some are taken on vacation at Disneyland, whereas in others he's dressed for work in a black suit. His detective badge sits on his hip and his arm is casually draped over another cop's shoulders, with both giving the camera a thumbs-up. Nate can't imagine Douglas ever showing that level of affection for anyone at LCPD. The other guy must be his partner from his previous police department. The one who died trying to save Douglas's six-year-old daughter. From what Madison told him, their families were enjoying a barbecue on their front lawn when someone Douglas helped convict drove past the day after his release from prison and gunned them down.

Looking at these images feels surreal. The difference between this Douglas and the guy who arrested Madison is vast, and it explains the depth of his despair over losing these people. To Nate, it clarifies why he wanted to end his pain.

These collages are Douglas's suicide note.

He heads back downstairs, where Madison is seated on the couch, wiping her eyes.

"When I lost Owen to child services after my arrest, I thought there was no greater pain," she says. "I felt like a part of me was missing because it was. Looking at those photos upstairs, I can understand why Douglas was the way he was. His pain was eternal. There was no hope of being reunited with his daughter one day, not in this world. It's hope that got me through my sentence. Hope that I'd be reunited with Owen one day. If I didn't have that..."

Nate sits next to her and rubs her shoulder. "I know." His own prison experience was different. He had no hope. Not until someone showed up years into his sentence and said they wanted to work on overturning his conviction.

They sit in silence for a minute, both fixing their eyes on the recliner.

"Wait a minute," she says, slowly standing.

"What is it?"

She looks at him. "The side table is empty. It was when we found him too."

He's not sure of the significance.

"Wouldn't an alcoholic have a drink before killing themselves? Wouldn't he have something nearby to comfort him? There should be a glass, a bottle of something, or at the very least a photograph of his daughter." She goes to the kitchen and Nate hears her open the refrigerator before rooting through the kitchen cupboards. When she comes back, she says, "There's not a drop of alcohol in the house."

Nate stands. "Let me check the garbage." The kitchen trash is half full with soda cans, coffee filters and food packaging. No liquor bottles.

Madison pulls out the sobriety coins and does a calculation in her head. "According to these he was three weeks sober. He was only suspended a little over three weeks ago, which means that triggered him into getting help right away. He wasn't drinking again when he died. He was getting better, not worse!"

"So what are you saying? That his suicide was staged?"

Her eyes are burning with fury. "That's exactly what I'm saying."

"But what about upstairs? That spare room?"

"His spare room is like that to provide comfort, not despair. When I lost Owen I would stare at a photo of him for hours on end, remembering what he sounded like, how he laughed, what he liked to play with. It was the only thing that brought me any joy."

Nate isn't so sure Douglas could have been murdered. "There were no signs of forced entry. And he used his service weapon, how would a killer get a hold of that?"

"Someone could've climbed in through a window and hid until Douglas was home. Or he could've left a door unlocked.

As for his gun, I don't know if he has a gun safe anywhere, he certainly doesn't have a lockable cabinet. Maybe the killer wrestled if off him. They could've taken him by surprise, while he was watching TV." She's getting more passionate as she works through her theory. "Then the killer positioned him to make it look like a suicide."

"But who would want Douglas dead?"

She blinks. "Where's his vacuum?"

"What?" He's confused.

She brushes past him and goes to the cupboard under the stairs. She pulls the vacuum out. It's a bagless, upright model and she disconnects the plastic cup that catches the dirt and debris. She holds it up and gasps.

"I don't get it," he says.

Madison slowly looks at him. "It's empty." When he doesn't reply she adds, "We think that whoever murdered Terri Summers vacuumed the house afterward and emptied the bag somewhere other than into her garbage. Probably outside in the wilderness where any evidence would have blown away. Yesterday Douglas's living room floor was spotless. His house was pristine. Sure, he's a tidy guy, but I'm willing to bet whoever killed him tidied up after themselves to destroy any trace evidence."

Nate doesn't know what to say. It's quite a theory, and one that would be difficult to prove without supporting evidence, something stronger than the fact that both victims had tidy homes. But Madison's instincts are rarely wrong.

"But why?" she says, thinking out loud. "Who would want to kill a homicide detective?"

Nate hazards a guess. "Someone who didn't want him around to solve the murder of Terri Summers?"

"But Douglas was suspended from duty. He wasn't working any cases. If that was their motive, they would more likely have killed... me." She swallows and a look of fear clouds her face.

He knows exactly what she's thinking; someone killed the wrong detective, and they had the balls to do it in his own home. It's not unrealistic to think they could come for her next. Or worse—for her son.

CHAPTER TWENTY-FIVE

Facebook Messenger

I'll be there in an hour.

Great.

I've bought a bottle of wine.

Thought we could do with it.

Are you trying to get me drunk?

Haha.

You haven't told anyone I'm coming, have you?

No.

Troy will be at the bar all night.

His favorite place.

Good. We have a lot of catching up to do.

And a decision to make.

Right.

I'm sorry you're caught up in all this.

I know you are.

See you soon.

CHAPTER TWENTY-SIX

Madison speeds straight back to the station to update Chief Mendes on what she found at Douglas's house, or rather, what she didn't find. When she gets there, Officer Goodwin is in Mendes's office, so she hesitates outside, as they're probably discussing his recent recklessness and how to avoid it happening again.

With Douglas due to be cremated in less than twenty-four hours though, she needs to act fast. She knocks on the door. Mendes looks up, irritated. She shakes her head at Madison and points to Goodwin as if to say, "Can't you see I'm busy here?"

Madison refuses to wait. She opens the door. "Sorry, Chief, but I have to speak to you urgently. It's about Douglas."

Chief Mendes crosses her arms. "You can't wait ten minutes?"

"Yeah, Maddie," says Officer Goodwin. "We're in the middle of something, have some respect."

Madison glares at him with barely contained rage. She doesn't have time for this punk. "I don't know who you think you're talking to, *Officer,* because that's not my name and it certainly isn't my title. I suggest you show some respect."

He rolls his eyes. "We work for the same team, *Detective*. So why don't you take that stick out of your ass?"

Madison's hands tense and she has to resist the urge to punch him in the face. Chief Mendes stands up and gets between them. "Officer Goodwin, give us some time. We can pick this up afterward."

Goodwin shakes his head as he gets out of his seat. He brushes past Madison with a look of contempt. Once he's gone, Madison slams the door shut behind him a little too hard. She doesn't have the patience to deal with assholes like him. Not today.

Mendes stares at her with raised eyebrows.

"I'm sorry. I know you're annoyed, but I had to interrupt." Madison tries to find a way to frame what she wants to say without being too dramatic but fails. "I think Douglas was murdered."

Chief Mendes opens her mouth but nothing comes out. She gives a little shake of her head in disbelief before responding. "What on earth has led you to that theory?"

Taking a deep breath, Madison tries to sum up everything she discovered at Douglas's house. "There was no alcohol in his house *at all*, his sobriety coins prove he was sober around the time of his death, there was no suicide note, he wasn't under the influence of any drugs because there was no drug paraphernalia in his house, and with no drink or drugs in his system he had no real reason to do it." She takes another breath. "Plus, like the home of Terri Summers, Douglas's house was recently vacuumed and the vacuum was empty. It wasn't emptied into his garbage. Someone was careful to destroy any potential evidence that they were ever there."

Mendes doesn't seem convinced. Instead, she looks worried. "Maybe now would be a good time to arrange for you to see that therapist we talked about."

"Wait. What?" She can't believe Mendes won't take her

seriously. "I'm fine. Nate and I were there, we saw for ourselves—"

"Madison, do I have to remind you that Nate Monroe is not an officer of this department? You shouldn't be taking him anywhere with you. I understand we're short-staffed but there is such a thing as confidentiality. We can't be giving him access to our investigations."

Madison shakes her head in frustration. Nate's the most reliable person she knows, he wouldn't leak anything to the press. "But this isn't an official investigation yet. None of that matters right now, Chief. You're not listening to me."

"I heard what you said, but just because Douglas wasn't drinking at the time he shot himself doesn't mean it wasn't suicide." She softens her tone. "Look, it's been a difficult few days for you and it wouldn't be surprising if you were reading too much into things. Douglas was your partner, after all."

"That's not it at all!" She's disappointed that Mendes is unwilling to listen. "Wait, let me get Steve in here." She opens the door and calls Steve over before repeating everything she told Mendes.

He listens, but then looks at Mendes instead of at her. "I don't know what to say. I don't think any of that is proof that Douglas was murdered. I mean, where's the motive?"

"That's what I need to figure out," says Madison, disappointed. "Ideally, we need an autopsy on Douglas, but I know you won't allow that without further proof, so I need Alex at his house immediately. There could be something besides the empty vacuum that proves he was killed."

Mendes is shaking her head. "Sorry, Madison. I'm not going to upset his father by saying he can't have his son's body back because my detective has a hunch about an empty vacuum cleaner." She softens. "I mean, can't you see how ridiculous this sounds?"

Steve turns to Madison, "I get that you're looking for

answers, but I have to say what you're working with right now is kind of a stretch. I mean, say he *was* killed by the same person who killed Terri Summers. What connection is there between the two of them? Did they even know each other?"

Madison's shoulders sink. When he says it like that it sounds crazy. "I have no idea if they knew each other."

"Could Douglas have been dating Terri Summers?" asks Mendes. "I remember you said Terri was possibly on a date with someone who wasn't her boyfriend when she died."

She gives Mendes credit for at least trying to piece her theory together, but Madison can't see Douglas dating anyone, especially not while he was concentrating on getting sober. It's not impossible, but she'd need to look into it. "I don't know. But if I find something else, will you at least delay his cremation while I look into it?"

Mendes remains hesitant. "If you find something else, I'll get Alex to process Douglas's living room. Otherwise, I have no credible reason to stop the cremation from going ahead."

Madison is unsure whether she can find anything in time. Twenty-four hours isn't long and she should be working exclusively on Terri's murder. But if she can prove the two are linked, she can solve both together.

"In the meantime," says Mendes, "I'm going to look for a therapist as a matter of urgency. Understand what I'm saying?"

Madison can feel Steve's gaze on her. Her face flushes hot. "I understand." She exits the office, but Steve stays behind, probably to talk about the state of her mental health. Is she crazy to suggest Douglas was murdered? She felt so certain at his house.

"Madison?" Stella calls her over to her desk.

"What is it?"

"Officer Williams just radioed in. The search team have found an empty wineglass lying under a bush next to Trent Road."

Her stomach leaps. "You're kidding? Did she say whether it had any remnants in it?"

Stella nods. "A drop of red wine in the bottom." With a glint in her eye she adds, "Looks like our killer slipped up."

Madison's elated. They can pull prints and saliva from it. And the other missing glass—or the wine bottle—could be nearby. She runs past the chief's office toward the exit, ignoring the concerned looks on Steve and Mendes's faces as she goes.

CHAPTER TWENTY-SEVEN

After Nate leaves Douglas's house, he finds an excuse to hang around in Ruby's Diner in the hope of bumping into Matt Rader. The guy's been difficult to pin down and has yet to return Nate's calls. He doesn't appear to be around right now though. The diner's pretty quiet this afternoon, with most people still having an hour or two before they clock off work for the day. Vince isn't around either and there are just two waitresses on shift right now.

He sips his coffee and stares out of the window. The sun has set, so the parking lot is bathed in an orange glow from the street lights. A dense fog is creeping along the ground, obscuring the tires of the parked vehicles. It gives the illusion they're all floating. He thinks of Madison and considers whether she's right to be suspicious of Douglas's death. On the one hand the guy was so repressed it wouldn't be surprising if he felt overwhelmed and wanted an out, but on the other he always seemed in control of himself.

The well-lit interior of the diner is reflected in the window and Nate spots Carla approaching so he turns to face her.

"Care for a top-up?" she asks.

He smiles. "Sure. Thanks."

"How was the special?"

He ordered tomato and basil soup, which came with a think chunk of freshly baked bread. "Amazing as always."

"I'll be sure to tell the cook." She turns to leave.

"Can I ask you something, Carla?"

With a playful wink she says, "If it's about a date, the answer's yes."

He laughs before getting serious. "Ruby Rader was your boss and presumably you knew her well. What do you think happened to her?"

Throwing a dishcloth over her shoulder she says, "Oh, goodness. I better sit down for this." She squeezes into the booth. "You know what, Nate? I'd like to think Ruby was having a midlife crisis and she took off to live in Hawaii or somewhere equally fancy, taking Oliver with her because she couldn't bear to be apart from him. I like to imagine they're bodyboarding in the surf and building sandcastles all day." She smiles sadly. "But I'm also a realist, and the sad reality is that when a woman goes missing, nine times out of ten she was taken against her will, sexually assaulted, killed and then dumped. And, sure, there's probably one in ten who might have disappeared because she wanted to, but I don't think Ruby would have left Vince and Matt behind. She had no reason to. Vince adored her, still does."

"And Matt?"

She considers her words before speaking. "He's changed, that much is obvious. He's more serious than he used to be and barely says a word to any of us, like we weren't here babysitting Oliver whenever he wanted back in the day." She sighs. "I was here when he dropped Oliver off that morning. There was no sign of any hostility between him and his parents. He simply went to work."

"And Jo Rader? How was she in the aftermath."

Tears come to Carla's eyes. "She was a broken woman. The light left her eyes and she would tremble constantly. Said she didn't know who to trust anymore, which is unsurprising. None of us did. When it became apparent they weren't going to be found, Jo wanted to get out of here. I wasn't surprised when she and Matt moved away, but Vince was devastated. He was left to deal with his grief all alone."

Nate feels bad for him. "You must hear a lot of rumors working here. Anything stand out?"

"Oh, please, these guys aren't worth listening to. They all suspect each other. That's what something like this does; it makes you suspect your neighbors. You wonder just what the heck is going on behind their drapes. Whether they're wolves in sheep's clothing. After all, killers have to live somewhere too, right?" She turns to look at the counter, where a line of customers is forming. "I better go." She stands up. "The sooner you find Ruby and Oliver's bodies and catch their killer, the sooner this town can find some peace." She fixes a friendly smile on her face for the customers and leaves.

He looks down at his phone. He's been researching homicides committed in Lost Creek around the time Ruby went missing. There are five from that entire year, which is a lot for a town this size, but none of them could be considered noteworthy with regards to Ruby's disappearance. They were mostly bar fights or domestic incidents coming to a head. One wife shot her husband and one guy killed his girlfriend with his bare fists.

His phone vibrates with a call. "Hello?"

"Hi. It's Joanne Rader. You left a message with my mom?"

He quickly pulls out his notebook and a pen, glad she decided to call him back. "I did. Did she tell you why I was calling?"

"Yes. And I'm not sure I want to talk to you."

He tries to keep her on the phone. "I'm just trying to find your son, Mrs. Rader."

"That's not actually my last name anymore. I remarried a year ago. My name's Joanne Letts now." Her voice is warm but wary. She's probably torn between desperately wanting someone to find her son, and not wanting to rake up old ground for no good reason.

"I'm sorry, I didn't know. How about you just answer whichever questions you feel comfortable with?" After a few seconds hesitation she agrees and he senses she might hang up at any minute, so he has to ask the most important questions first. "When Ruby and Oliver first disappeared, what did your gut instinct tell you had happened to them?"

He hears her swallow. "I thought they'd been abducted. It was the only explanation for them vanishing like they did."

"And at the time, who did you think could've taken them?"

She doesn't hesitate. "A stranger. Someone who just did it for the thrill. Maybe he was out with the intention of assaulting a woman, and he didn't see Oliver in the back seat of her car."

"Was Ruby's car ever found?"

"No. Detective Douglas thought their abductor must've stolen it, switched the license plates and sold it on elsewhere so it couldn't be traced."

Mindful of upsetting her, he asks a more difficult question. "And what do you believe now, all these years later and knowing what Detective Douglas covered as part of the investigation; who do you think took them?"

Silence. She doesn't speak for a long time, and when she does her voice is barely audible. "Matt doesn't have a solid alibi for the time they're unaccounted for. It kills me to even say it, but it's been eating away at me for years."

He's surprised she would give her ex-husband's name as a potential suspect, but this is what happens over time; allegiances change, people split up and move on. Once they're no longer loyal to a person, they're more likely to be honest about their suspicions. And they're more likely to become good witnesses. "Did you ever ask him if he was involved?"

"No, never. How could I? If he was, and he thought I knew, he might've killed me too."

So she thinks he killed them. "Is that why you divorced him and moved so far away?"

"I told my mom about my suspicion and she wanted me as far away from him as possible. She told me to move to Sacramento to be with her." She pauses. "I'm not saying he did it, Mr. Monroe. There was never any domestic abuse in our relationship. I was happy. I thought he was too. I'm just telling you he doesn't have a solid alibi. But equally it could've been a stranger. Maybe they were driven out of state and killed somewhere else. That would explain why they've never been found."

He nods. "Did Matt and Ruby have a good relationship?"

"I thought so, but he was money-orientated and we were going through a bad patch, financially. There never seemed to be enough money to pay the never-ending bills, you know? I thought maybe he asked his mom for a loan and she refused him."

"Had she ever loaned him money before?"

"I don't know, maybe. He didn't like to talk about money. He always pretended everything was fine, as if it was a personal failure to be like rest of America and struggling to pay the bills. Have you spoken to Matt yet? Mom said you told her he's back in Lost Creek."

"He is. But I haven't been able to meet with him yet. Vince has been helpful though."

"You know the crazy thing about all this? I miss Vince. I mean, I miss Ruby too, of course, but Vince was so kind. He and I had a thing where we'd team up against Ruby and Matt by making them the butt of our jokes. Nothing horrible, we liked to pull their legs a little. He has a great sense of humor, and Oliver adored him."

Nate smiles. "Vince misses you too. He told me he never heard from you once you moved away. Why is that?"

Quietly, she says, "I never knew if he was protecting Matt in some way. Once my son disappeared, I didn't know who to trust. It was unbearable. It still is."

"I understand." He pauses. "I heard you used to work for Angie McCoy a while ago. Can I ask what your relationship with Angie was like?"

"What's that got to do with anything?" She seems confused.

"I'm just looking into any potential motives for Ruby and Oliver's disappearance, and wanted to know of anyone you or Matt, or even Vince, might have had trouble with around that time. Anyone who could've been holding a grudge maybe."

"I didn't work for her for long. I didn't like her. Ruby tried to warn me that couple were bad news, and after what I heard about everything that happened down there this summer, I'm glad I moved away."

It's true that everything came to a head this summer for the McCoys, but it doesn't sound like Angie had anything to do with Ruby's or Oliver's disappearance, which is a relief. It means he won't have to pay Madison's sister a visit in prison. "One last question—I understand you were working the day they vanished. Which employer were you working for at that time?"

"It was a stationery company downtown, but they've since gone bust. I was their maternity cover, working on their accounts."

"What time did you get home?"

She sighs, as if she's repeated this a million times, which she probably has. "I got home around six, right when they were due back. But Ruby had a key to our place, she could've let herself in if she got there before me."

"When did you realize they weren't coming home?"

A minute or so goes by and Nate thinks she's trying to compose herself. "Ruby was rarely late for anything," she says. "So by seven I was worried. Matt got home just before eight. He went straight out looking for them. By then I was really scared, because he was taking it so seriously. I was relying on him to shake it off and tell me they'd probably got caught up shopping somewhere, but he was anxious right away, especially as her cell phone was switched off. He called Vince and they both went searching together. I can't remember at what point we notified the police. I think Matt or Vince made that call." She inhales deeply.

"Did the police ever manage to locate Ruby's cell phone?"

"No."

That's frustrating. "Vince mentioned Ruby appeared out of sorts in the days leading up to her disappearance. Did you notice that too?"

"No, sorry. I can't say I did."

Nate doesn't want to keep her any longer. He's written everything down and has enough information to fill some of the gaps he'd been wondering about. "If you think of anything at all that might help me, just call or message me, any time of day."

"I will. I'm not going to get my hopes up because I've learned from experience how soul destroying it is when nothing comes of an investigation, but I'm relieved someone is looking for them again. Please keep me updated with any significant leads. My cell number is the quickest way to contact me." She takes a deep breath. "Thank you for at least trying to find them, Mr. Monroe. I mean that."

"You can thank Vince. He's the one who wanted me to do this."

She doesn't reply, until. "Bye."

The call leaves him feeling drained. The sorrow in her voice was strong and he worries that despite what she says, he's got her hopes up for nothing. So when Matt Rader saunters down to the kitchen from the apartment upstairs, Nate gets straight up and goes to the counter.

Matt emerges from the kitchen with a piece of toast in his hand. When he sees Nate, he stops and stares defiantly without saying a word.

Nate stares back. "It's time we talked."

CHAPTER TWENTY-EIGHT

Angie McCoy is keeping one eye on the game of chess she's playing with Tracey, a fellow inmate, while also reading a crime novel from the prison library. The warden is yet to follow the example from other penitentiaries and ban crime fiction or true crime from the library, but it's just a matter of time. The book Angie's reading is called *Bitter Road* and it's based on a real crime that happened to two young girls. She wouldn't normally pick up this kind of crap, but the perpetrator was recently murdered in Angie's home town. And she's sharing a cell with the last person to speak to his killer.

Kacie Larson is a petite young girl who, on the face of it, wouldn't hurt a fly. It turns out she can hurt sex offenders though, which immediately earned Angie's respect. She looks out for Kacie in here and maybe once the girl is released, *if* she's released, she can do something for Angie. She'd better do if she knows what's good for her.

The noise of inmates catcalling distracts her from both the book and the chess game. She looks up to see what's causing their reaction. Expecting it to be a new inmate being brought onto the unit, she sees everyone staring at the TV instead.

The news anchor, a dumb blonde, is telling them about a cold case that's been reopened in Lost Creek, but not by the police. A private investigator is looking into the disappearance of Ruby Rader and her grandson.

Angie's fellow inmates are admiring a photo splashed on the screen of the PI, forty-year-old Nate Monroe.

"He can investigate me any time he likes," says Cat, a heavily tattooed mother of six. It's that way of thinking that gave her six different baby daddies, none of whom pay her any child support. Well, technically two of them can't since she murdered them in their sleep.

The other women laugh at her comment.

Angie closes her book and stands up. She walks toward the TV. "Shut up, goddammit. I want to listen." They silently watch the anchor.

"Mr. Monroe is hoping to pick up where the investigating detectives left off," says the reporter. "But with six years having now passed since Ruby and Oliver's disappearance, it won't be an easy task. This was him visiting Ruby's husband Vince Rader earlier this week. As many viewers will remember, Vince was a person of interest after his wife and grandson's disappearance."

An outside shot of Ruby's Diner is shown. It's a two-story building with a red neon sign outside and a large glass window overlooking the parking lot. It's surrounded on both sides by tall evergreens, the mountains standing proud behind them. Her stomach flips at the sight of something so familiar. They're not usually allowed to watch the news in here, because it gets everyone riled up, so they usually watch soap operas or *Real Housewives* repeats. Although, allegiances with the various housewives can cause more fights that any other topic.

Angie catches a glimpse of Nate Monroe stepping out of the diner. It provokes more whistles from the women. Sure, she can see his appeal—tall, sandy-haired and classically attractive—but he's not her type. She suddenly pictures her deceased husband, Wyatt. He wasn't exactly her type either but in life you play the cards you're dealt.

Monroe has a dog waiting for him in his car but it's who follows him out of the diner that makes Angie's blood boil. The other women turn to check her reaction and a couple even take a step back before finding something more interesting to go do in their cells. It's wise. Because the woman on screen, who often teams up with this PI, is also who killed Angie's husband, took away her stepson and got her locked up.

Madison Harper. Former convicted felon. Source of all her problems. And Angie's younger sister. As Angie silently stews, she decides it's high time her sister paid her a visit.

CHAPTER TWENTY-NINE

Madison pulls in behind one of the two cruisers parked on the private road where Terri lived. She pulls her rain jacket on as she gets out of the car. As the evening advances the thick gray clouds have returned and it feels like the heavens are going to open any minute. The uniformed officers performing the search have floodlights illuminating the area where the wineglass was found. As she approaches Shelley and Gloria, she can see the glass under a dense bush. "Find anything else?"

Gloria shakes her head. "We've searched the entire area up to the White Woods, and now we've lost daylight we should probably call it a day. It's dangerous in those woods in the daytime, never mind in the dark."

Madison agrees. "Bag it up and take it to Alex, would you? I'm going to speak to the neighbors."

"I've already spoken to them," says Shelley.

"I know, but I just want to follow up on a few things. Which neighbor told you Terri used to babysit their daughter?"

"That was George Ryan. He lives in the house left of the victim's."

"Thanks." Madison leaves them to finish up and walks the short distance to George Ryan's home, zipping her jacket as she goes. The wind is picking up and it feels like they're in for a stormy night. The neighbor's house is bigger than Terri and Troy's, and better maintained on the outside. She pulls a screen door back and knocks. It takes a couple of minutes for someone to answer.

A middle-aged guy in a red plaid shirt and blue jeans looks at her. "Help you?"

"Hi, I'm Detective Harper. I'm investigating what happened next door. Do you have a minute?"

He steps back. "Sure. Come on in."

Inside, the fire is burning, making it cozy. A girl around ten years old is on the couch reading a book. "Hi, what's your name?" asks Madison.

"Sophie. Are you a police officer?"

"I am, but there's no need to be alarmed. I'm just here to speak to your dad."

"Can I get you a drink?" asks George. "I have coffee or soda."

"No, thanks. I won't take up much of your time. I really just wanted to know if you or your daughter recognize this." She pulls the bag containing the beaded bracelet from her jacket pocket. Alex hadn't found any stranger DNA on it.

George shakes his head. "Nope, never seen it before." Turning to his daughter he says, "Have you ever seen Terri with this, honey?"

The little girl has a good look. "I don't think so. Can I have it?"

With a laugh, Madison says, "Afraid not. It might be important."

"Sorry we can't help you. All I know is that I heard a gunshot around eight-thirty that evening, but it could've been those damn turkey hunters. Deke, that's the guy who lives at the head of the road, said he heard a car drive by his place between eight-fifteen and eight-thirty."

Madison looks at him. "I didn't know about that."

"Well, Deke told me about it because we've been dissecting what happened. All the neighbors along here are considering more security now, and maybe pitching in for some street lights in case anybody tries to pull this again. He told that officer about the car, the one who shot Troy. Goodwin, is it?"

She nods and tries hard not to roll her eyes. It doesn't surprise her he didn't pass the information along. He was probably too worried about saving his own skin after shooting Troy.

"Deke didn't *see* the car, just heard it. Maybe it was Terri arriving home, who knows?"

Terri went to the gas station at six. She would've been home well before eight-fifteen. There's a good chance this was the killer arriving. She considers again whether this was a murder for hire and Troy paid someone to kill Terri for him. That would explain why he got so wasted, giving himself a credible alibi in the process. Terri could've been drinking alone that night when the assassin knocked on the door and forced her backwards as soon as she opened it.

But if she was drinking alone that wouldn't explain why she'd changed out of sweatpants and smartened herself up. And why would a paid assassin use Troy's gun and leave it where it would be found, ultimately framing him? No. That theory doesn't hold up and she thinks it's time to rule Troy out entirely. "Did Deke hear the car leave after?"

"No, he fell asleep in front of the TV within ten minutes of hearing it arrive."

Madison might be able to get footage of the car passing security cameras along the route now she knows what time she's looking at. "Thanks. You've been really helpful."

As he shows her out, he says, "I'm sorry to hear about Detective Douglas. He helped my girl retrieve her ball from the pine tree out front when he was visiting the other week. Seemed like a good person to go to all that effort of climbing a big old tree for her."

Madison stops dead in her tracks before turning back to look at him. At first, she's too stunned to say anything. "Detective Douglas was here recently?"

"Not here, next door. He was chatting to Terri about, I don't know, two weeks ago? And then again last week."

Her heart skips a beat. "Do you know what they talked about?"

He appears confused by her reaction. "No. He was only here twice that I know of. I assumed it was about Troy losing his temper with her, but Terri never said and I didn't like to pry." He shakes his head and takes a deep breath. "If it turns out Troy was responsible for her death, then I wish I'd convinced her to leave him a long time ago."

Madison swallows. Douglas was suspended. He shouldn't have been working. That's assuming it was a work matter. "Between us, Troy wasn't responsible for her death as far as I can tell."

Alarm sweeps over George's face. "Does that mean her killer's still out there? Because I'm worried for my daughter. What if he returns?"

She tries to reassure him. "I don't think there's much risk of that, especially considering the large police presence around town right now. Just keep eyes on your daughter at all times and make sure you lock up when you're home, whether it's daylight or not. If you see anyone around who shouldn't be here or at Terri's, you give me a call. Okay?" She hands him her card.

"Troy was there earlier. I was surprised he hadn't been arrested yet but now I know why."

"He was next door?"

George nods. "Left with a suitcase. I figured he either wasn't allowed to stay there yet or he didn't want to. I mean who would want to sleep in that bedroom after what happened, right?"

Troy's entitled to collect some clothes and toiletries, so she's not worried about that. Before leaving she stops to ask, "How long was Detective Douglas here the last time you saw him?"

He thinks for a second. "For the time it took me to wash my truck. About thirty minutes."

She's trying to figure out whether Terri was having an affair with Douglas, and that's what got them both killed. The more she thinks about it the less likely it seems. He wouldn't have come over in full view of the neighbors if Terri was cheating on her partner. Especially one as volatile as Troy. He would have been concerned for her welfare. And Douglas was an above-board kind of guy. If he had wanted a relationship with someone, he would wait until they were single. The whole situation is bizarre to her. "Thanks for your time, Mr. Ryan." She looks over his shoulder. "Bye, Sophie."

"Bye!" The little girl waves before turning her attention back to her book.

As Madison leaves the house her head is alight with possible explanations as to why Douglas was visiting Terri before both of their deaths. This new link between them is something solid that she can use to delay his cremation tomorrow.

The officers are gone by the time Madison returns to her car and the road is pitch black without the floodlights. It's creepy out here, especially with a killer on the loose. It's no wonder none of the residents saw anything without any street lights to illuminate the road. She slips into her car, locks the doors and switches the headlights on before checking her phone. A text from Alex is waiting for her.

Terri Summers has no FB account. She either deleted it before she was killed or her killer deactivated it.

Madison knows Terri *did* have a Facebook account before her death, so this is something else the killer thought to do, perhaps in order to hide evidence of their conversations. She needs Terri's cell phone records immediately so she messages Steve to see if he's had anything come through yet. He replies within a couple of minutes.

I've located her cell provider. Just waiting on the information to be sent through. Will forward it as soon as it does.

Then he adds:

Anything else on Douglas yet?

Before she can reply her phone rings. "Hello?"

"Madison, it's Chief Mendes."

"I'm glad you called. I just found out Douglas was visiting our victim as recently as last week. This proves there's a link between them and that they could've been killed by the same person."

Mendes is silent for a second. "Do we know why he was visiting her?"

"Not yet, but I'll find out." Although she doesn't know how, seeing as she can't talk to either of them and Troy never mentioned it, which means he didn't know they were talking. "Maybe she was making a complaint about Troy."

"But he was off duty," says Mendes. "She would've phoned it in to the station if she wanted to report him."

Madison's shoulders slump. "I know. I haven't figured it all out yet. I just need some more time. Can we postpone his cremation now?"

After considering it, Mendes says, "Find out why he was talking to her first. Maybe her mom or aunt know?"

Madison nods. "Fine. We have one of the wineglasses that

was missing from Terri's house. Alex will check it for DNA and prints."

"Understood." Mendes sighs heavily, like she's about to deliver bad news. "I called you because I've just had a call from the warden of the prison where your sister is incarcerated."

Madison's whole body tenses. That's the last thing she was expecting to hear.

"She says Angie McCoy has come forward with some information about the disappearance of Ruby and Oliver Rader."

"What? You're kidding, right?" How could Angie know anything about that?

"No, I'm not. Angie's stipulated she'll only talk to you and your friend Nate. Together. No one else. And it has to be in person."

Her heart sinks. Could Angie be bluffing in order to put her through the stress of a prison visit? She hasn't seen her sister since the day Angie was arrested almost five months ago. Right after she watched Angie's husband die a gruesome, painful death.

"Madison?" says Mendes. "How do you want to play this? I know we're not currently working on the Rader cold case but if she has some credible information, it's worth chasing up. If you don't feel up to it, I can go myself in the hope she'll speak to me."

"She won't speak to you." Madison sighs. "Angie likes playing mind games, and she hates me. She knows exactly what she's doing by requesting me and Nate."

Mendes is silent for a minute. "Think about it overnight. It's your decision. If you don't want to go, I'll tell the warden to try to get the information out of her some other way. If you do want to go, I have the warden's number for you."

Madison swallows. She doesn't want to go to the prison. Not just because her sister has betrayed her worse than anyone she's ever met, but also because she never wants to step foot back inside a prison. Neither does Nate. It took them both so long to get out of theirs. How could she put him through that after everything he went through?

On the other hand, if Angie knows something that could help Vince with the closure he so desperately needs, she has to go. It could mean Matt and Jo Rader finally get to bury their son.

With an uncertain voice she says, "I guess you'd better text me the warden's number."

CHAPTER THIRTY

"I've got nothing to say to you," says Matt Rader. His eyes glance over Nate's shoulder to check if any customers are listening in.

"Really?" says Nate, placing his empty coffee cup on the counter. "I thought you'd want to help find your mother and son by any means possible."

Carla walks by them, pretending not to listen, but she drops a glass as a result of not paying attention to what she's doing. "Oh, shoot!" It shatters on the floor.

"Look," says Matt. "My *dad* hired you, not me. I'm sure he's already told you everything you need to know."

Nate crosses his arms. "Vince has certainly been helpful. So has your ex-wife."

Matt's eyes narrow. "You've spoken to Jo?"

Someone enters the diner and walks up alongside Nate. He glances over and sees it's Madison. She looks pale and can't even muster up the energy for a smile. Staring at Matt, she says, "I'm glad you two are speaking at last."

"We're not," says Nate. "He's reluctant to sit down with me. Maybe because he has something to hide."

"For God's sake." Matt rolls his eyes and throws his toast in the trash. "Let's do this upstairs where we won't have the whole goddam diner listening in."

Nate turns to Madison and smiles at their small victory, but she doesn't return it. "Everything okay?" he asks.

She glances at her watch. "I have to talk to you, but I guess it can wait until you've questioned him."

Reluctant to miss this opportunity to question Matt, he says, "Come with me. You can verify whatever he tells us, seeing as you have access to Douglas's original investigation notes."

She nods. "Sure."

He follows her upstairs. Vince's apartment is spacious and filled with tasteful oak furniture and shelves full of books. It's the first time Nate's been up here, but he knows this is where Vince hosts his podcast. "Where's your dad tonight?" he asks.

Matt sits in a large leather armchair, not offering either of them a drink or a seat. "He's gone to visit Barbara Evans. He probably won't be gone long because that woman has a screw loose."

Nate bristles at his attitude. Barbara must have made good on her promise to call Vince and make amends. "I disagree. Barbara was extremely helpful when I visited her earlier."

Matt stares at him. "Is there anyone you haven't spoken to about my family?"

Nate takes a seat next to Madison on the couch. He doesn't often take an instant disliking to someone but this guy isn't doing himself any favors. "Only you."

Madison appears uneasy because of the tension between them. "Listen, Matt, we just need to ask you about what you know and then we'll be out of your hair. Nate's here to help, so drop the attitude."

Matt looks away. He seems to value Madison's opinion. "The last time I saw my mother and son was when I brought Oliver into the diner on the morning they went missing."

"What time was that?" asks Nate.

"Just after nine. Then I left for work. I was out at various addresses installing home security systems. I arrived home just before eight that evening. That's when Jo told me they weren't back yet."

"And you went to search for them?"

"Right."

"Why did you immediately assume the worst?" Nate watches his reaction closely.

A flash of annoyance crosses Matt's face. "What exactly do you think you can do that the detectives couldn't? I mean, you don't even have a law enforcement background, do you? You were never a cop."

Nate scoffs at the thought of being a cop. Like they're anything special. Most of the cops he's met have been crooked or hell-bent on convicting the wrong person, just to close a case. With the exception of Madison and her team. "No, I wasn't."

"Then what makes you think you can find them?"

"Maybe I can't," he answers honestly. "But isn't it worth a try? Wouldn't you do anything to get them home? I mean, what harm can it do to have a fresh pair of eyes on the case?"

"Of course I'd do anything to see them again, to find out what happened!" Matt's voice is getting louder. "But you're a stranger to me. How am I supposed to trust you? Especially with your history. I read you spent two decades on death row for killing your fiancée. You're not exactly the easiest person to trust, okay?"

Nate's surprised by how much his comments sting, even now all that is over. It's a reminder that he'll never outrun his past. Some people will always believe the salacious headlines over the facts.

Madison speaks up. "Matt? You're out of line. Bringing up Nate's past is just as despicable as us automatically assuming you killed your mother and child just because you're a man.

Especially as Nate's been legally cleared. And that's what he's trying to do with you: clear you from his list of suspects so he can move on to someone else. He may not have a police background but Nate's excellent at his job and he's helped me on various cases, including one that involved finding a missing child. Anything he lacks in official police background he makes up for in instinct, and arguing over this is just wasting precious time."

Nate's grateful Madison believes in him, because some days he wonders himself why he does this job.

Matt takes a deep breath and leans back into the armchair. "Listen, I don't know what happened. If I did, neither of you would be here right now because the case would be solved."

"But you must have thoughts? Suspicions?" presses Nate.

"I used to. I suspected damn near everyone at the time, even..."

Nate leans in. "Even who? Your dad?"

Matt looks at him. "I didn't say that."

"That's what everyone else thought back then," says Madison. "He went through hell and back."

"Some people still think it was him," says Nate.

"Do you?" Matt asks them.

Madison glances at Nate before shaking her head. "No. Neither of us do. But we need to know why you did, even if it was just for a brief time."

He runs a hand through his hair. "Because of the lack of other suspects. And then he started that stupid *Crime and Dine* podcast and got fixated on murders and missing people. It was creepy! I know people started talking about him, saying he turned into a conspiracy theorist. It was painful to watch. That's part of the reason I agreed to move away with Jo. Our lives did a complete one-eighty once mom and Oliver went missing. I didn't feel Dad was able to support me, and I knew I couldn't support him."

"It's obvious he uses the true crime stuff to try to piece together what happened to them," says Madison. "He's desperate for answers, and maybe the community of victims out there has been a comfort over the years. Because it's not like he had any family to turn to, is it?"

Matt lowers his eyes.

Nate actually feels sorry for the guy, despite his attitude problem, but Vince was suffering too. Just because his father couldn't emotionally support him doesn't mean he's capable of murder. Could Matt just be trying to pass the buck? Give them someone else to consider in order to take the heat off him? "What about Jo's parents? Did they live in town?"

"No. Jo's dad had already passed and Patricia lived in Nebraska when it happened. She was due to come stay with us for Thanksgiving that week, but she took ill and ended up in the hospital. She never made it to Lost Creek. She eventually moved to California."

"Did you have a good relationship with her?"

Matt looks up. "With Patricia?" He thinks about it. "I mean, we weren't super close but that's because she didn't live here. We got on well when she'd visit for the holidays, but she'd always take Jo's side in an argument. I wasn't surprised when Jo went to join her in California after we broke up."

"If you don't mind me asking, how was your marriage, before this all happened?" asks Madison. "Did you and Jo argue much?"

"About as much as any married couple."

Nate writes everything down. "Okay, so, knowing what you know now all these years later, which I understand is very little but humor me, what do you believe happened to Ruby and Oliver?"

Matt lowers his eyes to the carpet. "I watch all those documentaries on TV about people who've vanished. It's stupid, I know, but like Dad I look for answers. Patterns, I guess. To figure out the most likely outcome."

Madison wipes her eye and Nate can't tell if she's tearing up. "What conclusion have you come to?" he asks.

With a sigh Matt says, "Some of those people never get found. Their families eventually die off years later, never having got the answers they crave. On the other hand, I remember one woman had disappeared of her own free will, wanting to start a new life. She just left without telling anyone where she was going. She didn't take a single thing with her other than a hundred bucks in cash." He looks up at them. "Can you believe that? Her whole family was searching for her for *nineteen years* and it turns out she just felt like leaving. She never once contacted anyone to call off the search or reassure them she was okay. The cops eventually tracked her down thanks to a tip-off from the public." His face screws up in pain. "You should've seen the look on her mom's face when she realized her daughter had put her through all that for no good reason. How could someone do that to their family?"

Madison shakes her head. Nate stays quiet because he doesn't have an answer to that. It makes him think of Kristen Devereaux, the woman who helped exonerate him. She's currently missing without a trace. One day he'll find the mental strength to look for her, but not until he's ready to accept she might be dead. The last few years have taken a lot from him and he doesn't feel ready to deal with that final part of the puzzle yet.

Matt continues, "But the fact is the majority of the people on those shows are eventually found dead. Their skeletal remains buried in the woods, or under someone's house, or in a lake. They were murdered, of course. Because why else would they just disappear?"

Nate nods. "So you think Ruby and Oliver are dead." It's not a question.

"Of course they are." His face clouds over. "They were probably dead before we even knew they were missing. It's just a matter of finding who killed them and where the piece of shit buried their bodies." His voice catches at the end.

Nate tends to agree that they're dead. If they were still alive, there would have been sightings. He worries he's been too quick to jump to conclusions about Matt. His reluctance to sit down and talk to him could be due to fear of speaking the reality out loud, of making it real.

Then again, there's always the possibility that he just put on a good show for them, that they're being manipulated. The only way he'll know for sure is to find the bodies, because there's no crime scene he can investigate and hunting for a motive and a suspect isn't working for this case, which is why Detectives Bowers and Douglas didn't solve it.

He realizes it's time to put all his efforts into finding the killer's burial site instead.

CHAPTER THIRTY-ONE

SIX YEARS AGO

Ruby's a little shaken from her accident with Detective Douglas's car. He's already pulled away and she'd like to take a minute to compose herself but she can't because the cars she's blocking are honking their horns loudly now. It makes her even more flustered.

"Grandma? I want to see Mommy."

She risks a quick glance back at Oliver's pale face. "Don't be afraid, sweetie. These people are all being silly. We'll go and get some lunch now, okay?"

He nods but his T-Rex sits forgotten on the seat next to him and she can tell he's upset. He's probably overtired from the excitement of the dinosaur museum too. She'll see if he'll nap after lunch. That would give her time to do some digging into the problem that's preoccupying her.

She starts the engine and carefully drives them to Matt and Jo's house. Jo's mom will be arriving in town tonight or tomorrow—Ruby forgets exactly—to spend Thanksgiving with them all. She likes Patricia. She's a no-nonsense woman like her, and Ruby's grateful to have some help in the kitchen as Jo's not really interested in cooking.

She pulls up outside the house. It's a pretty one-story home that's not too big or too small, just right for the three of them, although they'll need an extra bedroom when they get around to having another baby. The pretty white plant pots she bought them for their wedding anniversary are sitting either side of the front door, and Oliver's grim-faced pumpkins—left over from Halloween—are slowly rotting on the front lawn. For some reason they remind her of one of those body farms, where human corpses are left to rot outside in controlled conditions all in the name of science. She shudders at the thought.

Once inside the house, Oliver appears to be happy as he runs to the TV and finds a strange cartoon about under-ocean creatures. Ruby pulls her wet jacket off and hangs it near the front door. As she walks into the living room, she notices a new couch. It's leather with two reclining seats at either end and a matching footstool in the middle.

"When did your dad buy a new couch, sweetie?" She takes a seat in the recliner and instantly relaxes back into it. "Oh, Lord. I need to get one of these."

"Some men brought it yesterday," says Oliver.

Ruby knows Matt's been working extra hours lately just to help make ends meet. The couch wouldn't have been cheap. She goes to the kitchen and starts making a PB&J sandwich for Oliver. Her eyes happen upon a fancy coffee machine in the corner. She leans in and pulls her reading glasses on. "Cappuccino, macchiato, latte. Wow, that's fancy for a home kitchen."

She suddenly feels uneasy about that and the couch; how can they afford them?

"That's an early Christmas gift," says Oliver, waiting to collect his sandwich. "Daddy said he was so good this year that Santa visited him early."

Ruby raises her eyebrows. "Did he really?"

Oliver nods, almost letting his sandwich slip off the plate in his hands. "I wasn't good enough to get an early gift, so I have to try harder." He wanders back into the living room to eat in front of the TV.

Ruby feels horrible for him. Matt shouldn't have said something so stupid and made his son feel that way. She'll have to talk to him about it. That's not the only thing she needs to raise with him. A ball of dread grows in her chest as she leans back against the kitchen counter. If her sources are correct, and it's not just a big misunderstanding, then the information she's been given could seriously damage her family and their reputation. That's if she tells anyone else about it. Or if Mrs. Hendricks does.

Rosemary Hendricks has been a customer at the diner from the minute the doors first opened, but more than that, she's a friend. Ruby cared for her when Rosemary went into the hospital for an operation on her back. She changed her dressings and even helped her to use the bathroom. The older woman has no family of her own; her husband has passed and they chose not to have children, and there's no one else to help her. They see each other almost every day for Rosemary's customary lunch of chicken salad with a side of fries. So when she recently called Ruby with some shocking news, Ruby didn't doubt it was true. It was only when the implications hit her that she started hoping there had been a horrible misunderstanding. After all, Rosemary is in her late eighties. She could be confused.

Ruby swallows. The only way she'll know for sure is to confront the person Rosemary has accused. But she can't bring herself to do that without first double-checking she got all the facts straight. So she checks Oliver is happy in the living room before pulling out her cell phone and calling Rosemary's landline.

CHAPTER THIRTY-TWO

It's eight o'clock and Nate's house is in darkness apart from the porch light. Madison can hear Brody on the other side of the door, patiently waiting for them to enter the house. She's only been here once before, when Nate first moved in, because he tends to visit her and Owen instead. Once inside, she crouches down next to Brody. "I'm sure you're getting a fat belly." He gently licks her cheek.

Nate laughs as he switches on some lights. "Blame Vince. He keeps feeding Brody diner leftovers. Take a seat." He wanders toward the kitchen. "What can I get you to drink?"

Madison doesn't hesitate. "Something strong. Don't insult me by offering me one of your pathetic decaf coffees because it's late and you wouldn't want me to have trouble sleeping." She hears him laugh. It's warm in here, so she pulls her jacket off and hangs it over a dining table chair before slipping her boots off, something that signals the end of the working day. She feels herself relaxing already, although her brain won't switch off from her investigation until she's asleep, and maybe not even then.

Nate's home is sparse of personal belongings which isn't surprising as he's lived on the road since his release from death row. All he owned when she met him was his car and his dead fiancée's rosary beads. She's pleased to see he's bought some furniture, but there's nothing of his personality in here yet.

When she hears the clink of glasses, Nate appears. "Let's go into the den."

She and Brody follow him. The den is small and cozy, at the back of the house. The lighting is soft and the couch is huge, probably because he has to share it with the dog. She spots the rosary beads hanging over a table lamp. She had noticed he'd stopped wearing them once his fiancée's real killer was arrested. She doesn't know if he still has faith, just that he's battled with it over the years.

They all sit on the couch, Brody between her and Nate.

"What's Owen up to tonight?" he asks.

She sighs. "He's at the new drive-in theater with a friend, apparently, but I suspect he's dating someone."

Eyebrows raised, Nate says, "That's great. After everything that happened with Nikki Jackson, it's good that he's open to that."

"I know, right? At least he's not mentally scarred." None of them will ever forget what happened to Owen's last girlfriend up at Fantasy World amusement park. The poor girl was killed on the Ferris wheel in the most horrific circumstances. That place should have been torn down years ago. Madison sips her drink; a generous double shot of bourbon with ice. The warmth slowly spreads down her chest.

Somewhat hesitantly, she turns to look at Nate. "I have something to tell you and you're not going to like it."

Unfazed, he smiles at her. "Have you noticed that's how all our best conversations start?"

She laughs and it feels good. "I don't know about that." For courage, she downs the rest of her drink. "Guess who wants me to go visit them in prison?"

Brody lifts his head like he can sense her anxiety. Nate frowns and a look of dread spreads across his face. "Who?"

"My sister."

His mouth drops open. "What the hell does Angie want? Surely she doesn't think she can convince you to be a character witness or something that will benefit her defense?"

Madison scoffs. "No, of course not. The warden contacted Chief Mendes to tell her that Angie has come forward with some information about Ruby and Oliver."

He shakes his head, clearly not believing a word of it. "Come on! Wouldn't she have come forward before now it that were true? She's making it up in the hope of striking a plea deal with the DA's office."

It's certainly possible. "Who knows with that woman?"

"So why isn't Mendes interviewing her if she really believes she's got credible information?"

This is the part Madison is dreading. She doesn't know whether to keep him in the dark about Angie's insistence he visits with her, or to fess up and see how he reacts. She doesn't want to upset him for no reason.

"What is it?" he asks. "What aren't you telling me?"

She sighs. "Angie says she'll only talk to you and me, together and in person."

He's lost for words. After a few minutes' contemplation, he downs his drink too and then looks at her. "She wants me to go inside a prison?"

She nods.

"Why? What's she got against me?"

"She'll know all about your history and how traumatic it'll be for you. Plus, you've helped me, her despised younger sister. She's trying to make you suffer for that."

He's silent again until, eventually, he gets off the couch to fetch something from the kitchen. Brody jumps down and follows him, leaving Madison regretting her decision to tell Nate. She should have just gone alone to visit Angie and pretended Nate was sick or something.

He returns with the bottle of bourbon and pours her drink before his own, then puts the bottle in front of them on the coffee table. Brody settles on the rug near the TV, leaving the couch to them. "Do *you* think she knows anything about the case or is she full of shit?"

She considers the timeline. Ruby and Oliver went missing while Madison was in prison, so she wasn't around to know what Angie and Wyatt were up to back then, whether they had any kind of relationship with the Raders, or any kind of grievance. "I honestly have no idea. I probably shouldn't have told you about it, I'm sorry. Don't come, it's not good for you to go back inside after your experience."

He smiles sadly. "By that logic it's not good for you either."

She focuses on Brody. "It's never going to end, is it?"

"What? Our pasts?" He scoffs. "Every day something reminds me of the injustice of what I went through. Every single goddam day." He looks at her. "It's like the universe conspires to make some detail in my day-to-day life trigger a flashback, or a feeling, or a thought. It's exhausting."

She feels hot tears behind her eyes. It's been a while since they got drunk together and had an honest discussion like this. Mainly because they both try to focus on the future and how lucky they are now. It upsets her to know he still feels haunted. "I thought things were getting better for you? You haven't been using cocaine, you've not had any depressive episodes lately..."

He looks thoughtful. "I want to get wasted almost every day. Rather than a day without drugs being an achievement, it's a day that's harder to get through. The coke made it easier to deal with my past. It helped me forget. Now I'm not using, I have no choice but to experience the flashbacks and the anger toward the assholes who ruined my life." He takes another swig of his drink before leaning his head back and turning to her. "I'm sorry. I know I should be grateful, and I am for a lot of things. You especially, and Owen and Brody. I guess we just have to keep on keeping on, as my dad used to say. I mean, what's the alternative, right?"

His eyes are a rich blue color. She can feel the intensity of his emotions. How he's desperate to move on and let go of the past, but the world won't let him. It's like trying to walk forward while being tethered to a brick wall with elastic. You might manage a step or two, but there's always something pulling you backwards, reminding you of the trauma you've experienced. She wonders if therapy would help him. Or maybe the church. But she understands his reluctance to put his faith in God again.

He leans forward. "Shit, I forgot to tell you."

"What?"

"I found out today that Matt's wife once worked for Angie."

She sits up straight. "She *what*? When? At the time of the disappearance?"

"No, before that. It wasn't for long—less than a year. She was helping with their accounts, presumably for the scrapyard business, but they didn't get on so Jo left. I wondered whether Angie could've done something to Oliver in retaliation, and maybe Ruby was caught up in it, but I can't believe your sister's capable of hurting a child, can you?"

She experiences a sudden sinking feeling. Without her knowledge or permission, Angie and her husband cared for Owen while Madison served her sentence. He still won't talk about what it was like to be raised by that pair, but he has told her he wasn't mistreated. If Angie was capable of hurting a little boy, she would have hurt Owen. That would have been the best way to get back at Madison. "No, I don't think she'd hurt a child. But the fact Jo worked for her means Angie might be telling the truth about knowing something. She could've been aware of any turmoil going on in that family."

Nate nods. "I guess we're going to pay her a visit then."

She studies his face. "Do you really want to put yourself through that?" Placing a hand on his, she says, "What if you have an anxiety attack inside, or feel overwhelmed and start using again? You've fought so many demons and I'd hate all that work to be wasted just to satisfy my sister's sick mind games."

He gives her a smile but it's not convincing. "Despite what I said, I'm stronger now. I must be if I'm able to resist the cravings. I just have to remember I can walk out of that prison whenever I want to, unlike last time."

Something about the vulnerability in his eyes makes her want to hug him. To protect him. "No. I'll tell her you're out of town and she has to talk to me alone. She'll agree to it because she knows I don't want to go back inside either."

He covers her hand with his free one. "I chose to become a PI, Madison. You can't protect me from all that entails. Besides, she may not be the only person I need to question inside a prison. This can be a test of how screwed up I still am. Hopefully, with you by my side, I'll pass the test." He smiles again, this time with a glint in his eye. "If not, you can get me drunk and find a therapist to fix me once and for all."

She snorts. "I don't have that kind of money."

He laughs hard at her joke.

"How do you do that?" she asks.

"What?"

"How do you manage to have a sense of humor after everything you've been through?"

He shrugs. "Like I said, what's the alternative? Besides, it could mean helping Vince. I'd like to see him get some answers. He's been through a lot."

Madison leans forward and grabs the bourbon. She has a nice buzz going on as she refills their glasses. "One more for the road. I guess I'll have to call a cab." She places the bottle back on the coffee table and pulls her knees up under her on the couch. She likes it here. The house has good energy and the den's coziness makes her feel safe, especially with Nate and Brody here.

Nate leans his head back against the couch and fixes his eyes on her. "Stay here tonight. I'd bet Owen won't mind having the house to himself. Especially if he's on a date."

She raises her eyebrows. "Are you seriously suggesting I allow my son to let his date spend the night?"

He smiles. "Well, someone should be getting some action."

Wincing, she says. "Don't say that! I don't want to know what he gets up to when I'm not there."

"Come on, he's almost eighteen. Let him have some privacy. You can have my bed. I'll sleep on the couch with Brody. I sleep down here some nights anyway."

Madison holds his gaze and thinks of what Lena asked her the other day, about whether Nate was single. She doesn't want to stand in his way of finding someone else, someone who really can help him start afresh. Because she and Nate come with a lot of baggage, and not just individually. They found each other at a time when they were hurting the most, after being released from the clutches of a corrupt judicial system with no help to reclaim their lost lives. They have seen the worst of each other as they struggled to cope with the unfairness of what happened to them. Madison can't help thinking that if Nate started seeing someone like Lena, he wouldn't have all that history weighing him down.

"What are you thinking?" he asks.

She takes a deep breath and leans her head back, like him. "Oh, you don't want to know."

He smiles and reaches out for the hand she removed. "Try me."

Her heart races. His touch is strong but tender, sending a

shiver through her body. She opens her mouth, unsure of what she's going to say. Before she can say anything her phone buzzes on the coffee table, making her jump. "Shit." Owen's name flashes on screen. "Sorry, I should get this."

Nate nods.

"Hey, Mom," says Owen. "Can you pick me up? I'm at the drive-in and my car won't start. It turns out my breakdown coverage has expired too, so I'll need to sort that tomorrow."

"You let your breakdown coverage expire?" She looks at Nate and rolls her eyes. "I'm at Nate's place and I've had a drink, so I'll be over once I can get a cab."

"Cool, thanks."

"Is it just you or do we need to drop someone home on our way?" she asks, fishing for details.

"My friend's left already."

"Okay, sit tight."

She orders a cab, wishing she didn't have to leave. Maybe she should let Owen get the cab home by himself, but she knows he would ask questions. Questions she doesn't have the answers to herself. She checks the time; it's getting late. She needs to be up early to focus on the investigation. Or maybe she's making excuses because she's too afraid to stay here with Nate. Their relationship could change. And there's no way of knowing whether that would be for the better or not. Is she willing to risk losing what they currently have?

She turns to face him. "I should go."

There's disappointment in his eyes, but he walks her to the kitchen where she pulls her jacket and boots on. "I'll come with you to the prison," he says. "Just let me know when. We can ride up in my car."

She looks at him. "You're sure?"

He nods. They step out onto the cold porch to wait for the cab. The wind is bitter now but the sky is clear of clouds, leaving the glistening stars free to shine brightly. It's beautiful to look at. Brody runs down the steps to find a suitable patch of grass for relieving himself.

When Madison shudders, Nate slips a warm, comforting arm around her. Being wrapped in his embrace makes her feel like as long as they remain in each other's lives, in whatever capacity, they can get through anything.

CHAPTER THIRTY-THREE

By the time she gets to work the next morning, Madison's feeling the pressure. She has six hours until Douglas is due to be cremated. That's six hours to find out why he was visiting Terri Summers and to prove a link between their deaths. Because once his body is burned, they won't be able to check it for any signs that he was murdered and, as it's already been released to the funeral home, Madison can't ask Lena to perform an autopsy. Not without Chief Mendes consulting with Douglas's dad, which would mean alerting him to the fact that his son's death might not have been a suicide. Until Madison can prove it wasn't, there's no way Mendes will want to upset him.

Sitting at her desk, she watches as Steve approaches. "Morning," she says, eyeing up the coffee in his hand. She hasn't even stopped to pour one yet.

"Morning." He hands her some paperwork. "This is the call and text history for Terri's cell phone number. The last message she sent bounced off of the tower nearest her house. They haven't been able to trace the whereabouts of her phone, which suggests it's likely been dismantled."

That's disappointing, but she eagerly reads the list of dates, times and phone numbers, looking for a pattern.

Steve leans in. "On the day of Terri's death, she placed one phone call, to Troy Randle's number around lunchtime. After that she didn't make or receive any calls or texts."

Her excitement dips because the logs don't tell her anything she doesn't already know. "This confirms she did most of her communicating through social media then, which we have no access to."

"Right. I have put in an information request with Facebook but I'm not holding my breath. I don't think we've ever been successful at gaining what we need that way." He finishes his coffee. "Douglas's number is on that list twice over the last two weeks."

That would make sense, he must've called Terri to arrange a time to visit her. But that doesn't tell Madison what he was visiting her about. "Thanks."

Steve returns to his desk and Madison watches Officer Goodwin walk in. He chats to Stella for a second, his back to her. She hears him ask if there's any word on whether Douglas's job is up for grabs yet. Madison shakes her head at the cheek of the guy.

Ignoring him, she stands up and walks around to Douglas's desk. It's been cleared of everything except the computer, monitor and desk phone. Pulling the top drawer open, she sees nothing but some stray paperclips. The middle drawer has his *Welcome Back* banner shoved inside. She pulls it out and sits in Douglas's chair.

The AA meeting she attended with him runs through her mind. It had been just as she'd anticipated: a room full of people taking turns to share their experiences. Some were just one day into their sobriety, others years. Douglas told her he didn't have a sponsor, something that didn't surprise her as he liked to solve his own problems, but he had managed to quit drinking anyway.

She thinks of Terri Summers. Could she have been in AA? That could be what Douglas had visited her about. Maybe he was her sponsor? No, she was drinking wine the night she died. "And no one has said she had a drinking problem," Madison mumbles.

"What's that, Detective?" Goodwin's amused. "Talking to yourself now?"

She ignores him and goes back to her own desk. Picking up her desk phone, she calls Lena's office and asks whether the toxicology results are in yet. Lena's assistant checks. "I'm sorry, not yet," says Skylar. "But the fetus's paternity results came in about an hour ago. I was just about to log them on the system."

Madison holds the phone a little tighter. "Is Troy Randle the baby's father?"

"Let me just check that for you."

Madison waits patiently while Skylar sorts through paperwork and then reads the results. "According to this, Troy Randle is ninety-nine percent likely to be the father."

Madison's disappointed. If Troy wasn't the father, that would give her a motive for the murder; that Troy found out another guy got his girlfriend pregnant and then hired a hit man out of revenge for her cheating. "Thanks."

"You're welcome."

At this rate they're never going to find any DNA linking the killer to the scene. She decides to check in on Alex and makes the long walk to his tiny office on the other side of the building. It used to be an evidence storeroom and still looks just as messy since he moved in. The heat doesn't reach this end of the building and he has only himself for company, until the cleaners turn up in the evening to grab their mops from the small cupboard on the other side of his office. When she gets there his door is open and he's studying his computer screen while listening to a podcast about blood spatter patterns.

"Knock knock," she says.

He turns in his chair. "Detective Harper! What brings you all the way over to the dark side of the moon?"

She snorts. "I was too warm and cozy in my office. Fancied some doom and gloom."

He laughs, delighted at her humor. Before she rejoined LCPD, Alex struggled to get along with both Detective Bowers and Douglas because they weren't keen on his dark sense of humor. They thought he was weird. That's probably why she likes him.

He switches the podcast off and clears paperwork from the only other chair in here.

"I've checked the wineglass that was found last night for fingerprints."

She sits opposite him. "Let me guess, only the victim's prints on it?"

"No prints at all, actually. So it had probably been wiped clean before being discarded. I sent off some swabs to the crime lab, taken from the rim of the glass. Perhaps we'll get lucky there if the killer didn't wipe his saliva away properly, unless it was the glass our victim was drinking from."

She takes a deep breath. "I hope we get lucky, but he seems to know what he was doing. I've asked Shelley to obtain any security footage from businesses out near Terri's address because one of her neighbors heard a car drive up the private road at around eight-fifteen. When she drops it off, see if you can spot a likely suspect and identify the car's make, model and license plate number, who was in the car, that kind of thing. I know it's difficult to identify any of that on grainy security footage, but even if you can get one of those things, it gives me something to work with."

"Of course."

Behind her, someone knocks on the door and Alex's face lights up. Intrigued at who could cause such a reaction,

Madison spins around. Shelley is there, looking bashful. "Oh, sorry. I can come back later," she says.

Madison stands. "No, it's fine. I'm done here. Have you had any luck finding security footage from the night in question?"

"Not yet. I'm planning on visiting the two gas stations next."

"Great." As she leaves, Madison glances back. "Should I close the door behind me?" They both blush so hard that she smiles. "I'm just messing with you." She walks away, leaving them to it and slightly jealous that they're in the best stage of a relationship; the early days. She checks her watch. It's just after ten, which means there are only five hours until Douglas's cremation now. The thought of running out of time makes her heart race. On her way back to her desk she sees Chief Mendes in her office. She knocks on the door and enters. "Morning, Chief."

"Morning." Mendes drops the file she was reading. "Have you made a decision about visiting your sister yet? I've had another call from the warden already this morning. Your sister's persistent, I'll give her that. She says it has to be today if you want the information."

Madison nods. "Nate and I will go. I didn't realize it had to be today though. I'm busy looking into Douglas's death."

Mendes sighs. "Still?"

She nods. "Where's Douglas's vehicle?"

"Still in his garage. Presumably his dad will come here to sort Don's belongings at some point."

"Can I check it over?"

Mendes frowns. "His car? What are you hoping to find? Not a suicide note."

"No, not a note. I seriously don't believe he killed himself. I've checked his house already and as we can't perform an autopsy right now, I just want to check his car. It's the only thing I've not seen for myself."

"You're like a dog with a bone." Mendes crosses her arms. "You're really not going to give up on this, are you?"

Madison bristles at her attitude. "Should I? I mean, one of our officers has died in mysterious circumstances and you expect me not to investigate it? I'd be pretty pissed if I were the victim here and no one bothered to check all credible options."

"But is it credible? That's my problem with this. You have nothing but a hunch and a weak link between him and your homicide victim. There's nothing concrete."

"But how can I get anything concrete if you won't let me follow my hunches?" she argues.

Mendes stares hard for a few seconds. "Fine. You can get the keys from Sergeant Tanner. But this is your last chance. I can't go upsetting his father, especially once he's cremated his son."

Madison spins around and opens the door. "Thank you."

"But do it after you've been to the prison," shouts Mendes. "We can't risk missing out on whatever it is your sister knows about that cold case."

Madison rolls her eyes. She wants to check Douglas's car first. That's more time sensitive. But, knowing her sister, she'll make good on her promise to clam up if they don't meet her demands. She's torn. Should she prioritize finding answers for Vince Rader or solving Douglas's death? She checks the time before quickly approaching Steve's desk. "Can I get Douglas's car keys? Mendes has approved it."

He looks surprised. "Are you onto something?" He passes them over.

"I don't know. Is the garage key definitely on here?"

"Yeah, it's the big one."

"Thanks." She grabs her jacket and rushes out of the station. This really is her last chance to find proof that Don Douglas was murdered. But first, she has to go back to prison, because Vince has already suffered long enough.

CHAPTER THIRTY-FOUR

After a call from Madison, asking him to meet her at Ruby's Diner so they can travel to the prison together, Nate is waiting for her to appear. When he first met her this past summer, he never dreamed they would still be working together now, especially once she got her job back at LCPD. He thought he'd have to go it alone while she worked with her new team. Luckily for him the local police department is small, and she still needs his help now and then.

He thinks about where they're going today. When he agreed to visit Angie McCoy in prison, he hadn't expected it to be this soon, but maybe that's a good thing. It means less time spent stressing about visiting a correctional facility.

When Madison slips into his car, she says hello to Brody in the back seat before noticing the two takeout coffees between them. She smiles widely. "Thank God. You don't know how much I need this. But wait until Owen finds out you didn't use that travel mug he got you."

Nate laughs. "I can handle Owen." He pulls out of the parking lot before glancing at her. She's clearly on edge, sitting on her hands and leaning forward with the seatbelt straining at her neck. "Everything okay?"

She nods. "Yeah. It's going to be a busy day, that's all. I could really do without Angie's distraction." He listens as she fills him in on the link between Terri Summers and Detective Douglas, and how she wants to search Douglas's car the minute they get back from the prison. It sounds to him like she could be onto something, considering Terri and Douglas were seen together not that long before her murder.

They settle into a comfortable silence for most of the journey. The trees along the route have mostly lost their leaves now, apart from the pine trees that are swaying in the cold blustery wind. The steady hum of the engine soon has Brody asleep on the back seat. Nate wishes he were that relaxed.

Eventually Madison breaks the silence. "Thanks for coming at such short notice. I only found out earlier that it had to be today. It appears Angie's calling the shots."

He doesn't say anything because his hands have started sweating and he's getting tiny shooting pains in his chest. Not like a heart attack, but noticeable enough to make him feel like it's something serious. He used to get this feeling all the time, so he tries not to panic, but that just makes the anxiety build even more. He desperately hopes he can control it once inside the prison, but the thought he might not be able to makes him even more tense.

"Maybe you should wait in the parking lot?" Madison picks up on his nerves.

"I'll be fine." He turns to her with a smile. "Just make sure I get out of there later. Deal?"

She smiles but he sees the worry in her eyes. "Deal."

Nate's legs are heavy as they walk toward the entrance of the prison. It feels like he's walking through mud and he hates himself for not having the strength to put his experience behind him and focus on what they're here for. But right now, he's not in control of his body. His emotions are.

Madison gives him one final chance to back out. "Nate, you look terrible. I'm sure Brody would prefer it if you waited at the car with him." Brody's sitting next to the car, watching them closely. He'd picked up on Nate's anxiety too, whining at him before they walked away.

He doesn't respond. He's putting all his energy into getting through those doors. Just driving through the secure perimeter fence and onto the grounds was difficult enough.

She holds the door open for him and they enter the prison. The first thing that hits him is the lack of fresh air and natural light. It's nowhere near as bad as on death row, but it's something only certain buildings have. Those built primarily to contain people. His lungs constrict, shortening his breaths. He lets Madison do the talking.

She steps forward with confidence. "Detective Madison Harper and Nate Monroe. We're here to see the warden." She flashes her badge at the security guard, whose face remains locked in a hostile glare. He's guarding the entrance to a large metal detector. Another guard stands on the other side.

"Take off all metal items, including weapons, and place them in the basket on the conveyor belt," he says as he checks his clipboard for their names. When he finds them, he adds, "Along with cell phones and any bags. I need to see photographic ID for both of you."

Nate isn't wearing a belt. He pulls his cell phone from his pocket and, once Madison is through the gate and slipping her gold shield back in place, he shows his ID, trying to keep his hand steady. The guard stares at it for a long time, certainly longer than he stared at Madison's. Does he recognize his name? Is there a warrant out for his arrest that he doesn't know about?

Nate's mind tries to trick him into believing his exoneration was overturned without his knowledge and law enforcement has been advised to detain him if they ever stumble across him. He swallows but his mouth is bone dry. The shooting pains in his chest increase and he's overcome with dizziness. It takes everything in him not to react to it, to remain ramrod-straight and composed.

The guard finally tells him to step through the metal detector before handing back his driver's license, which falls through his fingers onto the floor. Nate almost loses his balance to the dizziness as he crouches down to retrieve it. He feels Madison step closer to him, and discreetly leans against her leg while he waits for the dizzy spell to pass. When it does, he carefully stands up and sees a woman approaching them. She's tall and in her fifties, with thick, mousy brown hair. She's wearing a gray pantsuit and white shirt.

"Detective Harper, Mr. Monroe, I'm Julia Dabrowski. Thank you for coming." She shakes Madison's hand first, giving Nate just enough time to wipe his dry of sweat before she gets to him. "Can I get you a drink?"

Madison looks at Nate and then says, "Water would be great, thanks."

"Sure. Follow me." She leads them to her office, her heels click-clacking loudly the whole way there. Once inside, she has them take a seat while she hands them bottled water.

When Nate takes that first sip of water he doesn't want to stop. It's both refreshing and comforting and he nearly finishes the whole bottle. Julia pretends she doesn't notice that or his sweaty forehead and tense demeanor, which suggests to him she knows exactly why he's anxious. She's read up on who he is. It would be remiss of her not to, considering she's in charge of this prison, the inmates and those who visit them. It makes him feel a little better to know he won't have to explain anything about himself. Slowly, he's able to relax.

"I'm aware that Angie McCoy is your older sister, Detective," says Julia. "And I know she's capable of wasting your time and manipulating all of us." She takes a seat behind her large oak desk.

It's covered in a mountain of paperwork, two different landlines and a large mahogany and brass name plate, but no personal effects that Nate can see. No family photographs for instance. Perhaps she doesn't want the wrong people to be able to target her loved ones on the outside.

"She has some of her fellow inmates wrapped around her little finger," she continues. "And I recently had to switch her cellmate because of the influence she was exercising over the young lady, so I don't know if this is a big waste of all our time but when there are two missing people who could potentially be found based on what she tells us, I'm willing to take that risk. I just hope you feel the same way."

Madison crosses her legs. "I do. That's why I came. There's a high chance she's playing tricks, but Nate and I both know Vince Rader and we'd like to see him get the answers he craves."

Nate nods along, but doesn't say anything.

"I've told Angie she can only have up to an hour with you, mainly because I want her to get straight to the point. She's being taken to a private visitation room now and I'll have a correctional officer present during your meeting. I can't spare any time to sit in, but I suspect I'm not needed anyway."

"I'm sure we'll be fine," says Madison.

Julia stands up. "If it becomes clear she's just messing with you, feel free to end the meeting at any time. You'll be shown back to reception, and you can return to Lost Creek." She looks at Nate when she says this last sentence.

Logically, he knows he can walk out of here whenever he wants, but anxiety is rarely logical. He stands on shaky legs, still unable to gain full control of his body. It's the thought of being locked in a visitation room with a CO behind him, blocking the exit. Last time he was in one of those he was being given the news that he was going to be released. After seventeen years on death row and with a looming execution date, he hadn't believed his attorney. It was still months before his actual release, but he had been given something that had left him for so long: hope.

He follows Julia and Madison out of the office. They walk down a seemingly never-ending corridor, their footsteps echoing around the concrete walls as they go. Within minutes the sounds of prison life ring out—guards and inmates shouting, banging doors, jeering. And the worst sound of all for someone who has formerly been incarcerated—the jarring buzz that precedes the electronic release of a locked door.

He takes the deepest breath he can muster and prays to God for the courage to get through this.

CHAPTER THIRTY-FIVE

Madison enters the harsh, windowless meeting room normally reserved for lawyer visits, and stares at her sister as she sits opposite her. It's been almost five months since they last saw each other. Angie looks like she hasn't had a haircut since. She's forty-two but she looks older, her hair is less brown than gray these days and the bags under her eyes are those of someone ten years older. Her skin is pasty from a lack of sunshine.

Angie has her arms crossed tight across her chest and she's staring back at Madison with unsettling curiosity. Then she looks at Nate. "Are you my brother-in-law yet?"

Nate isn't fazed by the question designed to embarrass him. "Not yet, but never say never."

The way Angie's eyes narrow suggest she's annoyed she's unable to get a reaction out of him. "You don't want this one." She nods at Madison. "She's a born liar. And she doesn't know how to show anyone any loyalty."

"Yada, yada, yada," says Madison with a deep sigh. "Can we skip the insults and get straight to the real reason we're here? Some of us have a busy day planned."

Angie eyeballs her before smirking. "How's Owen these days? He missing me yet?"

Madison tenses but tries not to show it. She doesn't want this woman knowing anything about her son. "He's thriving now he's back with me. It's like the last seven years never happened."

Without missing a beat, Angie says, "He's welcome to come visit me anytime. You'd think the little shit would be more grateful for what I did for him while you were locked up. I guess he has a short memory."

Madison feels Nate's eyes on her and she knows he's hoping she won't take the bait. She doesn't. "I understand Joanne Rader worked for you and Wyatt. So tell me why you shouldn't be arrested for the murder of Ruby and Oliver Rader."

A flicker of panic crosses Angie's face. She's wondering if they've come here to pin this on her. "Because I had nothing to do with it and you'll never find any evidence to suggest otherwise. But I guess if you're still a crooked cop, that won't stop you."

She's referring to Madison's conviction for murdering her coworker, knowing full well she had nothing to do with that.

"It's time to explain why you brought us here, Angie," says Nate. "You obviously think you have some information to share." He's using his reassuring voice, the one that suggests he's on the criminal's side and there's nothing they can tell him that would make him think poorly of them. "Don't you want Vince Rader to be able to finally move on?"

"I don't give a shit about Vince Rader, although I will say he's far more interesting now his wife's dead. That podcast he does is hilarious. Used to listen to it on the outside. The senile old bastard thinks he can find answers by sharing in other people's misery. Then he goes and gets that crime writer killed." She shakes her head. "I was sharing a cell with Kacie Larson until just last week. She sends her regards."

Madison tenses. Surely they didn't put Kacie in a cell with Angie? That's a terrible combination. There's no doubt Kacie is a damaged girl who made some terrible decisions as a result of the trauma she experienced, but she's not evil. She has the potential to live a good life with her young daughter. She hasn't even been convicted of anything yet and there are plenty of people who would be happy to see a judge show leniency in her case. Madison can't resist asking after her. "How is she?"

"Angry that she got locked up for essentially doing your job; that is, clearing the streets of sex offenders."

"And I'm willing to bet you made her believe that's my fault?"

Angie smiles. "Of course. She was too dumb to see it herself. Still had some good left in her after everything she'd been through. Now she's resigned to her fate—spending life behind bars and letting strangers raise her daughter."

Madison shakes her head at the stupidity of the warden for letting Angie get in Kacie's head. The girl might never get the chance she needs to turn her life around now.

Angie's attention turns to Nate. "There's a few women in here who would love to be locked in this room with you right now. You have quite the fan base. I guess female killers are bound to be drawn to their male counterparts."

Nate tenses beside her.

"Shut up, Angie," says Madison.

"You still believe in God, Mr. Monroe?" Angie continues. "Or did you realize there is no such thing the minute you found your fiancée dead? The minute you realized there's no one out there to save us, not if a priest can end up on death row for something he didn't do." She leans back with a smug look on her face.

Madison looks at Nate. His gaze is steely, but he appears to be in control of his emotions.

He smiles at her sister. "If there's no God, then how come

I'm able to walk out of here today a free man while you'll be taken back to your prison cell?"

Angie shifts position in her seat and breaks eye contact. She's annoyed she can't rattle either of them and Madison realizes that, actually, Angie has no power without her husband or their money. Sure, she might be controlling some of the women in here, but she's pretty pathetic when you think about it. Madison stands up. "If there's nothing you want to tell us about the Raders, then we're out of here."

Nate stands too and Angie's eyes widen. "Sit back down. I've got plenty to tell you."

They do as she says. "So where were you and Wyatt the day they went missing?" asks Nate.

Angie laughs. "That's none of your goddam business. Neither of us were responsible for what happened to that woman and her grandson. He was a cute kid. Didn't deserve being murdered."

"How do you know they're dead?" he asks.

She crosses her arms again, with a smirk on their face. "Because I know where they're buried."

A cold shiver runs down Madison's spine. She doesn't want to have to tell Vince, Matt and Jo that their missing loved ones are dead. Of course, it's what they've all thought over the years, but to have it confirmed could destroy them. Angie's certainly convincing, but how could she know unless she was involved somehow? "If that's true, you'll tell us where to look for them."

Angie laughs before looking at her watch. "Hell, I've barely had ten minutes out of my cell. You think I'm going to give it up this early into our little reunion? How about you tell me what you think happened that day and I'll tell you whether you're on the right track."

Madison rolls her eyes. "So you don't know anything? You're just playing with us."

Angie goes deadly serious. "Ruby Rader should've kept her nose out of other people's business. That's what I heard."

Nate leans forward. "What do you mean, Angie?"

"She was snooping. Found out something that was nothing to do with her but couldn't resist digging. Don't you know all this? I mean, what kind of investigator are you? Obviously not very good if you haven't picked up on the rumors yet."

He ignores her. "So she and Oliver were killed out of revenge for Ruby discovering something she wasn't supposed to know?"

Angie nods.

"What did Ruby discover?"

"What do I get for telling you? No one's offered me a plea deal yet."

Madison wants to shout at her but Nate jumps in. "You know we don't have the power to offer you anything. That's up to the DA's office. Maybe you'd rather have this conversation with them? But then, you would have done that already if you really believed you'd get a reduced sentence in return. Which suggests to me you don't know anything. Or maybe it's just women in here running their mouths and you've formed some kind of story based on those unsubstantiated rumors." He pauses. "You'd look pretty stupid if you tell us something that turns out not to be true. Like if we find them alive."

Angie leans in toward him with a sneer on her face. "I know who killed them, why they were killed and where they're buried. That enough for you?"

He shrugs. "Only if you actually give up the information."

She leans back again, considering it, but Madison suspects she's not going to tell them anything. Nate must agree because he changes direction. "I heard you and Joanne Rader didn't get along. Is that right?"

"We did at first, that's why I hired her. She was sorting the accounts for the scrapyard and our fundraising efforts."

Madison tries hard not to scoff at that. Wyatt and Angie's fundraisers were nothing more than money-making scams. "I'll bet you didn't let her dig too deep into those, did you?"

Angie gives her a deathly stare. "She was weak and easy to control."

"A perfect employee for you then. Someone you could manipulate."

Nate glances at Madison, his eyes warn her to change her approach or they risk Angie clamming up. "Did something happen between you two that made her quit?" he asks. "Or did you fire her?"

"She quit. Managed to get a job elsewhere. She said she wanted to be closer to home but Gold Rock isn't far, so that was a lame-ass excuse."

"So, you don't really know why she quit? Did you speak to her much afterward?"

"Not really. Maybe I saw her once more."

Nate crosses his arms. "If you're not prepared to tell us what you know, humor me by telling me what you suspected happened at the time, when you first heard about their disappearance."

She laughs, clearly enjoying the attention. "I assumed Ruby got herself killed by a random psycho. Maybe he didn't know she had a kid with her until it was too late and then he had no choice but to kill the boy."

"He could've just left him there," he suggests.

She shakes her head. "Nah, the boy was four years old. He could've given the cops details. He was a witness. It's a shame he's dead. He reminded me a lot of Owen." She glances at Madison, who's heard about enough.

"Time for us to go." She stands up. "I would advise you to do the right thing and tell someone where Ruby and Oliver are buried, but I know there's no point because you're evil, just like your husband."

She turns.

"You visit Stephanie's grave much, Madison?"

She stops dead in her tracks. Stephanie Garcia was Madison's ex-girlfriend. She was raped and then murdered in the house Madison and Owen currently live in.

"You should do," says Angie. "Because you'll be buried next to her by the time this year's through."

The male CO finally walks toward them. "That's enough out of you, McCoy. Unless you want to be charged with threatening behavior."

"Oh, it's not a threat," says Angie. "It's a promise. Call it revenge for killing my husband."

Madison turns back and leans in so close to her sister's face that she feels her warm, nicotine breath on hers. Nate's hand is on her arm but she ignores him. "Your threats mean nothing to me, Angie. You know why? Because *you* mean nothing to me. You never have. That's why it's so easy for me to forget that you're even in this place, rotting away with no contact from anyone in your family. Especially not from my son."

She storms out of the room before Angie can say anything else.

CHAPTER THIRTY-SIX

Madison has Nate race back to Lost Creek as fast as the speed limits allow. It's almost one o'clock already and she's annoyed that she let Angie waste her time when she could be searching Douglas's car. Although, she can't help feeling unsettled by her sister's claims about knowing Ruby and Oliver are dead and buried. She was pretty convincing on that count. Maybe if they let her stew for a while Angie will tell the warden their location. She would probably be happy to watch Vince's life fall apart on the news while the bodies are recovered.

"I'm ruling out Angie as a suspect in their disappearance," says Nate as he drives across the covered bridge into Lost Creek.

She sighs. "I agree. If she was involved there's no way she'd incriminate herself by confirming the link between her and Jo Rader."

"Exactly. Maybe she does know what happened but I bet it's only third hand, nothing we could use to secure a conviction against anyone."

"She just wanted us to go through the pain of being back inside." She looks at him. "You did well today. I don't mean that to sound patronizing, but I don't know how you didn't run out of that place as we were leaving."

He smiles. "I wanted to. The minute that front door opened and I got a whiff of that cool fresh air, I wanted to kiss the ground in the parking lot."

"I'm not surprised. It was easier for me, but I think that's because I was worrying about you. I didn't have time to give the flashbacks any headspace."

His expression changes to sorrow. "You know, I half expected Rex to be standing there waiting for me, like last time I was released."

Madison squeezes his hand. "I miss Rex and I barely knew him, so I can't imagine how you feel."

"He was one of a kind, that's for sure. He'd be happy Owen got one of his cats though."

She laughs. "It's just a shame I can't bill him for the damage Bandit has done to my couch with his claws. And he brought up a hairball on it this morning. Owen couldn't clean it up because he kept gagging, so guess who had that honor?"

Nate laughs as he pulls up alongside Madison's car in the diner's parking lot.

Madison sees Kate Flynn approaching from her own car. She's alone, with no camera guy in sight. "Looks like Kate's found me." She turns to Nate before getting out. "Thanks for coming with me today, I appreciate it. I won't put you through that again. Not for Angie, anyway."

"It's fine. But you definitely owe me a drink or two." He smiles as she gets out of the car.

"Where are you off to now?" she asks before closing the passenger door.

"I have a few people on my list I've yet to speak to. And I want to call Jo Rader to ask why she quit her job with Angie. You never know, there could be something in that."

She nods. "Good idea. Catch you later."

As he drives off, Kate approaches her with a smile. "Hey. How are you?"

Madison hugs her before checking her watch for the millionth time. She has just two hours to stop Douglas's cremation now. The task feels impossible. "I'm good. How are you?"

Kate looks exhausted, and not as pristine as usual. Being on the local news at short notice means she's usually always camera ready, but not today. "Tired," she says. "The kids are keeping me busy."

She has two kids under six. They're both adorable, but Madison doesn't envy her. Owen was an easy baby with a cute smile that would attract women from across the room to coo over him. But he got a little challenging around four or five years old. He was one of those kids you see being dragged along the floor of the grocery store clutching the bottom of a shopping cart and screaming at the top of his lungs for no good reason. "You sure you're okay?" asks Madison. "If you ever need someone to babysit, just ask. I know I'd enjoy spending time with them."

Kate sighs. "Thanks, I appreciate the offer. Me and Patrick are arguing a lot at the moment, nothing serious, but maybe getting out one night would do us some good. Anyway, how's the investigation into your homicide going? Got anything for me to report?"

"Afraid not." She hesitates before looking around. "Off the record, I have no leads or suspects. No one is coming forward with any tips. It's like it was the perfect murder or something."

Kate frowns. "Surely, there's no such thing?"

"I hope not. What about you, what have you discovered?" Madison knows Kate's excellent at her job, and sometimes the community seems more willing to share information with reporters than with law enforcement.

"I'm not having much luck either. I did hear a rumor you've been back to Detective Douglas's house recently. Any reason for that?"

Madison tries not to give anything away. The last thing she needs is Kate—and the rest of the media—getting wind that Douglas's suicide might have been a murder. It wouldn't be fair on his family. Not until she has proof and they've been notified. "I just had to pick something up, that's all." She glances at her watch. "I don't want to be rude but I have somewhere to be. We'll catch up for a drink soon?"

Kate nods. "Sure. It's long overdue."

Madison feels guilty for shooting off but she's got to check out Douglas's car. The whole way there she keeps an eye on the rear-view mirror in case Kate decided to follow her. She didn't.

Once she arrives at Douglas's house she pulls on some latex gloves and goes straight to the garage, opening it with the keys Steve gave her. She has to switch the light on to see what's inside. The black SUV is sitting empty. It looks menacing from the front, probably because it's so quiet in here and she knows the owner is dead. She wonders when Douglas last used it and whether his killer had any reason to touch it. Ideally, she'd have Alex here checking for prints on the doors, but Mendes won't let her organize that yet.

She unlocks the car and pulls open the passenger door. As she slips inside, she's hit by the smell of Douglas's aftershave. It takes her breath away as she wasn't expecting to smell that scent again.

Trying to remain focused, she uses her phone's flashlight and rifles through the glovebox. There's a roadmap of the town, which looks like it hasn't been touched in a long time, a small first-aid kit and a pair of designer sunglasses, as well as several unused napkins from takeout chains. She tries to reach all the way to the back and her hand comes across something she can't see from her position. As she pulls it out, she realizes it's his pocket notebook.

She experiences a flutter of excitement as she opens it. There are pages and pages of names, numbers and locations, all of which she only glances at until she gets to the last entry. It's dated less than two weeks before Douglas's death.

> *Spoke to Terri Summers about the Raders. Reluctant to discuss what she knows. Left her to stew over what I said. Will return in a few days.*

Madison stops breathing. "The Raders?" she exclaims. "Why the hell was he talking to Terri Summers about the *Raders*?" Her mind buzzes as she tries to piece it together.

Turning back a couple of pages, she sees all of them listed: Vince, Matt, Jo, Ruby, Oliver. But half the page has been torn out so she can't see what he wrote next to their names. What *is* clear is that Douglas was reinvestigating the cold case while he was suspended from duty. He never disclosed that to her and he was never assigned to the case. Mendes didn't think it warranted reopening, not without some new lead or evidence, which was why Vince felt he had to employ Nate's services. So why was Douglas investigating it again after six years? Had Vince asked him as well as Nate?

She pulls out her phone and calls Vince. It takes him a while to answer, probably because of the lunchtime rush. "How can I help you, Detective?" he asks.

She can't think of a way to frame her question without alerting him to the fact Douglas was investigating his family. "Just a quick question; had you asked Detective Douglas to reopen the cold case for you recently?"

He's silent for a second. "Well, that's come out of left field. No, I didn't. Didn't see the point when Nate could probably do a better job."

Now she's even more confused. "What about Matt? Could he have asked him to?"

Vince scoffs. "Are you kidding me? He hated Douglas. There's no way he'd ask for his help."

He hated Douglas. She absorbs that for a minute. Did he hate Douglas enough to kill him? "Okay, thanks. That's all."

"Wait," he says. "Douglas was investigating it without your knowledge? When? During his suspension?"

She takes a deep breath. "It looks like it. Maybe he was just trying to fill his days, but he shouldn't have been questioning anyone in a police capacity while suspended, so I'd appreciate it if you didn't mention this to anyone." She doesn't want him to tell Matt. Just in case.

"If you say so. Seems odd to me. Maybe Douglas didn't want Nate to beat him to the truth and solve the case."

She nods. "That wouldn't surprise me. Sorry to bother you with this, Vince. I've literally just found out and I'll need to look into it further now I know it wasn't you or Matt who requested it."

"Not a problem. I'd be interested to know what you learn."

"Of course," she says, but it's unlikely she can tell him.

She ends the call as adrenaline shoots through her body. This notebook links Terri, Douglas and the missing Raders. And what they have in common is that they're all dead. Well, she doesn't know for sure about Ruby and Oliver yet but it's a good bet. It's not difficult to assume that whoever killed Terri did so because she was talking to Douglas, and now Madison knows she was talking to him about the Raders, it's clear what she has to do. She needs to join forces with Nate to find out what happened to Ruby and Oliver, and fast. Because if she can find *their* killer, she might just have Terri and Douglas's killer.

But first, she needs to stop Douglas's cremation from going ahead. Chief Mendes will have to listen to her now she has this new information. She gets out of Douglas's car, locks up the garage behind her and pulls out her phone again. Just as she's about to call Mendes it rings. Kate's name flashes up. Madison frowns. She's tempted to decline the call, not wanting to waste time, but it seems strange that Kate would want to talk to her again already. "Hey. Everything okay?"

"Madison, I'm so sorry to have to tell you this." Kate's voice is shaky and Madison can hear loud sirens in the background, along with traffic.

Fear grips her chest and she immediately thinks of Owen. He was planning to spend the day with his friend but she doesn't know what they were doing. Could they have been hurt? "What's happened? Is it Owen?"

"No, not Owen. But there's been an accident. It's Nate. His car was pulled over by the side of the road and he must've got out for some reason. I'm not sure why as there's no visible damage to it."

Madison's first thought is that he pulled over to let Brody relieve himself. "Is he okay?"

"No. He's been hit by a car."

Her blood runs cold. It takes her a second before she can form a sentence, and even that's short. "How bad is he?"

Kate doesn't respond, she's talking to someone else, maybe an EMT.

"Kate?" she shouts. "Is he alive?"

"He's unconscious. The ambulance has just arrived. We're on the road before the turning for Fantasy World." She pauses. "Madison?"

"What?" she whispers.

"I think you should hurry."

CHAPTER THIRTY-SEVEN

Time appears to slow down as Madison drives through downtown, not stopping for any red lights. She's careful, but fast, managing not to cause an accident herself. Angry car horns are just a faint distraction over the sound of her own heartbeat drumming in her ears. She's picturing the worst: Nate lying dead on the road, his body bloody and twisted. His eyes glassy.

She's unable to hold back tears. When her cell phone rings, she ignores it. She wants to see him before she hears news of his condition over the phone. She has to get to him. As she runs another red light, her next thought is of Brody. "Oh, God." If Brody wasn't hit too, how will he cope without Nate? She'll have to take him in. It's the right thing to do. Then she thinks of Owen's reaction but she won't let her mind go there yet.

Finally, she's approaching the stretch of road that leads to Fantasy World and she can't stop her left knee from trembling. She reaches a line of traffic and can see the flashing lights up ahead. Crossing into the other lane she maneuvers around them all, until Officer Goodwin signals for her to pull over.

When Madison goes to leave the car, she realizes she didn't even wear her seatbelt.

"He's pretty messed up," says Goodwin as he approaches her.

She holds her breath as she approaches the EMT's back. Jake Rubio is crouched on the ground, busy at work trying to save Nate's life. Nate's legs and arms are completely still. She stops dead in her tracks, covering her mouth with her hands. The blood on the ground, visible over Jake's right shoulder, makes her fear the worst.

Suddenly, Kate's next to her. "Come to my car with me for a minute."

Madison silently shrugs her off and continues forward to Nate. She crouches next to him, trying not to get in Jake's way, and looks at his face. He looks dead. The tears come thick and fast as she pulls his hand into hers. It's still warm. Leaning in to his ear she says, "Nate? Can you hear me?"

She studies his face. There's no movement. His eyes remain closed. She doesn't know if he can survive this much blood loss. Unable to speak, she looks at Jake for information but he's busy trying to stem the bleeding.

"You've got to save him," she says.

He remains focused on Nate. "That's the plan."

A second EMT, a woman she doesn't recognize, pulls her up and out of their way. Madison feels Kate's arm around her and leans in for a hug. She can barely see though her tears. Officer Goodwin hands Madison a tissue, which she accepts. It's a small gesture and much appreciated. She didn't think he had any compassion. "Where's the other driver?" she asks. "Do we have them in custody yet?"

"Afraid not."

Her heart sinks. "Any witnesses?"

"Williams and Sanchez are interviewing everyone in these vehicles." He points to the line of parked traffic. "Hopefully someone saw something."

The stretch of road they're on has no traffic cameras. It's the road out of town that leads to Gold Rock. It's probably safe to assume the other driver is long gone by now. Madison can't understand how someone could do this to another person and not stick around. Unless... She considers the possibility that Nate was hit on purpose. She looks at the ground and sees black tire marks that make a sharp turn in to where Nate lies. "Get Alex down here immediately. I want to know if this was deliberate."

"Deliberate?" says Goodwin, confused. "Does your friend have enemies?"

"Just do it, please."

He nods and walks away, getting on his radio.

Her teeth chatter as she wipes her eyes, but not because of the cold. It's the shock setting in. She suddenly remembers Brody. "Where's Nate's dog? Is he hurt too?"

Kate looks around. "He wasn't here when I arrived. He must've run away after the collision."

Madison frowns. "There's no way he'd leave Nate's side. Not when he's vulnerable on the ground like that." She walks to Nate's car and notices the back door is still wide open. "He must've pulled over to let Brody out for a second." Approaching Goodwin, she says, "Did you see a dog hanging around when you got here?"

"No. Must've made a run for it, which is dangerous on this stretch of road. Want me to go check for him?"

She nods. "Please. He's a German shepherd and Siberian husky mix. He needs to be there when Nate wakes up." She turns away from him so he can't see her tears. To his credit, Goodwin immediately gets in his car and drives away.

Madison can see other patrol cars farther along the road, controlling traffic. They might have picked Brody up. When she turns to where Nate lies, she sees the EMTs carefully sliding a spinal board underneath him. His head is packed with bloody bandages and he's still unconscious. She notices one sneaker is missing from his feet. Searching, she finds it way off in the long grass next to the road. Before he's put into the back of an ambulance, she slips his sneaker back onto his foot and rubs his leg. "I want to go with him."

Kate steps closer. "What about your car, and Owen? You should prepare him for the worst."

Madison looks at her with raised eyebrows and hot tears in her eyes. "You think he's going to die?"

Kate hugs her. "I'm sorry, I shouldn't have said that." She pulls back. "I just meant you need to be the one to tell Owen what's happened here before he hears it on the news."

She pulls away from her, disgusted. "You're going to report on this?"

Kate shakes her head. "No. But *they* are." She nods to the news crews that have appeared. They're preparing their cameras on the grass behind Nate's car.

Madison's blood boils. The media have already got their money's worth out of Nate over the years and she's determined they won't get any more. She storms over to Shelley. "Get them out of here. Make them wait as far back as possible and block the view of their cameras. I want his car screened."

Shelley gets right on it.

"And if you find Brody, call me immediately. He's missing." She turns and races to her own car, just as the ambulance pulls out. Kate's right; she has to break the crushing news to Owen before he hears it from someone else.

CHAPTER THIRTY-EIGHT

Madison moves her car to a quiet side road, ahead of all the building traffic. She can see the Ferris wheel at Fantasy World from here. It's only mid afternoon but the sun is already lowering and the wheel's bright neon lights shine brightly against the darkening sky. A faint rumble of fairground music and delighted screams reach her when she opens her window for some fresh air. Madison rubs her shaking hands together for warmth. She tries to relax her breathing because when she speaks to Owen, she wants to have a calm, reassuring voice. When she's ready, she selects his number and hits call.

He answers immediately. "That made me jump so bad. I was DMing someone."

Madison smiles faintly. She wishes she were calling to discuss something mundane, like reminding him to do his homework, or to take out the trash.

"Mom?"

"Sorry." She takes another deep breath. "Owen, honey, there's been an accident. It's Nate. He's on his way to the hospital." She says it all in one go as if she's delivering news to a victim's family. The more they know up front, the less they panic.

"What happened?" he asks, alarmed. "Is he going to be okay?"

She has to be honest with him, just in case the worst happens. "I don't know. He was hit by a car. By the time I got to him it looked like he was badly injured; he was bleeding from his head, and unconscious."

"Holy crap." She doesn't tell him to mind his language. He's quiet for a second. "Are you at the hospital?"

"No, I can't go yet. I have something urgent I need to sort first."

"More urgent than Nate? Come on, Mom!"

That stings. He'll understand when she explains it later but for now, she doesn't have time. The clock is ticking down to Douglas's cremation and she's no use to Nate while he's unconscious. "I'll explain when I see you. I wanted to ask if you would go to the hospital for me. I'll join you as soon as I'm able to."

He doesn't hesitate. "Of course I'll go. I can take care of Brody until Nate wakes up, assuming they'll let Brody in the hospital. I'll get someone to give me a ride."

Her heart sinks. "I'm sorry, but Brody's missing. He must've run away after the accident."

"Are you kidding me?" Owen clearly disagrees. "There's no way he would leave Nate behind."

That's what she had thought, but it's the only explanation. She can't imagine anyone would steal a dog after running down their owner. "Maybe he got scared."

He scoffs at the idea. "Brody doesn't get scared, you know that."

He's right. "I've got officers looking for him and I'm hopeful he'll turn up. In the meantime, get to the hospital and keep me updated on Nate's condition. I'll text you when I'm on my way."

"Okay. But, Mom, you have to find Brody."

"I'm trying my hardest, Owen." A tear runs down her cheek as she ends the call. She's never felt pulled in so many directions and all of them are urgent. She takes comfort knowing that Nate will have someone there with him when he wakes. *If* he wakes. On her phone she selects Chief Mendes's number. When Mendes answers, Madison updates her on what's happened and how Nate's currently being taken to the hospital.

Mendes is shocked. "Do we have the driver of the other vehicle? How many cars and people were involved?"

"It appears that only Nate was hit and the driver fled the scene. Hopefully we'll have witnesses shortly. My son's on his way to the hospital. He..." She was going to say he loves Nate but she can't bring herself to think about that. She tries to control her breathing. It's strained as she's so uptight. "Chief? You need to stop Douglas's cremation." She checks the clock on the dashboard. "It's happening in *thirty minutes* and we can't let it go ahead."

Mendes sighs. "I thought we'd been over this. We can discuss it later, once we know whether your friend is going to pull through."

"Chief? Listen to me. I found Douglas's pocket notebook in his car. He'd logged his first visit to Terri Summers. It says he went there to discuss Ruby and Oliver's disappearance."

There's silence for a second. "Why would he do that?"

"It seems to me that he was investigating the cold case while he was suspended. He must've been onto something and I suspect he wanted to beat Nate to resolving the case, you know what he was like. He hated unclosed cases. Saw them as some kind of personal failure." She pauses, trying to get her thoughts together. "Chief, his notes suggest Terri might've known something about their disappearance and he was planning to visit her for a second time, which I know he did do, but there's no update about that visit in his notebook."

"So you believe whoever killed Terri Summers killed Douglas, and that could be the same person who abducted the Raders?"

"Exactly. Terri must've known something damning about their disappearance and somehow Douglas found out. And now Nate's been hit by a car. It's too much of a coincidence that Nate's investigating their cold case too." Talking fast now she adds, "Chief, there are skid marks on the road that suggest he was deliberately hit, that it wasn't a random accident. I need Alex down there immediately."

Mendes exhales. "If you're right, this person is hell-bent on making sure no one finds the Raders. I mean, if they'd kill a detective, it's logical to assume they'd kill anyone."

"You need to stop the cremation so we can autopsy Douglas's body to look for signs of murder. It will buy us time to find his killer." She leans back in her seat a little. There's no more she can do to stop Douglas from being cremated. It's up to Mendes now.

"Leave it with me. I'll speak to Douglas's dad. Do you have any idea who could be behind all this?"

Madison considers whether it could have been Angie who arranged for Nate to be injured. They clearly rattled her at the prison earlier. She could have got straight on the phone to one of her and Wyatt's ex-employees, knowing that hurting Nate or Owen would be the best way to hurt her. But prison calls are recorded. Unless she spoke in some kind of code, she would be incriminating herself and she's just not that stupid.

Then there's Matt Rader. He took an instant disliking to Nate and was reluctant to even talk to him. And he hated Douglas. Maybe that's because Douglas was onto him. "I'm not sure. Maybe. I need more time." But she also needs to be with Nate.

"Do whatever you have to do in order to find this person. I'll brief the team and increase patrols further. I can hold another press conference to ask for witnesses to the hit-and-run if we need to."

"Thanks. And you'll arrange Douglas's autopsy?" Those are words she never imagined she'd ever have to say.

"Sure."

Madison swallows hard. "I'll head over to the morgue as soon as I can. I'd like to be there when Lena performs it. I want to know right away if there's anything we can find on him that could lead us to his killer."

"You're going to be busy," says Mendes. "I'll get the whole team on board so you can concentrate on leads. But..." She trails off.

It's not like Mendes to hesitate. It worries Madison. "What is it?"

"Just make time to check in on your friend first, in case the worst happens. You wouldn't want to regret not getting that final chance to be with him. I'll have my fingers crossed that he pulls through."

Madison's throat tightens and she can't even reply. She ends the call, takes a breath, and then phones Vince Rader's cell number.

"How can I help you, Detective?" he asks. She can hear the clatter of dishes and the noise of people chatting as they enjoy their coffees and snacks in the diner as if nothing is wrong.

"Hi. Is Matt there with you right now?"

"Why? Do you have an update?" He sounds hopeful.

"No, I just want to speak to him about something. Sorry to be vague. You know what's it's like."

Vince sighs. "Matty went out over an hour ago. He didn't say where he was headed. I can get him to call you back? Or you could text him."

She doesn't want to speak to him, she just wants his location. "That's fine, thanks."

"Has this got anything to do with the traffic that's building out near the amusement park? Folks are talking about it in here. Some kind of hit-and-run, apparently."

Anger builds in her chest. That's Nate they're all gossiping about, although Vince won't know that yet. "It was Nate. He's badly injured. The ambulance crew took him to the hospital." Her voice falters.

"That's terrible," says Vince. He sounds shocked—until: "Wait. You think Matty did it?"

"That's not what I'm saying. I was calling about something else. Forget it." She's about to end the call but he stops her.

"No, wait! Is there anything I can do? Look after the dog or fetch some clothes for Nate?"

Her eyes fill with tears at his kindness. She clears her throat. "Brody's missing. If you can find him, that would be a big help. Maybe he's gone home to wait for Nate."

"Leave it to me, I'll find him." He pauses. "How bad is it? Is Nate going to pull through?"

She takes a deep breath. "It's pretty bad, Vince. He was unconscious and there was just so much blood."

"Holy crap." He's shaken. "If I were still a religious man, I'd pray for him but I haven't done that since I realized my wife and grandson weren't coming home. So instead, I'll find the dog and bring him to the hospital."

"Thank you."

She ends the call and wipes her eyes knowing that, if she doesn't get her shit together, the person who mowed Nate down could get away with everything.

CHAPTER THIRTY-NINE

SIX YEARS AGO

Ruby gets Oliver out of the car seat and in his excitement to get to the store he tries to run ahead of her without checking both ways. "Wait!" She locks her car and grabs his hand. "You need to be more careful, sweetie. Drivers these days are too busy staring at their phones to look out for little guys like you, okay?"

"I'm not that little! Daddy says if I keep eating the way I do I'll be taller than him soon."

She laughs as they enter the store. She lets Oliver choose a shopping cart, even though they're bigger than him. "Keep one hand on the cart at all times, got it?"

He nods, but as soon as he's distracted by a shiny toy robot he shoots off down the aisle, ahead of her. Ruby's mind wanders as she selects the items Matt and Jo were running low on. She'd tried calling Rosemary earlier, but there was no answer, which means she's already at the church playgroup where she volunteers. Ruby intends to visit her at the church in a little while. They can discuss the issue that's bothering her in more depth. They shouldn't be disturbed once all the children have left. Dread fills her stomach again and she knows she can't live like this. She needs to get to the bottom of the allegations once and for all.

She realizes she's lost sight of Oliver but then hears him talking to someone in the next aisle. As she approaches, she recognizes Terri Summers, one of Matt and Jo's friends. Sometimes Terri will babysit Oliver when Ruby and Vince can't get away from the diner. "Hi, Terri. How are you?" Her eyes are drawn to Terri's shopping cart, where she has a selection of fondant icing and other cake decorations, alongside a six-pack of Diet Coke.

"Good, thanks," says Terri. "Oliver was just telling me about the dinosaurs at the museum."

Terri's always in a good mood and happy to stop and chat, and it's clear that Oliver adores her. "Oh, he loved the T-Rex," says Ruby. "It roared and moved its head and arms. I was a little scared to be honest with you!"

"I have one in the car," says Oliver looking up at them. He's so tiny and precious that Ruby's heart swells with love for her grandson. She wishes he could stay this age forever.

"In the car?" says Terri with wide eyes, feigning shock. "How did he fit in your car?"

Oliver giggles wildly before saying, "Not a real one, silly!"

"Phew! We don't need a T-Rex getting loose in Lost Creek! He might knock the Ferris wheel over."

Oliver runs away laughing and Ruby knows he's heading straight for the candy aisle. She turns back to Terri. "How's your mom doing? Her new hip working out for her?"

"Oh, sure. She walks faster than me now." Terri laughs. "She's good, but I wish she would get off my back about finding a boyfriend."

"She can't help it," says Ruby. "All mothers just want to see their kids settled. I'm sure you'll find someone soon enough, if that's what you want."

Terri sighs. "What I want is one of those." She nods in Oliver's direction. "But I suppose I've got to find a daddy for them first."

Ruby can't understand why someone like her hasn't got a line of men at her door.

"Are you having Thanksgiving at the diner?" asks Terri.

"No, we'll be working all day and then off to Matt and Jo's for dinner. They wanted to host it this year. Well, when I say *they*, you know I mean Matt. Jo's not much of a cook."

Terri laughs. "She sure hates cooking, but she makes a great cocktail!"

Ruby smiles. "What are you doing for Thanksgiving?"

"I'll be at my mom's with her and my aunt's family. I'm looking forward to it." Terri checks her phone. "I better go because I'm working tonight. I've just started at the Mountain View care home and I want to make a good impression by getting there early."

"How are you enjoying it?"

"I love it. The residents are fascinating. They tell me all these stories about the lives they've lived. It doesn't feel like work to sit and listen to them. I try to spend time with those who don't get any visitors as it really makes their day to have someone take the time to ask them about themselves." Her smiles falters. "I've been told the worst thing about working there is when one of the residents passes away. That's going to suck."

Ruby feels for her.

"Anyway, it was nice to bump into you, Ruby. Tell Jo I'll call her soon."

"I will. You take care now." Ruby watches her as she walks away. She wonders whether Terri might be a good person to quiz once she's clarified some things with Rosemary later. Because she's close to Matt and Jo, and one of them might have confided in her.

"Grandma, can I have these?"

She smiles as Oliver zooms back up the aisle toward her, a bunch of different candy bars in his hands. "Careful, you'll fall!" She lets him place the candy into the cart as she looks back at Terri.

"Are we going home after this?" asks Oliver.

"No, sweetie. We're going to the playgroup at the church. I need to speak to Mrs. Hendricks." She looks down at him. "You like her, right?"

He nods emphatically before zooming off again, leaving Ruby to wish Rosemary had never confided in her. Because the ramifications could hurt her precious grandson more than anyone else.

CHAPTER FORTY

Madison takes a minute before entering the morgue. She may have fought hard to get Douglas's body autopsied, but she wishes he could be allowed to rest in peace. Part of her feels guilty that she's the reason it's happening, but if Lena finds evidence he was murdered, it will be worth it and it could help her catch his killer.

Inside the room, it looks like Lena's already started the procedure as her long hair is tied back, she's wearing scrubs and talking into a recorder above the body on the table in front of her. There's a large tray of sadistic-looking instruments within easy reach.

As Madison walks farther into the cool, sterile room she braces herself for seeing Douglas again. But on approaching his body, she soon realizes that nothing could have prepared her. She inhales deeply as she stares at him and has to resist closing her eyes. The skin from his torso is cut open in a Y shape, the incisions starting from either side of his neck down to his collarbone, then meeting above his chest and going all the way down his torso to his pelvis. Some organs have already been removed, presumably for weighing. Before Madison's eyes reach his face,

Lena pulls his scalp back over his skull so she doesn't see what's underneath. Then she takes a step closer to Madison. "Are you sure you want to be present for this?"

Madison slowly nods. "He's gone. This is just his body."

Lena looks uncertain whether or not to continue. Eventually she flaps his scalp back over his closed eyes and leans in to examine the side of his skull. "Huh." She sounds puzzled. Madison looks away, prompting Lena to stand up straight. "There's nothing wrong with his organs, even his liver. His issues with alcohol must've been recent."

"There was no alcohol in his house when we found him." She pauses. "He was getting better."

Lena nods sadly. "I'll have to wait for the toxicology results to confirm whether or not he'd had anything to drink the day he died." She takes a deep breath. "One thing I have been able to ascertain is that there's no gunshot residue on his fingers. On either hand. Look."

Madison watches as Lena gently lifts his hands. The skin looks soft, and will soon slip off his bones like a discarded glove. "You're sure?"

"Positive. He didn't pull the trigger. Which means you were right to suspect he didn't take his own life."

Madison's overcome. She's been right all along, and Mendes didn't want to believe her. She leans against a counter. It's one thing to suspect her partner was murdered but it's another thing altogether to have it confirmed. She doesn't know whether to be relieved that he didn't take his own life, or angry that his death wasn't his choice. She feels a strange mixture of both and it's almost unbearable.

"Here." Lena hands her a plastic cup of water and waits as she drinks it all. "I've spotted something on his skull."

Her eyes widen. "What is it?"

"Can I show you, or would you rather not look?"

She hesitates. It's not that she's squeamish—she's in the

wrong job for that—but it feels too intrusive to look at Douglas's skull. Finding him dead was traumatic enough. She takes a step back. "You can just tell me."

"Of course. I'm pretty certain I see evidence that he suffered some kind of secondary trauma to the head, aside from the bullet wound."

"That would make sense," she says, thinking about it. "I couldn't understand how someone could get him to voluntarily sit in his recliner while they shot him in a way that made it look like suicide."

Lena crosses her arms. "With a hard enough blow to the head he could've been unconscious when they placed him there and shot him. They were obviously hoping the bullet's exit wound would hide the previous trauma but it hasn't. It's left behind a... Sorry, I won't go into details."

Madison swallows. As long as the full details are in Lena's report, she doesn't need to hear them now. "You really think he was unconscious when he was shot?"

"If he wasn't unconscious, he certainly would've been disoriented. He wouldn't have known what was happening to him."

Madison turns away and looks up at the ceiling in relief. The harsh fluorescent light has a fat black fly buzzing around it. She watches as the fly inadvertently makes its way to the insect control unit on the wall. A quick zap takes it by surprise, and it buzzes frantically before dropping dead onto the counter beneath. "That's something, at least."

Lena covers Douglas's body with a white sheet and her assistant Skyler appears, moving Douglas away from them. "I know my professional interest ends in this room," says Lena. "However, I can't help but ask; do you have any idea who did this to him? Because I don't feel safe with his killer out there, living in plain sight. I mean, Douglas was a *cop*."

Turning to face her, Madison says, "I think it was the same

person who killed Terri Summers and tried to mow Nate down today."

"Nate?" A look of realization crosses Lena's face. "That was him who got hit by a car?"

Madison nods. "He's in the hospital. I'm going there next."

"Oh my God, what is happening around here? Are *you* safe?"

She shrugs. "I have no idea. I need to go. Will you inform Chief Mendes that Douglas's death was a homicide?"

"Sure. I'll write up my report straight away." Lena pauses. "When you see Nate, send him my best wishes."

Madison can only hope she'll have the chance to speak to him again. "I will."

CHAPTER FORTY-ONE

When Madison walks into Nate's hospital room, the first thing she sees is Owen pointing to the TV and talking to Nate, whose eyes are closed. "So, this guy is this big environmental lawyer who never loses in court, and he's going after the—" He stops when he notices her. "Oh. Hi, Mom." He stands up but doesn't move anywhere.

"Hey. How is he?" She walks forward to the bed and hugs Owen quickly before looking at Nate. He has various tubes attached to him and an IV trailing from his arm, administering fluid. The blue gown he's wearing is loose, exposing some of his chest. She instinctively pulls it up to his neck, then takes his limp hand in hers. It's horrible seeing him like this, so helpless. He could've died. And for what? Doing his job? The heart rate monitor beeps steadily.

"Still unconscious."

"He hasn't woken at all yet?"

Owen shakes his head. "The doctor didn't really want to tell me anything until I pretended Nate was my dad." He flashes her a grin. "So call me Owen Monroe while we're in here."

She finds herself smiling, despite Nate's condition. "What did the doctor say?"

"That the head wound isn't life-threatening but he's going to have a hell of a headache when he wakes up. He's got a torn shoulder ligament and a couple of cracked ribs, plus some stiches in his head. Apparently, they shaved some of his hair off so he's going to look like Frankenstein under that bandage."

"Owen! Don't say that in front of him."

Owen holds his hands up. "He can't hear us!"

"Then why were you telling him who was on the TV when I walked in?"

He reddens. "That was just *in case* he can hear anything, but I don't think he can. He's not in a coma or anything. He's knocked out with drugs."

Madison's stomach lurches. She thinks of Nate's history with cocaine. What if he gets addicted to the painkillers?

"Don't worry, Mom. I told the doc he used to have a drug problem. It's on his medical chart now."

She looks at her son properly for the first time in a while. He's tall, and despite seeming immature at times—he is only seventeen—he's reliable in situations like this. She's dreading him leaving for college next year. She'll be alone again. And the fact she doesn't know how she'll pay for his tuition keeps her awake at night.

A strange sound scutters toward them from the corridor outside. They both turn in time to see Vince being dragged into the room behind Brody.

Owen's face lights up as Brody lurches for him. "You found him!"

Vince lets go of the leash and tries to catch his breath before closing the door. "The nurses can't know he's here. I had to bring him up the stairs."

"We can pretend he's one of those mental health dogs and

that Nate needs him to be here when he wakes up," suggests Owen.

"I don't think they'll fall for that," says Madison. Brody tries to get on the bed but Madison pulls him back. There are too many tubes he could pull out, and he could hurt Nate. He's not exactly small. Instead, she lets him put his front paws up and lick Nate's hand. She notices the blood on his paws and turns to Vince. "What happened?"

"We think he chased the asshole who hit Nate. Officer Williams got a report of a dog running across the bridge in the direction of Gold Rock and she managed to track him down. He was panting by the side of the road by the time she got there."

That's a hell of a long way for a dog to run, but it's so typical of Brody to want to catch the guy. She ruffles the fur on his neck. "Good boy. We'll get your paws taken care of."

"Did anyone see who hit Nate?" asks Owen. "Surely if Brody was chasing a car someone would've noticed."

"Officer Williams is interviewing people." Vince leans in to look at Nate. "At least his face is unscathed. He'll still be able to sweet talk the ladies."

Owen laughs.

Madison takes a deep breath. "Is Matt back at the diner yet?"

"He wasn't when I left to look for this one," Vince says, nodding to the dog. His eyes narrow. "You don't seriously think he did this, do you? Because I've got to be honest, Detective, I don't understand your reasoning."

She crosses her arms. "Okay, this is strictly between us three, so don't either of you dare tell anyone else, understand?"

They nod.

"Detective Douglas didn't take his own life."

Vince raises his eyebrows.

"What?" says Owen. "So he was murdered?"

She nods. "And I think the same person who murdered Douglas did this." She gestures to Nate.

Vince is confused. "But why? That doesn't make any sense. Nate isn't a cop."

"I have to assume it's because both Douglas and Nate were looking into Ruby and Oliver's disappearance."

Vince goes pale before taking a seat. "That would mean he's in here because of me."

Madison steps forward to place a hand on his shoulder. "The only person responsible for this is the guy driving the car."

"And you think this is all to stop anyone finding out what happened to my wife and grandson?"

"I have no proof of that yet, but it's too much of a coincidence. Especially as Douglas was seen talking to Terri Summers in the weeks leading up to her death."

Vince looks up at her. "Why was he talking to Terri?"

The way he says her name tells Madison he knew her. "He must've had some kind of hunch that she knew something about what happened to them."

He leans forward in shock. "Oh my God. Terri knew something this whole time and never told me? I can't believe it. She wouldn't let us suffer this long, surely?"

"I don't know that for sure, but I'm guessing that's why she was killed." After a pause she asks, "Just how well did you know Terri Summers?"

"She and Jo were close. I think they went to school or college together. She'd babysit Oliver if Ruby or I couldn't."

Madison's surprised, but that explains why Douglas wanted to talk to her. He was checking whether Jo ever confided in her friend. It's not unreasonable to assume they would have discussed what Jo was thinking after Ruby and Oliver's disappearance—who she suspected had taken them. Maybe Jo named someone. Madison wishes she'd asked Nate more about his investigation, because she feels ill-prepared with this cold case.

She only knows what Matt and Vince have told her. Before being injured, Nate had been planning to speak to Jo again, to ask why she quit working for Angie.

Madison has never heard Jo's version of events from the day Ruby and Oliver vanished. For all she knows, Jo might see things a little differently than her ex-husband and father-in-law.

The door to the room opens and a nurse stops in her tracks when she sees them all. Her eyes go to Brody and she puts her hands on her hips. "What on earth is that dog doing in here? He needs to go."

Vince stands up. "I'll take him." He grabs Brody's leash but the dog is reluctant to leave Nate's side. "Come on boy, let's get your paws taken care of."

"Before you go," says Madison, "could you text me Jo's cell number? I need to speak to her."

He does it right away then slips his phone back into his pocket. "Keep me informed. Meanwhile, I'll track Matt down so he can clear up where he's been."

She feels for him. He has a look on his face that suggests he has his own doubts about Matt. It makes her wonder whether Matt could have been having an affair with Terri. Perhaps Ruby found out and threatened to tell Jo? Is that enough motive for murder though? And what about Oliver? Surely Matt wouldn't kill his own son. Unless Oliver was a witness to any of it, like Angie suggested. After all, it's impossible to stop a child from talking.

She watches Vince leave and then asks the nurse when Nate might wake up.

"It's hard to say," says the nurse. "The doctor wants the swelling to go down before he reduces the meds. He'll be taken for another scan later today." She pauses. "I take it you're his wife and this is your kid?"

Madison glances at Owen, who offers an innocent smile. He might be able to get away with lying, but she can't. "Nate's a close friend of ours. I'm a detective and I'm investigating how he sustained his injuries."

The nurse raises an eyebrow at Owen.

"I'll organize getting an officer stationed at his door as I believe there's a risk to his life," says Madison. "Would you alert the hospital's security team to be on the lookout for any suspicious behavior near this room?" She pauses, wondering whether she's justified in asking them to be especially alert for Matt. She decides it can't do any harm. "I'm particularly concerned about a man in his mid-thirties, about six feet tall, with short brown hair. His name's Matt Rader."

"Of course." The nurse looks afraid but she writes it all down. "I'll tell them right away."

"Thank you. Owen, you stay here with him and let me know the minute he wakes up." She gives him a brief hug. She's not worried about his safety as she'll assign Shelley to the door. Shelley can be trusted to remain vigilant.

As she leaves the hospital to walk to her car, she spots news vans turning up. They will be hoping to get an update on Nate's condition. She slips past them before they see her. She doesn't have time for them right now. She needs to speak to Joanne Rader.

CHAPTER FORTY-TWO

Shaking off the cold, Madison sits in her car in the hospital's parking lot and makes some calls, one of which is to Shelley. She asks her to get to the hospital, and when her shift ends, to arrange for another officer to replace her outside Nate's room. Next, she needs to call Joanne Rader. She has her back to the news vans, so they haven't spotted her. It's pitch black now that it's early evening, so she's somewhat inconspicuous.

A woman answers the phone. "Hello?"

"Hi, my name's Detective Madison Harper from Lost Creek PD. Am I speaking to Joanne Rader?" There's a brief delay as the woman hesitates and Madison realizes she might think they've found Oliver, so she adds, "I'm not calling with any new information. I have some questions for you."

"My last name's Letts now. I've remarried." There's a long sigh. "What can I help you with?"

This woman is obviously low on patience when it comes to talking to cops, and who can blame her? The last detective she dealt with couldn't find her son. "Unfortunately, I have to tell you that Nate Monroe, the PI who was looking for your son, has been badly injured. It means I'm taking over the case for now."

With a softer tone, Jo says, "That's horrible, I'm sorry. Is he going to be okay?"

"I think so." She clears her throat. "I just need a few minutes of your time. Is now good?"

"I guess. I've just got in from work and I have the house to myself for a few minutes."

"Great. I'd like to start by asking you about the time you spent working with Angie McCoy, but before you say anything I need to disclose that Angie is my older sister." Jo remains silent so Madison continues. "You don't need to hold back on the truth to spare me. You see, it's safe to say my sister and I don't share the same values and if there's anything else she needs arresting for, I won't hesitate to do it."

"Still, it puts me in an awkward position," says Jo. There's a pause. "I remember your arrest. It was the year before Oliver and Ruby went missing. I'd just started working for Angie when you were convicted. I was at her house when we watched the guilty verdict announced live on the news. I thought you were going to pass out, you looked so shocked."

Madison tenses. She doesn't need reminding of that time but she's interested to hear what things were like in Angie's household when the news came through. "I imagine that was a good day for Angie and Wyatt?"

"They were ecstatic," says Jo. "It made me wonder whether Angie had anything to do with it. Like, whether you were framed. But I was new there, so I didn't know them that well. I assumed there was some bad blood between you that made her react that way. I mean, holding a party to celebrate your sister being incarcerated? That didn't sit right with me. I think I knew then that I wouldn't last long working for that pair."

It should probably hurt Madison to know that her sister went out of her way to celebrate her conviction, but it's unsurprising. When the time comes—once the trial date is set and Madison's called as a witness for the prosecution—she will make sure Angie stays locked up for as long as possible. "What were you hired for?" she asks.

"I was in charge of some of their accounts," says Jo. "Not for their fundraising antics though. I got the sense they didn't want me looking at those books and that was fine with me."

Of course they didn't, because the fundraising was just a front for all kinds of scams. "Why did you decide to stop working for her in the end?"

"I felt unsafe at that property. Their staff were gun-toting maniacs if you asked me. I mean, to be fair, I carry a weapon too, but—"

Madison cuts her off. "You do?"

"Sure. My dad was a hunter and he'd take me out with him when I was growing up. And when my best friend in high school was sexually assaulted, he bought me my first pistol. Told me to shoot any asshole who dared to touch me."

Madison almost smiles. He sounds a little like her own dad when she was growing up. "If you're comfortable around firearms, why would the fact that Angie's employees carried them make you want to quit your job?"

"Because the guys the McCoys hired weren't packing weapons for the same reason I was. They were bad people, Detective, as I'm sure you know, considering you're her sister and all."

Madison nods. "And Angie just let you go? There weren't any parting words or bad feelings?" She knows her sister. Angie expects loyalty from her employees. Loyalty and silence.

Jo sighs. "She wasn't happy about it, no, but by then I'd seen things that she wouldn't want me disclosing to anyone. She knew it was better not to upset me. She paid me for the whole month and told me I was welcome back whenever I needed work."

That's interesting. Angie must have wanted to keep her on

side. "You don't think she could have hurt your son in retaliation for quitting?"

Jo's response is immediate. "There's no way. She loved Oliver. She wanted kids of her own and doted on my son. She was happy for me to bring him to work anytime I couldn't get a sitter. At first I took her up on it."

Madison knows Angie can't have kids of her own for whatever reason and she's inclined to agree that her sister wouldn't harm a child. But there's that niggling doubt in the back of her head that tells her anything is possible with that woman.

"I know you've been in my position," says Jo. "I know you went years without seeing your son. How did you cope?"

Madison takes a deep breath. She wasn't prepared for that question. "When I was first incarcerated, I was told child protective services would find him a foster family just for the duration of my sentence, but that's not what happened and all contact from their end stopped soon after." The social worker responsible eventually paid with her job. Madison saw to that. "For years no one would tell me where he was. I didn't know whether I'd ever see him again." She realizes she could be upsetting Jo. "I'm sorry, it doesn't even compare to your situation."

"It does, actually. For those years that you didn't know where he was, that's what I'm going through every day."

But Madison knew someone was taking care of her son. She just didn't know who. Not until she teamed up with Nate to find him. Jo doesn't even know whether her son is alive. It's not comparable. "I want to find him for you," she says. "I'm going to try my hardest. You deserve answers."

Jo is silent—until: "I'm afraid of those answers now. I sometimes think it's better not to know. That's why I'm reluctant when anyone talks about reopening the case. I wouldn't be surprised if Matt is too. It simply hurts too much, you know?"

The sadness in her voice is hard to listen to. Madison changes the subject. "Am I right in thinking you and your husband were friends with Terri Summers while you lived here?"

"Terri? Sure, we went to high school together and remained friends for years. Why?"

Her stomach dives. Jo obviously hasn't heard the news. She would have thought Matt would have been in touch to tell her something like that. The fact he didn't could suggest their split was more acrimonious than he made out. "I'm really sorry, but Terri's dead. She was murdered a few days ago."

"Oh my God." There's a long silence. "Why? Who would do that to her?"

"That's what I'm trying to find out. When were you last in touch with her?"

There's a rustling sound of what could be a pack of tissues being opened, and then Jo says, "I haven't seen Terri since I left Lost Creek five years ago. We stayed in touch through Facebook for a while but eventually drifted apart like the rest of our high school friends. You know what's it like; you stop having anything in common with them as you grow older."

That's true. The only person Madison's still in touch with from high school is Kate Flynn. But they share a professional interest in catching criminals, so they never run out of things to talk about. They just don't get much opportunity to do it.

Jo starts crying down the line. "I can't believe she's dead. How did it happen?"

There's no way of breaking it to her gently. "She was shot at her home. It appears to be senseless, but can you think of anyone who might have wanted her dead? Anyone who had a grudge against her?"

"No, not at all. You don't understand what she was like, Detective. She was warm and had the best sense of humor. She didn't stick her nose into other people's business. She was basically the girl everyone wanted to be, and that's even before we talk about how beautiful she was."

That's pretty much what everyone else has said about Terri. "I do know that she was talking to my detective partner about your family right before she died."

Jo gasps. "Wait, what? I don't understand."

"I assume you remember Detective Don Douglas?"

"Of course." Her tone hardens. "I'll never forget him as long as I live."

Madison tenses. "I know Matt and Vince weren't happy with his investigation into your son and mother-in-law's disappearance and think he could've handled it differently. I take it you weren't happy either?"

"Well, he didn't find them, did he?"

Madison takes a deep breath. She could try to defend Douglas yet again but she doesn't have time for that, so she lets the comment slide. "He's been murdered too."

Jo's shocked into silence.

"He was working on your son's case again," says Madison. "I've recently discovered that he had been visiting with Terri in the week or two before her death but I don't know why, other than the fact it was about your family. So I need to ask; why would Detective Douglas believe Terri knew anything about what happened to Ruby and Oliver?"

"What the hell is going on in that godforsaken town?" Jo mutters tearfully.

"Did you ever have a suspect in mind for their disappearance and let Terri know what you were thinking?"

"I... I told the PI recently that I had fleeting doubts about Matt. But I don't have any proof."

Madison raises her eyebrows. Could it really have been Matt Rader all along? "So why do you suspect him if there's no proof?"

"When there's a severe lack of other suspects, you start looking at those around you more closely. He was on a break from work at the time they vanished, between appointments.

He'd supposedly stopped for something to eat, alone in his car. I just thought it was odd, and although his phone pinged off a tower near where he said he was, I've since wondered whether he purposefully left it there to give him an alibi. I've gone over it a thousand times in my head."

"There were no eye-witnesses who saw his car parked by the side of the road?"

"Not that the detectives told me, but they didn't tell me much. They treated us all with suspicion. I felt like a criminal."

It's sad that she felt that way. Some cops can be guilty of heavy-handedness with the victim's families in order to put pressure on them to reveal secrets, or to give up the perpetrators. It's a tactic that sometimes pays off but more often than not alienates the families. It's not something Madison would consider doing to anyone. "Is that why you divorced Matt? Because you suspected him?"

"Partly. Losing Oliver broke what we had. It turned into the only thing we had left in common. I had to get away from it all for my own sanity."

"Did you tell Terri you suspected Matt?"

Jo sighs down the line. "I don't remember specifically, but it's highly likely. We shared everything with each other. I'm sure I would've wanted to get her opinion on the thoughts I was having because she knew Matt too, and it's not like I could've talked to anyone else about it. Things like that soon become rumors that turn into facts when they're repeated by the wrong people. I didn't want the whole town treating him like a criminal when I had no proof. Maybe Terri came forward recently and told Detective Douglas what I said. She would've wanted to do whatever she felt was right. That's the kind of person she was."

"Wouldn't she have done that sooner though?"

"No. We were loyal to each other. She was more like my

sister. But I guess now that we're not so close, it could've been eating away at her."

Madison wonders if Matt found out they were talking about him behind his back. Perhaps he wanted Terri dead before she could tell Douglas. "Did Matt stay in touch with Terri too? After you both left town?"

"I have no idea. If he did, he didn't tell me."

Madison thinks he could have. Terri could have told him Douglas was sniffing around again, all these years later. "What about now? Do you still believe Matt's capable of murder? Because I have a dead woman, a dead detective and an injured PI on my hands, and it all happened around the time Matt returned to Lost Creek."

"Oh my God," Jo whispers. "I don't know. I really don't want to believe he hurt any of them, least of all his own mother and child." She breaks into a sob before trying to regain control. "I mean, what would that make me? I'd be a monster for marrying someone like that and subjecting our child to him."

Madison's heart goes out to her. This is a lot of loss for one person to go through, and the possibility that it was perpetrated by the man she married? That's going to be impossible to process. But something's bothering her. "If you genuinely suspected Matt was involved, why didn't you tell Detective Bowers or Douglas at the time?"

"For all the reasons I just mentioned; I had no proof. This was the man I was married to, Detective. How could I accuse him of something so heinous with no proof and just a gut feeling, and during our son's disappearance? What if I was wrong? Besides, Detective Bowers left most of the work to Douglas and I didn't trust him to handle it delicately. I thought he'd go in heavy-handed and arrest Matt immediately without doing any groundwork first." She pauses. "I'd seen Vince treated terribly by a small minority of the community, Detective. They painted *child killer* on his windows and slit his car tires. And he wasn't even arrested for anything; he was just named a person of interest. I couldn't risk that happening to Matt too. He was grieving." She breaks down again.

Madison shakes her head at the whole sorry mess. This needs to be solved once and for all. It's gone on long enough. If there was any physical proof, he would have been arrested a long time ago. So there's only one way to find out whether Matt was involved and that's by formally questioning him at the station. "I'm sorry to upset you. I can't imagine what it's like living through this. If you think of anything useful, get in touch with me immediately, no matter what time of day it is."

"Wait!" says Jo. "Are you going to arrest Matt?"

Madison hesitates. "I'm going to bring him in for questioning and take it from there. I'll try to keep you updated." She ends the call and exhales loudly. It's going to be a long night.

CHAPTER FORTY-THREE

Nate becomes aware of an all-consuming sharp, searing pain and at first, he can't even tell where it's coming from. As his confusion begins to subside, he realizes it's emanating from the back of his head, which he appears to be resting on but he's not one hundred percent certain. He desperately tries to remember what happened to cause it but draws a blank.

His eyes flicker open but the bright fluorescent light positioned above him makes them close again. "Jeez," he croaks. He tries to swallow and feels a thick layer of something coating his tongue. As he's injured his head, he's guessing it's blood. He moves his tongue around his mouth and winces. He's bitten it. And it hurts like a bitch.

He tries opening his eyes again, slower this time. He's staring at a white ceiling. He has a terrifying moment where he wonders if he's back in prison, but he can hear the beep of a heart rate monitor next to him. The steady beat quickens as he lifts his sore head and carefully looks around. He's in a hospital room, and he's alone.

He rests his head back and swallows again, the metallic taste making him grimace. He doesn't know what brought him here or why there's no one checking on him, and it makes him panic. The beeping quickens even more and he tries hard to remember what he was doing today. The window to the left of him shows the sun has set, but he couldn't say how late in the day it is. He wonders then whether this is even the same day as he thinks it is. His last memory is of visiting Angie at the prison. But that's it. He doesn't know whether Madison was with him when he was injured. His fists clench with worry. What if she's in here too? And where's Brody?

The door to his room opens less than halfway and he lifts his head, ignoring the pain in his neck. No one steps inside the room. They're talking to someone outside. A woman's voice drifts over but he doesn't think it's Madison.

"Hello?" he says, but it comes out as a barely audible whisper. He goes dizzy and lies back again, overcome with nausea. He worries he might choke on his own vomit if he can't turn onto his side quick enough, but he's drained of all energy.

Suddenly he gets a flashback: Brody by the side of the road, relieving himself while Nate checked his phone for messages. He heard a car's engine getting louder, menacing. Then the shrill skid of tires on the road. He turned around to see what was causing it and he reacted by moving as far out of its way as he could in the time he had.

"Shit." He was involved in a car accident. No wonder his head hurts so bad. The driver must have lost control. Oh, God. Did they hit Brody too?

Feeling like he's slipping into unconsciousness, he desperately tries to remember what he saw when he looked at the car. Relief swamps him as he remembers not only the color of the car, but also the driver's outline.

He tries to swallow as he hears Owen's voice outside his room. Nate knows he needs to tell someone what he saw. He needs to see Madison. But his whole body goes limp as he succumbs to exhaustion.

CHAPTER FORTY-FOUR

"Put out a BOLO for Matt Rader," says Madison to dispatch. "He drives a white Toyota Corolla but I don't have the license number. I want to question him asap. He's staying at Ruby's Diner but his dad doesn't know his current location, so he could have absconded already."

"Doing it now, Detective," says Dina Blake, the new dispatcher who took over the graveyard shift when Stella moved to days.

"Thanks. Is Sergeant Tanner at the station?"

"He is."

"Patch me through to him, would you?"

"Sure."

Madison tries to peer into the darkness to see if the news crews are recording yet. It looks like they're setting up their shots and assembling bright lights outside the hospital's entrance. She shakes her head, willing to bet they're hoping Nate dies from his injuries so they get juicer headlines for the evening bulletin. Then she thinks of Kate and feels guilty. Not all reporters are bloodthirsty. She's just in a bad mood because she has so much to do when all she wants to do is go to Nate's bedside and make sure he gets the best treatment possible.

Steve answers his phone on the second ring. "Hey, how's it going? Is Monroe okay?"

She takes a deep breath. "His injuries don't appear to be life-threatening but he's still unconscious. Do we have the driver yet?"

"Not yet. The ones we've questioned said he was already down by the time they passed him. It's possible we're out of luck and no one witnessed it."

She rolls her eyes. "Okay. So I need to ask a favor and you're not going to like it."

"Try me."

She smiles. Having a supportive team around her makes all the difference. She just wishes she still had Douglas as a partner. The thought of Officer Goodwin getting promoted into his position makes her feel sick because she doesn't believe she could ever trust him to have her back. "The disappearance of Ruby and Oliver Rader; I'm reopening the case. I have no choice now Nate's been mowed down and there's a link between Douglas, Terri Summers and the Raders. Did Chief Mendes fill you in on that?"

"She did. And I know what you're going to ask. I'm already on it. The case files Douglas and Bowers put together at the time of the disappearance are in front of me as we speak."

She leans her head back against the rest, relieved. "Perfect. Focus on the witness statements. I need to know if there were any leads that weren't followed, any evidence that wasn't processed or any suspects we don't know about."

"Sure thing. What are you doing next?" he asks.

"I'm going to bring Matt Rader in for questioning. His ex-wife thinks he might have been involved."

"Holy crap. Vince won't like that."

"I can't worry about that right now. Matt isn't answering his phone, so he could've left town already. Dina's issuing a BOLO."

"I'll update the chief. Be careful, Madison. If that guy's capable of murdering his own mother and son, *and* Detective Douglas, he's capable of killing you too."

Her chest tightens. "I'll call for backup if he won't come quietly. There's still a good chance this wasn't him. We need proof, and hopefully the old case files will have something we can use to get it."

"I'll let you know what I find," he says.

"Thanks. Do you know if the DNA results from the wine-glass have come back yet? Alex was sending off swabs from the rim, hoping for a saliva sample."

"Not that I know. I'll check in with him and get back to you. I've been watching the CCTV footage from the route leading to Terri's house but I haven't found anything significant yet." He sighs. "Whoever did all this was good at covering their tracks."

Madison agrees. It suggests the perp is someone who has experience. He could've killed before. It could be worth looking at any other cold cases from around that time to see if there's a link. Her stomach flutters with the thought they could have a serial killer on their hands. It's too soon to assume that because she doesn't yet have proof that any of these crimes are related. All she needs is that *one thing* the killer forgot to do. It could be a fingerprint left on a door handle, or some evidence they didn't discard such as Terri's purse or cell phone, any of Ruby's belongings. Or a witness who knows more than they initially admitted. "I've got to go."

"Sure," says Steve. "Just be careful. He's not going to like being brought in."

Which is why she isn't going in guns blazing and she won't be arresting him. She just wants to talk at the station to see if he suddenly becomes more helpful. The more he talks, the more likely he'll slip up and incriminate himself.

Slipping her phone into her pocket she starts the car's engine but before she can pull away her phone buzzes with a message. It's Vince.

Matt's here. Just got back. But if you're planning on arresting him at least have the decency to let him come out to you. Don't do this in here.

He's at the diner. Madison knows this is hard on Vince, so she's glad he's doing the right thing by disclosing his son's location. She shoots him a reply.

No arrest planned, just questioning at the station. On my way. Will wait in parking lot.

Her adrenaline kicks in as she races away from the hospital.

Madison sits in the dark and scans the diner's parking lot for Matt's Toyota. It's over in the corner. If he was the person who injured Nate, there would be something on the hood or fender of his car. Some damage or blood spatter. Making a split-second decision she jumps out of her car and cautiously approaches his. She checks no one is watching her as she lights up the hood of his car with her phone's flashlight.

There are some scratches on the fender and a lot of dirt, but no visible damage. She snaps some quick photographs with her phone and then quickly returns to her car where she stands, waiting. She's not expecting any trouble, not here in full view of the diner's customers. She'd like to think that Matt wouldn't do that to his dad, but then again, she's about to question him for the murder of his mother and son, so who knows? She sends a text message.

I'm here.

Vince replies immediately.

On our way.

She watches as Matt reluctantly leaves the diner and approaches her car with his father behind him. She didn't know Vince would come to see them off and prepares herself for an earful.

Standing opposite her, Matt crosses his arms defensively. "What now? I've told you everything you wanted to know."

"I just have some more questions. You're not under arrest but I would prefer to do this at the station. Mainly for that reason." She nods to the diner, where everyone seated next to the window is now watching them.

Matt shakes his head angrily and looks away. "I should never have come back to this goddam town."

"Can I join him?" asks Vince. "I'll keep my mouth shut."

Madison takes a deep breath. "I'm sorry, but I have to question him alone."

Matt looks anxious, as though he thinks he'll be arrested the minute he steps foot inside the police station. It's a possibility, depending on what he tells her. "It's fine, Dad. You go back to your friends. You can give them all the juicy gossip on your podcast later."

The comment hurts Vince. Madison can see it in his eyes. Matt's lumping his father in with the local community. The same community that failed to give up whoever took his mother and son. It's unfair and it does nothing to improve Madison's opinion of him.

"In that case," says Vince, "I'll head back to the hospital with Brody. He's restless. He knows something's wrong with

Nate." To Madison he says, "I'll let your boy head home for the night."

She doesn't know if Owen will want to leave but at least he'll have Vince for company if not. "Are you sure you don't mind?" she asks.

"Nate's in there because he was trying to help us. It's the least I can do. Guess I'll have to pretend Brody's a therapy dog or something, like Owen suggested, in order to get him past the nurses again."

As Vince turns and re-enters the diner, Matt's about to slip into the passenger seat of Madison's car, so she stops him. "Wait. I need to check you for weapons."

He raises his eyebrows. "I thought I was just being questioned."

"You are. It's precautionary. I don't want to be ambushed on the drive over there."

Matt shakes his head as she pats him down. "I can't get out of this town fast enough."

She stands up. "Well, that sure won't be tonight."

CHAPTER FORTY-FIVE

The evening advances too quickly for Madison. It's already seven-thirty by the time she arrives at the station with Matt Rader. They pass Officer Goodwin on his way out. Goodwin nods at both of them but gets no response from Matt, just a hostile stare.

"You ready?" she asks.

He turns back to her. "As ready as I can be when I'm being questioned for murder."

She ignores the attitude and gets him seated in a cold interview room. The light above them is harsh and the seats uncomfortable. It's not exactly conducive to a friendly chat, but they don't have much space at the station and she can't bring herself to put him in the more comfortable room reserved for victims and their families. Not if he really is capable of what his ex-wife suspects. "I'll be back shortly." She leaves to check in with Steve. It looks like Chief Mendes has left for the day as her office is in darkness.

She shows Steve a photograph of Matt's car. "I don't see any damage, do you?"

He looks closely and Alex joins them as he slips his jacket

on, ready to head home. Taking the phone off Steve, Alex zooms into the photograph. "Nothing to the visible eye but that doesn't mean there's nothing on there," he says. "Have you brought the car in? Because I'm more than happy to inspect it now."

She smiles at him. "Thanks, but it's not here. The owner's not under arrest and I have no warrant."

Alex hands the phone back to her. "Well, I have no plans for tonight, so if you need me to come back to the station, just say the word."

"I will, thanks."

"Goodnight." He leaves.

"Want me in on the interview?" asks Steve.

She wonders how long he's been at work today already. His desk is covered in dirty coffee mugs and food wrappers. He's been here for a while. "No, I'll be fine. Have you found anything in the old case files?"

He shakes his head. "No, Douglas was pretty thorough and methodical. We could repeat everything he did to locate Ruby and Oliver, but there are no obvious leads. I found Ruby's call logs from her cell provider but they don't show anything out of the ordinary leading up to the day of her disappearance. It looks like she spoke to the same people all the time, mainly her family. She made a few more calls than usual to an elderly friend, but in one of Vince's statements, when Douglas questioned him about it, Vince said the friend wasn't well and had no family to take care of her, so Ruby would check in on her and help with anything she needed." He sighs. "I've got a lot more to read through yet. I'm hopeful Douglas might've missed something."

"Okay. I'll come find you when I'm done with Matt." She walks back to the interview room. This is her chance to get Matt Rader to slip up or confess, and she's feeling the pressure. She hasn't had time to prepare questions, so she's going to have to wing it before he either lawyers up or skips town. She takes a seat opposite him and studies his face.

"Get on with it," he says, resigned. "I don't want to be here all night."

She leans forward. "Where were you today between 1 and 2 p.m.?"

He frowns before understanding why she's asking him. "You think I tried to kill your PI friend?"

"Where were you?" she repeats. "You weren't answering your phone and your dad didn't know where you'd gone."

He sits back and shakes his head. "You're just like Douglas. You want to pin everything on me or my dad, regardless of the truth." There's that animosity for Douglas again. Did he hate him enough to kill him? They'll get to that later.

"You still haven't answered my question."

He rolls his eyes. "I was visiting a friend. Ted Hardman, he lives on Malcolm Street. We used to work together and I was bored, so he said to drop by. Want his number?"

She nods, then writes it down as he relays it. It's possible he got himself an alibi by asking an old friend to cover for him, but she'll follow it up regardless. "What date did you return to Lost Creek?"

"On Thursday—Thanksgiving. I went straight to my dad's diner."

Terri and Douglas were killed the night before. "How did you travel here?"

He sighs. "I drove. Took me ten hours from Nebraska, with stops."

She knows that he and Jo moved to Nebraska when they left Lost Creek five years ago. Jo wanted to be nearer her mom and it was before Patricia moved to California and the couple decided to split up. "When did you set off?"

"About four on Thursday morning. I wanted to avoid rush-hour traffic. I arrived at the diner at around two that afternoon, I think."

The timeline is so close that it's possible he could have

arrived hours earlier, on Wednesday evening, killed Terri and Douglas, covered his tracks and then waited it out before making his grand entrance at the diner around 2 p.m. on Thursday. "Can anyone corroborate what time you left your home in Nebraska?"

He shrugs. "I live alone."

That's fine. She can try to get surveillance footage and phone location data if she has to. "Do you know where Detective Douglas lived at the time of his death?"

He frowns again. "I didn't even know where he lived when I was a local, so how would I know where he was living when he killed himself? Besides, what's that got to do with anything?"

Madison hasn't released information to the press yet about Douglas's death being murder, not suicide. She wants to stay one step ahead of his killer in that regard. Matt either still believes it was suicide or he's a good actor. "So if I get your cell provider to pull the location data from your phone, it won't show you as having been near Douglas's home the night before Thanksgiving? You know, when you were supposedly still in Nebraska."

He shakes his head in frustration. "I thought you wanted to question me about my missing family members, not about your partner's suicide. What's going on here?"

She changes the subject. "You were friends with Terri Summers, right?"

"She was Jo's friend really."

"But she visited your home and spent time with you both? Even babysat for Oliver on occasion."

"Right."

"Did you stay in touch with her after you and Jo split up?"

"Why would I? I didn't stay in touch with her at all once we left town. I think Jo did for a while, but I'm not certain." His face clouds over as he realizes where this line of questioning is going. "You think *I* killed Terri?"

She sits back and drops her pen. "Did you?"

He stands up, noisily pushing his chair back with his thighs. "This is ridiculous! I want a lawyer."

Madison sighs. If he lawyers up, it will make things much harder for her. "Sit down. If you weren't involved in her death then you have nothing to hide, right?"

"That's not how the police work though, is it?" he says, crossing his arms.

"Listen," she says, softening her tone. "I just have a few more questions, then you're free to go. I'm not trying to ambush you, Matt. I'm trying to rule you out as a person of interest. If you lawyer up now, you're making yourself look guilty and not just to me. Do you want the media on your back again? Do you want your dad to have to go through the humiliation of washing obscenities from his windows?"

He considers it. Eventually he sits back down but it's clear he's not happy. "I don't even own a gun, so how could I have shot Terri? And why would I? She never did anything to me. Like I said, I haven't spoken to her in years."

Owning a gun isn't a problem because the killer used Troy's in a bid to frame him for it. Madison can't judge whether Matt's telling the truth. "Are you willing to let us look at your cell phone? Access your social media?"

His face turns red with anger. "If you get a warrant."

She knows she doesn't have enough to get a judge to sign a warrant at this stage. It's time to disclose what his ex-wife suspects. "I've spoken to Jo."

He doesn't look surprised. "Is she okay?"

"She's fine. Upset that we're raking up old ground again but she understands why it's worth doing." She hesitates. "I asked her what she thinks happened back then."

His jaw clenches.

"She has some concerns about your alibi for the window of opportunity—the time they disappeared."

He rests an elbow on the table while rubbing his forehead. He's visibly shaken. Is he about to confess? Or is it disappointment that the mother of his missing child could think so poorly of him.

She gives him a minute before asking, "I understand you were between appointments for some of that time. You parked by the side of the road, to take a break."

He leans back, his face pale. "I had something to eat. I was there less than an hour, just killing time." He fixes his eyes on her. "Not people."

"Okay, but here's where I'm struggling. Why didn't you go to your parents' diner for something to eat? Why park by the side of the road?"

He shrugs wearily. "I spent most of my spare time in that place. Sometimes it's nice to have time to yourself. I don't know, it was a spur-of-the-moment decision. If I knew something that stupid would lead to my wife suspecting me of murder, I would've gone to the goddam diner and put on a show for people just to make sure I had a credible alibi. But I had no idea my wife had doubts about me. I had no idea my son was being abducted." His voice breaks.

Madison feels for him. She's starting to believe he wasn't involved, but she still wants to collect his DNA in case it matches whatever Alex managed to get from the wineglass. "I'd like to take a saliva sample from you. Would that be okay or do I need to obtain a warrant?"

He swallows hard. "You still think it was me?"

"I want to be able to rule you out. Having your DNA on record to match against any evidence we find will help me do that as fast as possible." This is a real test of his guilt. If he abducted Ruby and Oliver, or if he killed Terri or Douglas, he won't want anyone taking his DNA, no matter how careful he believes he was. Not unless he's planning on killing himself when he leaves here, to avoid jail time. He wouldn't be the first perp who gave up at the last hurdle. Some killers won't entertain the thought of being incarcerated, preferring to go out before it reaches that stage.

He lowers his eyes and nods. "I have nothing to hide. And if this proves it to Jo and to the rest of you, then do it. You can look through my phone too. I just want this to end."

She surprised. She assumed he'd lawyer up. But it gives her no pleasure that he's agreed. Instead, she feels as though she's kicking a man when he's already down.

CHAPTER FORTY-SIX

It's late, and as Madison drives home through the fog, she's exhausted and thinking of the long, hot bath she's planning to take. She just needs one uninterrupted hour of downtime to pull her thoughts together.

Matt's DNA is ready for Alex to process in the morning and she found nothing during a search of his phone. If she thought he was hiding something, she would have Alex forensically analyze it, but there were no messages to or from Terri Summers, and nothing in his other messages to suggest he was planning on hurting anyone. It's possible he has a burner phone, but she doesn't think so.

She tries to mentally switch off from work or she'll never get any rest. Owen sent her a text to say he's on his way home from the hospital where Vince is watching Nate. Apparently, there's been no change in Nate's condition. She doesn't know whether that's a good thing or not but the minute he wakes up she intends to head straight to the hospital to check on him and see if he remembers anything about the driver who ran him down.

When she pulls onto her street and approaches her house,

she sees a car parked in the driveway. A black SUV. "Great," she mumbles. "What now?" If it was someone come to hurt her, they wouldn't be parked on her drive for all to see. At least, that's what she has to hope.

Parking behind the SUV, she switches the engine off and gets out, one hand at her holster. The other car is in darkness, but when the driver opens the door, the internal light comes on. An older man slowly gets out. Madison stops where she is. The man leaves the door open and takes a couple of steps toward her. "Hey, Maddie," he says.

Madison gasps, her hand dropping from her holster. There's only one person in the world who gets to call her Maddie. "Dad?" Thanks to the light from his car, she can tell he looks a lot older now, too soft around the edges. And his thick hair is almost completely gray, with no hint of brown anymore. Didn't he used to be taller, too?

He walks right up to her, squinting to get a good look. "When did you get to be so old?"

She laughs, but it unexpectedly turns into a sob the minute he embraces her.

"Calm down, I was just kidding," he says into her hair. "You look beautiful. Just like your mother at your age."

His arms are still strong around her, just like when he hugged her that last time before leaving the family for good. She was only fourteen when he left her mom for another woman. She remembers as if it were yesterday. There was no messy ending. Being in law enforcement all his life he was always a tough guy, but he did shed a tear as he said goodbye to them all. Their mom was sad her marriage was ending but she always maintained it was better to end things amicably than to force someone to stay who didn't want to be there anymore. Madison had cried herself to sleep that night. Angie was newly married to Wyatt McCoy and on the path that would eventually lead her to prison. Madison's path to prison was a little different and not a result of anything she did.

She isn't sure whether her dad knows anything about what she and Angie have been through since he left. She stayed in touch with him as a teenager, with phone calls that mostly consisted of talking about what she was up to. They became fewer and further between as she entered adulthood, until eventually they dried up altogether. She missed him most when she was arrested. It was just pride and embarrassment that stopped her from trying to track him down and asking him to come rescue her.

"I'm sorry!" She pulls away and wipes her eyes. "I don't know where that came from. It's just a relief to have you here. Someone from my family, you know?"

He's still holding her arms but he has a look of confusion on his face. "I know your mom passed but what about your sister? Don't you two stay in touch?"

Madison grimaces. "I saw her earlier today, but she's... you know."

"She's what?"

It becomes clear her dad hasn't kept track of them at all. He has no idea his oldest daughter is in prison. He has no idea what Angie did to her. What Angie's husband did to her. Madison doesn't even know where to start. "Never mind. It's a long story. I'll fill you in later. Come inside, it's freezing out here."

He squeezes her shoulders as they walk side by side up her porch steps. "I've left the FBI now. I officially retired as a special agent at fifty-seven, but I stayed on as a consultant for a particular case."

She raises her eyebrows. "So that's why you came; you're bored."

He laughs and looks up at the house. "This is a nice place you've got yourself. You're married, I take it?"

Madison scoffs. "No, Dad. I don't need a husband to pay my way. This isn't the fifties."

"Oh, God," he says. "I forgot you're a millennial. I'm going to have to watch what I say, aren't I?" She looks at him to see if he's joking. A cheeky wink tells her he is. "I'm just busting your balls."

She laughs as she lets him into the house, thinking how easy it is to slip back into their roles from her childhood. He removes his coat and has a look around while she hangs it up. It feels so natural to have him here, despite not seeing him for over twenty years. She's overcome with gratitude that Owen tracked him down because she would never have found the time, or the courage. She just wishes they hadn't wasted so many years apart. Suddenly the kitten appears from upstairs. Bandit races down the stairs while vocalizing how hungry he is. He stops when he sees Bill.

Bill leans down and scoops him up. "Hey, little one."

Bandit immediately starts purring and flops against his chest. "So how do you afford this place on your own?" Bill asks as he follows her into the kitchen.

She prepares coffee. "It was left to me by someone who passed away."

His mouth drops open. "You lost a husband?"

Turning to face him, she hesitates. He doesn't know she's bisexual. He left too early on in her life to know. Hell, she didn't even know back then. Not really. It was a confusing time. "No. I lost an ex-girlfriend."

He raises his eyebrows.

"She was raped and murdered in the living room." That would shock anyone else but she knows her dad has attended more crime scenes than she has. Does she tell him who arranged for that to happen? No. He's not ready to hear that yet. One step at a time.

"Holy crap, Madison. I'm sorry you had to go through that."

He gently places Bandit in front of his food bowl. It's half full and the kitten tucks in. "So you weren't in a relationship with her at the time?"

She shakes her head. "No, we separated before I went to prison. But she helped me raise Owen before that."

He puts his hands up to stop her. "Whoa!" He stares hard at her. "Before you *what*?"

He doesn't know. It makes her question why he didn't care enough to keep tabs on them from afar. Guilt maybe? At leaving them behind. Goosebumps break out on her arms. He might leave when he finds out what happened. He might disown her. After all, he was an FBI agent and if his old coworkers find out he has a daughter who spent time in prison they'll never let him forget it. But it's so good to have him here, she doesn't want to lose him again. She crosses her arms and takes a deep breath. "I spent six years in prison for the murder of a fellow police officer. I assumed you would have heard." The look on his face is hard to read and she waits with bated breath to hear how he's going to react.

He studies her face. "Who framed you and why?"

She closes her eyes against tears of relief. He hasn't seen her in years yet he doesn't even consider the possibility she was capable of doing that. If only he had been around at the time. He could have cared for Owen after her arrest.

He hugs her again. "Tell me they've been caught? Because if not, I'll hunt them down myself and you better believe they'll regret messing with my daughter."

She knows he'll be satisfied when she tells him the person has been caught, but it won't last long when he finds out who was responsible. "They're in prison awaiting trial, well, one of them is. The other one is dead."

"Good for you." He smiles widely. "I couldn't believe it when young Owen tracked me down and told me my daughter went into law enforcement. A detective! And at my old PD? I was impressed. But I'll be honest with you, Maddie. Part of me worried you were too soft to be a cop. You were such a kind child, always seeing the good in people. It made me think the perps would run rings around you, but not now! Not now I know you're capable of looking after yourself. I bet that was the most satisfying bullet you ever shot, am I right?"

Madison swallows. "I didn't kill him with a gun. It was a little more... messy than that."

"Even better!" He laughs. "What about their accomplice? What are their charges? I assume there's no way he'll ever get out?"

She slowly meets his eyes. "Dad, you don't understand." She swallows. "Their accomplice was Angie."

He looks aghast and is lost for words at first. Confusion spreads over his face. "What? Your sister framed you for murder?"

"Right. Angie doesn't like me much." She waves a dismissive hand. "It's a long story."

He's shaking his head, clearly shocked. "I can't believe she would do something like that. I mean, she always courted trouble but you don't go against family." He rubs his jaw. "So, she's in prison now too?"

Madison nods. Her father is realizing that both his daughters have done time.

"Will she get a conviction?"

"I hope so. She shouldn't be allowed her freedom. She's dangerous."

The disappointment on her dad's face is heartbreaking. "Is there any chance she can be redeemed?"

Madison considers it. "I mean, it's always worth a try, right? Maybe she'd soften if you were to visit her." Or maybe her sister would turn their father against her. Tell him a whole bunch of lies. She gets a tight feeling in her chest at the thought of it.

"Maybe wait until closer to her trial. She will have had more time to think about the things she's done."

He shakes his head. "I've missed so much."

She agrees. Hesitantly she asks, "Why is that? Why didn't you ever visit? I mean, did you ever try to keep tabs on us? Because it doesn't sound like it."

He leans against the counter, full of regret. "I was calling once a week at first, remember?"

She nods.

"But you seemed so bored by my calls. We didn't have much to tell each other, and Angie wouldn't even come to the phone." He smiles sadly. "That girl can sure hold a grudge."

She raises an eyebrow. "Tell me about it."

"I guess I thought you'd be better off if you moved on without me," he continues. "I assumed it wouldn't take long for your mom to remarry, so I thought you'd have a stepfather soon enough. As for keeping tabs on you, it was too difficult. Not just because we didn't have social media back then, but because it hurt to think about you and your sister without feeling guilty. I'm ashamed to say it was easier for me not to think about you. I'm sorry."

She swallows back the hurt. His honesty is brutal. "I could've done with your support when I was arrested. You could've taken care of Owen for me."

He steps forward and takes her hand in his. "Listen, I can't change what's happened, but I want to be a part of your family again now, if you'll have me. I'm retired. The time feels right to come home and make amends. I don't want to spend my retirement in Alaska. It's too damn cold." He chuckles. "But I won't move back if you don't want me here. This is just a short visit to see you and Owen. I can leave if you want me to."

She looks into his eyes and can tell he's being genuine. It would be weird having him live close again, but her heart is almost bursting at the thought that she'll finally have some family around her. "Of course I don't want you to leave."

He smiles. Madison pours some milk into their coffees and leads him to the living room. When her dad takes a seat, she hears the front door open so she goes to the hallway. Owen appears. "Hey, how's Nate doing?" she asks.

"No change. He's still unconscious. The doctor thinks he might have internal bleeding so he might have to go into surgery overnight."

She shudders at the thought. "Will she call us if that happens?"

"Vince will. He's planning on staying overnight. Lucky for us the doctor's a dog person and once she found out Brody used to be a police dog she was fine with him being there as long as he's on a leash and he doesn't get in anyone's way." After taking his coat off, he asks who the SUV out front belongs to.

"Come see." She walks into the living room.

Her dad sets his cup on the coffee table and stands up straight. His eyes go past her and a smile lights up his face. "Well, well, well. Owen Harper. My first grandchild."

Owen glances at her with a look of surprise. "He came?"

She nods. "He came."

She moves out of the way as her dad comes over to shake Owen's hand. There's a little awkwardness between them, but that's to be expected. Seeing them together makes her fill up with tears and she notices Owen's eyes redden with emotion. He's felt the gap where family should be just as keenly as her. Isn't that what led him to contact his grandfather in the first place?

Owen asks, "What do I call you? Because you catch serial killers for a living, so Grandpa doesn't really fit."

Bill laughs as Madison frowns. "Serial killers? Really?"

"How did you know that, son?" asks her dad.

"I did some research online and found a list of all the

psychos you've helped catch. Alaska sounds even more messed up than Lost Creek."

He nods. "Something about the terrain brings out the worst in people, I guess. But I went all around the country over the years, not just Alaska. The sons of bitches like to move about to evade capture. Doesn't always work." He thinks for a second. "How about you just call me Bill? I don't mind Grandpa but it ages me with the ladies, if you know what I mean." He winks.

Madison shakes her head with a smile on her face. "Oh, God. You're not after another wife, are you? What happened to the one you left Mom for?"

The smile is wiped off of Bill's face and he goes deadly serious. His reaction confuses her. Eventually he says, "That didn't work out."

"Are there any serial killers you never managed to catch?" asks Owen.

His face clouds over and it's clear to Madison that he has unfinished business. "Oh sure. One son of a bitch has been taunting me for years," says Bill. "I've come close to catching him in the past but it's up to someone else to catch the asshole now."

He tries to act blasé but Madison thinks the one who got away will haunt her father until his dying days. She'll ask him about it sometime, when they can really get into it, and when Owen isn't here. She takes a sip of coffee. "I bet that was difficult—retiring when you know he's still out there."

He turns away from them and acts dismissive. "I've wasted enough of my time on him," he says. "I'm ready to move on."

"Will you tell me all about him?" asks Owen. "And I mean the details that aren't available online. The ones that only you would know."

"Owen, he probably doesn't want to relive his greatest failure," she whispers.

Bill takes a seat and looks up at them both. "The things I

could tell you about that guy would stop you sleeping for months. You don't want details, trust me."

Owen grins. "Cool."

Madison's even more intrigued, but it will have to wait. Because right now there's a killer in *this* town who needs catching.

CHAPTER FORTY-SEVEN

The next morning Madison wakes early to make breakfast for Owen and her dad, but they're both dead to the world so she forgoes her morning run, choosing to head straight to the hospital to see Nate instead, even though Vince has texted to say there's no change in his condition. Halfway there she gets a call from Steve and answers it hands-free as she continues the journey. She's not surprised he's at work already, even though it not even seven-thirty yet. He tells her that George Ryan—Terri and Troy's neighbor—has called dispatch to report seeing what looks like a flashlight bobbing around in the house next door as if someone's looking for something.

Madison grips the steering wheel a little tighter. This could be Terri's killer. "How long ago?"

"About forty minutes," says Steve. "He waited to see if anyone came out, in case it was just Troy Randle collecting more belongings, but no one did, so he went over and knocked on the door."

Madison groans. "He could've got himself killed."

"I know, right?" says Steve. "No one answered the door and

the light went out so George went home, locked his doors and called us."

"I'm not far away, so I'll head straight there now."

"Officers Sanchez and Goodwin are already dispatched and should be there already. Keep me updated."

"Will do."

Madison makes a U-turn and races to Trent Road. The whole way there she's trying to predict who it was. After last night's questioning she's no longer convinced Matt was involved in Terri's murder. She knows Troy is staying with a friend until the police are done with his house, and he would have answered the door if it were him, so without Troy or Matt as suspects, she's drawing a complete blank.

After pulling into the dirt road, she continues on until she makes a hard right into Terri and Troy's front yard. A squad car is already here but the officer must be inside the house. A glance over confirms the front door is open. She pulls her bulletproof vest from the back seat and slips it on.

It's raining this morning, not heavy but the fine drizzle that quickly soaks you. She rushes from the car to the porch, ducking the yellow tape and drawing her weapon as she goes. At the door she stops, cocking her head, trying to hear something, but it's silent. "Hello?" she shouts.

Footsteps approach from the rear of the house, so she raises her gun ahead of her and adds, "Lost Creek PD. Make yourself known!"

"Calm down, it's me." Officer Goodwin appears.

Madison rolls her eyes. "Why didn't you answer me sooner? You could've been shot."

He ignores her and instead says, "Property is empty. I don't know who the neighbor thinks he saw but there's no one here."

Disappointed, she holsters her gun and takes a closer look at the door. It's the only way in or out of the property. It doesn't look like it's been forced. "Are any of the windows open?"

He shakes his head. "I'll radio dispatch and let them know it's a false alarm."

Madison watches him leave. He's not even going to look around outside in case anyone's hiding. "Check the perimeter before you go, and the neighbors' backyards, just in case anyone's watching the place."

His shoulders sag as he walks away. He doesn't answer her. That guy has a serious problem with authority. Maybe he doesn't like taking orders from a woman. He wouldn't be the first. Madison intends to make Chief Mendes aware of just how difficult he is to work with. Anything she can do to stop him getting Detective Douglas's job will be worth it.

Another cruiser pulls up outside. It's Officer Sanchez. She leaves Goodwin to update him and closes the front door. She'd bet they both take off within five minutes. Goodwin bosses Sanchez around because he's older than their newest recruit. He's a bad influence on him.

The house is cold. No one has been here to warm it, and it looks exactly as it did the day Terri's body was found. She snaps on a pair of gloves so as not to leave prints behind. With it raining outside it's dark inside. She switches an overhead light on.

A shudder goes through her as she steps farther into the living room. It's deadly silent in here. She can still smell the blood faintly, but it's mixed with mildew now. With the heat off, the house is already feeling the effects of the cold, damp weather. She walks past the kitchen and checks the bathroom and bedroom to make sure she is definitely alone. There's no one here. The bedroom's closet door is ajar, and she can tell Troy has taken some of his clothes away. The bedding is all gone of course, bagged up as evidence. The blood spatter remains on the walls but some of it has been rubbed and sprayed by Alex as he took his samples, making it pinker than the rest.

Back in the living room she opens drawers and cabinets. There's nothing helpful. Her interest is drawn to the photographs on the sideboard. They're covered with a layer of fingerprint powder, which she wipes away. Various women smile back at her but she only recognizes Terri in most of them. There's just one of Troy. Another photo shows a family gathering with Terri, her mom, Sylvia, and her aunt, Maggie. It looks fairly recent. They all look so happy, and completely oblivious to what was to come. Madison shakes her head.

The final photograph is of a bunch of teenagers. It looks like they're at summer camp as the only adult in the picture is outnumbered by a row of girls standing next to each other. They're in front of a lake, with tall pine trees behind. Madison leans into the photo, trying to identify anyone in it. Eventually she spots Terri, probably no older than sixteen. She's one of two girls off to the left, who have their arms around each other's shoulders, and she's smiling brightly into the lens. That must be her best friend next to her.

Madison gasps as her eyes are drawn to their wrists. They're both wearing matching bracelets. And it's the same bracelet she found gripped in Terri's clenched hand the day she was found dead.

Considering the implications, Madison mumbles, "They both have the same bracelet. So what?" Is it significant that Terri was holding it when she died, almost twenty years later? She looks closely at the photograph but it's poor quality, taken before digital cameras were a thing. Could the other girl be Jo Rader? They were school friends, so it's not much of a stretch to assume they also attended summer camp together.

She pulls out her phone and googles Jo's name in the hope of finding a recent photograph of her, because it's been seven years since Madison last saw the woman in person and even then, they'd probably only ever said hi in passing at the diner. She didn't know Jo to talk to back then and didn't really know

Vince or Ruby well since they'd only run the diner for a year at the time Madison was arrested and imprisoned.

There are countless articles about Ruby and Oliver's disappearance online, some with images of Matt and Jo, clearly distressed during the search for their son. She zooms in on Jo Rader, who has chestnut hair and pale skin. She can't make out her eye color as the image is small. Looking back at the camp photo, Madison can see the girl Terri has her arm around is the same person. She's sure of it. Jo as a teenager has auburn hair, which could have darkened with age, and her face is covered in freckles, which are probably hidden under makeup now, but her features are undoubtably the same.

Conscious she may be jumping to conclusions, Madison has to consider whether Terri got her old friendship bracelet out for a reason that night—because her childhood friend was coming to visit her. Madison had been working on the assumption that Matt wanted to silence Terri in order to stop her from telling Douglas what she knew. But what if it was Jo Rader who wanted to stop her? In which case, just what did Terri know? Jo implied Terri was more like her sister, that they were loyal to each other. Could Terri have lied for her friend, to cover up Jo's involvement in the disappearances? It's possible. But if Terri knew something, she took it to her grave. Otherwise, Douglas would have acted on it immediately.

Madison's heart races as she considers all the consequences. If Jo killed Terri that would also mean that she killed Detective Douglas, but Madison can't see it. The woman she spoke to on the phone yesterday was devastated over her son's disappearance. Madison doesn't want to believe someone could fake those feelings, because if Jo killed Terri and Douglas, that means she also killed her son and mother-in-law.

"No. That can't be it," she mutters. "I must be missing something." There's one way to find out. If Jo killed Terri and Douglas, and hit Nate with her car yesterday afternoon, she could still be here in Colorado, hiding. Madison could try calling Jo's cell phone but that wouldn't confirm where she is, so she calls Vince instead.

He answers immediately. "Detective. I hear you went in hard on my son."

"I'm just doing my job, Vince."

Hesitantly, he asks, "So do you think he killed anyone?"

"I didn't arrest him, did I?"

He lets out a long sigh of relief. "Good. I don't think I could cope if he was involved."

A feeling of dread tightens her chest. She's tempted to ask how he would feel if his daughter-in-law was involved, but she doesn't. "How's Nate? Are you still at the hospital?"

"I am," he says. "I thought you would be here by now."

She would have been there by now if she wasn't trying to catch a killer. "Enough of the guilt trip, how is he?"

"Still unconscious. The doctors think he could have a bleed on the brain, but they're not telling me much. I get the impression they thought he'd be awake by now." Vince sounds worried.

She feels her legs go weak, so she takes a seat on Terri's couch.

"I'm not going anywhere," he continues. "I'll stay here until you're able to find the time to visit. Maybe you could send your boy over so I have someone to take Brody outside for bathroom breaks and to stretch his legs. He's getting bored of me. He wants his dad to wake up."

"Of course. I'll call Owen right away. He might bring someone with him. My, er, dad turned up out of the blue late last night."

"Really?" says Vince, with surprise in his voice. "I'd like to meet him. See if you're a chip off the old block."

She almost smiles, but then remembers why she called him. "I need Jo Rader's landline number, or an address in Sacramento so I can find it. I don't suppose you have that, do you?"

He's silent for a second. "Did the cell phone number I gave you not work?"

"It's switched off," she lies. "And I need to speak to her urgently."

He must be curious as to why she wants to speak to Jo urgently, but he doesn't waste time by asking. "I have Patricia's landline. That's her mom. I think Nate said he managed to speak to her on that number."

"Jo and her new husband live with her mom?"

"I don't know about that." He reads the number out for her and she makes a note of it.

"Thanks. Keep me updated on Nate."

"Sure."

She texts Owen quickly, asking him to get her dad to give him a ride to the hospital and help Vince out with babysitting duties. Owen responds with a thumbs-up, so at least he's awake. She wishes she could be with them all; she has so many questions for her dad, and for Nate's doctors. And what if he slips away without waking? She can't let her mind go there. She needs to focus.

Sighing, she calls the landline number. It takes a while but an older woman eventually answers. Madison introduces herself and checks she's talking to Patricia before then asking to speak to Jo.

"I'm sorry, she's at work."

Madison checks the time; it's only seven-thirty in the morning here, which means it's six-thirty in Sacramento. "Already?"

"She starts early and finishes early," says Patricia. Is that a hint of hostility in her voice?

"Okay, I'll contact her at work. What's her number there?"

"Why don't you just call her cell?"

"I have my reasons. What's the name of her employer?"

Patricia hesitates for a long time. "I don't give out personal information over the phone, Detective. I mean, who's to say you are who you claim to be? You could be a journalist for all I know."

Patiently, Madison says, "How about you call my police department and ask the dispatcher to patch you through to me? That way you'll know for sure."

Silence. Then: "I'll get Jo to call you instead." Patricia hangs up before Madison can protest.

She shakes her head. "Charming." This isn't exactly proof that Jo's not in Sacramento, but she calls Jo's cell phone before her mom can give her a heads-up. She gets a busy tone. Patricia beat her to it. "Shit."

In order to plan her next step, she decides to head to the hospital and quiz Vince about his ex-daughter-in-law.

CHAPTER FORTY-EIGHT

Voices echo in his head and Nate can't tell whether or not he's imagining them. They talk uninhibitedly, some close, some far away, but he can't make out the words. It's like listening to a radio station that isn't tuned in properly. In prison, he was only allowed a radio in his cell, no TV. He tenses at the thought.

Eventually he becomes aware of a heavy weight on his left arm and leg, pinning him down. Is he trapped under something? He tries to swallow but his mouth is dry, making it unsatisfying. He tries to open his eyes next, but they're heavy, as if weighed down with exhaustion. Now he's regaining consciousness he's aware of back and neck pain, as if he's slept in the wrong position all night.

"If we take him into..."

"See what we're dealing with..."

The words fade in and out, and he misses a lot of them. He doesn't recognize the voice.

"If that's what's best for him, then I guess we need to go ahead."

He recognizes *that* voice. It's Madison. He's sure of it.

His eyes flicker open but the harsh artificial light makes him wince. Suddenly a dog barks—close and loud—and the weight on his arm diminishes. Nate smiles. He should have known. "Hey, Brody," he croaks.

Brody barks again, excitedly this time. He sniffs Nate's face loudly, standing on the bed.

"Okay, time to get down."

Nate looks up. A doctor leads Brody off the bed and Madison is standing behind her, hands clasped together in front of her mouth.

"I've got him." Vince appears and takes Brody's leash before he says with a smile, "Welcome back to the land of the living. You had us worried there for a second."

Nate holds his hand out to Madison but the doctor steps in first. She shines a bright light into each eye before asking him a long series of questions about how he's feeling, where the pain is and what level his pain is at. Apart from some aching and dizziness, he doesn't feel too bad.

"That's because we've got you on strong pain meds," she says. "You may feel a little differently once we lower those."

"I need water."

Madison steps forward as he slowly sits up. She squeezes an extra pillow behind him before handing him a cup from the nightstand. "Here you go."

It might be the best cup of water he's ever tasted. He drinks the whole thing. The movement aggravates his shoulder and neck. "What happened? Why am I in here?" He can only take short, shallow breaths because of pain in his ribs.

"You were hit by a car yesterday afternoon and brought straight in," says Madison while the doctor makes notes on his chart at the end of the bed. "It's Sunday morning now. Do you remember anything at all?"

He tries to think. It feels like he's been asleep and had some crazy dreams. He looks at the dog, who is staring back intently, waiting for a command. "Was Brody hurt?"

"Only his paws," says Vince. "We think he chased the asshole all the way to Gold Rock, but wasn't able to keep up. He's been treated and his paws will heal in a couple of days."

Nate wants to call him back up onto the bed but the doctor is looking at Brody with a pained expression. "It's time he left. I understand he was here to comfort you and all, but dogs really aren't allowed at the hospital for this length of time. I could get in trouble."

Nate exchanges a look with Vince, who says, "I'll take him to my place when I leave shortly."

The doctor slips Nate's chart back into its slot and looks at him. "You seem to have got off lightly, which suggests the car only clipped you. It was enough to cause some cracked ribs, a swollen hip, a nasty head injury and some internal bruising. You lost a lot of blood too, at the scene, but it could have been a lot worse if you'd taken the full impact. We pulled some gravel out of the laceration on your head, suggesting it was caused by hitting the ground as you fell."

He tries to take it all in. "When can I leave?"

"I want to keep you in for at least another twenty-four hours, maybe more depending on how your recovery goes. I'll be back to check on you in a couple of hours. If you need anything in the meantime, press that red buzzer to your left."

Nate locates it and nods.

The doctor leaves, after stroking Brody's head on her way out.

Nate notices Madison check her watch and he tries to remember what case she's working on, but fails. She's probably itching to get out of here. She steps forward to say something but she's interrupted by Owen's arrival.

"You're awake!" says Owen. "How do you feel?"

"I'll be okay."

Madison glances outside the room before asking Owen, "Where's Grandpa?"

Nate's puzzled by the comment and thinks he mishears her.

"He's waiting in the car," says Owen. "Said he wouldn't feel comfortable turning up at some stranger's hospital room uninvited. Doesn't think it's right to see another guy half naked when he doesn't even know him." Owen finds that amusing.

"Have you caught the person who hit me?" asks Nate.

"Not yet," says Madison. "I'm working on some leads. I should probably get out of here now I know you're going to be okay. I was at Terri's place earlier and saw something that got me thinking." She turns to Vince. "I wanted to ask you some questions about Jo, actually."

The mention of Terri Summers reminds Nate of the cases Madison's working on. His thoughts clear and he wonders where she's at with everything.

"What do you want to know?" asks Vince.

"How was her relationship with Ruby for one. Did they ever fight?"

He frowns. "No. What gave you that impression?"

Madison hesitates and Nate wonders where she's going with this. Surely she doesn't think Jo was responsible for Ruby's disappearance? He gasps, and everyone turns to him.

"What is it?" asks Madison.

He tries to gather his thoughts. "I saw the driver."

"The one who hit you?" asks Owen.

The memory of it is a little hazy but he's certain. "I was waiting for Brody to do his thing on the grass and heard a car accelerate. It was pretty quiet along that stretch of road, so the noise stood out. I turned to see what was going on and realized at the last minute they meant to swerve into me. Before I turned away, I got a split-second look at the driver."

"Who was it?" asks Madison, pulling her phone out.

He shakes his head, trying to focus. "A reflection on the windshield obscured their face and they were wearing aviator sunglasses and a cap but I noticed their hair." He fixes his eyes on hers. "I got the impression it was a woman. The hair was long and dark, her shoulders narrow."

Madison heads for the door. "You're absolutely certain?"

He nods. "I'm not saying it was Jo Rader, just that it was a woman. She was heading out of town."

"What color was the car? Did you recognize the make or model? The license plate?"

"The car was blue. Some kind of Honda, I think." He leans back, exhausted. "But how would Jo get away with hiding in Lost Creek? Wouldn't someone have spotted her by now?"

"Depends where she was hiding," says Owen.

They all look at Madison, who's trying hard to figure out where to find her. After a long minute, a look of dread clouds her face. "Dammit." Before any of them can ask her what she's thinking she runs out of the room without saying goodbye.

Nate turns to Vince, who's gone deathly pale and is staring at the floor as if he wants to collapse. "You okay, Vince?"

He looks up. "Jo wouldn't do that to me and Matty. Would she?"

Nate wants to reassure him, but the one thing he warned Vince about from the very beginning was that the answers he so desperately seeks might be worse than he could have ever imagined.

CHAPTER FORTY-NINE

Madison takes the stairway to get out of the hospital as fast as possible. She feels like she might vomit and she desperately hopes she's wrong about where Jo Rader could be hiding, and that Jo is the killer she's been hunting. Because she doesn't want to believe the woman she bonded with over the phone when talking about their boys could so easily lie about not knowing what happened to her son. It's been six years. Is it really possible to cover up her involvement in her son's disappearance for all that time without cracking?

It would explain why she left town just a year after Ruby and Oliver's disappearance. Why she split with Matt and moved away to California. She wasn't escaping her grief. She was escaping law enforcement. And what about her mother; does Patricia know?

Panting, Madison reaches her car and realizes her dad is parked right next to it, waiting for Owen. She knocks on the driver's window and waits for him to lower it. "Sorry, Dad. I've got to shoot off. I'm sure Owen won't be much longer."

"Where you headed?"

"To catch a suspect."

"That's my girl." He smiles as he watches her slip into her car.

She races out of the parking lot and considers calling for backup. Not knowing whether her hunch is right, she wants to check first to avoid wasting anyone's time. She weaves through the morning rush-hour traffic, her wiper blades working hard to keep up with the rain. She speeds up as she heads over the bridge and out of town. The driver who hit Nate was headed toward Gold Rock and Madison thinks she knows why. All the things Jo said in their phone conversation run through her head.

I'm afraid of answers now. I sometimes think it's better not to know.

That's why I'm reluctant when anyone talks about reopening the case... It simply hurts too much.

And when asked who she suspected:

I had doubts about Matt.

If Madison's theory is correct, then Jo tried to frame her own husband for Ruby and Oliver's disappearance. What kind of person does that make her? She shakes her head in disgust. "A monster."

Jo is also experienced with guns. She disclosed that her dad used to take her hunting and bought her her first weapon. Terri was killed by Troy's firearm and Douglas by his own service weapon, but what if Ruby and Oliver were shot by the same weapon Jo owns now or owned back then? That should be easy to prove if her weapon was licensed, but not until Madison finds their bodies and has a cause of death. It's a foregone conclusion now, that they're dead. If they were alive, they would have come forward by now. There would be no reason for Terri and Douglas to have died. For Nate to be injured. The inevitability of it saddens Madison. She doesn't want to have to break the news to Vince and Matt. She saw Vince's face as he realized why she was asking him about Jo, and she imagines Matt's reaction will be even worse. The level of betrayal from Jo is unimaginable.

Nate had mentioned that Jo remarried a year ago. So where does her new husband fit into all this? He could know something. He could be here in Colorado with her. She considers whether Jo had any subsequent children in the last six years. Because they could be at risk from her too. She speeds up again and within twenty minutes Madison pulls up just short of a sprawling ranch in Gold Rock. She hasn't been here in months, neither has her sister. Angie and Wyatt McCoy lived here for over twenty years, but it's been abandoned since his death and her arrest. Both LCPD and the state police turned the place over during their search for evidence, all of which will eventually be used in Angie's trial.

The fact that Angie let Jo quit working for her without any repercussions has been bothering Madison. They must have been closer than either of them made out, which means it's logical to assume Angie would let her hide out here while she goes on her killing spree. Madison remains seated as she switches off the engine and peers out of the windshield. There are no vehicles parked outside the property that she can see from here, and there's no movement from inside. But Jo isn't stupid. She can't be if she got away with murder for six years. She could have parked her car where it isn't visible from the road, and she won't be using the lights in the main house. It's dark this morning on account of the rain, but she probably isn't intending to stay in town after today. She's done what she came for, unless she means to finish Nate off at some point.

Madison pulls out her cell phone and calls Steve.

"Hey, where are you? Owen phoned dispatch to say you took off from the hospital with a possible lead."

He must have been worried she wouldn't call for backup. "I'm at the McCoys' ranch. I think Jo Rader is using it as a base while she's in town."

"She's your suspect? For which part?"

"All of it."

"Holy crap. I'll send all units immediately. Do *not* go inside alone. Just sit tight."

"I have my vest."

"I don't care," he says sternly. "If you're right that she killed Douglas, do you think she cares about adding you to her list?"

No, probably not. She sighs. "Fine. Just hurry up."

"I mean it, Madison. If Jo Rader doesn't kill you, Chief Mendes will, for going in alone."

She rolls her eyes. "Alright, alright. Just get some backup dispatched asap." She ends the call. Steve worries too much. She stares at the house again. If Jo is hiding in there, it means she knew the place was abandoned, confirming she's still in touch with Angie. Madison shakes her head. Jo saw their accounts. She would have known what Angie and Wyatt were up to with their fraudulent charities. She could have told the police and chose not to. Which means she was in Angie's pocket. The pair had something on each other. The only thing Madison can think of that Angie had on Jo was what happened with Ruby and Oliver. Jo must have sought her help after killing them.

After fifteen minutes when not one car drives by and the only sound is the patter of rain on the windshield, a movement to Madison's right catches her eye. A blue Honda Accord is slowly and silently pulling forward out of the McCoys' scrapyard. "Shit." Nate thought it was a blue Honda that had clipped him. Madison starts the engine and drives forward to try to block the road outside the ranch, but the Honda takes off the minute the driver spots her.

Madison chases after the car. From her position she can't make out whether the driver is male or female but they're speeding through Gold Rock far too fast and heading north. She tries to keep up but the car in front is dangerously dodging other vehicles and she doesn't want to see anyone get hurt. On Main Street the Honda veers dangerously close to a mother and toddler on a bike. Madison holds her breath as she watches the driver cut a corner just ahead of them. The mother only just manages to get out of the way, with inches to spare, but she topples over on the bike, going down hard on the wet sidewalk. The little girl on the back of the bike cries loudly but appears unharmed. It's clear the Honda's driver doesn't care who they hurt as long as they get away.

Once they're through Main Street Madison hits the gas and tries to get as close to the other car as possible. It swerves off to the left, taking another corner far too late and almost going over. "Oh my God." Her hands sweat as she grips the steering wheel. They're getting desperate now, but Madison knows this dirt road leads to a dead end and the driver's about to be cornered.

Within minutes, the driver in front realizes this and makes an emergency stop. Madison slows but has to swerve out of the car's way in order to avoid hitting it. The Honda goes into reverse and starts backing out of the dirt road way too fast. The wheels spin in the mud but they eventually find grip and the car reverses out of sight. Madison calls dispatch and yells down the phone, "Suspect is on the run. They're heading north out of Gold Rock and they're driving recklessly!"

Calmly, Stella acknowledges her and says, "Officers should be at your location within minutes."

Madison drops her phone, makes a U-turn and goes after the driver. She makes it just in time to see them reverse into a ditch by the side of the road. The car lands awkwardly, tilting on the passenger side, and comes to a dramatic halt in the mud. Madison bolts out of her seat, pulls her weapon and yells, "Stop! Police! Put your hands where I can see them." She's quickly soaked as she stands in the rain, blocking the vehicle with her gun aimed at the driver.

When the wipers clear the windshield Madison sees who is

sitting in the driver's seat. Joanne Rader. Her hunch was right, but she can't take any pleasure from that. Not when the consequences are so horrific.

Jo clearly doesn't want to give up. She revs the engine as if she's going to try to get out of the ditch, but there's no way the car will move without assistance. To get her attention Madison fires a warning shot just above the roof of the car and advances toward the driver's side. The window is open a crack and Jo is leaning off to one side, with just her seatbelt keeping her secure.

Jo stares hard but she doesn't switch the engine off.

Madison tightens her grip on the gun and shouts above the rain, "Let me see your hands as you slowly get out of the car. Don't do anything stupid. Backup is about to arrive and they'll get you if I don't."

Jo stares at her and Madison has time to wonder whether she's armed. Jo could be weighing up whether to shoot her. After all, they're alone out here and no one would see her do it. A siren in the distance soon changes that. Madison can hear two or three cruisers advancing. A ripple of relief runs through her. "You've been caught. It's time to explain to your ex-husband why you killed his mother and child." She opens the car door and drags Jo out into the rain. The woman is armed, so Madison removes her weapon before cuffing her. Realizing there's nowhere for her to go, Jo doesn't resist arrest.

"Joanne Rader, or Letts, whatever your name is now, I'm placing you under arrest on suspicion of murder." Madison reads Jo her rights.

Once her hands are cuffed behind her back, Jo turns and stares blankly at Madison as rain drops run down her face. She looks dead behind the eyes. "You don't know what you're talking about."

"Oh yeah? I know you killed them along with your supposed best friend and a police officer. Or are you going to deny that too?"

Jo shakes her head wearily. "I would never intentionally hurt my child. I don't know how any mother could accuse me of that."

Something about the way she reacts has Madison wondering if she was wrong. But if Jo didn't kill them all, then who did?

CHAPTER FIFTY

Jo is taken to the station in the back of Shelley's cruiser. Once there, Shelley books her in before taking her to an interview room. Madison drops Jo's cell phone off with Alex before updating Steve and Chief Mendes.

"She's denying it right now," says Madison. "But I think if we get Matt and maybe Vince down here, she might break when she sees them for the first time in years."

"If that's how you want to play it, that's fine with me," says Mendes.

Steve nods. "I'll ask Vince to get over here."

"How certain are you that she's our killer?" asks Mendes.

Madison takes a deep breath. "Think about it; why else would she be in town while pretending to be in California? If she came because she wanted an update on the investigation, she would have let me know she's in town and she wouldn't be hiding at Angie's place."

Chief Mendes looks surprised. "She was at your sister's place? Does that mean Angie's involved?"

She really hopes not. "I guess I'm about to find out. I'll try to get what I can out of her but the minute she clams up, I'll bring

Matt into the room, and maybe Vince. If she has any remorse for what she's done, she's more likely to crack in front of them."

Mendes considers it. "Has the press got wind yet?"

She checks her phone. There are four missed calls from Kate, which doesn't surprise her. The way Madison, and then the cruisers, sped out of town and then back in again, it was just a matter of time before they started getting calls for information. "I think so. But they won't know any specifics yet. They don't know Douglas was murdered." Once that's out there the media attention will triple.

"Want me to sit in on the interview?" asks Steve.

"Maybe later on. I'm hoping to get her to open up about Oliver first, and she may do that if it's just mother to mother. But you can get Vince and Matt down here as fast as possible. Just don't tell them why yet. I want to be able to tell them myself once I know more."

"Sure."

"I've given Jo's cell phone to Alex. She wouldn't give up the pin code, so I don't know how long it will take him to access it, if he can get in at all. Let's try to get her call history from her cell provider as backup."

"I'm on it," says Steve.

"Okay," says Mendes. "Let's get this done."

Madison turns and heads straight to the interview room. Jo doesn't move in her chair as she enters. She's uncuffed now and Madison nods to Shelley, who's standing near the door watching. "Would you get us some coffees?" She feels windswept and soaked by the rain, and caffeine will help her focus.

"Sure." Shelley leaves the room.

Madison presses the button that starts the video and audio recording. She glances at the camera in the corner of the room to make sure the red light is on. It is. She drops Ruby and Oliver's case file on the table between them. Color photographs of both victims sit on top. Jo lowers her eyes, not wanting to look.

Madison asks, "Are you happy to answer some questions or do you want to wait for a lawyer?"

"I don't have a lawyer."

"I can make one available to you. It'll slow things down considerably but that's your right."

Jo shakes her head.

"For the record, Mrs. Letts has decided not to have a lawyer present at this moment in time but she has been advised she can ask for one at any time during this session." Madison takes a deep breath. "So, how long have you been in town?"

Jo's eyes are red and her body language is closed. She looks dazed, as if she never considered the possibility of finding herself in this situation. "I didn't kill those people."

"*Those* people? Are you referring to your family members?" She can't be that callous. She must mean Terri and Douglas.

Jo sniffs. "Please don't. I can't take it."

"I've only asked you two questions so far and things are about to get a lot more difficult. If you want this to be any easier for you, it's best you're open and honest about what you know."

Looking up at last, Jo says, "There's no way to make this easier on me. You don't understand, I've been living with this for six years!"

"So help me to understand. Tell me what happened, and why. What was so bad that you had to resort to killing your own child?"

Jo shakes her head and clams up.

It annoys Madison. She's not in the mood to play games. "Matt and Vince are on their way here."

Jo's mouth drops open and she's speechless for a second. "No. Please. I don't want to see them. I can't." She breaks into long, gut-wrenching sobs.

Madison can't help but feel sorry for her. She doesn't appear to be your average killer. There's no bravado, or attitude. She hasn't immediately lawyered up, and truth be told, she looks broken. Remorseful. That gives Madison some hope that she's more likely to tell the truth. "You're going to have to face them eventually, either here or in court. Don't you think they deserve answers after all this time?"

Wiping her nose, Jo says, "They don't want answers. Not really. The answers are worse than the loss."

So she's definitely involved. "Come on, Jo. Nothing can be worse than the loss of a child."

She appears to make a decision. "I'll talk to you if you make sure I never have to see them again."

"That's not a promise I can make." Madison thinks about it. "The best I can do is keep them away from you here at the station. But if this gets to court, I have no doubt they'll be there every day of your trial."

Jo groans.

"Let's start at the beginning," says Madison. "What happened to Ruby and Oliver? If you weren't involved, then now's your time to tell me. To put all this to rest."

Leaning forward with her head in her hands, Jo says, "Please don't make me relive it. I've tried so hard to block it out."

Madison's adrenaline is making her antsy. Her heart feels like it's going to burst out of her chest, because it's clear now they have the right person in custody. All Madison needs to do is link all four deaths, plus the attack on Nate, then she can find the two missing bodies and put this woman behind bars. With a softer tone, she says, "What did Ruby find out about you? Because that was why you killed her, wasn't it? She discovered something she shouldn't have."

Jo's hands are trembling. "How do you know that?"

She sits back and crosses her arms. "Angie told me."

With a look of disappointment, Jo says, "So she betrayed me. I knew I should never have trusted her."

Madison agrees.

"I thought you two hated each other?" says Jo. "Why'd she tell you?"

"Who knows? I gave up trying to figure out the motives of that woman a long time ago."

"Did she say anything else?"

"She wouldn't give up the locations of the bodies. Now let's stop stalling. What did Ruby know about you?"

Jo wipes sweat from her brow before tears spring up again. "It's all Mrs. Hendricks's fault. If she hadn't been such a goddam busybody..."

Madison frowns. That's a name she's never heard before. "Who the hell is Mrs. Hendricks?"

CHAPTER FIFTY-ONE

SIX YEARS AGO

Ruby drives through the dark to get to the church. It's almost 5 p.m. The wind howls around the car but the rain is holding off. It won't be long before she can get Oliver home to Matt and Jo for dinner and then she'll have to tell Vince what's going on. He'll know what to do.

But first she wants Mrs. Hendricks to show her what she discovered about Jo. She's clinging on to the hope that her daughter-in-law hasn't been embezzling money from the church and Lord knows where else. But the thought occurs to her that it might be the reason she worked for Angie McCoy: to help them cook the books. Or maybe she learned it from Angie, who knows? Ruby's heard the rumors, that the McCoys aren't as charitable as they make out. That, actually, they're committing charity fraud. That's just the tip of the iceberg though. She's also heard they've been offering bad loans and when someone can't keep up with the extortionate interest rates, they lose their home and possessions. But it's all based on rumors, which a town like this thrives on, so she doesn't know what's true and what's made up.

She thinks of the new couch and expensive coffee machine

at Oliver's house, then remembers Jo's driving a different car these days. It's newer than her old car, and must cost more to lease. Is that where all this money is coming from, the church? From donations people willingly give to help out those less fortunate than them. How could anyone steal that? And for what—home comforts like fancy furniture and a nicer car? She wonders how much is squirreled away in bank accounts Matt might not be aware of. Is Jo planning on leaving him? Her heart thuds at the thought Jo will leave and take Oliver with her to start a new life.

Ruby shakes her head in disappointment. If the embezzling accusations are true and someone besides her and Rosemary find out, it's just a matter of time before Jo's arrested. She'll go to prison for fraud. And if the church isn't the only place she's stealing from, she could get a long sentence. Oliver will grow up without his mother. The whole town will know her daughter-in-law is a thief, and the worst kind. Their customers might stop coming to the diner. Ruby could lose her business. And Oliver will grow up with his mother's conviction hanging over him. "How could she be so stupid?" she mutters.

"What, Grandma?" says Oliver.

She meets his eyes in the rear-view mirror and her heart breaks for him. Would Jo really risk going to prison and losing her son? "Nothing, sweetie. Just talking to myself. We're almost there."

"I'm hungry."

She smiles. He's always hungry. "I'm sure Mrs. Hendricks has something in her purse for you." She doesn't go anywhere without some candy for the kids.

He chats away about his favorite candy as she looks over at the church, waiting to turn into the parking lot. It's dimly lit but she sees a figure standing at the top of the steps. The church is in darkness, all lights switched off. It must be Mrs. Hendricks about to leave, which means Ruby's too late for play group. At least she'll catch her before she drives away. Ruby looks closer. Someone approaches Mrs. Hendricks from behind and pushes her hard. She goes flying down the steps.

"Oh my God!" She can't believe what she's seeing. The perpetrator descends the steps and stops at the bottom, staring at poor Rosemary.

Ruby has to do something. She pulls straight into the parking lot and tries to grab her phone from her purse with her spare hand. She needs to call the police, or an ambulance. Her headlights illuminate the steps as she approaches.

She gasps when she sees who is standing there.

"Mommy!" says Oliver, recognizing Jo. "Can I get out now, Grandma?"

Ruby's lost for words. Rosemary is crumpled on the ground at Jo's feet. Jo stares into the headlights, shielding her eyes from some of the glare. She's supposed to be on her way home from work right now, so why is she here, doing this? Ruby can't understand it. "Stay here a second, sweetie. I'm just going to help your mom."

"Mommy!" he shouts, waving through the car's windshield.

Ruby's trembling. With her phone in her hand, she gets out of the car.

"She fell," says Jo, her face expressionless.

Ruby rushes forward and crouches next to her friend. There's a faint pulse in her neck, but her head is leaking blood. "Rosemary? Can you hear me?"

There's no response.

Ruby stands up, not knowing what to do. She unlocks her phone, intending to dial 911, but Jo takes it from her. "But we need to call an ambulance! She could still be saved."

"No," says Jo. "She's gone." She looks over at the car, where Oliver is desperate to get his mom's attention.

"Mommy," he says through the window. "What's wrong with Mrs. Hendricks?"

Ruby closes her eyes. He's seen Rosemary. He's a witness now.

"Why did you come here, Ruby?" asks Jo. "You shouldn't be here."

With a shaky voice she says, "I wanted to talk to Rosemary."

Jo studies her face. "She told you, didn't she?"

Ruby's heart sinks and it's then that she realizes she's in trouble. She's suddenly scared of her daughter-in-law. This isn't the woman who married her son. "I had to check for myself. I didn't believe you were capable of it. But now..." She looks down at Rosemary and it's clear she's gone. They didn't act fast enough to save her. Tears spring to her eyes. "You didn't have to do this. You could've come clean, or given the money back."

"No," says Jo. "She threatened to tell Pastor Graham and my boss. They would've both checked their accounts and found what I've been doing. I would've been arrested before long. And if the police extended their investigation to look at what I was doing for the McCoys, I have no doubt that Angie would have me killed for exposing them like that."

So it's true; she was helping the McCoys commit charity fraud and she's gone on to steal money from the church she volunteers at and from her employer. Ruby's heart sinks as she realizes how deep in trouble Jo is. She made a deal with the devil and felt that killing Rosemary was her only way out. She almost wishes she hadn't stumbled across them, that she had arrived just ten minutes later and was able to naïvely believe that Rosemary tripped down the steps in the dark.

Taking Ruby's elbow, Jo says, "Come with me."

Ruby glances back at the car before letting Jo lead her away. "You wouldn't hurt Oliver, would you?"

A tear runs down her daughter-in-law's cheek. "Neither of you should be here."

They reach the other side of the church, hidden from the

road and surrounded by pine trees. "I won't tell anyone, I swear. And Oliver didn't see a thing, he was looking the other way."

Jo turns her back on Ruby and steps forward as if she's trying to come to a decision. Ruby uses the opportunity to dial 911 on her cell phone but before she can hit call, Jo spins around. "What are you doing?" She pulls out a gun and aims it at her.

Ruby's hands are shaking so bad that she drops the phone in fear. "Jo, think about this for a minute; it's just money. It's nothing you can't fix. Pay the money back and no one will ever know. I can help you. Vince and I... We have some savings."

"What about Mrs. Hendricks?" says Jo. She has tears streaming down her face. She's losing control.

"We'll say we found her together. That she slipped on her way home." Ruby would never do such a thing to Rosemary. She intends to tell the police what really happened as soon as she gets away from her daughter-in-law. Oliver can't live with a woman who's capable of killing an old lady to cover her crimes.

It looks like Jo's seriously considering it. Her expression is pained. It gives Ruby hope that she'll do the right thing. "But if *you* saw what happened, Oliver might have too. He could tell Matt, or Vince. I'd be living in fear, waiting for him to blurt it out one day."

Ruby swallows. She doesn't know how much Oliver witnessed. Her hands are sweating even though it's cold and blustery. "Please, Jo. Don't make this any worse. Think about Oliver. If you kill me, he'll be without his grandma."

Jo wipes tears away with her spare hand. Her expression has changed. She's made a decision. "It's better than being without his mom, which is what will happen if you tell the police what I did to Mrs. Hendricks and why I did it. I'll be locked up, unable to see him for years. He'd be all grown up by the time I got out of prison. If I ever got out." She slowly shakes her head. "I'm sorry, Ruby. I wish there was another way. I wish you hadn't come here tonight."

Ruby's lost for words. She's about to risk bending down to pick up her phone and call the police but a shot rings out through the darkness. It's loud and shocking, and it temporarily deafens her. Within seconds she's winded, unable to inhale. She crumples to the ground, clutching her chest. As she struggles for air, she hears Oliver crying. He can't see them where he is but the gunshot would have scared him. He can't understand why his mom and grandma won't go to him.

Jo passes her as she walks toward the car. Ruby manages to grab her ankle. "Don't hurt him," she splutters. "Please. Think about Matt."

Jo pulls herself free, leaving Ruby to die alone on the cold, hard ground just feet away from Mrs. Hendricks.

CHAPTER FIFTY-TWO

Madison struggles to remain composed as Jo recounts what happened that night. How she went to the church intending to silence the elderly volunteer, but got caught in the act and felt she had to silence her mother-in-law too. Madison pictures Oliver sitting in the back seat of the car, in a pitch-black parking lot, afraid and confused about what was happening.

"Ruby died quickly," says Jo, somewhat detached from her own actions. "I made sure to shoot her in the chest so she wouldn't suffer for long."

Madison scoffs. "How caring of you."

Jo glares at her before saying, "I need to use the bathroom. And I'd like another drink. Water. My mouth is dry from all the talking."

Madison's reluctant to break while her suspect is readily talking, but the truth is she's ready for a break too. She needs time to absorb what she just listened to. It's worse than she imagined and she feels like she needs to mentally prepare herself for learning what happened to Oliver. She leaves Jo in the interview room and heads outside to where Shelley is waiting expectantly. "She wants to use the bathroom. Would you go in with her? I think she could be at risk of harming herself."

Shelley nods. "Sure. Did she admit anything yet?"

Madison nods. "She killed Ruby."

Shelley turns away, hands on hips, as she gives herself a moment. Everyone knew Ruby. In a small town like this the diner is the epicenter for the locals. Shelley's reaction reflects how everyone else will feel once the news is out. "Matt and Vince will be devastated."

"I know." Madison places a hand on her back. "She also killed a woman called Mrs. Rosemary Hendricks. She was a volunteer at the church. Would you ask Steve to check whether there was ever an investigation into her death?"

She nods as she inhales deeply. "He wants to talk to you when you get a second. It sounds like some guy's turned up with information."

Madison's intrigued. She opens the door to the interview room. Jo stands and Shelley leads her away. Madison follows them as far as the bathroom then heads to the open-plan office. Steve isn't at his desk. He's in Chief Mendes's office with the stranger. Madison walks straight in.

Chief Mendes looks stressed. "Madison, this is Gary Letts. Jo Rader's husband."

Madison's heart skips a beat as she wonders how he knew his wife was here. Shouldn't he be in Sacramento?

"He and Jo have been married for just a year," continues Mendes. "But it seems his new wife hasn't been honest with him."

Gary looks at her. "When we met, she went by the name of Joanne Jones. So when I found an old passport of hers this week, using the name Joanne Rader, I was confused. She mentioned she had been married before and kept her ex-husband's last name of Jones. And Rader isn't the maiden name given on our wedding certificate, so I realized she had a whole life under a different name that I never knew about. I couldn't understand why she lied, so I googled her. That's when I read about what happened down here in Lost Creek six years ago."

"She never mentioned she lost her son and mother-in-law in suspicious circumstances?" asks Madison.

He shakes his head. The poor guy looks like he's caught up in a nightmare, with the strain evident on his face. "She'd already left for Colorado when I found her passport. I was looking for mine because I'm due on a business trip to the UK next week."

"What reason did she give you for coming here?"

"She said she was visiting a family member in Colorado, but she didn't specify where. I couldn't believe it when I read what had happened. And the fact she never told me any of it... Our cell phones have family tracker apps activated. I checked to see exactly where in Colorado she was, which is when I realized she'd come here." He shakes his head. "That's why I flew out here. I wanted to confront her about it but then I heard on the news that you'd brought her in for questioning."

The press knows about it. Someone must have recognized Jo in the back of the cruiser on her way to the station.

"I'm glad you came," says Madison. "I'll have a lot of questions for you. But for now, I need to get back to interviewing your wife as I'm at a critical point." She turns to Mendes and Steve. "She's already made certain admissions."

"Go right ahead," says Mendes. "Steve can talk to Mr. Letts."

Madison's about to leave when Gary says, "Wait. I think you'll want to see our son first."

She stops dead in her tracks and turns to face him. "Your son?"

"Yeah. I brought him with me but left him waiting in the car for now because I didn't want him to hear any of this. I can't have him hearing anything negative about his mother. It wouldn't be fair to him. He's a sensitive kid."

Madison's whole body is overcome with goosebumps. "I just need you to be clear; are you talking about a child you've had with Jo?"

"No," he says. "I'm talking about the ten-year-old boy from her previous marriage. Oliver."

Steve turns away, with his hands to his head. Chief Mendes looks lost for words. Madison has to swallow the lump in her throat. She struggles to speak. "He's alive?"

Gary nods.

"And he's right outside?"

"Let me go get him."

Dazed, Steve leads Gary out of Chief Mendes's office. When they're gone Madison breaks down. She covers her eyes, relief pouring out of her. Chief Mendes surprises her by slipping an arm around her shoulder and saying, "Thank God. It's not often we get good news."

Once she composes herself, Madison wipes her eyes with a tissue. "What if it's not the same boy? Gary could be confused. This is all new to him."

Mendes goes to her desk and picks up the phone. After a couple of seconds she says, "Alex? My office, now. And bring a DNA testing kit." She slams the phone down and looks at Madison. "Come on."

They head to the front desk behind Officer Goodwin, who is leaving the station to start his shift on patrol. Officer Brett Cooper is in charge of the front desk and he's calmly ending a phone call that sounds heated. Even though the doors are closed it's always freezing in here and no one likes it when it's their turn to work the front desk. It's not just the cold; the random walk-ins off the street are usually trouble, wasted or delusional. They seem to think this place is their own private bathroom too, sometimes taking a leak in the corner. It's the officer's job to

keep the area clean, hence the lack of enthusiasm for working
out here.

Madison and Mendes peer out of the front window and
watch as Gary opens the back door of his car. He leans in for a
second to talk to the boy. Another car pulls into the parking lot
and Madison recognizes it as Matt's white Toyota. Vince is
seated in the passenger side. "Oh, shit. They're going to be
blindsided if they spot Oliver out there. I want a chance to
prepare them first."

"It's too late," says Mendes.

The ten-year-old boy who gets out of the car is wrapped up
in a thick coat, scarf, gloves and a hat. It's unlikely anyone
would recognize him easily. Steve and Gary lead him toward
the station just as Matt and Vince get out of their car,
completely oblivious that their son and grandson is just inches
away from them. She had asked Steve not to tell them why they
were wanted at the station. They have no idea Jo's here, never
mind Oliver. Madison doesn't know how they're going to react,
she just knows their reunion can't happen in the parking lot.
She steps forward and opens the entrance door.

Oliver smiles politely at her and says hello as he walks in.
He's pale, with dark hair poking out from under his hat. The
resemblance to Matt is striking. It occurs to her that he's the age
Owen was when she was arrested. She missed out on seeing
Owen grow up, but Matt and Vince are going to get that opportunity with Oliver. And she couldn't be happier for them. "Hi,"
she says as brightly as she can muster. "Come on into the
warmth."

Gary enters behind him and Chief Mendes moves to whisk
them away before Vince and Matt enter, because Madison
needs to prepare everyone separately before the reunion
happens.

Steve has no option but to hold the door open for Vince and
Matt, who enter behind him. Matt is talking on his phone. The

conversation sounds work-related. Madison steps in front of them, trying to give Mendes the opportunity to dash off. But Oliver looks over his shoulder before following her, curious about who else has arrived.

Madison watches his expression when he sees his father and grandfather, and she's immediately choking back tears. Vince, who is looking at her instead and asking why she wanted him and Matt down here, spots her reaction and looks puzzled. "What's the matter?" His face clouds. "You've brought us here to give us bad news, haven't you?"

Oliver stops in his tracks. "Grandpa?" He recognizes Vince's voice now too.

Matt is in the corner, still talking on his phone. He hasn't noticed a thing. But Vince looks over at the boy. "No, son. I'm not your—" He stops and the color drains out of his face. He takes a step back in shock, grabbing Madison's arm for balance.

Madison's helpless to stop her emotions boiling over. She's thinking of the moment she was reunited with Owen after seven years apart. She covers her mouth with both hands, but when Vince looks to her for confirmation, she nods.

Vince's eyes redden immediately. Gary, Steve and Chief Mendes watch as Vince goes over to Matt. He takes his arm, swings him around and points to Oliver.

"What?" says Matt, confused.

Oliver steps forward, away from Mendes. There's recognition in his eyes. He was four years old when he last saw his father but some faces you never forget. "Dad?"

Matt's phone slips out of his hands and hits the floor, instantly breaking apart. He falls to his knees and his face crumples in anguish. Doubt, followed by confusion, plays out on his face and eventually he allows himself to believe it. He covers his eyes with his hands. Madison goes to Oliver and takes his hand so she can lead him to Matt, who is too overcome to move.

Oliver places his hand on his dad's shoulder. "What's the matter, Dad?"

Matt looks up, wraps his arms around his son and squeezes him tight. He's openly sobbing and Madison checks the faces of Gary, Steve, Mendes and Officer Cooper behind the front desk. There's not a dry eye in here.

"I thought you were gone," says Matt into Oliver's hair. "I thought you were gone." When he lets go, Matt sits back on the cold, concrete floor, just staring at his son.

Vince goes to the boy and scoops him up in a massive bear hug. "You don't know how much we've missed you, young man." His voice breaks and it feels like he's never going to let go of him.

"I missed you too, Grandpa. I remember the chocolate milkshakes you and Grandma used to make me. Chocolate's still my favorite, just so you know."

Everyone laughs through their tears and Vince places him back on the floor.

"Is Grandma here?"

Vince's smile immediately vanishes. It's heartbreaking to watch him understand that Ruby isn't here with Oliver. Madison can't stand it. She steps out of the station, into the cold, and breaks down again. Vince doesn't know yet. He doesn't know what Jo did to his wife.

She feels someone approach. Steve pulls her in for a hug. Eventually he says, "They'll be fine. They have their boy back. Ruby will be looking down on them, ecstatic about this."

She nods and pulls away, desperately trying to compose herself. Vince joins them outside. "Well, Madison, I sure hope you never play poker." He's never called her by her first name before, usually preferring more formality. "I take it from your reaction that my wife's dead? And that your recent interest in my daughter-in-law means she killed her."

Madison's throat clenches. This might be the worst news

she's ever had to deliver because she knows Vince. She knows how final this is for him. He can no longer hope his wife might come home one day. "I'm so sorry, Vince." That's all she can manage.

He nods thoughtfully. "Do we know where she is?"

"Not yet." She wipes her eyes. "I'm not done with questioning Jo yet. I'll get it out of her."

"Please do," he says, with watery eyes. "I'd like to give my wife a proper burial."

Steve puts a hand on his back. "Let's go back inside. We have to take a DNA sample from Oliver, just to be sure."

"I know my own grandson, Sergeant. That's definitely Oliver."

"I don't doubt it for a second, Vince, but you know how it is. We have to tick those boxes."

Madison watches them go back inside. She has a lot of questions for Gary and Oliver, and even more for Jo. But first she just needs to take a minute.

CHAPTER FIFTY-THREE

"What took you so long?" asks Jo in the interview room. She isn't angry at the delay, instead she looks like she's resigned to her fate.

"My chief wanted an update." Madison tried to hide her tears by splashing cold water on her face. If Jo notices she was upset, she doesn't react, so Madison returns to her seat opposite and tries to focus. She can't let her know that Gary and Oliver followed her here. She might clam up. "It would be helpful if you would provide the pin code to your cell phone."

Jo lowers her eyes. "I don't want to do that."

"Why? You've already admitted killing two people. What's on your phone that you don't want us to see?"

Silence.

"Fine," says Madison. "Let's get back to it then. What did you do with Ruby's body?" Steve had checked out Rosemary Hendricks and found her death wasn't treated as suspicious. The church pastor found her at the bottom of the steps the next morning and assumed she'd fallen by accident. She had no family to raise concerns over the manner of her death, but even if she did, Madison thinks it would have been difficult to tell it wasn't an accident. Jo could have got away with the perfect murder if Ruby hadn't turned up and complicated matters.

Jo hesitates. "I know you think I'm some cold-blooded killer, Detective, but I never planned for all this to happen. Yes, I needed to silence Mrs. Hendricks, but I consoled myself with the thought that she was old and had no family. She'd lived a long life and there was no one to miss her, yet if I went to prison, my son would suffer." She lowers her eyes. "It seemed a fair trade-off to me back then. If I'd known Ruby would turn up, I would never have risked it. I would have tried to repay the money." She looks up. "You have no idea how much I regret it. My life ended the night Ruby's did. Everything changed for the worse."

For Madison, this remorse is too little too late. And what about Terri and Douglas? She'll get to them. "You didn't hurt your son, did you?"

"Of course not. He's the reason I did any of it." Jo takes a sip of water. "My mom had just arrived at a motel in town. She lived in Nebraska at the time but was visiting for Thanksgiving. I called her and told her to meet me at the church. I had to admit what I'd done. I can't even begin to tell you how horrific that was." She wipes her eyes. "Eventually, she took Oliver home to Nebraska with her."

They took him away and hid him. And when her mom moved to California soon after, presumably to stop anyone finding him, Jo followed. Gary said Jo had lied about her last name. She was living under an alias, and Madison would bet Oliver's last name was changed to match. "But why? Why take Oliver away from his father?"

"There was no other way. I had to hide Ruby's body, and Oliver was a witness to everything. He could've told his dad, or anyone else who asked questions, where we'd been that night, or when he'd last seen Ruby, and what happened to Mrs. Hendricks." She's getting upset. "One wrong word from him and both their deaths would have been for nothing because I would've been arrested."

"And your mom willingly helped you?"

"Not willingly, no. She was horrified." Jo wipes away a tear. "My mother adores her grandson even more than she loves me, and she didn't want him to grow up with his mom in prison. She knew she'd never see Oliver again if that happened. We didn't have long to decide what to do. I'm not saying we made the right choice, and I'm sure she's regretted it every day since, but it was too late. Once she left with him, she was implicated."

Madison takes a deep breath. She's going to have to bring Patricia in for questioning. She helped harbor a criminal. "So where did you take Ruby?"

"After we moved Oliver to my mom's car, we dragged Ruby into the back of her car. I didn't want her to be found by her cell phone so I took it apart and destroyed it. What's left is in the vehicle with her. Once we'd done that, Mom reluctantly left for Nebraska with Oliver. I drove to Gold Rock."

Madison's stomach lurches with nerves. "To Angie's place?"

"No, of course not. But I did phone her for help."

And there it is: even more proof that Angie is one of the most despicable people on this planet. "What did she do?"

"I told her what had happened. I was a complete mess, even threatening to shoot myself. If it wasn't for Oliver, I would have done it." She takes a second. "I needed somewhere to hide Ruby's car and body. Angie recommended one of the old silver mines in Gold Rock that had been closed for years."

Finally. They have a location. No wonder she was never found. Douglas and Bowers had been focusing their searches in Lost Creek. "How far from Angie's place is it?"

"About two miles north. It has a dried up well to the left of it. I drove as close as I could get, left the handbrake on, got out and pushed the car inside. Angie sent one of her guys to give me a ride home. He was in charge of making sure Ruby's car would never be found. She told me later that he had managed to seal the entrance by exploding something." She shakes her head. "Every single day after that night I expected a surprise knock at the door by Detective Douglas because I didn't know if Angie would betray me. I soon realized she needed me to keep her secrets, so she was glad to know one of mine."

Angie had told Madison and Nate that Oliver was dead too, despite knowing he wasn't. Probably to send them off on a wild goose chase that would lead them further away from the truth.

"Detective Douglas always looked at me like he suspected me," Jo continues. "I felt like he had a hunch but he couldn't prove it."

That's not unusual. Madison thinks anyone who ever came into contact with Don Douglas felt they were under suspicion of something, warranted or not. Maybe because experience had taught him that everyone is capable of murder. "Is that why you killed him too?"

Jo wearily shakes her head. "I didn't kill him, or Terri. I would never hurt Terri."

Madison thinks she's lying. She pulls out the bracelet Terri was holding when she died. "Recognize this?"

Jo glances at it and freezes. "She still had that?" Tears start to fall.

"She was holding it when she died. I know you had one too, I've seen a photo of you together at summer camp. Why would she be holding this if you weren't visiting her that night?" Lowering her eyes, Jo doesn't answer. It angers Madison that she's unable to admit to this. "Did you know Terri was pregnant when you killed her?"

Her mouth drops open and she looks Madison in the eye. "You're lying."

"No. There's only one liar in here and it's not me."

Jo's expression is pained. "I wasn't even in town when she

or the detective died. You can check with my boss in Sacramento. I would never hurt Terri."

Madison's confused. How could she not have killed Terri and Douglas? She was sure their deaths were linked to Ruby and Oliver's disappearance. Was she wrong all along? She will have to verify Jo's alibi but it doesn't sound like she's lying. "What about Nate Monroe? He said he saw a woman behind the wheel of the car that mowed him down, and the car I found you in fits the description. I take it you were getting desperate at that point. He was the last person who could expose you for the killer you are."

Jo shuts down. "I'm tired. I can't talk about this anymore, not right now." She wipes her eyes with her sleeves and she looks emotionally drained. "All I can say in my defense is that I never set out to cause so much pain. If I could go back in time, I would never have gone to work for the McCoys. I saw how easily they conned people out of money and I guess I was sick of living pay check to pay check. I got greedy. I wish I could take it all back. I just want to see my son. I wish he was here." She breaks into sobs.

Madison stands. She doesn't think they're crocodile tears but she still has no sympathy for this woman. "Your son is here."

Jo looks up. "What?"

"Gary found an old passport of yours that listed your last name as Rader. That wasn't the name you were living under with him, and it wasn't your maiden name. It didn't take him long to figure things out. He followed you here with Oliver, to confront you. Your son is with his real father right now." Madison picks up the case file. "You'll never get custody of him again. I intend to make sure of that."

She leaves the room, slamming the door shut behind her. Today has been intense and she wishes she had a partner to share the burden with. Feeling shaky and drained she stops at the kitchen and pours herself a mug of coffee. Thinking of her own son, she texts Owen to check he's okay. He texts back to say he's at home with her dad. They have Brody with them as Vince dropped him off on his way to the station. That means Nate's alone in the hospital.

Madison calls him. She needs to hear his reassuring voice. When he answers she says, "Hey, how are you?"

"Bored." He sighs. "Daytime TV sucks, and don't even get me started on the food. The portion sizes are small and there's no wine menu."

She smiles, unsure whether to burden him with everything that's going on. He should be relaxing.

"I've seen on the news that you have Jo Rader in custody," he says. "Is she talking?"

Madison scoffs. "You could say that." She decides to fill him in on everything she's learned, if only to help her make sense of it all.

He's as horrified as she is and concerned about Vince's reaction. "So Ruby's remains were close by this whole time," he says.

"I know. If Jo had admitted what she'd done sooner, she could've saved them all that extra heartache."

"Having Oliver back will help them heal faster. Vince must be over the moon about that."

"He is. The whole reunion was so emotional."

"You cried, didn't you?" he jests.

"Listen, it was so intense that even Chief Mendes had a tear in her eye."

"Wow. I'm impressed."

She sighs. "I have to go. There's still so much to do. Jo's saying she didn't have anything to do with the murders of Terri and Douglas, so if she's telling the truth, I'm back to square one with those."

"Really?" he sounds as skeptical as she is about that. "I wish I were helping. I feel useless in here."

"Trust me, I wish you were here too. I guess I'll call you when I'm done. If you need anything and you can't reach me, call Owen."

"Sure. Good luck."

She says goodbye and slips her phone away. After downing some coffee, she heads to Steve's desk, but not before glancing in at Chief Mendes's office. Matt, Vince, Oliver and Gary are all squeezed in, answering each other's questions about the last six years. Without Ruby, it's not the best outcome Madison could have hoped for, but it's better than what everyone had feared.

Standing in front of Steve, she says, "I have the location of Ruby's body."

Steve leans back in his seat, his relief evident. "Thank God. I thought it would never happen. Where is she?"

Madison tells him. "Would you organize the search party? I still have so much to do. Jo says she wasn't in town when Terri and Douglas were killed and that her boss will corroborate it."

He nods. "Yeah, Gary said she only left Sacramento two days ago—on Friday. As Terri and Douglas were killed Wednesday night, she's telling the truth about that."

Her heartbeat speeds up. "But that means we've got two killers." Madison crosses her arms. "I was so sure all the cases were linked." It could be time to give up on that theory. "We need to get the Sacramento police to her mother's house. Apparently, Patricia helped Jo move Ruby's body and helped with the whole cover-up of where Oliver was."

Steve raises his eyebrows. "Jeez. Nice family. I'll notify the local PD now."

She steps away from his desk as Alex appears. "Hi, Detective. I have the DNA results from the saliva on the wineglass found outside our victim's house."

"And?"

"No match in the system. However, now we have a suspect in custody, I can take a sample from her and see if they match."

"They won't," she says. "Jo Rader wasn't in town for Terri's murder."

Alex frowns. "Ah. Okay, well I haven't been able to break into her phone, so I'll need the pin code. Is she still resisting on that front?"

"She is. But let me see if her husband knows it."

Madison heads to Chief Mendes's office and quietly squeezes in. "Sorry to interrupt. Gary, do you know Jo's cell phone pin?"

He shakes his head. "Sorry. She never told me any of her passwords. Now I know why."

"Are you talking about Mom?" asks Oliver.

His eyes are red and watery, and Madison realizes he became overwhelmed while she was gone. This must be the most confusing for him. She wonders what Jo told him about his dad after Patricia took him away. The poor kid must have been bewildered to suddenly move to his grandmother's home, never see his dad again and only see his mom when she could get away from Lost Creek. Plus, he doesn't even know his mom is here at the station. She smiles at him. "That's right. Have you ever used her cell phone?"

"Sure, lots of times. She has cool games on it."

"So you know her pin code?"

He nods and gives her a four-digit number. "It's the year we moved to California with Grandma Patty and changed our last names to Jones."

Madison swallows. The poor kid has no idea what his mother and grandmother were doing. He's going to need help understanding why his mom will go to prison. The thought leaves her feeling sad. "Thank you. That's very helpful."

She slips out of the room and gives Alex the pin. It works, the phone wakes up and they now have access to all her texts and social media accounts. She breathes a sigh of relief. Alex takes a seat at Douglas's desk and starts scrolling through with laser focus. Madison returns to Mendes's office.

"I want to see her," says Matt. There's anger in his eyes but he's keeping his voice steady for Oliver's sake. "Just give me five minutes with her. I deserve answers."

Madison agrees about that but it's not the right time. She promised Jo she wouldn't have to see Matt or Vince at the station. She might stop talking if Madison breaks that promise. "That's not a good idea right now as I'm not done questioning her. I suggest you all head to Vince's apartment and spend some time together without any of us getting in the way. I'll bet Oliver's ready for that long overdue chocolate milkshake, am I right?"

He nods.

Vince stands and shakes Madison's hand before shaking Chief Mendes's. "Thank you. I mean it. And I'll thank Nate too when I visit him later today. If he hadn't agreed to look into the case, I have no doubt this department would never have reopened it."

Chief Mendes straightens. "Mr. Rader, you must understand—"

He cuts her off with a raised hand. "I know your reasoning. You and your predecessor declined my request more than once on account of having no new tips or leads. It doesn't matter now, does it? Nate breathed new life into this cold case, even though it seemed like an impossible case to solve." He takes a deep breath and softens his tone. "I can't wait for him to meet my grandson."

Madison doesn't want to tell him they have a location on Ruby's body. Not yet. She needs to be sure, as Jo could be lying.

CHAPTER FIFTY-FOUR

Nate's trying to stay awake. The doctor has reduced his pain meds but he's still drowsy. He can't wait to get out of this place and go home. It's impossible to sleep for any decent length of time because of the constant interruption from nurses, doctors and staff bringing food and drink. He appreciates the care and attention but he just wants to be out of here as fast as possible. The fact he can't just get up and leave whenever he wants to unsettles him.

His cell phone rings. "Hello?"

"Is that Nate Monroe?"

"It is." He recognizes her voice. It's Patricia. He sits up.

"Where's my daughter right this second? I saw online that she was seen being taken in for questioning. Is it true?"

She's right to be anxious seeing as she was harboring a killer. Nate struggles to feel sorry for her. "Jo's fine. She's being questioned at Lost Creek PD about the murder of her mother-in-law."

Patricia gasps. "Why on earth would they think she was involved in that?"

Nate shakes his head in disgust. It's clear this woman is going to keep up the pretense for as long as possible. "Because your daughter has admitted to killing her, that's why."

Silence.

"We know where Ruby's body is now, so you need to start cooperating with the authorities like your daughter is. She's being honest at last, so it's time you were too, because there's no going back now." He doesn't tell her that the local police are probably already on their way to arrest her for her involvement.

"But I don't know anything. And I don't believe it's true." She doesn't sound convincing.

"No? You didn't take your grandson home with you to Nebraska the night Ruby was killed? You didn't then move to California with him and change his last name so no one would know who he really was?"

"Stop! Please just stop. I can't take it."

He takes a deep breath. "I imagine you covered for your daughter because you love her and you love your grandson. You thought you were doing what's right for both of them. Believe it or not, I can understand why you would want to protect them."

"You can't understand. Not unless you have children. I'd do anything for them." She blows into a tissue.

He softens his tone. "Listen, the best thing you can do for your daughter right now is to be honest. Judges and juries respect honesty. Jo's admitted killing Ruby and the church volunteer, and we suspect she was involved in the murder of her best friend and Detective Douglas."

After a few seconds of silence, he thinks she's abandoned the phone, but she eventually speaks. "Jo made a terrible mistake that night. Horrendous. I can't condone it and I couldn't believe it when I turned up at the church and saw that old woman lying at the bottom of the steps. Then she led me to Ruby's body and my knees buckled, I almost fell down. The only thing that stopped me reporting her to the police that night was Oliver. My grandson was just four years old. He couldn't lose his mother at that age. I couldn't break his heart. But I also didn't know what to do. Neither did she. She was too distraught to think straight."

He frowns. Madison made it sound like Jo quickly came up with a plan. "So if it wasn't either of you who came up with the idea of taking Oliver home with you and hiding Ruby's body, who did?"

"Jo hasn't told you?"

She might have told Madison by now but she also might have clammed up, so Nate needs to push Patricia to reveal it. "I'm guessing it was someone close to her."

After a moment's hesitation she says, "It was her step-brother."

Nate's mouth drops open but he has to hide his surprise. He never knew about any siblings. "Her stepbrother?"

"He was living in Nebraska with his dad at the time—that's my ex-husband. I never really saw eye to eye with him, so we didn't have much of a relationship, but he and Jo stayed in touch over the years. He was in training at the police academy at the time this happened, so she thought he'd be able to tell her what to do."

Nate's stunned. Not just that Jo has a stepbrother on the force but that he would advise her to hide a body. "And he didn't tell her to turn herself in? He didn't call LCPD himself?"

Patricia scoffs. "You know those crooked cops you hear about on the news who are in law enforcement for all the wrong reasons?"

Nate knows those kinds of cops extremely well. "Sure."

"That's him in a nutshell. He told her what to do and he kept her secret. Probably knowing he could use it for his own personal gain at some point. But then..."

Nate wishes Madison were here to listen to all this. He needs to call her immediately. "What?"

"I keep an eye on the news down there, Mr. Monroe. We both do. Because Jo has always worried that the police will stumble across Ruby's body one day, and that she left something behind that would lead back to her: a fingerprint on the car, or a hair on the body. So when I saw on the news that poor Terri Summers had been murdered in her own home, I just about broke down. Terri didn't deserve that. She was a beautiful person." She sniffs back tears.

"Where was Jo when Terri was killed?"

"Here in Sacramento. It wasn't her. She wouldn't do that to Terri. Then I heard about Detective Douglas's suicide and my heart beat out of my chest. I thought..."

"What? Did you suspect someone?"

"Jo's stepbrother. I mean, he got a job at LCPD, so it would've been easy for him to stage something."

"Wait, what?" The heart rate monitor next to him goes crazy as adrenaline races through his body. "You're telling me Jo's stepbrother works for LCPD? What's his name?"

There's a slight hesitation. "Dan Goodwin. He's a police officer."

Nate almost drops the phone in shock. Then he realizes Madison's in danger. "Why would he kill Terri?" he asks, palms sweaty.

"Jo broke down one night in the weeks after Ruby's death, when it was all getting to her. She confided in Terri what had happened and where Oliver was."

"And Terri never told the police?"

"You have to understand something. Terri and Jo were best friends since high school. They loved each other like sisters. Terri was Oliver's godmother. She took the news hard, and I know she battled with keeping it a secret because she felt so bad for Matt and Vince. But Jo pointed out that Oliver would be left without his mom if she went to prison for what she'd done, that his life would be ruined. I think Terri stayed silent for him."

Nate shakes his head. Jo emotionally blackmailed her friend.

"Terri recently told Jo that Detective Douglas had come around asking questions about what happened back then. She thought he knew something, and she didn't feel she could keep the information to herself any longer. She wanted to tell him everything for Matt's sake, so he could see his son again. She pleaded with Jo to come clean so that she wouldn't have to do it for her."

Terri was in an impossible position. "Did Dan Goodwin know any of this?"

"Yes. Jo told him. He was angry and said Terri was a liability. If Terri told the police what had happened, Dan would be implicated too, for helping us plan the whole cover-up, and for not contacting LCPD the minute Jo told him what she'd done that night. He seemed far more worried about what would happen to him than what would happen to us. He talked Jo into pretending to Terri that she wanted to meet up and discuss turning herself in. He wanted Terri to be alone that night, so that he could turn up in Jo's place."

Nate shakes his head. Terri was killed for wanting to do the right thing. It sounds like Douglas was building a case against Jo and using Terri as a witness. That's what got them both killed. "Do you believe Dan killed Detective Douglas?"

"In my experience, that boy was born bad and he's capable of anything." She sighs heavily. "It's a huge relief to finally talk about all this. I didn't ask for any of it to happen. I made a split-second decision that I thought would benefit my grandson. I was sorely mistaken. Our lives ended that night too. Sure, we had Oliver with us, but we couldn't fully enjoy it. We were terrified someone would find out who he really was." With a thick voice she asks, "Where is my grandson, Mr. Monroe? I want to hug him one more time before I get locked up." She finally breaks down.

Nate ends the call without replying. He's disgusted with her and her daughter and he doesn't owe them his sympathy. He has more pressing issues. Madison needs to know she's working with a cop killer.

CHAPTER FIFTY-FIVE

Madison's phone won't stop ringing. It's Nate. As Matt and Vince prepare to leave the station, she answers it. "What's wrong?" she asks.

"Listen," he says, out of breath. "Jo Rader's mom just told me that Officer Dan Goodwin is Jo's stepbrother and she suspects he murdered Terri and Douglas."

Madison gasps and almost drops the phone in shock. She's rendered speechless as she considers the implications. That arrogant asshole has been hiding in their police department this whole time. He was there as she detailed her investigation into Terri's murder. He attended Douglas's farewell drinks. Her blood boils. "I'll need to call you back in five minutes."

"Sure."

She turns to Matt and Vince, unsure how they'll react. "Did you know Officer Dan Goodwin is Jo's stepbrother?"

Vince turns pale as he shakes his head. Matt says, "I thought I recognized one of your cops when you brought me in for questioning but I wasn't sure where I recognized him from."

Madison remembers they passed Goodwin as she was

taking Matt to the interview room. "Surely you'd know your former brother-in-law?" she says.

"No, I've never met him. I didn't even know his name. All Jo ever told me was that she had a stepbrother from when Patricia was living in Nebraska, but the marriage was short-lived. I saw a photo of them all together once, but that was years ago."

Madison turns to Mendes, who looks equally shocked. She goes to her computer and brings up his personnel file. Having only been in Lost Creek for five months herself, Mendes won't know much about any of her staff yet. After reading the screen she says, "He's only been with us for a year. He was previously an officer at a small PD in Nebraska." She stands. "How close is he with his stepsister?"

Matt says, "She never really talked about him, so I imagine not close at all, but she's obviously capable of deceit, so who knows?"

Vince speaks up. "You don't seriously believe a serving police officer was involved in any of this, do you?"

That's exactly what Madison thinks. It makes sense—the fact that Terri and Douglas's killer was able to cover their tracks so well. He was a *cop*. He knew exactly what to do. "I need to go. If Officer Goodwin approaches either of you, get away from him. In fact, I'm going to send an officer home with you, just in case."

"What's going on, Dad?" Oliver is scared.

"Nothing," says Matt with fake breeziness. "Let's go to the diner. You remember that place, right?"

Oliver nods and Madison leads them over to Shelley, who's filling in paperwork at her desk. "Shelley? Would you escort them home to the diner?" She leans in to whisper into her ear, "Goodwin is Jo's stepbrother and I believe he was involved in Terri and Douglas's murder. He might come after them."

Shelley looks up at her in disbelief. She clearly has a lot of questions, but, ever the professional, she smiles widely at Oliver as she stands and pulls her jacket on. "Sure. Would you like to ride in my police car?"

His eyes light up with excitement. "For real?"

"If that's okay with your dad."

Matt smiles wearily. It's been a long day of revelations for him. "Of course."

"Wow, thanks!" Oliver's excited.

They follow Shelley out of the station and Madison returns to Chief Mendes's office, where she calls Nate back and puts him on speakerphone. Steve enters as Nate fills them in on what Jo's mom told him. They stare at each other as they all try to come to terms with the realization that they have a killer on their team.

"It's highly likely that Goodwin killed Terri and Douglas to save his own ass," says Nate. He sounds exhausted. "You need to locate him immediately."

She thinks of how arrogant Goodwin has been about going for Douglas's job. Did he really think he'd get away with killing him? Yes. Because he almost did. She shudders. He could have been Douglas's replacement. Then it dawns on her. "He was the first person at Terri's crime scene. Is that because he wanted to double check he'd done a good enough job of covering his tracks?"

"He was quick to shoot Troy Randle too," says Mendes. "If he'd been a better shot, Troy would've died."

"Which is probably what he intended," says Nate down the line. "Because a dead guy can't prove his innocence."

Madison nods. "Goodwin couldn't have known Troy would stay out all night getting wasted, giving himself an alibi in the meantime. He used Troy's gun to kill Terri in a bid to frame him for it, but when he saw an opportunity to silence him completely, he took it."

"There was nothing about a stepbrother in Douglas's case

file," says Steve. "Goodwin was never interviewed after Ruby and Oliver's disappearance."

"Jo wouldn't have told Douglas about his existence because he was her accomplice," says Nate.

"And besides," says Madison. "He lived in Nebraska at the time. Even if Douglas had been told about him, he wasn't a credible suspect."

"Guys, the doctor wants to speak to me," says Nate. "I've got to go."

"Sure. Speak to you later." Madison ends the call and walks to the door of Mendes's office, her heart pounding in her chest. "Goodwin left the station just as Vince and Matt arrived. He must've seen that Jo was brought in and then slipped right on out of here before she revealed anything in her interview. He could be anywhere by now." She runs over to Stella on dispatch. "Stella? I need all units to be on the lookout for Officer Dan Goodwin and to bring him in immediately. He's dangerous and may resist arrest. He's a suspect in the murder of Terri Summers and..." She pauses, taking a second to compose herself. "And Detective Douglas."

Stella's eyes widen, but she immediately slips on her headset and gets on the radio.

Chief Mendes approaches Madison. "Here's Goodwin's home address."

Madison takes the slip of paper. "He won't be there, it's too obvious. But while everyone's searching for Goodwin, Alex and I can search his house to see if we can find anything incriminating. We never found Terri's purse or cell phone."

"I guess I'd better call a judge about a search warrant," says Mendes. "And I'll hold a press conference to make the public aware we're looking for Dan Goodwin. I'm sure there's plenty of people in town who would be more than happy to help us locate a crooked cop." Before she turns away, she adds. "You were right all along about Douglas not taking his own life. Good work, Madison. Your instincts are impeccable."

Madison hasn't got time to feel proud of herself, but she hopes this means Mendes listens to her sooner next time she has a hunch. She walks over to Alex, who is glued to Jo's phone. "Found anything?"

"I'll say." He's about to launch into an explanation, so she picks up a spare bulletproof vest and throws it in his lap.

"Tell me on the way. We're off to Dan Goodwin's house. Bring your kit."

Alex looks at the vest. "I've always wanted to wear one of these."

The adrenaline coursing through Madison's veins makes her bolt out of the station as fast as possible.

CHAPTER FIFTY-SIX

As Madison speeds out of the parking lot with Alex in the passenger seat, she has to dodge the convoy of news vans heading into it. She hopes they all make the press conference in time because she wants Goodwin to pay for what he's done and the media can help with that. The quicker news spreads about Douglas's death being a homicide and Goodwin being the primary suspect, the sooner they'll locate him. She thinks about what Goodwin will go through once he's caught. She's been accused of the same thing and she knows how fast the media and the community turn on cop killers. Except Goodwin is guilty of it. She wasn't.

"All these old pumpkins," says Alex looking at the houses they pass. "Did you know that in some cases they take longer to rot than a human body?"

She glances at him. "I bet you have a million facts like that about dead bodies, don't you?"

He smiles. "Maybe not a million."

She wonders if he tells Shelley stuff like that on their dates. "Okay, hit me. What's on Jo Rader's phone?"

He scrolls though a few apps. "In Facebook Messenger

there are several exchanges between Jo Rader and Terri Summers where they're arranging to meet up on Wednesday evening."

The night Terri was killed. "So Terri expected Jo to turn up that night." That's why Terri got the old bracelet out, to show her friend and remind her of happier times. "But instead, Goodwin showed up."

Alex shakes his head. "You know, I knew there was something off about that man. He was just like the person who bullied me at school. He seemed to enjoy tormenting people."

Madison glances at him. "Anything else?"

"Yes, several text messages between Jo and a mystery number saved under *anon*. I'd bet that's a second phone Officer Goodwin owns, because they're discussing Terri and what to do about her meeting with Detective Douglas." He scrolls through the messages. "This anonymous person goes on to discuss how they need to silence her, and he needs Jo's help by faking a visit to her house."

"Anything about Douglas's murder on there?"

"A message from Jo on the day news broke about Douglas's suicide shows her asking this anonymous person if he was involved. He replied with a wink emoji."

Madison clenches her jaw. It's damning but it's not good enough to get him sent down. It sounds like Jo went along with Goodwin's plan to get Terri alone on Wednesday night, but there's nothing to suggest Jo was involved in planning Douglas's murder. That was all Goodwin.

Alex says, "Now I have the DNA from the wineglass taken from Terri's house, I just need a comparison sample from Officer Goodwin. Because it doesn't match Terri's DNA, which means it was the glass the killer drank from."

"That wineglass bothers me," she says. "I mean, did he really share a drink with her before killing her?"

Alex shrugs. "Jo and Terri were friends for years, so it's

likely she would've met Jo's stepbrother at some point, meaning he wasn't a complete stranger to her. All he had to do was turn up and pretend Jo was running late. Terri probably felt obligated to invite him in."

Her stomach churns at the thought of how trusting Terri was. Then again, Goodwin was a police officer. And the stepbrother of her best friend. He *should* have been trustworthy. Madison wonders exactly when Jo told Goodwin that she had confided in her friend. It could be the reason he moved here last year. To keep an eye on Terri and make sure she didn't tell anyone what happened that night.

When they reach Goodwin's house Madison's phone rings. She parks before answering it. "Dad?"

"Hi, honey. Owen and I have been watching your police chief give a press conference on the news. Sounds like you've got a lot on your plate."

"You can say that again."

"I wouldn't normally bother you at a time like this but when your chief confirmed a cop was involved in your partner's murder, I thought it best to keep an eye on the street outside. Just in case."

At first, she wants to laugh. It's well known that retired cops and agents have a hard time letting go of the action and relaxing, but then her heart drops into her stomach as she realizes what her dad's implying. Goodwin wouldn't go to her house, would he?

Of course he would. He already hated her. Now she's got his accomplice in custody and a warrant out for his arrest, he has nowhere to run, nothing to lose. "Oh my God." She starts the engine and does a U-turn in the middle of the road. "Have you seen anything?"

"Yeah. There's a brown Nissan parked all the way at the end of the street, with a guy inside. I can't see his features, but he has no reason to be sitting there this long."

She doesn't know what Goodwin drives but her heart skips a beat. "Where's Owen?"

"Don't panic, he's with me."

"Are you armed?"

He snorts. "Honey, I'm an ex-Fed. Of course I'm armed. But a little backup wouldn't go amiss."

"I'm on my way. Is Brody still with you? He's got K9 experience. He can help."

"Huh. I wondered why he was pacing back and forth by the front door. Wants me to let him out but I thought he'd get himself shot."

"He won't. He knows what to do." But does her dad? He may be an ex-Fed but he's not a young man anymore. His reflexes will be slower. Goodwin could easily overpower him. What if she doesn't get there before Goodwin acts? "You've got to keep Owen safe, Dad. That's who he'll go for."

"Well, the asshole won't get anywhere near him without a fight."

She throws her phone onto Alex's lap and speeds through downtown faster than she's ever driven.

Alex is clutching the dashboard.

"Call dispatch!" she barks at him. "Tell them Goodwin's at my house."

He calls it in. Madison can only hope her dad is able to protect himself and her son until she gets there.

CHAPTER FIFTY-SEVEN

By the time she and Alex pull up a few houses away from hers, keeping their distance so Goodwin can't see them, the Nissan at the end of the road is empty and patrol are nowhere to be seen. She looks at Alex. "Do you carry a weapon?" He isn't issued a service weapon as a forensics tech, but she's hoping he carries his own.

He shakes his head. "It's not something I feel comfortable with, being British and all."

She hands him her car keys. "Drive someplace safe and wait for backup. I can't risk him shooting you if he gets away."

Alex swallows. "Are you sure? I know karate."

Madison fixes her eyes on his. "Sorry, Alex. With no gun, you're no help to me." She tears out of the car and runs toward her house, careful not to be seen from a window. Reaching the side of the house she draws her weapon and listens. She hears Alex drive away, but nothing else. No yelling, and, more bizarrely, no barking. Dread fills her chest as she fears she's too late. Goodwin could have shot Brody first, knowing he was the most dangerous.

A text makes her glance at her phone. It's from Mendes.

Goodwin's girlfriend watched the press conference and called in about a box of junk he stored in her garage. She looked through it and says there's a purse inside. Fits the description of the one Terri owned.

Her heart sinks. There's no doubt now that it was Goodwin. She forces herself along the house toward the backyard. As she turns the corner, the backyard appears to be empty. He could be hiding in the cornfield beyond her land, or in the large barn off to the left, but the silence from the house is more troubling. She peers into the kitchen window. There's no one there. Maybe her dad took Owen and Brody upstairs to buy time for the cops to arrive.

When she turns around, her heart jumps into her mouth as Goodwin appears as if out of nowhere and grabs her hard by the arm. He swings her around and manages to grip her in a head-lock. His spare hand has a knife to her throat. She tries to breathe in but her throat is constricted and she only manages a tiny gasp of air.

"You think I'm interested in hurting your kid?" he yells in her ear. She can feel his spit on her face. "If I'm going down, I want the pleasure of killing *you* first, you condescending bitch."

He's still wearing his police uniform. Something he never deserved to own, let alone wear. Anger builds in Madison's chest as she pulls at the arm around her neck. "You killed Douglas," she croaks. Trying to delay the inevitable, she says, "Tell me how you managed it." The blade is cold against her throat and she has no doubt that he would go through with it. She needs to remain calm in order to get out of this.

"You can't prove that," he says. "You can't prove anything. Just because my stepsister killed the Rader woman doesn't mean I was involved. That's got nothing to do with me. It doesn't mean I killed Douglas or Troy Randle's girlfriend."

She cautiously tries to straighten a little in his grip, to get her feet hip-width apart, because she needs all her weight behind her if she's going to get him off her. A quick glance at the house makes her realize no one is coming to save her. There's no movement at all and she can only hope that he hasn't already killed everyone inside. "Yeah? Well this is a strange way to prove your innocence."

He scoffs before tightening his hold of her neck. "I don't have to prove anything to you."

Fighting a tight, panicky feeling in her chest she breathes in as deeply as she can before clenching her fist and elbowing Goodwin as hard as possible in his chest.

The wind is knocked out of him and the pain reverberates down her arm. Her elbow connected with one of his ribs and she sees stars for a second. He temporarily lets go before grabbing for her again. He gets a handful of her hair before she can swing around, so she kicks backwards like a horse, managing to hit his shin hard.

"Fuck!" he shouts, trying to stay upright. He drops the knife and rubs his shin, looking meaner than ever.

She's free now, and gasping for air. Her head hurts and she sees a clump of her hair in his hand. She manages to put some distance between them but within seconds he pulls his service weapon on her. He's smirking now. He has the look of a madman with nothing to lose. She's still clutching her own gun and knows that, unless she does something to distract him, whoever survives this showdown will be the person with the quickest reflexes. "If you had nothing to do with Terri's murder, then how come her purse is at your girlfriend's place?"

The smirk is wiped off his arrogant face.

"We found one of the wineglasses from Terri's house too, by the side of the road near her house. I'm guessing you wormed your way into her home and accepted her offer of a drink." She shakes her head and ever so slowly lifts her gun to point at his chest. "Terri was just trying to be nice to her best friend's step-brother, and you killed her."

He stares blankly but he must be trying to calculate whether there's still any way he can get away with what he's done now he knows they have evidence.

"I'm guessing you stupidly dropped one of the glasses on the way to your car afterward," she continues. "Thanks to that mistake Alex has the killer's DNA."

Sweat breaks out on Goodwin's brow as the full implications hit him. Juries love DNA evidence. He's going down for this.

Biding time for backup to arrive and for Owen and her dad to get away through the front of the house, she continues. "I know you staged Douglas's murder as a suicide because Lena found a second injury to his head and he had no gunshot residue on his hand. You attacked him from behind because you knew he could easily overpower you otherwise. You're a coward and a cop killer."

His face flushes red with anger. "I should've killed you instead of Douglas." He takes aim.

Madison doesn't even have time to react. A gunshot rings out and echoes around her and it's quickly followed by a tirade of aggressive barking from inside the house. She's shocked when Goodwin stumbles backwards instead of her. A wet patch builds on his uniform shirt. It must be blood coming from his shoulder. He looks above her head in surprise and she follows his gaze. At the bedroom window, above the kitchen, her dad has his gun trained on Goodwin.

Relief spreads through her that he and Owen are safe, but when she turns back to Goodwin, his weapon is raised again. This time at her dad who is looking over his shoulder, into the bedroom. He must be talking to Owen. Goodwin manages to fire off one round before collapsing. Her dad yells out in pain and disappears from view.

"Dad!" she screams.

Time appears to slow down as Owen opens the back door, making her want to yell at him to stay inside. But he's letting Brody out. The dog races to Goodwin and pins him down, barking menacingly the whole time. Madison knows he'll bite if Goodwin dares to move. She advances, gun aimed at Goodwin's chest. He's struggling for breath, so she shouts to Owen, "Call 911. We need two ambulances immediately!" She wants to go inside and check on her dad, administer CPR if she needs to, but she can't leave Goodwin alone.

She retrieves both his gun and the knife, and that's when the sirens come. Loud and plentiful. She considers cuffing Goodwin but he needs treatment and the cuffs could hamper that. She looks at Brody, whose face is right above Goodwin's. "Don't let him move."

Goodwin is young and was hit in the shoulder; he has a good chance of survival. She has no idea where her dad was hit and he may need immediate assistance. She races upstairs, past Owen who's talking to dispatch. In her bedroom her dad is sitting on the floor and leaning against the wall. He's clutching the top of his arm and she hopes it's just because that's where he was shot and not because he's having a heart attack. The blood is spreading down his torso and onto her carpet. "Dad. Are you okay? Do you have any chest pain?"

He grins at her, which is more like a grimace because of the pain. "That was the most action I've had in years."

He's sweaty and pale, fast turning gray. She's worried about him. All she can do is hold his hand until the ambulance arrives and pray he'll be okay.

CHAPTER FIFTY-EIGHT

It's dark as Madison and Owen enter the hospital in silence. It's been a long, emotionally draining day and she's not looking forward to what's yet to come. She had called Maggie, Terri's aunt, to let her know they've caught Terri's killer. Maggie was overwhelmed at learning the reason for her niece's murder and Madison knows she and Terri's mom will have a lot of questions over the coming days. But not yet. They need to let it sink in. Maggie told her that Sylvia was slowly getting better after her stroke, and she should be released from the hospital soon. Getting answers about why a loved one was murdered is often bittersweet but Madison hopes the fact that she has identified and captured Terri's killer gives them some comfort.

Thankfully Chief Mendes is in charge of telling Douglas's dad what really happened to his son. Madison doesn't envy her. Steve had volunteered to let Troy know what happened the night his girlfriend died. Troy was outraged that the killer turned out to be the same person who tried to shoot him dead. Steve thinks there's a hefty lawsuit coming their way.

The media are going crazy over the fact LCPD has itself another case where an officer was killed by one of their own, even dragging up all the old footage of Madison in cuffs from seven years ago. She just hopes they remember to point out that it had nothing to do with her last time.

Owen gives her a reassuring smile as they take the elevator up to Nate's floor. She smiles back at him. "I'm glad you're safe. If my dad hadn't been there..." She trails off, not daring to speak the words aloud.

"Brody would've saved me. It was pretty cool though, Grandpa was badass."

She looks at him. He called her father Grandpa for the first time. She wonders how long it will take her to get used to hearing that.

They enter Nate's room and Vince is already there, as she knew he would be. Nate had given her the heads-up. There's a six-pack of beer on the nightstand and some takeout packaging from Ruby's Diner that suggests he's rewarding Nate for taking on the cold case.

Leaning in, she hugs Nate for a long time and feels his warm hands on her back. Having been confined to a lonely existence on death row for so long, he used to hate hugs when they first met. They made him uncomfortable. "How are you?" she asks as she pulls away.

"Full. Thanks to Vince I've just eaten like a king." He looks tired but he has more color in his face than he did the last time she saw him. The bandage around his head has been reduced to a smaller version that just covers the wound.

Vince smiles, clearly happy to be of service.

Madison can't meet Vince's eyes. On the way over here, she received word from Steve that they've located Ruby's car in the silver mine. They haven't been able to unearth it yet but one of the team had managed to shine a flashlight into the rear window. Ruby's skeletal remains are where Jo said they would be, on the back seat. She was left there to rot alone in the dark for six years.

"You okay?" asks Nate. He takes her hand in his and she has to blink back tears.

When she has the courage to look at Vince, she says, "We've got Ruby."

The smile vanishes from Vince's face and he turns away from them all and inhales deeply. Madison doesn't mention how Lena will need to perform an autopsy in order to try to confirm Ruby's cause of death. It's been so long that it may be difficult to prove she was shot in the chest, unless the bullet hit a bone. Regardless, Vince doesn't need to hear any of that right now.

"When can I bury her?" he asks, turning back to face them with watery eyes.

"Not long."

He nods and smiles sadly. "She deserves a proper burial." After a second, he says, "What will happen to Jo and Goodwin?"

Madison composes herself. "Goodwin's in surgery but he should pull through, which means he'll be arrested for the murders of Terri and Douglas, among other things. Alex has compared his DNA to that found on the wineglass and it's a match, placing Goodwin at her house the night Terri died. He must've dropped it during his rush out of there. He stored Terri's purse at his girlfriend's house."

"What is he, stupid?" asks Owen. "Why didn't he just get rid of it?"

"My guess is he was going to plant it on someone, probably Troy, until he realized Troy had a good alibi. Either that or he was certain he'd never be a suspect himself. He got cocky." She inhales. "As for Jo, she's already been arrested for Ruby's murder, as well as that of Rosemary Hendricks."

"Rosemary?" says Vince, surprised. "I remember when she died. I thought it was an accident."

Madison shakes her head. "I'm afraid not. There's a lot you don't know."

He holds a hand up. "Just tell me two things. Why she killed them, and whether she's sorry for what she's done."

Madison considers it. Jo certainly showed some remorse in her interview. "She was embezzling money from the church and her employer. Mrs. Hendricks found out and Jo needed to silence her. Ruby unintentionally witnessed the murder."

A look of disgust clouds his face. "This was all about *money?* I would've given her whatever she wanted."

Madison doesn't doubt it. "Jo has displayed some remorse. She wishes she could take it all back. I believe she was in too deep and couldn't see a way out once Ruby knew what she'd done."

He shakes his head. "I don't want to hear any more. Not now. I just want to focus on Matt and Oliver for the next couple of days. There's a lot to process, you know?"

"Sure. I understand."

Footsteps approach the room and suddenly Brody appears, followed by Madison's dad. He's in a white hospital gown and pushing an IV along. "So this is where the party's at," he says. "The damn nurse said I couldn't keep the dog in my room any longer, something to do with hospital policy. A stickler for rules, that one. She'd make a good Fed."

Vince steps forward and holds out a hand. "Vince Rader. Pleasure to meet you."

Bill shakes it. "Bill Harper."

"Your daughter's quite the cop," says Vince. "She's solved some tough cases already and she's only been back on the force a few months."

"Oh yeah?" Bill eyes him up. "You in law enforcement?"

Smiling, Vince shakes his head. "No. I'm in the diner business. And I'm ex United States Navy."

Bill raises an eyebrow and nods, impressed. "You like to drink, Vince?"

"Sure do. Whiskey. But only the good stuff."

"Then maybe we can share a drink sometime and you can tell me what my daughter's been up to. If I wait for her to tell me, I'll be in my grave."

Madison rolls her eyes. That's all she needs, these two pairing up as friends. His arm wound is nothing to worry about, thankfully.

Brody jumps onto the bed and Nate breaks into a wide smile. "Hey, boy."

Bill steps forward. "So you're this Nate guy Owen won't shut up about."

Madison notices Owen face reddens. It makes her smile.

"I am," says Nate. "Pleasure to meet you." They shake hands awkwardly, since Nate's ribs are injured and her dad's arm is bust up.

"According to my grandson, you and my daughter are pretty close."

It's Madison's turn to blush now. She looks at Owen, who shrugs and says, "What? You are. I didn't say you were sleeping together or anything."

Vince laughs, clearly enjoying her discomfort. Bill focuses on Nate and says, "I don't care whether you're screwing or not as long as you don't hurt my daughter in any way."

To his credit, Nate is unfazed. "Wouldn't dream of it, Bill. Especially now I know her dad was a federal agent."

Madison wonders whether Nate's bothered by the fact her dad worked for the FBI, given his mistrust of law enforcement. If he is, he doesn't show it.

Nate strokes Brody's head and says to the dog, "I hear you stopped another perp from getting away?"

Brody's tail thumps against the bed and he does one of those weird vocal yawns that sounds like he's answering.

Vince ruffles his fur. "He gets free diner food for the rest of his life. You all do." He looks at Madison and then Nate. "I don't know where I'd be if you pair hadn't come back to town this summer."

"Does the free food apply to me too?" asks Owen.

Vince claps him on the back. "You too, kid. Until you leave for college, anyway."

"Speaking of which," says Nate. "I know your mom's been stressing about how to pay for that." He glances at Madison. "I want to use some of my exoneration payout to cover his tuition fees."

She gasps. "Nate, you can't. We don't expect that."

He waves a dismissive hand. "Listen, I want to. It's not like I have anything else to spend my money on, is it? Consider it an investment for the next time one of us gets arrested." He smiles. "I might need him to represent me one day and he can't do that if he can't afford to graduate."

She laughs. The same thought had occurred to her when she first found out Owen wanted to be a lawyer.

Nate looks at Owen. "But it's on the condition you pass all your exams. Deal?"

Owen nods. He looks so happy that Madison's heart could break. "Deal. But I might fail a couple. I mean, it takes years to become a lawyer. I need to get through college before law school. Think how many exams that involves in total." He starts bartering with Nate about the ratio of fails he can get away with, sounding a lot like a lawyer already.

Madison looks around the room and feels a sudden rush of gratitude. Her dad spoils it.

"When you say exoneration payout," he says to Nate. "What do you mean, exactly?"

Nate takes a deep breath. "I spent seventeen years on death row for murder."

With raised eyebrows, Bill looks at Madison. "Jeez. You sure know how to pick 'em."

Madison laughs. She feels guilty for being able to experience small moments of joy like this when Detective Douglas has lost his life. And when Vince and Matt still have some difficult times ahead, what with having to bury Ruby and sit through the murder trials that will follow. But she's reminded that no matter how bad her job gets, and how horrendous the crimes she investigates, she's helping people find the answers they seek. And with the people in this room around her, she feels like she can handle whatever this town has to throw at her.

A LETTER FROM WENDY

Thank you for reading *Gone to Her Grave*, book 4 in the Detective Madison Harper series.

You can keep in touch with me and get updates about the series by signing up to my newsletter here, and by following me on social media.

www.bookouture.com/wendy-dranfield

When I started writing book 1—*Shadow Falls*—I had no idea whether readers would be interested in reading about a former detective who had been convicted of manslaughter, and a wannabe priest who had spent almost two decades on death row. But it turns out you are! I've been blown away by the response to the series so far. I'm so pleased you're enjoying their unique stories, as well as the supportive relationship between the duo.

If this is the first book in the series that you have read, you might have been confused or intrigued by some of the references to previous events. I believe a crime series is always more satisfying when read in order as we get to see a character's history and development, so if you want to discover what the young waitress (Kacie Larson) did to land herself in prison, or how Nate and Madison originally met, or learn about Nate's history on death row and how he managed to get off, or even to see how Nate ended up adopting Brody the former K9 (who is a reader's favorite!), then do go back and start the series from book 1.

Following Madison and Nate's journey back to some kind of normality has been great fun, as well as emotional at times. They're not done yet though, and now Madison's retired father is back in her life I have a feeling things may get a little complicated for her, especially as he had to retire knowing that the serial killer he chased his entire career managed to get away with his crimes. That's got to be something that will haunt him forever. Unless, perhaps, Madison and Nate can help him solve the case...

If you enjoyed this book, please do leave a rating or review (no matter how brief) on Amazon, as this helps it to stand out among the thousands of books that are published each day, thereby allowing it to reach more readers and ensuring the series continues for many more books to come.

Thanks again,

Wendy

facebook.com/WendyDranfield1
twitter.com/WendyDranfield

ACKNOWLEDGMENTS

Thank you to the readers first of all. I always keep you in mind as I write, and I love hearing from you on social media. Your feedback perks me up on days when I'm doubting what I'm doing.

Thank you to the advance readers and book bloggers who share reviews of my books online. Your enthusiasm is contagious!

As always, thank you to everyone at Bookouture who has worked on this latest book in the series.

And special thanks to my husband for buying the best coffee machine ever, allowing me to work longer and more efficiently in the hope he gets to read the next manuscript sooner!

Made in the USA
Coppell, TX
09 April 2022